Upon the upland road
Ride easy, stranger:
Surrender to the sky
Your heart of anger.

— 'High Country Weather', James K. Baxter

SURRENDER

Donna Malane

The New Zealand Society of Authors (PEN NZ Inc)
PO Box 7701
Wellesley Street
Auckland 1141

Designed by Anna Egan-Reid
Typeset by Pindar NZ
209 Great North Road, Grey Lynn
Auckland 1021, New Zealand
www.pindar.co.nz
Cover design by Keely O'Shannessy for Pindar NZ
Printed by AstraPrint, New Zealand

Lines from 'High Country Weather' quoted on pages 2 and 299 from James K. Baxter *Collected Poems*. Ed. J. E. Weir. Auckland: Oxford University Press, 1995, p. 32. Permission generously granted by the James K. Baxter Trust.

ISBN 978-0-473-17414-9
A catalogue record for this book is available from the National Library of New Zealand.

For Essie

CHAPTER 1

I was scowling at my computer screen when something made me turn around. He was just standing there in the doorway of my office looking at me. There were signs that keeping his stomach flat actually took some work now – in fact, I'd be willing to bet he put on fluttery nylon shorts every morning and pounded his way around Oriental Bay. Definitely on the downward slide towards forty but I knew he wouldn't take that lying down. I won't claim that as instinct or clairvoyance. I have to put it down to experience. He was my ex-husband, my 'husband-once-removed', as he referred to himself recently in an uncharacteristic fit of pique. Once I introduced Sean as 'my ex'. I thought I was just being accurate but he took offence, thought I was being flippant, I guess, and months later repaid me with the 'husband once-removed' number. Cops are like that – they never forget.

Accuracy is one of my strong points. I don't have a lot of strong points so bear with me if I'm accurate to the point of pedantry. You see, I'm not being entirely accurate when I say Sean was in the doorway of my office. It was actually my laundry. I could call it my ex-laundry since as with my ex-husband I've turned the taps off and pulled the plugs out, but I'll stick with 'office' to avoid confusion. The room functions perfectly well as a workplace with my laptop on an old door that I'd nailed on to some four-by-twos, and two of the un-Gibbed walls covered with cheap office files. After a while you don't even notice the closed-off taps sticking out of the other wall. I use them to hang Wolf's lead on. I was aware Wolf hadn't barked at Sean's arrival – in fact, he had his nose shoved right up against the muscle behind Sean's balls. It's Wolf's inimitable way of being affectionate. You'll have to take my word for it that he didn't learn it from me.

Sean eased himself into the one spare chair, jerking the knee of his trousers up. I'd already heard on the radio news that the body of a middle-aged Caucasian male had been found in upper Cuba Street, and that Detective Sean Callum was heading the investigation into 'what appeared to be a homicide'. I didn't suppose Sean had me down as a suspect but I was keeping an open mind about that. Divorce does funny things to the way people think about each other.

'You heard about the body we found this morning?' He made it sound like an everyday occurrence. Bodies had never bothered him before and I doubted he was going soft now, apart from around the hips, that is.

I swivelled my chair around to face him. 'I heard you found *a* body. What's so interesting about this one?' Bodies hadn't bothered me for some years either.

'You knew this body, Diane, even if you weren't exactly bosom buddies. It was James Patrick Wilson, aka Snow.' With that Sean stood up, mumbling about coffee as he backed out of the doorway.

He was always good at leaving me alone. Maybe too good. He remembered to duck his head around that last shelf in the hall – funny the things you remember. The traitorous Wolf followed him into the kitchen, his nails clicking optimistically on the wooden floor. Sean had always been a soft touch for something from the fridge.

For some now-forgotten reason I'd set my digital photo album as screensaver. I stared at the monitor, hypnotised by the images it randomly threw at me from my past. Snow dead was the end of something for me. A year ago my sister's body had been found on the Island Bay golf course. Niki had a fatal 'hole in one' between the shoulder blades where, according to the pathologist's report, a seven-inch, smooth-bladed boning knife had been embedded. Her killer had never been found.

I'd spent the next nine months following every lead, every hint, every development, every dead end of the police investigation into her killing. And I'd done a fair bit of investigating of my own. I'd looked at every known and suspected murderer, rapist and basic sicko whose criminal record I could get my hands on. Running a missing persons' business gave me the skills, and the work I did for the cops linking missing persons to corpses allowed me access to police files – off-the-record access, of course. A degree in criminology gave me the bullshit respectability I needed, and being married to a cop, which I was until six month ago, did the rest.

Well, that was the theory. In reality, when it came to Niki's case, none of it did me any good at all. I became convinced the cops had let the killer slip from their fingers. Snow had a record of petty but escalating violence against women, dating back to his first offence against his sister when he was fifteen.

I'd badgered Sean and when that got me nowhere I went after the cops working Niki's case, starting with the O/C Suspects and finally ending up in the office of the C/O Inspector Frank McFay, though I'm pretty sure it was McFay who called that meeting.

He told me to, 'Sit down, shut up and listen up', and then he lectured me on how tolerant he'd been of my 'harassing' his men about Niki's case, but that it had to stop. I replied that I wouldn't have had to if he'd done his job properly, or something along those lines. McFay reminded me that he had no obligation to tell me anything about the case but that, given the unusual relationship I had with the police (I wasn't sure whether he was referring to Sean or my work), he was prepared to tell me that the crime team investigating Niki's death had looked at Snow and 'eliminated him from their enquiries'. He said Snow had admitted to a casual relationship with Niki and that's why his prints were at her apartment and hers at his.

I buttoned my lips at that. I knew Niki's taste in men and although they could never be described as 'boys next door' they didn't run to Snow's type. McFay said he'd checked Snow's alibi for the night of Niki's death and it was bulletproof. He went on to remind me that Snow had no motive to kill Niki and 'furthermore' they had absolutely no evidence Snow had anything to do with Niki's death. As if that had ever stopped them.

McFay finished his little lecture by saying that they'd continue to keep an open mind but at this stage Snow was not a suspect and he was not 'authorising any further investigative resources in that area'. I was fluent enough in cop-speak to know that a rough translation would be, 'We know the bastard did it but we can't nail him for it.'

You don't want to know what I said to McFay next, but I haven't had any police jobs since. So, I finally stopped harassing the cops working Niki's case. I left McFay alone. I gave up.

That was three months ago.

On the computer screen was a photo of me squinting suspiciously into the camera. It was probably Sean who took that photo. He'd be the invisible person behind the lens, the one looking. Yep, that would be Sean all right.

I heard coffee being ground and then knocked into the little Italian percolator I'd given Sean as a birthday present a couple of years ago. I hoped he wasn't going to ask for it back. I tapped the keyboard to wake the laptop from sleep. The photo was replaced by the text I'd been working on – a written report on the job I'd just finished for a television company making a series about missing persons. I really must do something about that photo album screensaver. Having my laptop dreaming images of me in its sleep mode is downright unhealthy.

The coffee pot was on the gas ring and the mugs were on the table. The fact that Sean still felt at home in my kitchen caused me some less-than-lofty feelings, and he was fondling the intelligence bump on Wolf's head in a way I definitely found unsettling. Not that Wolf was complaining. His one good eye had glazed over and now resembled the other. Sean used to joke that Wolf was the only police recruit ever thrown out of the force for being one-eyed. Wolf had lost his right eye in the line of duty and was going to be rewarded with a quick bullet to the temple unless some idiot actually wanted a one-eyed dog. Sean got him for me saying he thought we suited each other. He was right. Wolf and I suit each other just fine. I've always found Wolf easy to understand. When he wags his tail, he's happy. When his ears flop low on his head like a beret, he's sad. When he drools, he wants either food or sex. I was never able to read Sean that well.

I sat at the table so I could face Sean. I noted the signs of tiredness – the pinched skin around his eyes and mouth. Working on homicides did that. I had a fair bit of pinched skin myself.

‘Well, much as I fantasised about killing Snow, I’m afraid you’re wasting your time. It wasn’t me, Detective.’

Sean didn’t seem to think my joke was very funny. He turned the coffee pot off and frowned at it. For a moment I thought he was remembering that it was his but then I started to get a strange feeling down my back. It was a bit like ice water being trickled down my spine. A bit like the feeling you get when your husband says, ‘We have to talk.’

‘Pleasant though this is, is that why you’ve come? To tell me Snow’s dead?’

Sean swivelled the coffee pot around three times. I counted.

‘It’s to do with Snow. And it’s about Niki’s case.’

Something was causing the hairs on my neck to stand on end. He was behaving like an odd mixture of the Sean I knew intimately and the more formal Detective Callum that I didn’t particularly want to know.

‘I thought Niki’s case was closed. Now that Snow’s dead, I guess it’s closed for me too,’ I said.

Sean poured the coffee. ‘McFay asked me to come and see you.’

I was fighting the desire for a smoke. I’d given up two months, three weeks and two days ago. Not that I was counting. As if reading my mind, Sean took out a packet of cigarettes and began tapping it against the table. I had to control a sudden desire to suck my thumb, giving weight to the theory that smoking’s all about oral deprivation in infancy. Thumbsucking wasn’t uppermost in my mind however. If McFay had sent Sean to tell me something about Niki’s case, I wanted to know what it was. I sipped my coffee and gave Wolf, who was leaning affectionately against Sean’s thigh, the same squinty look I’d just seen in that photo Sean had taken of me. Overly sensitive, he crawled under the table and lay on my feet. Wolf, that is.

‘So, tell me about Niki’s case, Detective Callum,’ I said, keeping my voice casual.

Sean began pacing, tapping the cigarette packet against his leg. I sat on my hands to keep my thumb out of my mouth.

'Diane, this isn't easy . . .'

He sat down again. I found myself concentrating on his hands. I wondered if he was going to take out one of those damn cigarettes or not. I hadn't seen one close up for a while and I was wondering how I'd react to it.

Sean switched to police-speak. He did that when he was nervous.

'Some months back now, new information came to light that suggested we should have another look at Snow as a suspect for Niki's murder.'

'Jesus H! What'd I tell you?'

'Hear me out. It was a tip off and Gemma reckoned it was a reliable source. She's a good cop, as you know.'

'She's the best. Come on, Sean. For Christ's sake, what happened?'

There was a metallic taste in the back of my throat. The sound of Wolf scratching was loud in the silence of the room. Sean was frowning into his coffee cup, concentrating on its emptiness. He picked up that damn cigarette packet again, flicking his thumb against the lid. He avoided looking at me – I suppose I was meant to feel grateful.

'McFay thought it was a waste of time and told Gemma to drop it. She couldn't. She was convinced you were right and that Snow had killed Niki.' Sean's hand went up to stop me before I could even open my mouth. 'We all thought he did it. You know that. We just couldn't prove it.'

This was the first time Sean had ever said it outright. I waited.

'Gemma was convinced she could get him to spill. More than convinced. There was no talking her out of it. She stopped thinking about Snow as a suspect – to her he *was* the killer. We all do it, but it's dangerous to think you know a suspect is guilty. You develop tunnel vision and can miss the real perp because you're so busy trying to prove *your* killer is the one.'

My hand strayed to the comfort of Wolf's head under the table. 'Spare me the new recruit lecture, Sean. What happened?'

Sean let out a lungful of air. 'Sorry. Okay. So Gemma set Snow up. She was wired of course. I . . . um . . . I kept tabs on her from the car.'

I didn't trust myself to speak so I just nodded.

'She posed as this wealthy woman, husband beat her up all the time, she wanted him taken out – that sort of thing. She made it sound simple, said her husband went jogging on the outskirts of town each morning before dawn and that it'd be easy enough to make it look like a hit-and-run. It was the kind of scrotey job Snow would be tempted by.'

'And he bought it?'

'Well, no one ever said he was bright.' He flashed a grin at me but I was in no mood for it and he quickly flicked back to serious mode. Sean's better at reading me than I ever was with him. 'Anyway, it paid off. Snow wanted in. Gemma had a wad of cash with her and baited him till he was drooling. When she had him hooked she said she wanted proof he could go through with it. She went all wide-eyed, said the rumour was he'd killed a prostitute, sorry, but you know, and well, he went for it and spilled over. He told her everything. He was still boasting about killing Niki when Gemma snapped the cuffs on him. We had it all on tape.'

'How do you know he wasn't bullshitting?'

Sean softened his voice. 'Snow knew stuff, Diane. Things he couldn't have known unless he'd done it.'

'Like?'

We looked at each other. Sean knew I wouldn't let it go. He shrugged.

'The way her body was left, what items of clothing had been

removed, details we hadn't given out to the press. He did it, Diane. You were right.'

I had a flash of the last time I'd seen Niki. I saw her body in the coffin, the life gone out of her, skin waxy and damp-looking. Gone, gone, gone.

Sean stood up and paced to the window. I stared at his back, saw his shoulders heave in resignation.

'So what happened?'

'He got himself a flash lawyer. The tape was deemed inadmissible. He denied everything. Gemma got three months' suspension for "behaviour unbefitting a police officer". I got off with a censure, a rap over the knuckles.'

So, I *had* been right. Snow had killed Niki and now he was dead. I would never have the satisfaction of spitting in his face. Was that what I would have done – spat in his face? Something was nagging at me. An insistent feeling I was missing something.

'McFay was worried you'd go after Snow if you found out he'd confessed.' Sean was keeping his voice neutral. 'He embargoed the whole thing. That's why Gemma hasn't been around here for a while. She didn't think she could face you without spilling.'

He picked up that damn cigarette packet and began tapping it on the table again. Wolf clambered to his feet, banging his head on the underside of the table. Normally that would have made me laugh.

'Do you think I could have one of those?'

'I thought you'd given up. These things can kill, you know.'

And suddenly that nagging question illuminated like one of those little light bulbs above a cartoon character's head when they have a great idea. I didn't have a great idea but I had a pretty good question.

'How did Snow die?'

Sean lifted his head to look directly at me. His gaze was a lot steadier than my hands. 'He was stabbed.'

'Any chance it was suicide?'

'Not unless he stabbed himself in the back. Snow was a tricky bastard, but not that tricky.'

I was sorting all this through. Niki died twelve months ago, stabbed in the back. Snow had finally admitted killing Niki. Now Snow was dead. Sean was watching me as I ran this through the old minus-two-megabyte soft drive called my brain. When I'd got to that point, he answered the question before I had a chance to ask it.

'It looks like Snow was stabbed between the shoulder blades with a seven-inch boning knife.'

CHAPTER 2

I wound down both back windows of the car so Wolf could hang his head out one side and his tail out the other. I could hear the percussive flapping of his tongue against the glass, punctuated by little yelps of pleasure. That's one of the great things about dogs – they remind you how simple happiness can be.

As I waited for the lights to change, I thought about the last time I'd seen Niki. Not that time in the coffin. That wasn't Niki any more. The last time Niki and I had talked, we'd argued. Well, actually, I'd argued and she'd gone quiet. She'd done that since she was a little girl whenever she was upset or frightened: she'd just pull into herself and go very still and silent. Inaccessible. It used to drive me mad. I hated the way she could remove herself so totally, and it just made me yell at her even more. Twelve months ago she was removed for good. No amount of yelling was going to change that.

I slid the car through the intersection and up Pirie Street. Wolf whimpered with desire as he breathed in the aroma of greasy fried chicken from the nearby KFC. It's never had that effect on me, but then Wolf has a similar response to week-old possum carcasses so maybe that says something about the Colonel's secret ingredient.

Niki and I had argued about her working at the club. When she'd first told me she was occasionally dancing at a strip club for extra money, I'd given her the lecture about how women who sold their bodies undid all the good work of women before them. How women had fought to be treated as equals, not property to be bought, sold and discarded. How it was soul destroying to sell your body for money. I might even have mentioned slippery slopes and thin edges of wedges.

Yeah, exactly. I'd never learnt to keep my mouth shut or my opinion to myself, despite it being suggested to me on a regular basis by a number of people in my life. Niki wouldn't remember what our mother had sounded like because she'd died when Niki was born, but I was six years older than my baby sister and I remembered. When I made that slippery-slopes speech I suspect I sounded just like her. By default, when our mother died I'd taken on the role of Niki's surrogate mum. I don't know which of us hated that more.

When my lecture ran out of steam, Niki peered at me in what I suspect was a mirror image of my own squint, and told me that actually she found dancing 'empowering'. I guess she'd heard me use the word and was using it right back at me for effect, but maybe not. Maybe dancing around a pole while a whole bunch of men drooled into their laps did empower her. What did I know? She'd invited me to come along and watch her some night. She said she was 'a really hot dancer' and guys loved her.

At barely twenty with a girl-next-door face and a gorgeous, sexy body, it was no surprise to me that the guys loved her. Or that she was a hot dancer. What did surprise me was how much I hated her doing it. I'm far from being a prude and I had plenty of girlfriends who'd stripped and danced 'exotically', though I'd be hard-pressed to explain exactly what made sliding up and down a pole 'exotic'. I'd always been cool when friends did it, but for some reason I hated that my little sister did.

I pulled into a park outside Gemma's place and wound the back windows up enough so Wolf could still stick his nose out and sniff the breeze. He gave a whine of displeasure when he realised he wasn't coming with me but then settled down for a nap. Wolf is much better at waiting than I am.

Gemma lives alone in a two-storeyed, wooden house squeezed between impressive turn-of-the-century villas, perched on the slopes of Mt Victoria. The way Gemma's place was built, just forward of and on a rise above the houses on either side, makes it look as if it's leaning into the wind, like the prow of a ship. An assortment of men's work and tramping boots lay scattered in the porch at the front door. Either Gemma was making the most of her suspension and having a lot of fun at home this morning or she'd put the boots there to ward off would-be burglars. Although I hoped for her sake it was the former, I was pretty confident it was the latter.

Gemma opened the door on the first ring. She looked untidy, weary, bad tempered and emotionally bruised. That was fine. She's looked like that all the time I've known her. When she saw it was me, her mouth contorted into a great big toothpaste commercial of a smile, only on Gemma it looked more like a photo from a medical text of facial deformities.

'It's okay. Sean's told me everything,' I said quickly.

The smile was replaced by her normal scowl.

'Thank Christ for that. Come in,' she said, turning her back on me and heading into the house.

I followed her through the hall to the back, picking my way through a maze of stacked magazines, odd pieces of discarded furniture, and what looked like a pile of broken toys. The toys were a strange addition because not only does Gemma not have kids, but I'd known her to recoil from them.

I'd ask about the toys some other time. It was unlikely I'd get a satisfactory answer from her anyway. Despite, or maybe because of, her slender frame and delicate features, Gemma comes from the 'if you can't beat 'em, join 'em' school of women. She's one of the guys. It's pretty hard to be anything else if you're a female cop.

I manoeuvered the jug around a sink full of dirty dishes, filled it and plugged it in. Gemma never offers coffee so I knew this was the only way I'd get one. She'd wedged herself between two piles of books on her sofa and was studying me.

'So does it lay any ghosts? Make you feel better knowing you were right?'

I ran a couple of cups under the tap before answering. I knew there wouldn't be any clean ones in the cupboard. I've known Gem for about five years but there are still things about her I can't reconcile. She has one of the most disciplined, ordered minds I've ever known, yet she lives in total domestic chaos.

I thought about her question – in fact I'd been thinking of pretty much nothing else since Sean's visit.

'No. It doesn't lay anything at all,' I said. 'Certainly not the ghosts.'

Gem wouldn't lie to me, but she wouldn't necessarily tell me all the truth either.

'Snow did it, Diane. You can trust me on that,' she said, giving me that direct, eye-contact look they teach new recruits to use on juries, but in Gem's case it comes naturally.

I sat at the table on the one chair not piled with junk. It put me at an odd angle to her and I had to twist my neck around to meet her gaze. It made me feel at a disadvantage. She didn't seem to notice, but with Gem it's always hard to tell.

'Any idea why he did it?' I asked.

She walked to the steaming jug, keeping her back to me. I saw her fine shoulder blades shrug beneath her thin cotton shirt.

'I gave up years ago trying to figure out why scumbags do things. As they say, that way lies madness. Why do they burn little kids' legs with cigarettes? Beat the crap out of some poor kid delivering pizzas for a living? Rape little old ladies? Who knows why they do anything. Who the fuck wants to know?' She poured water on to the instant coffee, spilling a fair bit on the bench and ignoring it.

'He didn't give you any reason? He just killed Niki for the hell of it – because he could?'

Gemma put a cup on the table in front of me, pushed a pile of books on to the floor and sat on a chair opposite. For the first time I saw the faint sketching of fine lines around her eyes. The signs of ageing in friends always bring out the best in me but that's probably just me making some kind of unholy pact with the future.

Gem nodded at my mug as if daring me to drink. 'How are you these days, babe?' she asked, and peered at me through her coffee steam.

'Great,' I lied. 'Really great in fact,' I elaborated. I took a sip of the coffee, giving Gem time. I knew she was watching me, checking me out. For the first three months after Niki died I'd totally lost the plot, then three months after that I'd lost Sean, though in a very different way. Actually, I thought, maybe not so different. Separation is a kind of death, as any dog watching its owner leave the house would tell you if they could. Since Niki's death my behavior had been pretty ropey and Gemma knew it. Plus she'd witnessed my uncontrolled showdown with McFay that had lost me any police work.

It wasn't that I'd now come to terms with Niki's death or anything as mature as that, but I'd learnt how to keep my reactions hidden from everyone. Even my friends. I made a point of taking another casual sip of the ghastly coffee. Real nonchalant. It's unlikely I fooled Gem but she let me play it out.

Gemma flicked through some CDs in a drawer beneath the stereo and then slid one across the table to me. I looked at the label: *Herb Alpert and the Tijuana Brass*. My heart was thumping and not because I have a liking for '50s swing. In fact I hate it. That girl from Ipanema could just keep walking as far as I was concerned.

'You made a copy?'

Gemma looked away and shrugged. 'No way. McFay would hound me off the job for good if I'd done that.'

I grinned at her as I dropped the disc into my jacket pocket. 'I'll borrow old Herb if you don't mind.'

'Be my guest. I hate swing,' she said, dropping one eyelid in what I hoped was a wink. Or else she'd just had a little stroke. Either way, it would be bad mannered of me to draw attention to it.

We chatted about inconsequential things while we finished our coffee but neither of us is good at small talk and we were drying up long before the coffee did. The CD was burning a hole in my pocket, and there were the unspoken thanks I owed her for risking her job to get a confession out of Snow. Risking her life too.

I tried a hug and murmured thanks as I was leaving, but Gem gave me a pat on the arm that I'm likely to carry the bruise of for some time to come, and assured me she didn't need to be thanked. We stood companionably shuffling and avoiding eye contact for some time until I finally made the move and headed back towards to the car. Christ – and they say men aren't good at showing emotions. Still, I hoped she knew how grateful I felt. I owed her big time.

I drove the remaining fifty metres up Pirie Street and parked beside the Mt Victoria Bowling Club. From the shrieks of laughter I could hear coming from the green it was obvious the old silverbacks were having themselves a hell of a time. I let Wolf out and whistled him quickly through the kids' playground, ignoring the glares from protective mothers who wanted so badly to lecture me about dog leads and the proper use of them on a dog rather than looped over my own neck. Wolf zigzagged ahead of me up into the first set of pines. I filled my lungs with the balmy, pollen-filled, late afternoon northerly, and followed Wolf who, head up into the breeze, was being reeled in by an invisible line of scents.

I kept my hands deep in my pockets as I walked. My left hand scratched at the fluff accumulated in the seam; my right tapped at the casing of the CD – not the *Tijuana Brass* as the label warned, but a recording of Snow telling Gemma how he'd killed my little sister. It made me sick just thinking about it but I knew I had to listen to it – had to know the ghastly details of how she died. Surely the reality couldn't be worse than my nightmares, I told myself, knowing that was bullshit.

As I watched Wolf lumber up the slope in search of a pine cone to chase, I remembered a documentary I'd seen about a guy killed and eaten by one of the wild bears he'd been filming. His camera was running at the time of the attack but the lens was pointed in the other direction so no images were caught on film. But the microphone picked up every last yell and scream as he tried to fight off the attack, and then every last bone crunch, lip smack and slobber as the bear consumed him. The recording ended up in the possession of the dead guy's girlfriend but she'd never been able to bring herself to listen to it. In the documentary, the director listens to the tape and then tells the girlfriend she must never, *ever* play the tape. It's just too horrible. She agrees to lock the recording away, unheard.

I ran my thumb along the edge of the disc. I guess that girlfriend and I are just different.

CHAPTER 3

Heaps of people go missing. Some do it deliberately and don't want to be found. Others go missing for the prime purpose of being found: they want the reunion. They want to hear that all is forgotten or forgiven. My job is to locate the missing people and find out to which of those two groups they belong. The deal is that once I've located them I get to decide if I hand over the details of their whereabouts to the client paying me, or not. Either way I keep the deposit and my integrity. I take on jobs for individuals, for PI firms, for lawyers looking for witnesses to crimes, insurance companies, television companies, all sorts really.

Until my showdown with McFay the police service had been

a good source of work. I guess being married to a cop for five years inevitably meant I'd end up doing work for them. The police jobs were not usually about finding a missing person, but about finding the people who should be missing them. When bodies, or sometimes bits of bodies, turned up on beaches or were unearthed in pine forests, I got the enviable task of trying to find out who the corpse might once have been.

Mostly they were suicides and it was a matter of going back, sometimes as far as fifty-odd years, through police archives to try to match the remains. Often there was nothing more than the record of a phone call to police to say someone had gone missing. Sometimes not even that. They're the saddest ones. Those poor buggers unnoticed in life and unmissed in death.

The police work, which until recently was my staple, means I've ended up with office folders packed with photos of corpses in various states of decomposition. Yeah, I know, nice work if you can get it. But decaying bodies have never really bothered me. Well, not dead ones anyway. Still, I've learnt from experience that it's best for me to view work material during daylight hours. I've also learnt not to leave photos of corpses lying around on the kitchen table where Girl Guides can see them and go complaining to their parents who then pay me 'a serious visit'. After that particular sobering little event I made two vows: one, to keep all the ugly work stuff in my office, and two, never to open the door to Girl Guides.

I decided to approach Snow's confession as if it was just part of my job. Ugly work stuff. I didn't want him invading the rest of my home, and anyway I reckoned he was in good company with the rotting corpses. So, early morning, still in my pyjamas and dressing gown and clutching my small percolator of coffee – okay, Sean's percolator of coffee – I checked my emails and then, as if it was a routine job, I opened the plastic CD case, dropped the disc Gemma had given me into my laptop and clicked play.

I squashed in beside Wolf, who was curled like a shell on the small sofa, ready to spend the morning contentedly sniffing his own farts. For at least thirty seconds the only sounds were the whirr of the CD drive and the thump of my heart. I was about to get up and check the player when Gemma's voice filled the room.

'So, how will I know when you've done it? Will you contact me?'

Wolf lifted his head long enough to check Gemma wasn't in the room and then continued with his previous preoccupation. He needed to get out more. Obviously Gemma had given me an edited version of the original recording and for that I was grateful, but there was going to be no gentle lead-in and I readied myself for the hard stuff.

'You'll know because he'll be dead.'

I recognised Snow's voice immediately. For a big man he had a surprisingly whiny, high-pitched voice. Gemma's next question suggested she was thinking the same thing.

'How do I know you've got the balls to do it?'

Wolf's head shot up optimistically at the word 'balls'. Despite the nausea I was feeling I couldn't help but smile. I'd have let Wolf chase Snow's balls any time he wanted. In fact, I'd have paid good money to watch.

'Lady, your husband won't be my first, you know what I mean? Knocking over hubby with a car will be like eating peanuts. The last one I did was real up close and personal. I watched her eyes roll back when I stuck the knife in. They were pretty eyes, but they went real flat-looking once she was dead. So don't talk to me about balls because I got them all right. Nice big ones.'

There was a rustling sound that was no doubt Snow grabbing Gemma's hand and shoving it in his crotch. Nice. Knowing

Gemma, it would have taken real restraint for her not to use the opportunity to twist them right off.

'Okay, I'm sorry. I'm just a bit nervous. It's not like I've hired a hit man before. That's the correct term, is it? Hit man?' Gemma laughed, a bit unconvincingly, but like Sean said, no one ever accused Snow of being smart. I could hear Snow shifting in his seat, probably readjusting himself.

'You can call me whatever you like. It's not like we're in a long-term relationship or something. You pay me cash, I do the job, and we never see each other again. That's the deal. I'll be like an enforcer.' Snow chuckled as if that was real funny.

Gemma's voice cut in. 'If you don't mind my asking, was that a job, too? The one you just mentioned, I mean. Were you hired to do that? It's just that, I imagine, being hired to . . . *remove* someone is quite a different thing from, well, a personal killing.'

Gemma had adopted a breathless 'posh lady enjoying a bit of rough' tone that seemed to be working on Snow. She was inviting him to brag.

'What is this – a *This is Your Life* show or something?'

Snow's question was wary but it didn't sound like he was on to Gemma. Not yet, anyway. Gemma giggled – something I'd never known her do in real life. I heard the plastic seat covers creak, then Snow, languid now, enjoying himself.

'I don't do personal and I don't do freebies. Like that guy with the funny hair says, it was just business. She was a whore. Dumb too. Thought she could walk away when she felt like it. "*I don't want to do it any more*",' he mimicked in a girly voice. 'Well, it doesn't work like that. But, you know, upmarket nice-looking lady like you, I might be prepared to consider a discount.'

I was pretty sure this wasn't a threat. He even sounded a tad begrudging.

Gemma spoke up quickly. 'Listen, money's not a problem. I've got it here.' I could hear crinkling. She must have had the cash ready in a paper bag. 'There's five thousand dollars here, all in ten and twenty dollar notes like you said. And I'll give you the other half when you've done the job. That seems fair. Because I don't have any proof that you can actually see this through. I mean, despite what you say, I don't really know you've killed anyone before. You could drive away with my five thousand and that's the last I'll hear from you. You could have read about that girl, the prostitute, in the papers and then gone around telling people you did it, so as to – well, I don't know, to impress them.'

Gemma's voice had gone up an octave as she searched for a convincingly aggrieved, indignant tone. She was pushing her luck and she would have known it. I imagined I could hear the faint, fast beat of her heart, but it could have been my own pulse racing.

I imagined Sean listening to all this from the car nearby. Tense, alert, hand on the door handle. Ready to respond as soon as she gave the signal. I bet he was swearing at Gemma under his breath, at the risk she was taking in pushing Snow that hard, and maybe regretting he'd agreed to be part of this. I'd heard him mumble and swear like that often enough when he was frustrated with me. The memory made me smile.

'Well, I'll tell you what wasn't in the papers.' Snow's voice boomed out as he moved his lips so close to the microphone I could hear the sibilant click and pop of spit against his teeth. Gemma's wire would have been attached near her collar. I could picture Snow's lips and teeth, feel his breath hot and moist on her neck. 'I stuck that bitch with a knife right between the shoulder blades. I thought she'd die pretty much straight away but it took eight minutes. Eight fucking minutes. I timed it. Jesus, there was enough time for an ad break! I thought about sticking her again, get it over with, but it was kind of interesting to watch. She fought it. That chick really did not want to die.'

My hands were shaking so badly the coffee was spilling.

I placed my mug on the floor. The room was retreating and expanding like lungs. There was just Snow's voice. Nothing but his voice. Bile rose in my throat.

'And you know what? I thought of doing her in those eight minutes. I got her dress hitched up, and I was all good to go, but she was wearing these panties – like kids' panties with fucking puppies and balloons or something on them. Well, I may be some things, but I'm not a pervert. Those little kids' panties put me right off.'

Wolf yelped in pain. I was clutching the roll at the back of his neck so hard I'd hurt him. I didn't want to hear any more. I tried to stand but my legs wouldn't support me. Snow hadn't finished. He laughed. A thin, unlikely laugh for such a huge man.

'By the time I'd ripped them off her and was ready to go again, she was dead. I thought about doing her anyway but . . .' Snow was still laughing as I staggered across the room and slammed down the laptop lid, shutting him up.

The room had retreated entirely, leaving me in a black void. There was a roaring in my head and I was pretty sure it wasn't the beating of angels' wings the nuns used to talk about. I took deep breaths, willing myself not to pass out. That film director had been right: the bear-man's girlfriend should never, *ever* listen to the sound of her loved one being mauled.

Rabbits. On her underwear. When Niki was five she went through a phase of what's now called obsessive compulsive disorder, shorthanded by the familiar to OCD. Dad had yet another new live-in girlfriend who found his youngest child 'difficult' and there were murmurings that perhaps Niki should spend some time getting 'the kind of help she deserves'. In other words, Dad's girlfriend thought life would be a lot more fun without this creepy kid hanging around touching everything three times and counting her footsteps and generally being a pain in the arse and an embarrassment at dinner parties. Even

I could see that unless Niki stopped doing that shit she was going to be locked up and therapied to hell.

She'd become obsessed with the idea of luck. Good luck, bad luck, how arbitrarily it was handed out. Not that she talked about it like that as a five-year-old, but it's how I later came to think about it. Back then, at eleven, all I knew was that I had to stop her walking three times one way, then three times the other way around every lamp post between home and school. If I let her, by the time we got to school it was time to turn back around and come home again. That happened a couple of times, which led to the live-in girlfriend suggesting Dad get Niki 'twenty-four hour *quality* care'.

I knew that meant 'lock her up and throw away the key' so I used every trick I could think of to keep Niki from circling lamp posts. I'd hold her hand all the way from home to school to stop her crossing her fingers over each other, which she did once for twenty-four hours, crippling her hands so badly she couldn't hold a pencil or her knife and fork for a fortnight. And I worked hard at distracting her from her compulsion to touch every piece of wood between our home and the school gates, to go in search of black cats, cross her eyes, walk backwards . . . you name it.

I figured she wasn't so much trying to attract good luck as warding off the bad. If I worked at it and stayed attentive, Niki was pretty much okay with me, but as soon as I went to my own classroom or left her alone in the house for more than five minutes, she reverted to those maddening, obsessive-compulsive behaviours.

Things were looking bad for Niki and I was losing ground with her. Then one day as I admired a blue sparkly nail polish in the $2 Shop, I spotted a 'Good Luck Specials' bin full of tubes of nylon panties. The panties were emblazoned with rabbits holding bunches of balloons that read *Good Luk!* With only the briefest glance of regret towards the nail polish, I used all my pocket money to buy them. I told Niki they were magical good-luck knickers but that they would only work if she kept them secret and stopped doing all that other weird shit. I told her all those other things would reverse the good-luck charm. I did a good job on her and she bought it. Yeah, okay, I admit it's pretty easy to bullshit a five year old, but I was only eleven.

Niki secretly wore the good-luck panties and stopped all the weird crap, and after a couple of months she semed to have forgotten about the whole thing. I'd forgotten about it anyway until just over a year ago when I'd spotted the same knickers in the $2 Shop. Bizarrely, they had SM size complete with bunnies holding *Good Luk!* balloons. I gave them to Niki for Christmas. I thought she'd laugh and either throw them at me or spend the rest of the day wearing them on her head – a party favourite with both of us. When she first unwrapped them, she grinned at me, maybe expecting them to explode or something, but then her face changed as the memories began to surface.

And then to my horror I realised she was crying. I told her I was sorry, it was just a joke, something I thought she'd remember and laugh about. She did laugh then, but it was strained and fake and made me feel like shit. I tried again to apologise, suggested we swap presents because hers to me was actually very cool – a six-inch-tall 'Dolly Surprise' with waist-length hair that retracted into a hole in her head when you cranked her arm like a windmill – but Niki wouldn't swap. She plunged those stupid damn knickers into her purse. She said she was keeping them. She said she was sure they'd bring her luck. Maybe even *luk!*

Two weeks later she was murdered.

My legs gave up the effort to keep me standing. I slumped to the floor, wrapping my arms around my knees. I heard great howling sobs come out of me, sobs that must have been lodged somewhere deep in my stomach ever since I'd been told Niki was dead. So, that's where the grief had been hiding for the last twelve months. It was a relief to let it go. Warm, comforting and awful, like wetting the bed when you're a kid.

Wolf whimpered and I turned to him. He was sitting bolt upright with the lead hanging from his mouth, head cocked in that inimitable Disney cartoon way. That's another great thing about dogs: they do their best to be sympathetic to us, caught up as we are in the ugliness of being human, but they never lose sight of their own priorities. It was time for a walk.

I dressed, hunched myself into my walking jacket, and went in search of Wolf's collar. I forced myself to think dispassionately about what I'd learnt from the recording. Gemma had edited the original and all I'd heard was the damning bit – the five minutes before the cavalry, aka Sean, arrived and dragged Snow out of there. Not that I needed to hear any more, that was for sure. Snow had done it all right. He'd killed Niki. But I already knew that: his confession was just confirmation of what I'd known for a long time.

I looped the collar around Wolf's head and strung the lead over the back of my neck. I never actually use the lead on Wolf but I do like the feel of the cold chain on my neck. That little quirk is something I don't share with many people.

What I'd learnt from the recording was that killing Niki was a paid job. Snow had said he didn't do personal and he didn't do freebies, and so, bizarre as it seemed, someone must have ordered a hit on her. Who would have paid Snow to kill Niki? Had Niki got deeper into the seedy world of strip clubs and prostitution than I'd thought? Did she know too much about the workings of the club – the money laundering, the drugs? Was there someone at the club who didn't want her breaking out of their control? The club's owner, maybe?

I hadn't taken up Niki's invitation to watch her dance. I'd never been inside the doors of the club, though sometimes, when I couldn't sleep, I'd park across the road from it and watch the men enter and exit. I'd looked out for her all her life and it was a hard habit to break. Sometimes I'd see her leave, waving a girlish goodbye to the security guys on the door. Watching from across the street was the closest I'd got to the place. I had no idea who Niki worked with or for.

I had two options: front up to the people at the club and find out about Niki's life there before she was murdered, or go undercover, get myself hired as an 'exotic' dancer and find out what I could that way. I checked out my body in the hallway mirror. The Doc Martin boots, faded jeans and dog-hair-covered hoodie didn't make for a hot look, and the chain over my neck added a decidedly punk touch, but I knew the twenty-eight-year-old body beneath wasn't in too bad a shape. At around five foot eight, I was always picked for the netball and basketball teams and my height gives me a leggy look. The actual legs are pretty good too, particularly if I remember to shave them. Wide hips, long torso, flat stomach, and breasts which, though not large, always look alert and ready for action. I couldn't claim to be a great dancer but if I held on to that pole like I'd seen them do on TV, I reckoned I'd be able to shake and roll my body around it okay.

I'd just convinced myself that undercover was the way to go when I caught sight of my scowling face. As long as I can remember, well-meaning friends, elderly relatives, colleagues, boyfriends, husbands – they've all told me I'd look 'nice' if I'd just stop frowning. The more positive tried the 'You look so nice when you smile' version. Neither approach worked. I've never wanted to be nice and it's too late to change the set of my face now. I suspect I'm not bad looking, but my habitual glower is undoubtedly a man turn-off for all but the most intrepid. And I doubt that men who have to pay girls to take their clothes off are intrepid types but that may just be a prejudice of mine. Unless I was prepared to wear a paper bag over my head while

I danced, or – more difficult option – actually smile at the punters, undercover probably wasn't going to work.

I whistled Wolf out the door, letting it slam behind me. Immediately I felt better. There's nothing like being outdoors with a dog trotting along in front of you to lighten your mood. Okay, I decided, I'd just have to front up to the strip club and suss it out that way. Wolf lifted his leg and let out a long, satisfying stream against the lamp post. I stopped with him, admiring, as I'm sure he did, the way the steam swirled into the cool, early morning air.

I'd been so caught up thinking about Snow killing Niki that I'd forgotten the most recent development: Snow's death. Snow had killed Niki by knifing her in the back. Now it looked like Snow had been murdered in the same way. Although I had no wish to bring his killer to justice, in fact, I'd be tempted to shake the hand of the guy who did it, there was no doubt Snow's death and Niki's were inextricably linked.

It was no use going to the club until late at night, so that gave me the whole day to finish the report on my last missing persons job, and fire off the invoice so I could pay the mortgage and fill the fridge. Only one serious problem remained. What the hell does a girl wear to a strip club?

CHAPTER 4

I settled on what I hoped was a sophisticated look: black silk trousers, open-necked, white silk blouse nipped at the waist with a three-inch-wide, Mediterranean-blue belt. I don't do heels, partly because of my height but mostly because I like to be able to run if I need to. Checking myself out in the hallway mirror, I was pretty sure I'd achieved the look of a liquorice allsort rather than one of sophistication but it would have to do. Anyway, it seemed unlikely with naked women dancing around the place that there would be many looks in my direction. What I couldn't understand was why I felt so nervous about going to the club. What was I afraid of – being hit by flying pussy?

I found a TV park outside, locked the car and headed

towards the neon lights of the tritely named Pussy Galore. Two imposing men in fine charcoal-grey suits stood guard at the door, hands clasped in front of their groins and legs slightly apart, the way they must be trained to at security guard school. Actually, I reminded myself, they probably learnt it at karate school and I should wipe the smart-arse sneer off my face. Samoan, well over six feet, broad-shouldered and flashing wide smiles of perfect white teeth, they made the kind of handsome pair I could, after six months of abstinence, happily imagine as bookends – with me as the book.

As I passed between them into the entrance alcove I made a real effort to erase my scowl. I even attempted a smile. One of the Bookends, surprisingly quick for a guy of his size, slipped ahead of me, barring the interior glass door with his arm. I'm pretty sure my scowl returned.

'I have to stamp your hand first', he said, indicating my clenched fist. 'Then I'll buzz you in.'

He manoeuvred his bulk behind a little plywood island and I felt like a five-year-old holding out the back of my hand. He applied the stamp with a studied concentration, throwing me a shy smile as he let me go. Sheesh! I'd been expecting grimaces, sneers and crass gestures. Instead I was being treated with deference and a polite but low-key welcome. It made me uneasy.

'It's ladies' night,' he smiled, as if that explained everything.

A button was hit somewhere and the opaque glass doors etched with reclining pussycats slid apart. My Bookend lifted his eyebrows in the time-honoured Pacific gesture, and motioned with his head that I could enter. I glanced back at the guy still on the street and in that moment a look, maybe a signal, passed between them. I stepped into the club and the pussy-etched doors slid closed behind me.

My first thought was that the place was on fire. After the cool evening air, the blast of heat was like stepping from a plane on to the tarmac in the tropics. Roils of smoke swirled around me and flame-red horizontal LED lights flickered and spun directly into my eyes. The bass was so loud my teeth buzzed with the vibration. I took a step forward and could make out a dozen or so semi-naked girls seated around a catwalk the size of a gangplank. Perched on stools in chattering groups of two and three, the girls resembled a flock of Easter chicks fluffed up in pretty, pastel feathers. Faux-harem silks wafted dreamily in the warm air of the industrial blow heaters. The occasional pussycat tail was absentmindedly swirled like a skipping rope.

I circumvented the gangplank, smiling at girls who looked back at me with blank disinterest. If any were wondering why a single woman was at a strip club, they kept their interest well hidden, but my appearance did seem to set off a domino effect of languid movement. Several of the girls slid off their stools and began shifting their weight from one foot to the other. They might have been dancing or just trying to get their circulation back after sitting for too long. For the first time in my life I felt overdressed.

I made my way to the back of the room where two tomato-red vinyl sofas were installed at right angles to each other. A girl appeared at my elbow. She was naked except for tiny lace knickers that glowed the startling greenish white of a skeleton in a ghost train ride.

'Hi, I'm Chloe, I'll take that for you,' she offered, draping my coat over her arm. She looked about seventeen, wore dramatic Egyptian-style eye make-up to complement her sunbed-bronzed skin. Her hair was held off her face by an Alice band made incongruous by the enormous metal ring with flashing stars pierced through her right nipple. I winced, clasping my hands to keep from cupping my own breast in sympathy.

'Thanks. And could I have a drink?' I asked, reaching for my wallet.

She flashed her teeth which, like her knickers, radiated a

startling, ghoulish green-white. 'Sure. You want to buy me one too?'

I'd been wondering how I was going to get to talk to the girls about Niki but at this rate it might be easier than I thought.

'Okay.' I hoped I wasn't making some ghastly blunder. For all I knew, agreeing to buy her a drink was a euphemism for an all-night orgy.

'I'll just take a swipe of your credit card now, and then at the end of the night I'll give you a receipt. You don't have to worry about anything while you're here, because it's all taken care of.' She voiced exactly my suspicions. Misinterpreting my hesitation she added, 'Don't worry, everything you spend here will appear on your bank statement as a donation to the Feline Protection Services.'

'Great. I'll have a red wine and yeah, sure, you order what you want for yourself.' I shrugged and passed her my credit card, mentally adding up my credit balance and hoping for the best.

As Chloe clicked off towards the bar the music changed to a deep, throbbing, sexual rhythm. I glanced behind me at the DJ who sported a brilliant red, pubic-like strip of hair down the centre of his otherwise butt-naked pate. I followed the direction of his gaze. A short, tidily dressed Asian man was leaning towards one of the girls on the stools, a proprietary hand on the back of her neck. She was looking away as he spoke, but then obediently slid off the stool and clambered up on to the catwalk. She took custody of the pole and began swaying around it, her tiny hot pants and lace bra so luminous a diffuse halo outlined her body. She walked four steps to the pole at the other end and swayed some more. I had a horrible suspicion it was my entrance that had set this enervated movement in motion.

The Asian man had settled himself in a prime watching position next to the stage, but all his attention was on his mobile which he thumbed intently. I scratched at the door of my memory for anything Niki might have told me about this guy. Gordon? Gordy? Something like that. I think she said he'd inherited the club from his uncle. He glanced up as a group of young men entered. They formed a huddle on the far side of the catwalk, their movements jerky and nervous, their laughter loud and forced. The girl on stage didn't seem to register them. Gordon went back to his texting.

Chloe leaned over, tits swinging like udders, and placed my wine on the low table, then she dropped on to the adjacent sofa. She was holding what looked like a club soda that had probably cost me twenty bucks of feline protection.

She held out thin pale fingers for me to shake. 'I'm Chloe, but I think I might have already told you that.'

I squeezed her fingers in what I presumed was a girly version of a handshake. They were surprisingly cold given the heat of the room.

Chloe started right in. 'If you want a lap dance that'll cost a hundred bucks and a VIP lap dance – that's touching and stuff – costs a hundred and fifty. Or you can just buy 'pussy dollars' for the stage dancing, but it's, you know, better for us if you want a lap dance. I'm really good at it but you don't have to have me. You can pick any of the girls.' Chloe smiled, her teeth and tiny panties flashing luridly.

'Look, I'm sorry.' I was feeling out of my depth. 'I just want to talk to you. About a girl who used to work here. Her name was Niki. Niki Rowe.'

Chloe shrugged. 'Okay. Whatever. That'll cost fifty bucks for ten minutes and I won't do more than ten minutes, okay?' She crossed her legs, swinging one long limb over the other, and took a sip of her drink. She smiled again, apparently waiting for me to start.

'Do you remember Niki? She worked here for about six months. She left about a year ago,' I prompted her. 'She was your age, maybe a bit older, and she looked, well, a bit like me only younger and prettier. Definitely smilier.'

Chloe's hands flew to her mouth and her eyes widened. 'Oh my gosh! You're for real!'

Actually, right then, in that place, having that conversation, I was having serious doubts about that.

She giggled. 'I thought you wanted me to talk dirty,' she explained cheerfully. 'You really want to talk, as in *talk* talk? Like conversation?' She uncrossed her legs and leaned in for her drink.

'Ah, yeah. That would be good. Is that a problem?'

She took a sip, eyeing me across the top of her glass with those heavily made-up eyes. Her mascaraed lashes stuck together at the far corner of each eye. In an attempt to separate them she would squeeze her eyes shut and then open them wide. It gave her a peculiar, animated look. The things we women do . . .

'No, that's cool, but it still costs the same. I mean, I have to earn, okay?'

I nodded my agreement and took a sip of the red wine which immediately paint-stripped the roof off my mouth. I replaced the glass carefully, worried for the table.

'I just want to find out about my sister, Niki. She worked here until a year ago. She was killed. I want to find out about her – who she spent time with before she died.'

I kept my eyes on Chloe's, doing my best to ignore the video on the wall behind her head where a girl wearing nothing but high heels was doing an act which involved flaming torches being passed between her legs. She'd either had a Brazilian, or at some point she'd misjudged the flame action. Whatever the cause, she seemed intent on making sure the camera paid close attention to her hairlessness.

Chloe reached a hand up to release tendrils of hair caught beneath her Alice band.

'Oh, you mean Bonnie,' she said. 'We only ever use stage names here. It's kind of like acting, you know?' Chloe's attention was wavering. Her finger twirled a strand of hair as her gaze drifted towards the dancer now swaying listlessly in front of a mirror at the end of the stage, her dreamlike absorption with her own image somehow touching and more intimate than anything else she'd done.

'You knew Niki as Bonnie?' I prompted, forcing Chloe's attention back to me.

'Yeah. She was a really cool chick. We got on great. And she was an excellent dancer. She made shitloads on a good night. She liked to dance on stage, you know? Most of us don't. The money's not in it. I mean, look at those guys.' She stared angrily at a row of men leaning against the stage.

The tableau of guys stood close together, shouldering each other in companionable aggression. They reminded me of cattle stamping and peering through the slats in an abattoir truck. I watched the dancer separate herself with reluctance from her own mirror image and turn back towards the herd of men. Leaning over to grasp her ankles she obligingly presented herself to them.

'They pay their twenty bucks at the door then just perv at the girls,' Chloe added with disdain.

It seemed an unreasonable complaint given what the dancer was doing right then, but before I could say anything in the guys' defence, the music changed and a new dancer climbed on stage. This one wore a nipped-waist, soft cotton blouse and long, layered skirt that fell in feminine folds to below her knees. She was the only female in the room, apart from me, who had any actual clothes on. As she reached up to clasp the pole I noticed her feet were bare. In a room of women wearing nothing much more than shoes, those wriggling toes looked extremely naked. Instead of gyrating against the pole, she clasped it and climbed those little bare feet right up between her hands, her bronze ponytail falling back towards the stage, her skirt rucked up to reveal bikini pants.

She flipped and landed, giggling shyly towards the men who, as one, had reached to catch her fall. Caught in these beseeching gestures, they shuffled self-consciously and shoved hands in pockets or grabbed at their drinks. The drowning men drank deeply, their shoulders slumped in defeat. The dancer smiled at them and modestly rearranged her skirt.

'Vex is brilliant isn't she?' Chloe whispered, echoing a version of my thoughts. 'She's got quite a fan club. She only dances Tuesdays and Thursdays and those guys are here both nights.'

I noted a young man sitting alone near the far end of the stage. Unlike the others, who all could have been contenders for Young Businessman of the Year, he was dressed in black jeans and T-shirt, a suit jacket thrown on top, no doubt to get him past the dress-code police at the door. He was hunched over his beer glass and, unlike every other punter, seemed more interested in his drink than in the dancer.

'What about him? Is he a regular?'

Chloe followed the direction of my gaze. 'Oh, that's Stoke. Funny you should ask about him actually because he was really close to Bonnie. Bonnie, Niki, whatever – your sister, I mean. He was totally into her.'

I studied his face, sure I'd seen him somewhere before. Now he too was watching the ponytailed dancer who'd abandoned the pole and was dancing to her own reflection in the mirror at the end of the stage. The buttons on her blouse had come undone as if by accident. Captured as she was by her own image, she seemed oblivious to her audience. The dazzling LED lights caught the copper and bronze highlights in her swinging hair. She looked like a young girl practising dance moves in the privacy of her bedroom. Somehow in this very public place she had managed to turn us all into secret voyeurs. This girl's dance routine made me feel dirty.

I angled myself back towards Chloe. 'How does it work here? Do you get paid by the dance or by the hour or what?'

'Oh, no way. We have to pay to dance here. That's why we hate it when punters just pay the door charge and then spend the night perving at us.' She saw my look of confusion. 'Gavin gets the door fee, except girl customers don't pay a cover charge on ladies' night, that's tonight. We don't get any of the door money.'

Gavin. That was right. The owner of the club was called Gavin.

Chloe counted the facts out on her fingers as if I was a slow learner. 'And we have to pay Gavin two hundred bucks a week to dance here.' She lifted her eyebrows at me, possibly as a gesture of bewilderment or perhaps it was the mascara problem.

'So how do you earn?' Even as I heard myself ask the question I knew I sounded stupidly naive.

'Well, the guys buy pussy dollars and they put that money in the dancer's garter. Well, except Vex. The guys don't get to touch her when she's dancing. They have to put the money on the stage and she collects it at the end.'

At the mention of her we both turned back to the dancer now doing up the buttons on her blouse and giggling. Chloe took a sip of her drink and eyed me flatly before continuing.

'But mostly, you know, we earn our money by lap dancing. Like I said before, there's the ten, fifteen or twenty-minute no-touch lap dances. Most guys pay upfront for twenty minutes but only last five, if they're lucky.' She grinned. 'Only two minutes if *we're* lucky. There's no refunds,' she added, flicking the fringe from her eyes. And then there's the VIP lap dances that involve, like, touching, and we charge heaps for those, though Gavin gets a cut too, of course.'

'Of course,' I agreed. I was totally out of my depth.

Chloe was warming to her role of teacher as she filled me in on the finer details of the commerce of sex. 'I can make seven or eight hundred bucks a week, easy. That's nearly all from lap dances though. The deal is we have to dance on the stage even though it doesn't earn us much, because it's kind of what the place is known for, and it brings the paying customers in. Then it's up to us to get the punters to buy lap dances. It's mostly regulars here, and they're, you know, easy, really.'

This burst of animated discourse seemed to take it out of Chloe and she slumped back against the vinyl, peering at a lock of her hair for split ends. I sat back too, feigning casualness. The club was filling up with groups of men dressed in their best, their jaws shiny and abraded from recent shaves. It seemed touching that they wanted to make a good impression on these girls who were working the room now, leaning close, whispering, brushing against the men, touching them, and then withdrawing again.

'And my sister – did she have regulars?' I asked.

Seeing the real trade under way, Chloe was losing interest in me. 'Sure. Like I said, she was real popular.' She knocked back the last of her drink.

'And would any of these regulars be pissed off if she told them she wasn't going to do this any more? Like Gavin, the guy who owns this place. Would he have tried to stop Niki leaving?'

Chloe stood and adjusted her tiny panties with a snap. 'Gavin? No way. He's useless.' She waved dismissively in his direction. 'There was one guy,' she added, tapping the nipple ring to bring it back to life. 'Loads of money but, you know, a bit of an arsewipe, actually. He got totally obsessed with Bonnie. Wanted her all to himself, that kind of bullshit. She was a bit freaked by him, I think.'

My palms went sweaty and it wasn't the heat. I stood but even my height was no match for Chloe's heels.

'Any idea of his name? How I could find him?' I asked.

'Richard . . . Browning? Brownlee? Something like that. He was into buildings but I don't know in what way.' Chloe held out those long, cool fingers for me to squeeze again. 'He was a nutcase, if you want my opinion,' she said and smiled. I squeezed the offered fingers, resisting the urge to blow warm breath on them.

'You've been a great help, Chloe. Thanks.' I scrabbled in my wallet and handed her three twenty-dollar notes. She palmed the money and with a little finger wave, tottered off on her heels towards a man who'd just entered. He appeared to be saluting but was more likely shielding his eyes from the riddles of pulsing lights.

I made my way past the stage to where the guy Chloe had called Stoke still leaned. I was sure I recognised him, but still couldn't figure out where from. He had a narrow canine face framed by shaggy auburn hair – maybe it was just his resemblance to Wolf that made him look familiar. He was hunched over, but he straightened as I drew near. I saw his jaw slacken in recognition. So he knew me too. I was about to speak to him when someone tapped me on the arm. I turned and was handed my coat and credit card by a completely naked girl with a radiant smile. I had to fight the urge to wrap the coat around her. By the time I'd signed the receipt for the drinks and turned back, Stoke was gone.

Standing this close to the stage, I could see fine blonde hairs on the legs of ponytail girl who was still dancing on the catwalk. Actually, she was skipping with a wooden-handled skipping rope. The smell of male sweat and aftershave swamped me and suddenly I needed to leave. Quickly. I pushed through the stamping, jostling males towards the exit.

At the door I glanced back: the punters all wore the tragic expressions of drowning men surfacing for their final breath. They were real sirens these girls, luring the guys to the depths. I caught one last glimpse of the ponytailed girl on stage. She seemed to be looking in my direction, her lips parted in a china doll's smile.

CHAPTER 5

The cool night air hit me like an avalanche. I hunkered into my coat, grateful for the excuse to hug myself. I'd finally had a glimpse into Niki's world and what I'd seen didn't make me feel that great. The Bookends were still there, filling the entranceway, shoulder to shoulder now, stamping their feet and puffing their breaths into the cold air. Separated from the herd, they looked bored and adrift. Politely, they made room for me to pass between them.

Tall though I am, their shared bulk dwarfed me. Feeling dwarfed doesn't happen to me a lot. Obviously, standing eye to eye with a woman didn't happen to them a lot either. I plucked out the little notepad I always carry with me and flipped it open.

'I'm investigating the death of James Patrick Wilson,' I said, consulting my notepad. 'Also known as Snow.' What I read was not Snow's alias but a shopping list I'd been meaning to do something about for days, but they couldn't see that. 'What can you tell me about the guy? He spend a lot of time here?' I gave the ballpoint an authoritative click, keeping my manner relaxed and confident, just like every cop I'd ever known. The Bookends glanced their suspicion at each other but my height and demeanour seemed to convince them I was the real thing. Or maybe it was my ballpoint pen action. The bigger of the two hunched his shoulders towards me.

'Yeah, Snow spent time here. He hung out with the girls a bit.'

'Any girls in particular?' I kept my eyes on the pad.

The talkative Bookend shrugged, making his neck disappear like a turtle's. 'Vex, maybe,' he said, his eyes darting to his partner for confirmation. The partner was eyeing me closely. I wrote 'Snow' and drew an arrow towards 'Vex'. From the look of the big guy it was just a matter of time before he told the chatty one to shut up. I got straight to the point.

'What about . . .' I flipped through pages of domestic lists and GST workings, pretending to look for my own sister's name. 'Niki . . . Niki Rowe. Working name Bonnie. You see Snow with her a lot?'

The Bookends looked at each other. The talkative one tapped his forehead and chest in a sketchy attempt at crossing himself. 'She's dead. Bonnie died about a year ago.'

'Yeah, we got that,' I said, sounding as much like a cynical cop as I could.

'You look like her,' the silent one said. 'Like Bonnie. You're her sister, eh?'

I smiled weakly, feeling pretty dumb now.

'She talked about you a lot. She was real proud,' the quieter one said and he put a hand the size of a dinner plate on my arm.

My guess is, in another place, another time, he was one of those guys who could lumber up the sideline with a footy clapped in one hand like it was a tennis ball. 'I'm sorry about what happened to Bonnie. She was a real nice girl,' he added. He might be working at a strip club but he was a well-brought up, polite, Christian boy, and the wet eyes were for real. I felt mine well up in response.

Before I could say anything, the glass doors behind us slid open and the small Asian man, Gavin, the club owner, stepped out, in a miasma of smoke. I shoved the notepad back in my pocket. The Bookend took his paw from my arm, after giving it a friendly squeeze to increase the size of the bruise Gemma had inflicted. Gavin walked right up to me, which, given the height difference, wasn't a good idea on his part.

When he tilted his head to speak, he seemed to recognise his disadvantage and took a step back, flapping his hands in a histrionic gesture.

'What you want? This business. Dancing business, not talking business. You go away now. I don't want trouble.'

I would have moved off without a fight but he made a shooing gesture, and being shooed is not something I like. I closed the space between us, towering over him.

'Well, you've got trouble, mate,' I said, 'because my little sister worked here and she was murdered by one of your heavies. Now that heavy's been killed too.'

'Not *my* heavy. Snow not my heavy. I only hire Asian heavy,' he informed me with surprising candour. He indicated the Bookends who had resumed their default positions either side of the door. 'These guys big. They look good to punters. They stop fight before it happen.' The Bookends straightened their shoulders in pride. 'But they're no good for real jobs. I use Asian heavy for real jobs.'

I may not be a fabulous judge of character, but I was pretty sure Gavin was telling me the truth.

'Snow not Asian,' he added helpfully and then made that shooing gesture again. 'You go away now. You're *no* good for business. You scare off punters.'

With that he turned, the doors slid open, and like a magician in a tacky stage show he disappeared into the smoke. Despite him, despite the place, despite the realisation that this had been Niki's life, I laughed.

So, I scare off the punters eh? Yeah, well, ain't that the truth!

At home Wolf was waiting at the door, toenails clicking as he danced from paw to paw in delight. I have a theory that if lovers greeted each other the way dogs do, there would be no such thing as divorce. The only downside I could think of was how long you'd have to grow your toenails.

I showered in the hottest water I could stand, letting the hard pellets pound into my skull. Eyes closed, I replayed the scene at the club. It was obvious Niki had been selling sex. I hadn't realised how much I'd hoped she was just dancing like she'd claimed she was.

Then I remembered the ponytailed girl's dance routine. In some ways, maybe selling sex was cleaner, more honest, somehow. A straightforward commercial transaction. Sex. In theory I had no problem with the buying or selling of it. I had no religious or other belief system that instructed me to object to it. Prostitution was a win-win, I reasoned. The girls got money, the guys got . . . actually I wasn't sure what they got from the deal. An orgasm, obviously. Well – you'd hope.

I lathered my shoulders and neck with coconut soap, mixing the steam with its sweet, cloying tropical perfume. I remembered asking Sean if guys told their mates they'd had sex with a prostitute. I assumed they'd be embarrassed, almost ashamed – that it was a kind of admission they couldn't get it for free so had to buy it. But Sean had laughed. I smiled, remembering how his hair fell across his forehead when he laughed like that. Sean said that men boasted of using prostitutes and that other guys were impressed. I didn't understand that.

I lathered my breasts, feeling the nipples harden. Six months without sex was the longest I'd been celibate since I was a virgin. I was beginning to suspect there's truth in the warning 'use it or lose it'. Even masturbation was becoming a bore. I was going to have to do something about that. But where does a girl go for sex? If there was the equivalent for women, like a strip joint where women paid men to lap dance, would I use it? I doubt it, but who knows? Maybe paying for it is like 'Sex, Jim, but not as we know it'. Separating the lips of my own sex, I spent some time not thinking about anything much at all. And it wasn't too boring either.

I have a recurring dream. I'm in my house. Not the one from my waking life, but a special dream house. I'm always walking through it, locating new rooms that I didn't know existed. Sometimes I wander through luxurious, well-lit, big, open rooms and I have a real sense of liking this place. Other times the dream turns nightmarish and I come across dark, dank cellars or dusty mote-filled attics that I'm afraid to enter. Someone told me once that the house was my subconscious. Yeah, well, maybe. I don't go in for that stuff.

Whatever it is, no sooner had Wolf curled into his bed beside mine than I plummeted into a dream of the house. This time I was searching, running from room to room in a slow-mo dream run. I was looking for Niki. I started to panic. Where was she? I went through room after room, dragging my paralysed sleep-legs, forcing them to move. Snow was in one room, his head in his hands. He seemed to be crying. In another room were the dancers I had seen earlier, huddled in a corner of the room like frightened chooks. But no Niki. I went on, room by room, searching. Then suddenly I stopped. Something was behind me. Some*one* was behind me.

No sooner had I thought this than whoever it was jumped me and I landed hard on the floor, the weight of my assailant pinning me to the ground. I twisted my head, trying to see who it was. Fear hit me: he was going to stab me in the back the way he had stabbed Niki. I struggled. I was hot with the effort, sweating, but still I couldn't get him off me. It was all in slow-mo, my attempts weighed down by sleep.

And then with a huge effort, I twisted hard and finally I saw my assailant. It was me. The shock of it startled me awake. Wolf had crept on to my bed during the night and, not content to take Sean's side – I mean the side formerly known as Sean's – had spread himself across the bed, pinning my legs. So that explained my nightmare.

Almost.

CHAPTER 6

Despite my dream I woke refreshed, and while I brushed my teeth I went over what I'd figured out so far. Niki wanted out of the sex business and someone had paid Snow to kill her rather than let her go. The obvious suspect was the club owner Gavin, who last night had given me a succinct lesson on his selection criteria for employing security guards. I needed to find out more about this guy but at first meeting he seemed way too pragmatic to order a hit on Niki just because she'd decided to quit working for him. I figured girls must come and go in that place with inevitable regularity.

I'd just spat out my toothpaste when the phone rang.

'Diane? It's Inspector Frank McFay,' he said, giving me his

full title as if we didn't already know each other. 'I've got a job for you.'

McFay hadn't spoken to me since the day he'd thrown me out of his office after our little set-to. Ringing in person to propose work was probably his version of a peace offering. I made a noise to suggest he should continue but I knew from experience that once McFay was in full flight he would keep going whether I joined in or not.

'A body's turned up in the Rimutakas. The local boys reckon it's been there for a couple of decades at least. We don't have the manpower to waste trying to find out who this joker is, so I thought of you.'

This was classic McFay. Definitely old school, was Frank.

'Gee thanks, Frank,' I said, confident the sarcasm would fly right past him.

'I told the Wainuiomata boys you'll be out there by ten this morning. It's no use asking me about it,' he continued, as if I'd assailed him with questions. 'The boys out there know all there is to know, though I gather there's not much to go on.'

I walked the phone through to my office and reached for a pad and pen.

'Who do I see out there?'

McFay continued crankily as if I hadn't spoken. 'I don't want you racking up too many hours on this. The boys did a cursory check on persons reported missing in the area over the last couple of decades, but they came up with zip in the way of a match, so it might just remain a John Doe. Any questions?'

'Is this a peace offering?' I asked.

'What kind of guy would offer you a rotting corpse as a peace offering?' he shot back, though I thought I could detect a grin. 'Listen here, Diane. If I get word you've been sniffing around for information about the Snow homicide, I'll pull you off this missing persons like a shot. You hear me?'

His voice was so loud I suspected my neighbour could hear him. I lowered myself on to Wolf's sofa.

'Any leads, Frank?'

'I told you. There's not much to go on. Been a bit of flooding up there recently and looks like the body got washed down from further up in the forest. Could be twenty, thirty years ago.'

'I'm talking about Snow's case,' I said. 'Are you looking at anybody for it? Because, you know, whoever knifed Snow knew exactly how he had killed Niki.'

'I warned you, Diane!'

'Yeah, okay. I'm just saying.'

Before Frank could start in on his lecture I told him that my mobile was ringing and I had to go. I told him I appreciated the job and that I'd be in Wainuiomata in an hour. I told him I'd leave Snow's case to the cops and not sniff around getting in anyone's way. Since I promised him all that, I thought I should make at least one of those promises true. I'd have to dress and drive fast to get across the hill by ten.

I hated leaving Wolf at home, especially as I was heading to his favourite walking track, but it was risky to take a dog when checking out a skeleton. In his days as a cop Wolf wouldn't have misbehaved but in his retirement years he'd let himself go a bit on the discipline front. Wolf is keen on bones and I could imagine him embarrassing me in the worst possible way. I did my best to ignore his reproachful look as I left.

I drove out of Wellington along SH2. The harbour was white-capped, the sky prison-grey. A few dog walkers on the Petone beach leaned into the gale, their puffed up jackets making Michelin Men of them all. Their dogs squinted into the wind-blown sand, ears pressed back against their skulls.

I swung the car through the roundabout and accelerated past the Gracefield ESR laboratories and on up the Wainui hill. The odd camber of the road created a tilted facsimile in my parking mirror of the wide, pale Hutt River snaking its way towards the larger basin of the harbour. Peppermint-green willows dotted the valley. The harbour was an expanse of indigo; the fingernail settlement of Petone appeared almost pretty. I could just make out those little marshmallow walkers and their dogs on the beach below. From this distance the whole scene looked idyllic. I guess everything's about perspective.

I located the Wainuiomata Police Station at the rural end of the town, squatting between the local bowling club and a run-down outdoor swimming pool where chipped concrete dolphins leapt at faded beach balls. The community cop shop was a no-nonsense, state-house designed brick bungalow. A butterfly or garden gnome decoration wouldn't have looked out of place.

Work boots, their tongues hanging out in apparent exhaustion, were lined up in the porch, giving the place a homely touch. The hardboard tacked over the bottom section of the glass door made it identical to the suburban front doors I grew up alongside. It was probably the etched stag at bay that had been kicked out. Personally, I'd always had a hankering to do that.

In the waiting area, four enormous Māori guys balanced on tiny wooden chairs, the only ones provided. They were all reading *Women's Weekly*s, their legs stretched out in identical postures of relaxation. Seven entirely different coloured socks were on display. One naked foot sat proud in this company. None of the men looked up when I entered.

Directly in front of me was a chest-high counter where a uniformed cop leaned, reading the paper, a lock of sandy hair falling over his forehead. His finger traced a line of text, lips moving as he silently read. He straightened as I approached, flicked the hair back, and looked directly at me. He kept his finger planted on the paper.

'Hi. I'm Diane Rowe. Inspector McFay said you'd be expecting me,' I said, noting his eyes were the warm, deep brown of bush honey. He held my look for a moment and then his free hand disappeared below the counter.

'Yeah, sure.'

A loud buzzer sounded and a light went on above the door next to the counter, indicating it was now unlocked. It always surprises me how easy it is to get into a police station, but I guess it's the getting out that's meant to be difficult. I stepped into an empty office. A couple of desks were piled with report forms, ring-binder case files and dirty coffee mugs. On the wall was the ubiquitous girlie calendar alongside a whiteboard listing the station's jobs for the day. According to the 'urgent' list, Lou should ring his mum ASAP.

The cop from behind the counter was right behind me.

'I'm on my own here, sorry. Pat and Lou are out doing warrants, so I'm going to have to juggle you with the desk.' He hesitated, and then held his hand out. 'Rob. Robbie. Robert. Take your pick.' He bobbed his head shyly towards an invisible crowd of people clamouring to pin a name on him.

Robbie wore his good looks as casually as a favourite T-shirt. He must have been at least six foot three or four but hunched his height down into his shoulders with a slight stoop. Very broad shoulders they were too, but he didn't seem the gym bunny type, so my guess was he played a bit of sport.

I shook his hand. Firm. Warm. Dry. A lot of men have trouble shaking hands with women. Some make their hand go all limp and take yours in their fingers like it's a half-dismembered rat the cat has presented them with. Others crunch your knuckles in an attempt to make some point or other. But Rob, Robbie, Robert's handshake was plain . . . nice. I let him go. Reluctantly.

'You can use my desk if you like.' He smiled.

'Thanks. That'd be great. But listen,' I said as he stacked papers and cleared an area for me. 'You don't have to babysit me. I know my way around a case file.'

'It's not exactly what I'd call a case file,' he said, tapping a slim manila folder. 'This is it, I'm afraid. A couple of report sheets and some snapshots of the remains.'

I picked up the folder. 'Okay. Well, I'll have a read and then maybe you could take me out there to look at the body in situ.'

I looked at the half dozen photos paper-clipped to the inside. The first photo is always a shock, but then it gets easier. This one was a close-up of what I recognised as a femur. The bone was bleached white, with what remained of the muscle stretched the length of the bone and attached tenuously at each end. It resembled an overcooked leg of roast mutton.

Robbie screwed up his face. 'Can't do that, sorry.'

I slid the photo out to reveal the next one. 'I don't mean now.' I said. 'I can come back when it suits.'

The next photo was a close-up of the ribcage. There was no flesh on the bones but patches of what looked like fine mesh or filament adhered and draped into the chest cavity.

Robbie shifted his weight. 'It's not that. I can take you out there but it wouldn't be any use.' He scratched his upper arm in a nervous gesture.

'Actually, Robbie, seeing the body is a lot of use to me,' I said.

Robbie cleared his throat and shuffled again. He didn't seem the sort of cop who would stonewall me just because I was a civilian, but he was definitely holding something back. I put the folder on the desk.

'If you can't take me, fine. Just give me directions and tell whoever's up there keeping an eye on the body that I'll whistle as I approach. That way I won't catch them having a pee or whatever.'

Robbie looked at me silently, then crossed to the back door, pulled back the bolts and indicated that I should follow him.

The backyard was like any small-town, suburban backyard, complete with rotary clotheslines set in a leaning square of concrete, and a garden shed at the end of the recently mown lawn. A neat line of tea towels was pegged alongside a plastic, purse-shaped peg basket. Intrigued though I was by this, I didn't know Robbie well enough yet to ask him about it. He led the way to the garden shed and opened the padlock.

'You might wanna . . .' He indicated his nose as he pushed the door open.

I took a step into the shed, breathing through my mouth. Draped nonchalantly in a wheelbarrow was what was left of John Doe.

Robbie shrugged apologetically. 'The ranger was a long way into the valley laying possum traps when he found him. He went back to the hut, got the wheelbarrow, loaded the body, then went on laying his traps. He didn't bother to bring him in until the following day. I guess he reckoned that after a couple of decades another day wouldn't bring him any closer to being alive again.'

My knee clicked loudly as I bent to get a closer look. It was more a skeleton than a body, though some muscle, a tendon, and dried skin the colour of kauri gum linked the bones together. There was no skull. To me, a body doesn't look human without a head, but maybe that's my prejudice.

I peered at the collarbone and ribcage, noting the patches of adherent filigree that I'd seen in the photos. Robbie bent over beside me. I could feel the heat of his body and we weren't even touching. He spoke quietly, almost in a whisper.

'I reckon that's his undershirt or singlet. There might have been some kind of synthetic thread in it and that's why it lasted. It might help date him, eh?'

He was right. The lace filament was all that remained of the fabric after exposure to the elements for who knows how long. I stepped around the wheelbarrow, partly to move away from Robbie's distracting body heat, but also to see the back of the John Doe's neck. I was hoping for the remains of a shirt label but no such luck.

Breathing through my mouth I could almost taste the sickly, sweet odour of decay. I circled the body, ending up at the right foot. Only a few shreds of the sock remained, but the boot itself was in relatively good condition, though it gaped at the toes in a smiling, Chaplinesque way. The bootlace was tied in a perfect double bow. A couple of the fingers that had tied the bow were gone.

'Lots of pigs in the Rimutakas. They go for the stomach first then they start in on the digits and . . . things.'

'And no sign of the head, huh?'

Robbie's shoulders went up then down again. I was close enough to smell his aftershave: ck one, if I wasn't mistaken. It was a relief from the smell of the John Doe. I wondered if Robbie was staying close to me for the same reason. Ironically, I was wearing Eternity.

'I went up there yesterday and had a good hunt around, but it could be anywhere. The body was washed downstream – that much we know. But the stream has changed course so many times even over the last ten years, and this guy might have been up there much longer than that.'

We squatted together in the dark. Silent, but companionable like a couple of kids having found an old uncle drunk in charge of a wheelbarrow.

'In the end, we don't know who he is, where he died, when, or how.' Robbie summed up for us both.

'So you've nearly got the case solved then?'

He threw me a grin that hitched up one corner of his mouth with quotation-mark creases. Then he turned his attention back to the body. I watched that grin until the lines dissolved. When he spoke again his voice was a whisper.

'If we had a head, it might have a hole which would tell us one story. But right now we don't know if it's a suicide, an accident, or a murder.'

I was still looking at him when he turned towards me.

'I guess that's where you come in.'

He gave me the full smile this time, maybe a bit embarrassed because he'd caught me checking him out. This smile hijacked his entire face and made it impossible not to smile right back. Actually, it wasn't just my face responding to Robbie.

I stretched to my full height and, hands on hips, surveyed the room in a purposeful fashion as if my intention was other than breaking the eye contact between us.

'Was there anything else near the body? Backpack? Anything that might suggest he'd been tramping or hunting up there?'

I don't know if I fooled him but Robbie stood too.

'Nah. Well, yeah. Sort of . . .' He shuffled some more and even in the dim light of the shed I thought I detected a blush. He motioned for me to follow him out into the backyard and over to the fence.

Mesh wire was attached to the top of the picket fence over a length of roughly three metres. Maybe one warm, crime-free summer someone had decided to grow tomatoes or beans there, though nothing grew on it now. I looked from the fence to Robbie who was running his hand through his hair. I still didn't get it. I looked at the mesh again and this time saw what looked like tiny threads clinging to the wire diamonds. Up close, I saw tiny patches of interwoven fibres similar to those on the body. Some were almost gossamer, others thicker mesh. I reached out to pluck one off but Robbie touched my wrist.

'I wouldn't do that.'

'Why? What is this? What did you hang here?'

Robbie was about to speak when a magpie shrieked. He shaded his eyes and glared up with what seemed unreasonable rancour. The bird paced the branch and shrieked at him again. The heavy beat of wings announced the arrival of another bird. Robbie glared at them both. At least half a dozen magpies were squabbling with each other in the nearby branches. Robbie gazed at them with disgust as he spoke.

'When the ranger wheeled the body in, I didn't know what to do with it. I was here on my own and when I rang the Sarge he was still having his breakfast and he said to just wheel it out to the shed until he got in.'

Several sparrows hopped along the palings towards me. A large blackbird, with bright orange beak and beady eye, bounced through the dry grass in our direction. Robbie and I watched the blackbird's advance. This police station backyard was a regular Disneyland.

'I was halfway down the yard when the wheelbarrow tipped and, well, John Doe fell out. I did my best to put him back in the way he was, but a bit of his clothing fell off and, well, a bit of our John Doe came away with it and I thought, since it didn't smell too good, I'd hang it out here rather than stink the shed out.'

The blackbird was within kicking distance. Its beady eye focused on the fence wire – and what was sticking to it. The magpies bobbed impatiently, annoyed no doubt that we were standing between them and lunch.

'So, you hung John Doe's clothing, along with a bit of John Doe, out here on the fence, and the birds ate it?'

Robbie looked like he was about to throw up. 'I used to like birds,' he said.

I didn't think Robbie was ever going to make sergeant.

The aluminium exterior door clanged open and another uniformed cop came out, hitching his belt with one hand, slapping a brown envelope against his thigh with the other. Robbie's shoulders slumped.

'Diane Rowe, this is Acting Sergeant Lou Watts,' he mumbled as the big guy joined us.

Lou wore the anticipatory smirk of a guy brimful of punchlines.

'The death squad boys are here to pick up the John Doe,' he said, grinning at me. 'You want to roll him round to the hearse or shall I just get the birds to fly him there?'

Robbie obliged with his one-sided grin, despite no doubt tiring of this joke. I'd been around cops long enough to know he'd never shake this one off. Lou's eyes shifted from my face to my chest. His tongue darted out to his lower lip and he gave himself a flick with the envelope. He was looking at my tits with the same beady avarice as the blackbird eyeing the bits on the fence.

'McFay said you'd be coming out to look at the file. Robbie give you everything you need?' He was one of those men who make everything sound sexual. The tongue darted out again, the pants were hitched. 'I got one of the boys to run copies of the remains for you.' He thrust the envelope at me. 'They make pretty rough viewing.'

This wasn't so much deference to any sensitivity on my part, but more a pitch for him to act as comforter. I put the envelope in my shoulder bag.

'Yeah, I'm good thanks, Lou,' I said, knowing he'd hate me using his first name.

The long black snout of the hearse crept into view down the side of the building. Robbie threw me an apologetic glance and set off towards the shed. Lou winked at me. There's not much I hate more than being winked at.

'Maybe you could put a call in to the ranger, tell him I'd like to see where the body was found and have a bit of a talk. It would help if you could smooth the way for me there,' I said, watching Robbie's departure only partly to avoid looking at Lou.

'Better still, I could take you myself,' Lou said. I turned back in time to see his eyes shifting between my left and right tits.

'Shall I bring these two along as well?' I asked innocently.

It took him a second, but when he got it he hitched his pants again and scowled.

'If you're accompanying the John Doe remains back to town,

tell tweety-bird he can stay here and clean out the shed. It doesn't need the two of you, guarding a wheelbarrow of bones.'

I watched Lou head back into the station, safely removed from my dangerous mammary glands and even more dangerous smart mouth, and then I went to help Robbie.

We found an old piece of tarpaulin to drape over the body. With one pushing the wheelbarrow and the other steering from the front, we managed to manoeuvre it across the grass. At the back of the parked hearse the two attendants sucked on their cigarettes and scuffed their leather shoes in the gravel. We squabbled a bit about how to best lift the remains from the wheelbarrow to the gurney without further destruction of evidence, and without drawing the attention of the kids splashing and squealing in the swimming pool next door. We might have gone on arguing for some time if circling seagulls hadn't hurried us along. In the end we lifted the whole wheelbarrow into the hearse; the pathologist could sort it out at his end.

Robbie and I washed our hands under the outside tap. It's a ritual for me to wash my hands after being in the company of the dead. I suspect the hand washing was more Lady Macbethian in motive for Robbie.

'You said the ranger brought the body into the station in the wheelbarrow.'

'Uh-huh. He had it on the back of his ute.'

'So, who took the photos of the body? They were taken in situ, right? Where the body was found?'

Robbie tore off a handful of grass sticking out from under the weatherboards and used it to scrub his palms.

'Yeah, that's right. The ranger took the photos then loaded the body into the wheelbarrow.'

I wiped my wet hands on my jacket. 'That was . . .' I searched for the word, 'helpful of him.'

Robbie was too engrossed in his hand washing to respond. I

decided not to pass on Lou's message about cleaning the shed. Robbie was still scouring as I went to the hearse.

The two attendants were already waiting, engine running. They shuffled together so I could join them in the front seat. The interior smelt strongly of peppermints which I guessed from the synchronous jaw movements both guys were sucking. Without comment, the peppermint roll was angled towards me. A Lifesaver. Hang out with cops, pathologists and funeral directors long enough and you get to associate the smell of peppermint with the stench of death.

The driver was just starting to reverse when Robbie appeared at my window. He handed me his card and I scrabbled in my shoulder bag and then handed him mine. He murmured about having written his home number on the back and I nodded.

There wasn't much talk on the drive back to town. These guys weren't going to let conversation get in the way of their impressive sound system, so we listened to Ben Harper sing about fighting for his mind. I suspected the boys had mixed a bit of leaf with their tobacco, but I didn't mind. They drove the whole way under fifty kilometres per hour which suited me just fine. One of the smoothest rides you'll ever get is in a hearse. Wasted on the dead, I thought, as I tapped the numbers from Robbie's card into my phone, telling myself it was simply because I was always losing business cards.

I sucked powerfully on my Lifesaver and settled in to enjoy the trip back over the Wainui hill. I thought about John Doe resting languidly in his wheelbarrow in the back. In all likelihood I'd never discover who he was. He'd lie around the Wellington Hospital morgue until the coroner made a call on how he'd died, and then if no one claimed him, he'd be cremated and his ashes stuck in an unmarked hole in the 'memorial wall' at the Karori Cemetery. At least he'd have company there.

I thought about the old custom of bribing gravediggers

to bury paupers in existing plots. When Mum died my aunt arranged to have her buried in the old family plot. During the arrangements with the sexton, she uncovered historical records that listed two unnamed strangers buried alongside my great-grandmother. My aunt was horrified and wanted these uninvited guests removed, but I was strangely comforted by the thought that Mum wasn't lying there with only her own ancestors – that some strangers had dropped in. A gregarious person in life, I reckoned Mum would have liked that.

We'd driven all the way to the Basin Reserve before Ben stopped singing. I noticed how people in the cars alongside the hearse glanced nervously at us and then looked quickly away. The boys beside me stared straight ahead. I don't think they realised the music had stopped.

'Is Smithy doing the autopsy on this one?'

The guy next to me shifted his feet around what I had thought was a KFC takeaway box but now realised was someone's ashes.

'Yup,' he said, reaching to push the now ejecting CD back in. 'I think he's on all this week.'

I thought I'd try my luck before Ben started up again. 'Did he handle that stabbing from Cuba Street?'

Ben drowned out his response, but I caught the nod and at the same time a cry went up from the Basin. I don't think anyone was celebrating the news that Smithy had cut Snow open from sternum to pubis, but I'd be happy to join in if they were. More likely someone had just hit a six on the cricket grounds. The traffic lights turned green, Ben Harper whined again about fighting for his mind, and the hearse purred forward into Adelaide Road.

I helped the boys unload the wheelbarrow and roll it into the hospital morgue discreetly hidden away in one of the older buildings of the spanking new hospital. While they went in search of munchies from the tuck shop, I checked the paperwork and read that pathologist Dr Grant Smith, aka Smithy, was down to perform the autopsy on my John Doe at ten o'clock the next day.

I took the opportunity to flick back a few pages, and confirmed that Smithy had also performed the autopsy on one James Patrick Wilson (aka Snow). There was no clue to the findings of the autopsy – that would have been too easy – but the forms noted that Snow's body had been released to Hooper Funeral Directors. Killers often go to their victim's funeral, which is why cops attend the funeral as well. Families think cops are being sensitive. If they knew the funeral was also being filmed they might rethink the sensitivity bit. I hadn't seen Snow at Niki's funeral. I hadn't really seen anything except that coffin. It occurred to me I'd never asked Sean if Niki's funeral had been filmed.

It was only when I waved goodbye to the Ben Harper fans as they drove off and I stood looking blankly at the empty car park space that I remembered my car was still parked outside the Wainuiomata Police Station.

CHAPTER 7

I knew enough about Snow to bluff the telephonist at the Hooper Funeral Directors into believing I was a relative of the deceased who wanted to attend the final service for my good old cousie Snow. I was relieved I didn't have to taxi over there to bullshit her in person. She told me the service was at two thirty today at St Joseph's – a big, modern hybrid of a church that motorists swing past between Regional Wines and the Mt Victoria tunnel. Having a church at the entrance to a tunnel seemed appropriate somehow.

I had about half an hour to get there. Given my carless state and the fact I hadn't yet eaten, the timing was perfect. I've always considered stomach rumbling at funerals bad mannered, topped only by farting and taking phone calls during the service. I would behave well at Snow's funeral for the sake of those poor bastards who had loved the prick at some time in his useless excuse for a life. If it had just been between me and Snow's ghost, I'd have had no qualms about dancing naked on his coffin, stomach rumbling, farting and singing loudly into my phone.

The walk from the Newtown hospital to Mt Victoria and the seafood-with-double-cheese sandwich en route made me feel better in opposite yet strangely complementary ways. I was at the church in plenty of time to pick out the tinted-window van parked in Brougham Street from which the cops were filming the arrivals, and to find myself a place in the church where I could watch the grieving mourners without being too noticeable. I'd been to funerals at the U-shaped St Joseph's before and knew that the best sight line was over by the organ to the far right of the entrance.

The church was filling up but I excused my way past the few people already seated and shuffled to an empty possie at the right tip of the U. From there I could see pretty much everyone face on, except those directly in front of me. The design and architecture attempted a fusion of modern and classical, Christian with secular. A big ask but they'd done their best. I craned my neck at the ceiling – looking heavenward is what you're supposed to do in a church. The architect had gone for a lofty form with dark-stained, arched beams ribcaged across the ceiling, presumably in an attempt to simulate flying buttresses of the gothic variety.

It made me feel as if I was trapped underneath an upturned boat but it didn't seem to be having that effect on anyone else. It was hard to tell though, given that most of the fifty or so people were looking distressed anyway. Funerals do that to you. Floor-to-ceiling stained glass window panels separated the congregation on either side of the altar but there were no shepherds or bleeding hearts for the rosy light to shine through. Instead they'd gone for safe geometric shapes which were popular in the '70s as background to shagpiled conversation pits.

The coffin was centre stage, one step down from an almost aggressively simple linen-covered altar. There was a pervasive smell of alcohol – either the mourners had been drowning their sorrows already, someone had gone overboard with parallel import aftershave, or the priest had been sampling the altar wine. Perhaps all three.

A trio of large, black-clad women was hunched together in the pew nearest the coffin. I was pretty sure the one in the middle was Snow's mother, Maureen, which would make the props on either side Snow's twin sisters, Peaches and Cream. Could have been worse, I guess. They could have been called Bubble and Squeak or Benson and Hedges. I remembered Sean telling me that Snow's first criminal offence had been a charge of assaulting Peaches. The remainder of the congregation had given this central cast a wide berth.

Looking around the room, I recognised a few of the small- and not-so-small-time crims Snow must have had dealings with. Okay, maybe they were his friends, too, although it's not easy to think of your little sister's killer having friends or being liked by anyone. The cops scattered through the congregation stuck out like the proverbials. It wasn't so much their dress, though they all had that tidy-casual look adopted only by guys who have been in the forces, spent their formative years in boarding schools, or who play golf. It was the way they stood, legs slightly apart, hands clasped in front of their genitals, head slightly bowed, that gave them away. I watched as one of these cops lifted his sleeve to his mouth, as if to stifle a cough. He was wired, in both senses of the word. I could tell from his shoulders and neck muscles that he was tense.

Someone had ordered Snow to murder my sister. A year

later someone had killed Snow using exactly the same method. That looked like a message to me and I was pretty sure by the number of cops in the church that they thought the same. The crims might be Snow's friends but I was willing to bet that every one of the cops was there on business. The wired cop was scanning the room, studying each face, memorising it. I did the same. The cops knew, and I knew, that there was a good chance Snow's killer would show.

The entrance of the priest brought everyone shuffling to their feet, blocking my view of the congregation. As master of ceremonies the priest made a little speech about forgiveness, but I wasn't buying it. I tuned out by studying the neck of the guy two rows in front of me. Something about it was familiar. I'd seen it recently.

As if feeling my X-ray eyes, he half turned and lifted a hand in greeting. I'd seen him at the strip club. I scanned my memory for his name. Dope . . . Spiff . . . Stoke! That was it. Even that night he'd seemed familiar, but I'd put it down to his uncanny resemblance to Wolf. His scruffy-haired hangdog look was definitely German Shepherdish.

The priest led the mourners into the first song. I couldn't imagine who chose Dean Martin singing 'Green, Green Grass of Home'. I hate singing in public. I've been known to mime 'Happy Birthday' at friends' parties but I didn't even bother with that pretence for Snow. I kept my mouth clamped and tried to figure out why Stoke had seemed so familiar at the club, and even more in this different environment. Or maybe not so different. I guess the worship of sex and the worship of god have a kind of synergy.

I picked out Stoke's voice as he volumed up for the chorus. And suddenly I remembered. My skin went cold and the sandwich reminded me it hadn't been digested yet. It was the singing. I remembered him singing. I'd heard Stoke singing at Niki's funeral. And I'd heard him sobbing.

The funeral reached its finale. Snow stayed dead in his coffin. I couldn't ask for more.

Keeping Stoke in my sights, I joined the stragglers as they filed out. The wired cop was right behind Stoke, shadowing him. I slowed my step – it wouldn't be smart to be caught on tape talking to a suspect. I was picturing the look on McFay's face if he heard about that particular field tape, when I felt an all-too-familiar hand in the small of my back. The kind of familiarity only an ex-husband exercises. I allowed Sean to shepherd me into an alcove next to the room where sandwiches and sausage rolls were laid out on trestle tables. He started right in.

'What are you doing here, Diane? You're supposed to be deep in the Rimutakas checking out a missing person.'

So it had been Sean's idea to send me out of town. Or more likely, he and McFay had cooked up that little job for me together.

'I'm paying my last respects to my sister's killer, that's all. What's wrong with that? You think I might dance on his coffin or something?' I tried to make it sound unlikely.

Sean wagged his head non-committally. He'd seen me do worse.

'We're working here, Di. You know that. Seriously. What are you doing here?' He stood between me and the departing mourners, keeping his voice low. I tried to keep mine down too but I was the one facing the departing congregation.

'What do you think I'm doing? I want to know *who* killed Snow,' I hissed. 'And *why* would be good too,' I added, 'but I'd settle for *who*.'

I didn't like the sensation of my back against the wall and I stepped up eye to eye with Sean. It was a position we'd been in many times before. Being this tall also brought me pelvis to pelvis with him. It wasn't the first time for that either. We held each other's look for some time before he raised his hands in mock surrender and stepped back to give me room to move.

'How about we grab some fresh air,' he said, touching my wrist for attention and sliding back his cuff to reveal the tiny microphone. It seemed to me that Sean and I had always spoken in code.

Knowing we were being recorded for a possible court case, if not posterity, we made small talk as we walked along Brougham and into Ellice Street. When we reached the traffic lights at the Basin Reserve, Sean lifted his wrist to his lips and told the guys back in the van that he was switching off and going to lunch. He'd see them back at the station. He threw me an all-too-familiar rueful look as he discreetly slid his fingers between shirt buttons and unplugged the mike from the battery taped to his chest. I responded with an equally all-too-familiar look.

We crossed the road and meandered into the cricket grounds, where we settled ourselves on the grass bank and chatted for a while about inconsequential things, easing into it. There were a couple of people in the stands eating lunch and a groundsman, hands in pockets, staring glumly at the pitch. That exultant cry I'd heard from the hearse must have been someone at practice.

Sean asked about the John Doe. I told him how the body had been delivered to the station in a wheelbarrow. I told him what a jerk I thought the sergeant was. I didn't mention Robbie or his nice handshake and smile. Then there was a bit of a pause and I readied myself for the dressing down I knew was coming.

'You know you're going to have to stay away from this case, Di,' Sean said, brushing grass from his palms. 'You're just going to have to trust that we're on it. *I'm* on it.'

I watched him flick blades of grass from his sleeve. He was going easy on me and I appreciated that.

'It's got nothing to do with trust.'

I felt his eyes on me but I kept my gaze on the Ladies' Stand. Someone was sitting up there. Probably a cricket fan remembering games past – that big six they almost made if only they hadn't played the ball on to the stumps. I could feel myself choking up and the last thing I wanted was to break down in front of Sean. I needed to convince him I was calm and cool and not going to lose it any more. I didn't trust my voice so I waited until the swelling in my throat subsided.

'So what *is* this about then?' he asked.

'I need to know why she died,' I said, my voice breaking on the last word.

Sean must have heard it because he breathed in deeply then reached out and rested his palm on my knee. He gave me a minute before speaking.

'There is no "why" Niki died. You know that. You heard Snow's confession.'

I shot him a look and he shrugged apologetically. 'Gemma told me she'd given you the tape.'

I looked back at the cricket fan. Of course Gemma would tell Sean she'd given me Snow's confession tape. I didn't blame her.

'Snow killed Niki – end of story. He did it because he could and now he's dead.' He took his hand off my knee and hunched forward. 'And like it or not, it's my job to find out who killed him.'

'It was your job to find out who killed Niki. Now the bastard's dead and you act like that's the end of it. Well, it's not the end of anything for me.' I didn't mean to get so angry. I didn't know I still could.

Sean put his hand back on my knee. I felt the dry warmth of it through my jeans.

'Let it go, buddy.'

Sean used to call me buddy when we were first together. It was the closest we ever got to pet names. I loved it because it was such an understatement. We were always so much more than buddies. I fought off those memories. My throat was so tight it felt like there was a noose around it.

'I can't, Sean. Letting it go would be like letting her go. The only way she goes on living is if I remember her.'

It sounded weird even to me and I'd said more than I'd meant to. I didn't want to talk to Sean about Niki. That's all I talked to him about for six months after she died. He was great about it at first but there came a time when he wanted to talk about something else and I wouldn't. I knew it was driving him away – knew *I* was driving him away. I needed Niki in the foreground of my life. I needed to live and breathe her all day, every day. It was my duty, because if I forgot her, even for a minute, then in that minute she didn't exist. She was nothing. I had to keep Niki alive by thinking about her, by remembering her. I didn't blame Sean for leaving me. Well, I did blame him, but I understood it. I suppose in my better moments I even forgave him. I wasn't so forgiving about the girlfriend he took up with pretty much straight away.

'Look, Sean,' I said. 'I know it's your job to investigate Snow's murder and I'll keep out of your way, I promise. But I'll never stop trying to find out why Niki died. You know that about me.'

'Yeah, I know a lot about you,' he said. I couldn't argue with that.

'The thing is,' I explained, 'Snow was just the enforcer. Someone else ordered the hit on Niki. I need to know who that person is and why they wanted Niki dead.'

I could feel Sean's impatience growing. He tugged out a handful of grass.

'You don't believe that crap Snow was on about, do you?' he said, chucking the grass away. I hoped the groundsman wasn't watching. 'No one ordered a hit on Niki. She probably laughed at his tiny dick and that was enough to set him off. Snow murdered her because he was a scumbag.' He finally turned directly to me. 'Listen to me, Diane. McFay has cut you a break and you're back working with us. Don't blow it.

Let me investigate this homicide without stumbling across you every five minutes. If I find out anything about Niki's death in the process I'll tell you, okay? But, please, for your own sake, stay out of this.'

If I didn't let it go he'd have to tell McFay. I knew Sean didn't like delivering this warning. But he was right of course. I was risking both our careers.

'Okay,' I lied. 'But since we're on the subject of Snow's homicide – have you got any leads on who might have killed him? Just so I can send the guy a happy-face balloon, you know?'

I didn't expect an answer but I did appreciate the grin. Sean was always generous with those. He forgave easily. Much more easily than I did. We were companionably silent for a while. Then, just as I was about to stand, he hunched forward and ripped out another handful of grass. He had something else to say. I leaned back on my elbows and waited.

'Listen, Diane,' he said, running his fingers through his hair and combing in some blades of the Basin Reserve's finest green. I resisted the urge to pluck them back out. 'Since you're back at work, and most likely you'll be working out of HQ, there's something you should know, and I thought it was better coming from me.'

I watched his shirt rise and fall as he took in a couple of deep breaths. He aimed his voice towards that guy in the Ladies' Stand.

'Sylvie's pregnant. I mean, we are. We're having a baby.'

My world tipped and that sandwich made its presence felt again.

I think I congratulated him. I know I walked back with him to his car and accepted a ride to town but declined his offer to sign me into Central. I'd sort out my access to HQ tomorrow.

I'm pretty sure I even kissed him goodbye on the cheek. Best of all, as I moved the case file from the passenger seat to the back, I managed to read Snow's last known address. Not bad considering I had to read it upside down – an old party trick of mine that I always knew would come in handy one day. I guess I'd gone on to automatic.

I crossed the road and used the toilets in the public library. Being a multitasker I wrote Snow's address into my notepad while I peed and switched my phone back on. Then I held my wrists under the cold tap and stared at myself in the mirror. I looked pretty much like I always did. So how come I felt like I'd been hit by a train?

I was drying my hands when my phone rang. It was Robbie offering to drop my 'vehicle' off the following night. He would drive it into town and a mate would drive Robbie's 'vehicle' so they could get back home. Robbie said maybe we could have a drink together and he could hand my car keys over personally rather than putting them back under the front seat where he'd found them. He suggested meeting at The Tasting Room, a bar in Courtenay Place that I knew quite well.

He said maybe I could bring a friend along so his mate had someone to have a drink with as well. He said all this without taking a breath. I said that sounded like a good idea and suggested eight o'clock the following night. It was only after I'd rung off that it dawned on me I'd just agreed to a double date.

They say timing is everything.

CHAPTER 8

The library was busy but I didn't have to wait long for a computer to come free. At Pussy Galore, Chloe had told me that Richard Brownlee was the one client she thought would be totally pissed with Niki for deciding to leave the sex business. That he was obsessed with Niki and jealous of any other guys spending time with her. I googled the name, highlighted the New Zealand icon, and hit the search button. Six hits immediately appeared on the screen. I opened them all in separate windows and clicked through each of them.

I learnt that Richard Brownlee was the managing director of a property development company, Brownlee Property. The ghosts of a couple of companies he'd been involved with that had gone belly up appeared, but I'd need to dig deeper than the internet to uncover what they were all about. They may have been genuine failures or, more likely, created for the purpose of shuffling money across a pack of companies which were then deliberately folded.

A school class photo on an 'Old Friends' site didn't tell me much, except that in year nine he was the shortest kid in the second row, olive-skinned with very dark, straight hair, and that he, along with every other boy in his class, had struggled with the myriad physical side effects that accompany puberty.

Richard's name appeared in a number of applications to the city council, mostly to do with rezoning issues. There was no R. Brownlee listed in the White Pages, but there was a 'J' and 'R' with a residential address in Karori. Possibly he'd listed his wife's initial first to avoid searches, or of course he could be a really modern, liberal, Mr Nice Guy who thinks it's just fine to have his wife's name first in the phone book, and who also happens to be a regular client at a strip club where he nurtured an obsession with my now-dead sister.

I was prepared to keep a totally open mind about him, at least until I met the prick.

Brownlee Property had a landline number listed in the White Pages but no business address other than a postbox which I could tell by the numbers was in the Marion Street post office. It might have been that he shifted his business offices into whatever site he was developing at the time and then moved on as soon as he'd sold it. On the other hand, it could be that he didn't like being found too easily. You can't be subpoenaed via a postbox.

I gave up my terminal to the schoolkid waiting in line to use it, but not before deleting the history cache. Then I rang Brownlee Property and asked to speak to Richard. The receptionist said he'd gone for the day. I angled my head to see the library clock. It showed five thirty, so he'd cut loose early.

I told her I'd catch him at home then, making it sound like I did that all the time. She snorted a derisive laugh but I didn't know if it was aimed at my pretence that I had his home number or the idea that Richard would be home any time soon. She told me she wasn't supposed to tell anyone where he was, not ever, but that I could find him at a bar in Cambridge Terrace called Charlie's Angels where he'd be 'having a meeting with a bunch of other jerks'.

She managed to weight the word 'meeting' with a tonne of irony. When I said I might drop by the bar now, she told me to knock myself out and that she, on the other hand, was going home to have a very hot, very cleansing shower, and then she was going to find a new job on Job Search and never have anything to do with that cock Brownlee ever again in her entire life.

I guess I got her on a bad day. Or a good day, depending on your point of view. I thanked her and wished her luck finding a new job. She said 'Ta' and told me to feel free to tell the arsewipe that she'd quit and pocketed the petty cash as her severance pay.

The bar now calling itself Charlie's Angels had been operating as a drinking hole under different names for as long as I could remember. It had been used as a money-laundering joint by a series of owners over the years and I didn't imagine this reincarnation was any different in that respect. The room itself was impressive with an eighteen-foot stud and walls painted icing-sugar white. The bar was a room-length sweep of dove-grey Cararra marble behind which the tuxedoed staff, men and women, polished glasses with Irish linen cloths which they tucked into their pristine knee-length aprons.

Remembering I'd been messing around with a decomposing body in a shed in Wainuiomata that morning, and then less than an hour ago lying on the grass at the Basin Reserve cricket ground being delivered a cruel bouncer from my ex-husband,

I gave my jeans and sleeves a bit of a brush down. That would have to do.

I ordered a Campari and soda from the young woman behind the bar who, I couldn't help noting, was dressed a damn sight better than me. She had the whole 'white shirt and bow tie with starched apron over well-pressed suit pants' thing going on. She made it look styly, androgynous and immaculate. Try me in that number with the apron, and I'd look like someone's itinerant grandmother.

The drink was delivered to me with a flourish. When I lifted the glass to take a sip, the tiny circle of pink fizz left on the bar surface was wiped away with a murmured apology. From this close I could see that the grey marble was shot through with pale brown capillaries. I swirled my oily pink drink with the swizzle stick and checked out the clientele.

I spotted Richard Brownlee immediately. He was in the middle of a group of suited men at a high table next to the windows. The other guys squatted on stools but Brownlee remained standing. I guessed he didn't like his legs to dangle. He didn't look too different from his school photo: in his mid thirties now, he still seemed to be struggling with puberty. Nature hadn't helped him with the doubtlessly much anticipated teen growth spurt. It had sucked his frame up to a lofty five foot five, before cruelly abandoning him.

He was wearing a royal blue, extra-wide pinstriped suit. I could hear the salesman's pitch that the vertical stripes would give the illusion of added height. They didn't. He'd used a fair bit of hair gel which gave him a slippery appearance, although I think he would have managed that look without any help. My guess was that slippery came naturally to Richard Brownlee. He'd cultivated designer stubble which only emphasised his triple chin. A glass of beer was clutched in one hand, his phone in the other.

I stopped myself from picturing Niki having sex with this

guy, but not before I'd imagined his hands on her. I knocked back my Campari in one hit, caught the attentive eye of the bartender, and had another one delivered. When it arrived, I picked up my glass and approached the flock of preening peacocks.

'Richard Brownlee? I'm Diane Rowe,' I said, holding my hand out.

His swagger at being singled out by a woman in a bar was quickly replaced by dismay when he registered our height disparity. No way was standing beside me going to make Richard Brownlee look good, which was fine with me. He hitched his butt cheek up on to a stool and studied me, paying particular attention to my crotch and tits.

'Have we met before? You look familiar.' He wiped his beer hand down his thigh before taking my hand. His shake was a damp bone-cruncher. The other guys formed a casual ruck facing away from us, though I could tell from the set of their shoulders they were listening and I caught a couple of winks pass amongst them. Charming.

'No, we've never met, but I'm told you knew my sister,' I said, getting straight into it.

He looked genuinely confused. 'Really? Well, I know a lot of people, babe. And if your sister is as good looking as you are, I certainly hope I do know her. What's her name?'

'Niki,' I said, watching him closely. 'But you knew her as Bonnie.'

I saw the memory kick in and a fleeting look of fear pinch up his face. It was erased as quickly as it appeared and replaced with a broad smile. His teeth were wide-spaced and resembled little tombstones.

'Yeah, I knew Bonnie. Nice girl. I was sorry about what happened to her, but, well, you know, she played rough . . .' He left the sentence unfinished. I really wanted to knock those little tombstones over. 'They ever find the guy who did it?'

I took a sip and carefully put my glass down. That way it had less chance of ending up in his face.

'Actually, Richard, that's what I wanted to talk to you about. You see, the cops know who killed her, but they believe someone paid that person to do it and I was thinking, maybe that person was someone who didn't want other people knowing they'd become obsessed with a young dancer. That mightn't be good for family relations or it could be bad for business. So I was thinking, Richard, that maybe you might know who that person is.'

During my little speech, the other guys had given up all pretence of not listening and had formed an intimidating scrum around me in support of their buddy. Richard was still grinning those teeth at me but sweat had popped on his forehead.

He held his hands out in an inclusive gesture 'What do you say, guys? Shall I set this girl straight, do you think?' They grinned and swaggered, not sure where he was going with this, but prepared to step in no matter what he said.

Richard nodded at them. 'Look at us. Do you really think it's bad for business if our clients know we go to strip bars? That we pay good money for gorgeous girls to have sex with us? Honey, I'd be putting it out there that I was living the high life even if I wasn't – you get my drift? But trust me, I *am* living the life because I'm a successful businessman.' He moved his sweaty face close to mine. 'You got it all wrong, babe. Clients love it and you can go ahead and feel free to tell anybody you like that Richard Brownlee buys good booty. I'm not going to deny it. It's *good* for business.'

He was a cocky little bastard.

'And having Niki killed? Is that good for business too?'

He tensed his shoulder muscles and dropped the false smile routine.

'Listen. I understand you're upset about your sister dying and all, but you'd better be very fucking careful about what you accuse me of, because I've got a reputation to uphold and I won't have you coming in here to a public place making suggestions that I was involved in her being killed.' He shrugged and threw a peanut in his mouth but that didn't stop him talking. 'It's a dangerous sandpit that girl played in, but from what I could see no one was forcing her to do it. She made good money on her back.' He grinned at his mates for support. 'Hell's teeth,' he said, eerily mirroring my observation, 'I wish that was all *I* had to do to make a buck.' He popped another peanut. Warming to his subject, he indicated my glass. 'Listen, let me get you a drink, eh? We'll raise our glasses to Bon. I don't mind doing that. It's on me,' he offered, all generosity of spirit.

He was about to jump down off the stool but thought better of it and instead raised his arm and yelled at the young woman serving drinks to the nearby table.

'Hey, babe' he yelled, hooking a finger at her, 'get over here.'

This show of finger-waggling machismo seemed to give Richard back his confidence. Now he was including his nearest buddy in the joke. The guy's jacket was a comedy routine in itself – a baby-blue number with extra-slim lapels and a royal blue faux silk hanky in a faux pocket – but I don't think that was the source of their mirth. Richard had turned to his friends, effectively dismissing me.

I said to his back, 'One of the girls at the club told me you had a bit of a thing for my sister.'

Richard sighed theatrically and rolled his neck to look at me over his shoulder. 'What kind of thing would that be, babe? No offence, but she was a whore.'

I was determined not to let him get to me. 'She said you didn't like other guys spending time with Niki. That you liked to have her all to yourself. I heard you were jealous.'

Richard barked a laugh. 'Now that would be pretty stupid, wouldn't it?'

'Yep,' I agreed pleasantly. 'But then, you see, that would fit nicely with my assessment of you so far.'

A couple of the guys hooted at that but I kept my attention on Richard who swivelled the stool around and angled his crotch in my direction. He popped another peanut in his mouth. Not many seemed to end up in his stomach – they just got crushed up and filled the gaps between his teeth.

'I'll tell you this for nothing – Bonnie was a lot of fun. A lot more fun than you are and that's for sure. But let me explain something. Your sister and me, we weren't in a relationship. I paid her. I had sex with her. End of story. I don't think she had anything to complain about with me. In fact, I'd say she enjoyed it. Maybe you should try it some time. You look like you could do with a bit of enjoying it – you know what I mean?' All theatre now, he made a show of taking out his wallet and flipping through a couple of hundred dollar notes. 'What would you cost? Hundred? One fifty? Name your price.'

His mates all roared with laughter and slapped each other on the back. Richard Brownlee only stopped laughing when I poured his beer on to his crotch. I was just doing him a favour. That suit really had to go.

I needed to walk Brownlee out of my system and I knew just the dog to help me do it. I don't walk in the town belt at night. It's not because I'm scared: I'm pretty confident Wolf would relish the memory of his police training and attack anyone who thought of harming me. There's something about walking the streets at night that I've always loved and Wolf gets to schmoozle in and out of people's front yards, which I can't let him do in daylight. It's the voyeur in me, I guess. I love to glimpse people's lives through partly closed curtains, love the smells from dinner, the clanging of dishes, the flickering of television screens or thud of music, the sounds of little kids giggling and running up stairs, probably on all fours. It's like that old song says, 'homes full of people'.

When Sean and I first moved in together we used to walk the streets. It started as house hunting but then we developed this game where we'd each pick out the house we liked and make up a story about us in it. We'd invent a life for ourselves. We were a couple of kids playing house, I guess. Playing mothers and fathers.

After we'd done that for a while we'd go back to our two-room bedsit and crawl under the sheets and make love until we were exhausted and aching, our limbs wrapped around each other, the heady fug of sex enveloping us. No matter how hard we tried, we knew there was no comparison. Our life together was far better than anything we could make up. Even then, right at the start, we'd talked about getting pregnant, but knew we were too selfish. We couldn't get enough of each other and neither of us was ready to share the other person with a demanding baby. We liked to talk about it though – the idea that what we were doing could create a life made up of the two of us was an aphrodisiac. I always knew when I was ovulating and it was as if Sean's body knew too. He'd thrust harder and deeper and then just hold himself there, deep inside me, and wait. He'd look at me and we'd both just *know.* Is that how it was with him and the little blonde Sylvie? Did he look at her and did they *know*? I had no right to ask. I had no right to even imagine how they conceived their child together. That's the terrible thing when you let your partner go – their life's got nothing to do with you any more.

It was a cool night and most people had their curtains pulled tightly shut so there wasn't much to see in the way of happy families. Wolf was cheerfully occupied with trotting from fence post to lamp post inhaling urine odours, but tonight all those lights behind curtains, those voices and thuddings on floorboards made me feel excluded. Here I was at twenty-eight, walking the streets on my own, envying other people's lives, with only an empty fridge and even emptier bed to go home to.

Wolf's ears pricked up and his body tensed some moments before I saw the cat on the letter box, eyes glassily reflective, its long, albino fur translucent in the streetlight. Wolf's training kicked in and he immediately came to heel and sat, leaning his right shoulder into my calf. Tension quivered through his body as he restrained the impulse to rush at it.

I knew that in his own canine way he saw that cat running ahead of him, felt the hot-breath exhilaration of the chase, the final lunge and satisfaction of that warm, silken body in his jaws, the glorious, killing shake and then the heavy body, limp and acquiescent, the taste of blood. Instead, he waited for my command, straining against the invisible lead of his training. Every fibre of his being wanted to chase that cat and kill it, but he'd been conditioned not to. No physical restraint, just self-imposed control.

It was both remarkable and strangely tragic to witness. He was no different from us humans, really. I cupped the bump on the top of his head.

'Good dog,' I told him. 'You're a good dog.' And though his tail gave one swift whack in response, his body still quivered with the effort to restrain his natural yearning.

Usually I discourage him, but I let Wolf climb onto the bed with me. I was woken some hours later by rhythmic jolts as Wolf lightly yelped and growled. He was after that cat in a dream-chase, his paws twitching, his good eye glittering beneath the half-closed lid. I lay back, careful not to wake him.

I really hoped he caught that blonde bitch of a cat.

CHAPTER 9

I spent the morning doing domestics and clearing emails, quite a few of which were a complex cross-referencing, cc-ing and no doubt bcc-ing, clutter of communications from various levels of police hierarchy, arranging my readmittance into HQ. They promised me desk space on the third floor with a computer giving me access to missing persons' files going back to the 1980s. If I needed earlier information I'd have to go down into the dungeons and hunt through the archived files not yet entered in the database. All of this I knew, of course; I'd been doing it for years. This was McFay's way of reminding me I was back on trial only, and that if I strayed outside the parameters of this particular case and tried to go hunting for information about Snow's killing, he'd know about it. McFay's name featured in shouting capitals in all the emails.

McFay hadn't mentioned clearing me for access to Central. I guessed that would happen if I passed this first little test. At least at HQ I wouldn't be banging into Sean or his pregnant girlfriend every five minutes. HQ wasn't even within spitting distance of Central, though depending on my frame of mind I might be tempted to give it a go.

Smithy was performing the autopsy on my John Doe at ten and, given the state of the body, I didn't think it would take him more than an hour. My plan was to call in at the hospital around midday and see what I could get out of him. The written report to the coroner could take weeks and I wanted a couple of preliminary answers before then.

In the meantime, while Wolf settled himself on the sofa, I sipped coffee and started a file on the John Doe. I didn't get far before my first question mark. *John* Doe? I don't know much about the human body. I vaguely know where my pancreas and liver are, but if I was served them both on a plate – an unlikely scenario, I admit – I probably wouldn't be able to tell them apart.

But I know two differences between male and female skeletons. The male pelvis is pretty much straight and parallel; females' flared hips create a chalice-shaped cavity, and in mature adult skeletons, this difference is obvious. Less obvious, the elbows on females twist outward to accommodate this purpose-built design difference, whereas men's elbows have no twist. Esoteric stuff but useful for the work I do. I'd get confirmation from Smithy later, but from my initial eyeball of the skeleton, I'd go with my amateur-pathologist assumption that this was a John and not a Jane Doe.

I slid the John Doe photos from the envelope Lou had given me, and held them under my desk lamp. The photocopies weren't as lurid as the originals but they were sharp and had been enlarged for detail. The body in situ looked more tragic than it had propped in the wheelbarrow. The right arm was thrown up and over where the head should be, as if warding off a blow; the body was on its side and curled into itself. It looked like it had been placed in the recovery position, which, I realised, was almost identical to the foetal position. It's also the way we lie when we're in pain.

I spent the next twenty minutes writing up the very few details I already knew and the little I could glean from studying the photos. The written statement from the ranger who had found the body was one double-spaced page of typed text. It told little more than I already knew: he'd been laying possum traps in a densely bushed area in the Orongorongas, when he came across the body. The traps were set every 250 metres or so near a newly formed stream, water courses being the best trap-laying points since possums come there to drink.

The next two paragraphs waxed lyrical on the pros and cons of bait versus gin traps, with the ranger, a Scott Wilborough – I checked the signature at the bottom – firmly of the opinion that the latter were brutal and inhumane. He really went to town on this point, expressing himself with fluency and passion, and then returned to the matter in hand, i.e. the human body he'd found, reverting to a flat, pragmatic prose.

He described tersely how he'd taken photos of the body before lifting and transporting it in the wheelbarrow. He'd walked out of the forest on what he referred to as 'the shortcut', wheeling the body down the wide, stony, dry bed of the Orongorongo River to the coast. I'd once done the reverse tramp from the coast road into the forest along that rocky riverbed as far as the camper's picnic spot, and it had been neither easy nor short. Presumably Scott had been some way further in than the picnic area if he was laying poison traps. It would be quite a feat pushing a laden wheelbarrow over stones for that distance, and I was starting to look forward to meeting this guy.

I slid out the only other document, a one-page police report giving details of the body's arrival at Wainuiomata Police Station. Robbie had made a note that he'd given the ranger a receipt for the wheelbarrow and a promise to return it once the body had been 'relocated'. Robbie's delicately looped signature at the bottom of the page reminded me I'd agreed to the date with him and his mate. Sometime soon I'd have to think about which single girlfriend I could ask to be the double part of the date. Robbie's mate was, without doubt, a cop, because cops don't have any other friends. That goes with the job.

I scribbled a note for Damian, my dog-walker, letting him know I hadn't taken Wolf out this morning. I suggested a good long lope would do him good. Wolf, that is. Damian lives a couple of doors down and the deal is he walks Wolf every day whether I've already taken him or not, but he appreciates a heads-up as to whether Wolf's priority is exercise or company on any given day. Wolf whined and drooped his ears but it was a half-hearted performance, and since I knew Damian would be taking him out with a bunch of other dogs within the hour I didn't take the tragedy of my leaving too much to heart.

I found Smithy in his little office next to the autopsy room. He was bent over his keyboard, head angled at the lopsided screen of his faded cream 1980s computer monitor. I could have sworn it was made out of Bakelite. I knew he was a bit deaf so I knocked on the open door. Smithy reared up, knocking over his empty plastic water cup.

'Sorry, Smithy, I didn't mean to scare you.'

'No, no, come in, come in.' He patted his pockets nervously. He'd given up smoking thirty years ago but his hands still remembered where the packet should be. 'You're looking grand,' he added, though I was pretty sure he hadn't glanced at me yet.

Actually, it was Smithy who was looking grand. He'd dropped about ten kilos since I'd last seen him, had his hair cut by a professional instead of his usual own-goal attempts with a scalpel, and had replaced his hand-knitted cable-stitch jersey with a plain black sweater. He'd even hedge-clipped his eyebrows and wrenched out the tufts that usually protruded from his nostrils like boar tusks. The thought made my eyes water in sympathy.

It was an open-and-shut case. Smithy had gone and got himself a girlfriend. Smithy's wife had died on her fortieth birthday and though I knew that in the subsequent two decades he'd seen a number of lady friends, as he quaintly called them, none had meant enough for him to have gone under the nasal tweezers. I took the office chair he was thrusting at me and placed it so we were both facing the computer screen.

'I've just started to write up the John Doe now but I suppose you want a preliminary chat,' he offered.

In green text on a black screen was the beginning of the autopsy report. The cursor, a little white square, was blinking in mid sentence.

'Smithy, this machine is truly ancient. Why don't you order yourself an upgrade?'

Smithy leaned forward and wrestled with the monitor. 'I don't need a new one. This is just fine.' He released the monitor which rocked back into its lean. He glanced shyly at me. 'It's good to have you back, Diane. I thought you might have given up on our lost-and-found friends.'

'Nah, it was just me I lost there for a while, Smithy,' I admitted. 'But I think McFay's got me on trial, so I'd better deliver on this one.'

'Yes, right,' he said, rubbing the bridge of his nose where glasses used to be. He blinked rapidly, a new addition to his usual tics and mannerisms. I suspected it was to moisten his new contacts. 'Well, it's not the easiest case to get back on the proverbial horse with. It's a John Doe.' He threw me a complicit smirk.

I took out my notepad and started making notes as Smithy talked.

'Probably about six foot two in the old measurements, but without the skull that's only an estimate. Long-limbed. Slimmish build. Had the odd fracture when he was a child, I'd say. Nothing unusual there.'

'Any idea how old he was when he died?'

'Early twenties.' He watched me make a note. 'That's my informed guess, at this stage, nothing more.'

'Sure.'

Smithy scrolled through the text on the screen. 'To be safe, I'd say between twenty and twenty-five. Fit and healthy too, as far as I can tell.'

'Apart from having no head,' I contributed.

'Yes, well, there is that.' Smithy looked depressed at the thought. 'Oh, there is evidence of a fracture in the left talus.'

I blinked. 'Isn't that what Dr Who travels in?'

Ever the gentleman, Smithy responded without a hint of sarcasm. 'I think you'll find that's the Tardis, Diane. The talus on the other hand occupies the middle and upper part of the tarsus, supporting the tibia above, articulating on either side with the malleoli, and in front with the navicular, and resting upon the calcaneus below.'

'Oh,' I said, buying for time. Then I got it. 'You're telling me he broke his ankle?'

'Yes, well, it's hard to tell if the fracture occurred pre- or post-mortem, but my guess is before, because, unless I'm mistaken, there is an indication, a very, very faint indication, of the beginnings of a heal.'

I must have given him my 'Duh?' look because his hand flew to his mouth as he suppressed a giggle.

'Heal on an ankle, that's a little pun isn't it? I must make a note of that.' He sobered, no doubt giving himself a silent reprimand. 'I meant *heal* as in healing. My guess is that the fracture to the talus happened about a week to ten days before our John Doe died. I'll get Brian to have a look, too. He's got a new-fangled camera that will help us get a bit closer.'

'So, you're thinking maybe it was an accident? He fell over, broke his ankle, tried to crawl to a hut or for help . . . ?'

He shrugged. 'Of course, just as likely a scenario, since we don't have a skull, is that something or someone smashed his head in.'

'Or put a bullet through it,' I suggested helpfully.

'Indeed.'

I sucked the end of the ballpoint and stared at the blinking cursor for a full minute before asking the next question.

'Why do *you* think the head is missing?'

Smithy squeezed his hands together between his thighs. 'Good question, Diane. And as with all good questions, the answer is elusive.' He pushed those invisible glasses back again. 'It looks like there was a snap break to the neck which could of course mean he hanged himself – the break in the neck would make it more likely for the head to become separated from the spine when the flesh rotted away.' He waggled his head as if in sympathy with the missing skull as he went through the possible scenarios. 'Then again, the neck could have been broken post-mortem if the body was thrown around or dragged downstream, for example.'

I made some notes, aware Smithy was reading everything I wrote. Obviously I wasn't the only one able to read text upside down.

'I couldn't see any signs of decapitation. Normally you'd see slice marks from the blade on the vertebrae if that had been the case. I can't entirely rule it out but I don't think so.'

'Not a Triad execution, then? Great, well, that really narrows it down.'

We grinned at each other, and then lapsed into thought, me sucking the pen, Smithy blinking rapidly. There's a special kind of intimacy that develops when two people think together. I took the opportunity to praise him on his weight loss. He blushed as if I'd referred to the size of his genitals rather than his waistline.

'Yes, well, health and all that,' he mumbled, self-consciously patting a little stiff curl cantilevered over his forehead. The touch to his head acted as a reminder.

'It's possible of course that our John Doe was shot in the head, but without a skull, and in the absence of organs, it's impossible to say yay or nay on that one.' He tapped me on the knee with his index finger. 'Find me the skull with a bullet hole in it and Bob's your uncle.' With that he stood and rubbed his stomach which grumbled in complaint.

'I'll do my best, but finding his head after all this time is going to be tricky.'

Smithy yanked open the door of a small fridge tucked under a corner desk, and stared despondently at the contents.

'Pigs are the most likely culprits to have made off with it,' he said, taking out a pottle. It had a sticking plaster on the lid with 'lunch' written in red felt pen.

'Any idea how long ago he died?'

'Well, that's going to be difficult.' He removed the lid and sniffed at the contents. 'I've sent samples of bone and tissue to the lab so we'll see what they come up with, but it's going to be hard to date without more specific information.' He dipped his index finger and licked it. His expression was of resigned disappointment.

'What kind of information do you need?' I asked.

'Well, if we knew whether the body was out in the open all the time, or sheltered for some of it, that would help to calculate the dates. As I say, I'll have ESR run some tests, but in reality it's pretty much impossible to pinpoint exactly how long he's been out there.'

He put the lid on the pottle and placed it back in the fridge, keeping the door open with his knee.

'All we can really do is narrow it down.'

I joined him in his lonely perusal of the fridge contents.

'So all I've got to go on, really,' I said, 'is that he was a guy in his early twenties, with a broken ankle and maybe or maybe not a bullet in his head, or who had or had not hanged himself, who went missing some time in the last hundred and fifty years.'

We both stared mournfully into the fridge at the only things keeping that little lunch pottle company: a half container of trim milk with a suspiciously clogged opening, a single bruised pear and a six-pack of low-fat yoghurt.

'As far as the body itself goes, at this stage, yes, that's about it.' Smithy removed his knee and the fridge door aspirated shut. The soft gasp of the seal seemed to spark a memory. 'Ah, but I do have something for you, though.'

'Go on – excite me,' I grinned.

Smithy blushed crimson. He handed me a plastic evidence box containing a boot.

'This is from John Doe's right foot. I cleaned it up a bit and I think you'll find it quite a clue to pinpointing the era the body went missing.'

He was right of course. With the mud removed and good hosing down, the manufacturer's label 'Lowa' was clearly visible on the inside ankle. From the style of the boot I could see it was probably made around the 1960s; checking out the label with the manufacturer should narrow the date down even more. It would at least give me the earliest possible date for the body to have been out there. I resisted the urge to kiss the top of Smithy's head. It was the little varnished, transparent comb-over that did it.

I packed my notepad away and tucked the evidence box under my arm. Smithy was staring at the fridge again and my own stomach rumbled in sympathy. I suggested we grab a burger together at the hospital café but he declined. I thought

I saw tears in his eyes. It was probably just those damn contacts giving him trouble.

Smithy said he'd hang on to the body for a couple of weeks, but if I hadn't found a solid lead as to who this guy was by the end of the month, he'd have it cremated and the ashes stored in what was affectionately known as the dungeon. Space in the city is at a premium, even at the morgue. As they say, location, location, location.

I gave Smithy a peck on the cheek and thanked him for his time. He seemed distracted – by hunger I suspect. I said goodbye, went out the door, closed it, counted to ten, then opened it again. Smithy pretended he was bending to tie his shoe lace. I didn't buy it. Not least because he was wearing slip-ons. I suspect he was in the middle of his first callisthenic.

'By the way,' I said, real casual. 'Anything of interest in the autopsy on Snow?'

He didn't even bother to straighten. 'Sean's already told me not to talk to you about that.'

'Oh well,' I admitted. 'It was worth a go.'

Smithy didn't respond. He's not usually so churlish. I put it down to the new diet. As I was about to close the door he relented.

'The phrase "frenzied attack",' he said, straightening, 'along with the single word "unexpected", for some reason spring to mind.' He gave a wink accompanied by his fullest, most rigor mortis-like smile.

Shit, I thought, he's had his teeth capped too. This new girlfriend better be worth it.

CHAPTER 10

It was a ten-minute taxi ride to Molesworth Street where I grabbed a melted cheese and relish panini from a trendy café next to the National Library. Haunted by images of a wasted Smithy, I sat on a bench in the sun and devoured my lunch. Ah, the things we do for love, I thought, which took me back to the Basin Reserve and Sean telling me his girlfriend was pregnant.

I'm really superstitious about pregnant women. I've known too many who have miscarried to feel anything but a nervous, Tourette-like compulsion to celebrate the announcement of every pregnancy. Babies should hear only exclamations of welcome while they're tucked away inside, before they make the break into the big, wide world. It seems reasonable to ask that of people, at least until the child has been born. After that, well, they're fair game like the rest of us. So even though some inner voice muttered dark thoughts about this joyfully anticipated event, I shouted it down and praised Louie or Gaia or whatever bloody deity was responsible for the fusion of Sean's sperm with that bitch's ovum. I was doing my best!

Police HQ squats at the top of Molesworth, a big black Stalinist building with reflective glass on all its windows. They don't open. Not from the outside or the inside. I waved my way past Joey, the security guard. As I waited for the lift I saw him pick up the phone to alert level 3 I was on my way. Like the windows, Joey's for show, really, because each floor is secured off with bulletproof glass and the only way anyone can enter or exit offices is with a swipe card through the outer doors, then a security code into each inner office. Fort Knox has nothing on this place, which is odd because Central, where all the actual criminal stuff goes on, is just a simple buzz-through affair. Typical. The brass protecting their arses while the workers get theirs put on the line.

I stepped out of the lift at level 3, knocked on the thick security glass, and finger-waved to Tilly when she looked up. She came swinging around the reception desk, keyed the first security pad and then swiped her card through the second door. She held it open for me and repeated the process in reverse. Tilly, in a strange reversal of Smithy's condition, had put on at least ten kilos since I'd last seen her. Maybe the same weight just got shifted around amongst people.

'I know,' she said, as if reading my thoughts. 'I'm a blimp.'

It would have been plain wrong to argue the point so I went for a lateral approach and asked what the latest goss was in cop-land. She gave me a withering look.

'You mean apart from your ex moving in with Sylvie the sucker?'

I truly, honestly and without doubt did not want to know why Sylvie had ended up with that little nomenclature. I knew she worked in the legal division of 'the service', doing what . . . I'd never bothered to ask, but I didn't know anything else about her except that she was pregnant to my husband. Okay, *ex*-husband, but still. I hoped the nickname came from some foolish professional act she'd committed rather than other actions I didn't want to visualise.

It took the next ten minutes for Tilly to issue my security clearance cards, walk me through to the little room I'd been allocated next to the kitchenette, and acquaint me with the latest updates to their internal, digital seek-and-find system. That done, and coffee mug in hand, Tilly walked me past the other offices on the level and made sure I knew everyone, which, tragically, I did. Not much changed at HQ, particularly on this floor.

Mostly people were nice and offhand, which is much the same thing, though a couple of the guys got that shifty look when they greeted me. I knew what those looks meant: these guys hung out with Sean and Sylvie and didn't think they could handle the whole 'good mate, good mate's new girlfriend, plus good mate's ex, working for the same company' thing. Either that or they'd heard rumours about how I'd lost it when my little sister was murdered and become a liability to my cop husband because I wouldn't butt my nose out of the investigation.

I wasn't in a reassuring mood, so after I'd thanked Tilly and promised to catch up for a real bitch session with her in the near future, I settled down in front of my computer, typed in the password she'd given me, and opened the search engine.

I spent the next half hour locating Lowa, the boot manufacturer's, contact details, then spending a shitload of tax payer's money ringing people all round the world trying to get a handle on when this particular batch of boots came on the market. I had some interesting conversations, including one with a shoe-fetishist, animal rights activist in Bavaria, however that didn't bring me any closer to finding out about the John Doe boot. It was fun, though, and reminded me how much I used to enjoy these jobs for the police.

I had trouble finding anyone who could tell me if the German-based brand had been exported to NZ in the 1960s, and I got sick of confirming that, 'Yes, New Zealand is a beautiful country,' and breaking the surprising news that 'No, I didn't know Peter Jackson personally.' Occasionally, just for the hell of it, I lied and said I did know PJ, and followed it up with some interesting anecdote that I made up on the spot.

But in the end, perseverance paid off and I found out that our batch of boots went on the retail market in 1969. I've always thought 1969 had a lucky ring to it, and I hoped that would be the case here too. There was no style name on the boot but after describing it in detail I ascertained that this particular line was discontinued five years later in 1974.

I did the maths. If the earliest John Doe could have been wearing those boots was 1969 and if he was twenty-something when he died, he must have been born around 1949. I jotted a couple of figures down; he'd be sixty or more now if he'd lived.

I sat back in my chair and stared at the blank wall as I thought through the dates. If the boots came on the market in 1969, the body couldn't have been there before then. So, earliest date, 1969. The only thing that could give us a secure latest date was a forensic path report, and Smithy had already admitted that the date was going to be difficult to pinpoint, given the variable effects of weather and environment on a dead body. I chewed my pen some more. Still, 1969 was a starting point.

I switched to the internal missing persons' search engine and put in the start date of 1969. I left the 'latest' date blank and filled in male for gender and, to be safe, typed 20–30 for the age range. I had nothing for distinguishing features, since the absence of a head was unlikely to have been a feature when he was alive.

While the computer had a think about it, I did too. I made sucking noises on the pen and the computer made those little clicking noises. I've always suspected that was just a sound effect built in to discourage the technologically illiterate amongst us from getting impatient and banging keys to hurry the process.

I stopped chewing as several hundred names scrolled on to the screen. I was going to have to narrow my search. Start narrow, and if I had no luck I could always expand. I went back to the original search page. This time, I made 1969 the earliest date and 1974 the latest. Five year brackets seemed a good way to start.

The names appeared at once. Only two men in their twenties went missing in that period, and remained missing. Only two, I reminded myself, who were reported to the police. The first, a Malcolm Robertson, was described as thick-set, with a 'square' build and a height of five foot seven. I checked my notes which confirmed my memory of John Doe being six foot two – give or take the variables of head size. Didn't sound like a match, but I wasn't ruling Malcolm out yet. I clicked on the other name, Steven Grigg. He'd gone missing in 1970. Height six feet. Slim build.

I jotted down the case number and took that through to Tilly who was in the middle of an intense phone conversation. She gesticulates and pulls faces when she's on a call, as if the listener is standing right in front of her. She argued for some time with the person on the other end about his cleaning up the kitchen mess after himself, and I hoped it was her son she was talking to and not her husband. She suddenly bored of the conversation and ended it. 'Boys', was all she said, so I was none the wiser, but whoever they were I hoped for their sakes that they did wash those dishes and wipe down the bench and put the cleaned toasty sandwich maker back in the cupboard when they'd finished.

I asked Tilly if she'd mind getting the Steven Grigg file for me and handed her the case number. Since my photo ID pass wasn't yet security cleared, we both knew it was quicker and less problematic if she went down to the dungeon for it. She asked me to mind the desk and I said I was more than happy to do that, but once she'd key-padded and swiped her way out and disappeared into the lift, I realised that my answering the phone would be pointless as I had no idea how to work their system, and since no one could walk in without their own swipe card, that limited the amount of foot traffic.

I decided to do as she asked and mind the desk, so I hung about, leaned on it occasionally, gave it the odd rub with my elbow. I was doing just that when Carol Pritchard swiped her way through the doors.

She gave a very bad performance of gobsmacked surprise when she saw me, which only confirmed what I'd already suspected: Tilly had alerted everyone that I was there, including Queen Carol, senior legal advisor and privacy officer to the police commissioner. 'Privacy officer' was the joke on levels 3 and 4 because Carol was known as the biggest gossip in both sworn and unsworn sections of the police force, or police *service* as it prefers to be known. What Carol doesn't know hasn't happened yet. She schmoozed and cooed at me sympathetically before going for the jugular.

'I'm so sorry to hear about Sean and Sylvie,' she crooned excitedly. 'You must be devastated.'

I've never been able to play this game – where women say one thing but mean entirely the opposite. Carol was eyeing me in the same way I'd looked at my panini lunch. I mumbled about it not being a problem, and Sean and I still being friends, and my having nothing against Sylvie – all of which goes to show that I must know more about the female bullshit than I let on.

Gemma told me once that the best thing to do with women like Carol – in fact I'm pretty sure it was Carol she meant – was to turn the tables and try and get as much information out of them as possible. This, according to Gemma, had the twofold outcome of gaining information and stopping yourself from giving any. Backed into a corner, literally, I had nothing to lose.

'Did you know Sean is handling the homicide of my sister's killer?' I asked as casually as I could.

Her eyes went very wide. She looked like a big, brainless, china doll, and I never did like dolls.

'You mean the body found in Cuba Street?'

I tried for a complicit look. 'And I hear he's got a really good lead on who might have killed him.'

'That's what I heard too.' She lowered her voice for effect. 'I heard he's thinking it was some kind of payback.'

Things were just getting interesting when a ting announced the arrival of the lift. Tilly, clutching a manila folder, approached the outer door, swipe card at the ready. Carol glanced over and, suggesting we 'do lunch sometime', hurried to take advantage of the open door. I was one of the few people in the world who knew Tilly's full name was Chantilly, and right now I was tempted to remind her of that, but she had no idea what she had interrupted, so I thanked her and took the folder back to my office.

It took less than twenty minutes to read. Steven Grigg had gone missing on the 4th of March 1970, exactly one month after his twenty-second birthday. His father had made the initial call to police, and it was obvious from the dismissive reports and follow-ups over the next few days that the cops were confident he'd turn up under his own steam. But the parents never let up, and there was even a terse report of Mr Grigg senior assaulting an officer whom he accused of not doing enough to find his boy.

After a couple of weeks of parental harassment, and the fact that Steven didn't turn up, it was easy to read the escalating concern as weeks and then months went by. But although Steven never returned, there was never any reason – no evidence, that is – for the missing person case to be ramped up to anything more serious. The parents insisted that the only reason their son wouldn't contact them was because he couldn't. Unfortunately, that hadn't been enough for the cops to upgrade the investigation to homicide.

I sympathised with the parents, as no doubt the cops at the time did, but they could do nothing unless there was a clear sign of an offence having occurred. Or foul play, as they used to call it. The case officer had done his work, interviewing all of Steven's workmates and friends and canvassing the neighbourhood for any sightings. He'd even parked a police caravan in the street where Steven lived, and another one near his workplace, but there was no new information, no leads. Nothing.

There were a couple of photos of Steven in the file which I studied closely. I didn't expect to see a resemblance between him and the headless skeleton, but I was hoping for a sign or a feeling, a whisper of something. I didn't get anything. All I saw was a skinny guy in tight, faded denims and open-necked shirt, white sneakers and oversized sunglasses. He had shoulder-length, wavy, dark hair and looked as though he could use a shave.

In one photo he was shading his eyes, pointing and grinning at the camera. In the long fingers of the pointed hand a cigarette sat proud, and when I held the photo under the lamp I could make it out as a rollie. He was a good-looking guy, but his full, pouting lips gave him an indulged look. I suspected that if I met him I'd want to bite that lip – and not in a good way.

I checked through the other photos, studying the footwear, hoping to spot my tramping boot. I knew it was a long shot and wasn't too disappointed when I didn't get a hit. Okay, I thought, Steve Griggs could be my John Doe. He was certainly worth a look.

According to the file, Steve's parents were Margo Alice and Steven Alphonse Grigg. Starting with the main cities, I did a quick White Pages internet search under those names but found nothing. Not surprising since his parents, if alive, would be in their eighties at least. I checked the file again. Steven had two brothers and a sister. The elder brother had been blessed with his father's middle name, Alphonse. I did another White Pages search for Alphonse Grigg and got a hit in Wellington. Bingo. I jotted down the inner-city apartment address in my notepad, and exited the computer.

Tilly had already gone for the day but she'd left my new laminated ID card in a big envelope on the desk that I'd minded so faithfully. I checked out the photo. Yep, I was scowling again. Which just goes to show that I am, if nothing else, consistent.

CHAPTER 11

Alphonse Grigg lived on the sixth floor of an apartment block in Marion Square. By day a vaguely grubby but entertaining part of town, by night it's where the local trannie prostitutes ply their trade in doorways. It's definitely one of Wellington's more colourful areas. I pushed the intercom for apartment 6B, expecting to give name and explanation into the grill, but I was buzzed in without saying a word. So far so easy.

When I stepped out of the lift I saw the apartment door open in readiness. I tapped on it, called out a greeting, and waited. Nothing. I was about to call out again when a square-shaped man in his sixties appeared, with a towel around his waist and his face covered in what I hoped was shaving cream.

'Mr Grigg? Alphonse Grigg?'

He lifted the bottom of the towel to his mouth, revealing more than I needed to see, and wiped a hole for his lips. He looked me up and down several times.

'You're not my five-thirty, are you?' he said, ducking his head to look down the hall.

I didn't think I wanted to be his five-thirty.

I introduced myself, told him about the John Doe being found, and why I was there. Feeling like a magician with a rabbit, I produced the oblong evidence box containing the tramping boot. All the time Alphonse stood motionless in his towel skirt and cream Santa beard and stared at me. When I stopped talking, he told me I'd better come in then. He returned to what I presumed was the bathroom and shut the door.

There was only one room to wait in, so I waited in it. I placed the box next to an empty coffee mug on the tiny table, uncomfortably aware of the similarity between the shoebox and the room itself. Even the colour of the apartment, which probably had a name like *Void* or *Infinity*, was exactly the same as the interior of the box. Nothingness. The only interesting thing in the room was the splatter of snapshots above the bed. I was studying these when Alphonse spoke behind me.

'That one on the far right is Steven. It was taken a couple of weeks before he went missing.'

Alphonse was now, thankfully, dressed in chinos and black T-shirt. The shaving cream had been wiped off except for a tiny blob on his earlobe. I resisted the urge to lean over and tweak it away. He was stalled by the table, looking at the tramping boot in the open box but not touching it.

I turned back to the photo of Steven. It was the only one I could see of the missing brother, pinned up separate from the others. Alphonse came close, enveloping me in a musk of shaving cream. He pointed out a young guy holding a surfboard.

'That's my younger brother, Charlie. He was only fifteen when Steven went missing. Just starting out.' His hand pressed the photo like a blessing. 'He was a lovely boy. And that,' he said, touching a black and white photo of a young girl in a miniature wedding dress and veil, 'is my sister Robyn. This was taken at her first holy communion.'

So she *was* a child bride then. The invisible groom being good old God himself. I waited, knowing Alphonse would get there eventually; he just needed to do it at his own pace. Finally he unpinned a tiny black and white photo curling at the edges and handed it to me.

'That was us before Steve buggered off. I'm not saying we were anything special. Just an ordinary family. Mum, Dad and the kids.'

I studied the photo. The little group did indeed look like an ordinary family, their image forever fixed in the midst of what looked like a big work picnic. Mum and Dad were caught in the act of laying out food on a tartan blanket. Robyn, this time in shorts and t-shirt, was standing on one foot, clasping the other behind, her head thrown back for balance. Two boys, who I guessed were Alphonse and Charlie, were tying their ankles together with torn-up pantyhose. They were sharing a complicit grin in anticipation of the three-legged race. I glanced surreptitiously at Alphonse; he'd kept the same surprised smile that he had as a kid, but that was about it.

'We won that day. Can't remember what we got for it. Nothing, probably.'

The smile was gone. I studied the third boy in the photo. I hadn't noticed him the first time I looked. Older than the other two, he stood at the edge of the picnic blanket, looking away from the family towards something off camera. No one else in the photo was seeing what he saw.

'This is Steven?' I asked, sure it was but wanting to keep Alphonse talking. I had a feeling this guy opened and shut like a valve. Alphonse took the photo and studied it as if for the first time.

'He didn't bugger off until a couple of years after this was taken, but this is the last time I remember us all being together as a family.' He pinned the photo back on the wall. 'He was always a selfish prick.'

The pin went in dangerously close to Steven's head.

'We lost our parents the day Steven went missing. I had to take over being the grown-up and I didn't do too good at it. Charlie killed himself a week after his seventeenth birthday.' Alphonse walked stiffly to the table and picked the boot out of the box. 'And Robyn might as well have,' he added cryptically.

I watched him weigh the boot in his hand, the sole flapping like the jaw of a ventriloquist's dummy. He'd gone somewhere else – somewhere I didn't want to follow him to. I thought he might throw the boot at me and took a step towards him just in case. The movement seemed to remind him I was in the room.

'One day Steven just up and disappeared, and for all that Mum and Dad noticed us after that, they might as well have gone with him.' He placed the boot carefully back in the box and held it out. 'This isn't his.'

'You're sure?'

'Steven had huge feet right from when he was a kid. Poor kids remember things like that. I wore his hand-me-downs. Anyway, I never saw him in any kind of boots. He sure as hell wasn't a walker. My bet, he got himself killed over some drug deal, but who the fuck knows.'

I left Alphonse in his little shoebox apartment, scraping over the coals of memory, blowing on the embers of resentment. I felt bad about reviving the hurt although it hadn't seemed too deeply buried before I started digging. And when his five-thirty passed me in the corridor I stopped worrying. From the look of her, I figured Alphonse wouldn't be thinking about his family for the next little while. At least, I hoped not.

I grabbed a coffee from Floriditas, a café in Cuba Street with large windows. Wolf's walker Damian works the odd shift there, so it's a useful haunt for me when I'm in need of a bit of staring out of windows. The coffee's pretty good, too.

I had no reason to disbelieve Alphonse when he said the boot didn't belong to his brother, but this was an annoying dead end. There were only two missing persons on the police database that fitted the timeline and only one of them was in the probable age bracket of my John Doe. Now it looked like he wasn't a match.

That left two possibilities: the initial autopsy evidence was wrong, or my John Doe had never been reported missing. Smithy would be the first to say his initial report to me was premature and therefore likely to be incorrect, but from experience I thought that unlikely. Smithy is the best and I couldn't remember him ever being wrong in his initial assessment.

Which left me with the other alternative: my wheelbarrow JD had never been reported missing. That wasn't so unusual. There are far more loners in this world than we'd like to think, and when those people disappear they can just slip-slide away, unremarked and unnoticed by anyone. What I needed to do next was try and figure out if this particular JD wanted to disappear or whether it was someone else's idea. I needed to go back to where the body was found. If I could establish where he died, that could help me with how and maybe even why. With those answers in place, I might be able to have a go at the most important question of all: *who*.

Damian wasn't on duty at the café, so I scribbled a note asking him to drop the shoebox off at my house tomorrow when he came to walk Wolf, and handed the note and evidence box to the manager to put in Damian's locker. Maybe it was the coffee, maybe it was that little cubicle Alphonse was scratching his life out in, or maybe it was the address I'd seen in my notepad while I was scribbling the note to Damian – whatever it was, I needed a walk, which was handy since I wouldn't get my car back until I met up with Robbie later.

I'd walked as far as the D.Vice sex shop when I remembered I'd agreed to bring along a friend tonight. I didn't want to consider if there was a connection between the shop and that recollection. As I walked I rang Gemma and asked if she'd like to join me for a drink at eight thirty. It's true I mentioned neither Robbie nor his mate, and I certainly didn't use the words 'double' or 'date', but it was better that way for two reasons: one, Gemma would actually turn up; and two, I wouldn't have to listen to her scornful laugh before she hung up on me.

It was also, I admit, insurance for my own safety. One of my few good points is that when I say I'm going to be somewhere I *always* turn up, unless something really serious happens to prevent it. People know that about me. If I didn't turn up for drinks, Gemma would know something was seriously amiss – she'd know I was in trouble. And tonight, if that happened, she'd have two other cops on hand to share her concern with, though admittedly she didn't know about the other cops yet.

I paused outside the little junk shop beside the charcoal chicken outlet at the top of Cuba Street. I knew from the newspaper report that Snow's body had been dumped in the gutter outside this shop. With no security cameras in this part of town, and with little vehicle or foot traffic in the wee small hours, there had been no witnesses. If anyone in the apartments nearby had seen anything they sure as hell weren't rushing forward to tell the cops.

According to Sean, the police theory, backed by minimal forensic evidence, was that Snow had been killed elsewhere and his body tipped here from a moving vehicle. It seemed such an appropriate place to drop him – in a gutter outside a junk shop – that I couldn't help but wonder if the killer wasn't making a metaphorical statement. Then again, maybe it was time I cut down on my television crime-show viewing.

I looked along the gutter and the shopfront edge of the pavement but couldn't see anything of significance. The shop window displayed a collection of tobacco tins, and tragically discarded soft toys leaning together as if for comfort, all covered with a thick layer of dust. The sign on the door said 'Back in 10' but I doubted it. It looked like the place had been locked up and deserted years ago.

I continued on up Web Street and dodged the traffic to get to the dairy on the corner of Willis, then made my way up Aro Street, checking off the house numbers as I went. Outside the Aro Street video store I stopped and rechecked Snow's address in my notepad. Having read it upside down in Sean's car, it was possible I'd written an incorrect number, but this looked like the right place – a little run-down cottage up a long driveway that snaked between the video store and a block of apartments.

The bland and soulless apartments had replaced a garage called MM Motors. Rumour had it that the initials were short for Mickey Mouse Motors, an apparently fitting name for a business run by a bunch of cowboy film-makers from the seventies who specialised in 'blowing shit up in movies'.

Under the guise of checking out the video store's specials bin, I made sure there were no cars parked up the driveway directly outside Snow's place.

On closer inspection the cottage looked derelict and deserted. I checked my watch. It was just after seven. I had time to have a quick look around inside the house, get back home, change, and still be on time for drinks downtown with Robbie at eight. Although I wasn't anticipating trouble, Gemma would be expecting me at eight thirty and if I didn't turn up she'd know something was wrong.

All I had to do was figure out how to break into Snow's place.

CHAPTER 12

I knocked, waited a full thirty seconds, then knocked again, louder this time. Still nothing. The gravel underfoot crackled like cornflakes along the narrow alley between the house and a concrete retaining wall. I glanced at each of the windows along the side of the cottage ready to wave a confident hello if anyone suddenly appeared – but they were too thick with dust and cobwebs for me to see inside. I knocked loudly on the back door to be sure no one was inside, and then I clasped the door handle. Nothing ventured and all that, but this time nothing was gained either.

I glanced around the back porch. We're a funny bunch, humans – each thinking we're different from the rest. That we're the only one with a particularly bizarre fear or desire. That we've each got our own quirky, exclusive ways of doing things. It's what keeps us believing we're individuals in control of our own destiny. It's also what keeps us lonely, but that's another matter. The fact is, eight out of ten people put their house key under the welcome mat at the back door. Though I know it drives cops and insurance brokers up the wall, I find that little example of human frailty endearing. A free-thinking four per cent of us put the key under a pot plant, brick, gumboot or sneaker within a metre of the door it opens. The truly maverick stick it on a ledge above the door.

I looked in all these places but found nothing, which proved that my suspicions about Snow were correct – he wasn't like the rest of us. Then again, the cops might have taken the key from one of these 'hiding' places after they'd been through the place, and maybe the only thing that set Snow apart from the rest of us was that he'd stuck a knife in my little sister's back.

A fine drizzle had started to fall, and a gloom had set in, probably a summer storm brewing. If I was going to climb in through a window I should do it before dark – neighbours are usually less suspicious of daylight break-ins. That's another of those odd little human foibles.

I tried to wriggle my fingers under a couple of the windows along the southern side of the house but an amateur paint job had stuck the frames to the sills and it would take a putty knife to free them. I didn't need to check my shoulder bag to know I didn't have one of those on me.

Refusing to be daunted, I turned my phone off, slipped the bag strap over my chest commando-style, and tried the windows on the northern side. On the last one I struck gold. The bottom sill was hip height, and with the tips of my fingers I edged the frame up the first tricky couple of inches and then used my shoulder to heft it up far enough to duck my head underneath. I nearly strangled myself with the bag strap, but

I finally managed to get some purchase. For one vulnerable moment the weight of the window rested on my neck while I scrabbled for a decent hold with both palms, then shoving it up, I swung one leg over the sill. Once my foot tapped the floorboard inside, I manoeuvred my crotch over the sill.

As I ducked my head inside a voice in the room froze me to the spot. Shit! This wasn't only the most uncomfortable position to be caught in, it was the most vulnerable. Too late to pull out. I had to risk it.

Leaping in, I let the window fall shut after me. I'd like to add 'in one smooth movement', but it was far from smooth. I'd badly scraped my shoulder, and the windowsill had bruised me in a way that would have meant abstaining from sex if I'd been having any sex to abstain from.

I spun around to confront the speaker, mentally searching for my excuse. That book I'd read on worst case scenarios didn't cover breaking and entering. I was on the point of blurting something about fire and kittens when I realised there was no one in the room to pitch this implausible excuse to. Other than me that is, and I sure as hell wasn't buying it.

The voice was coming from a radio clock by the bed.

I breathed again in relief, and took a moment to rub my shoulder and ease the seam off my bruised clitoris, while I listened intently for any other sound in the house. The clock was flashing 7.10. I made myself stay completely still and listen for a full three minutes before I was confident that the only sounds were my own heart pounding and someone on the radio whingeing about the latest cricket team selection. When the clock flicked to 7.13, it was time to do what I'd come to do.

Until that moment I hadn't figured out exactly what that was – I just knew I needed to look at where Niki's killer lived. I thought that maybe I'd find something of Niki here, although I'd rejected the idea of any intimacy between killer and victim. Ever since I'd listened to Gemma's tape, the one I shouldn't have listened to, I'd had to fight against the awful fear that Snow might have taken a souvenir from Niki, something to remind him of the killing. If he'd done that, I wanted it back.

Piles of clothes were scattered on the floor. Possibly someone was sorting them for collection, or they'd been searching for something. The room smelt of dirty socks and another musty, animal smell I didn't want to try too hard to identify. I took a step towards the centre of the room, breaking into a sweat at the creak of the floorboards.

On the chest of drawers was an empty bottle of Boss aftershave and a greasy-looking hairbrush riddled with blond hairs. It occurred to me for the first time that Snow was given that nickname because of his hair, probably in childhood. I knew I shouldn't pick it up, but the brush was in my hand before I could stop myself.

The thing I find really hard to come to terms with about the sickos who cigarette-burn kids, or torture animals, or stab little sisters in the back with boning knives, is that they also do the same, ordinary things the rest of us do. Things like brushing their teeth or hair. Like enjoying the smell of a flower or laughing at the same jokes. Crying at the same, sad movie as the rest of us, for all I know. I can never get my head around that. I find it hard to believe people like that are the same as me, but here was simple domestic evidence of it. I didn't like the mix of emotions it produced in me.

The drawers had all been emptied and left hanging open, and the wardrobe had been cleared out as well. Presumably everything of Snow's was now on the floor. Keeping my hands in my pockets, I kicked through some of the clothes but there was nothing I could see of any interest. I glanced around for a possible hiding place. Lightshades are good but nothing was stashed in this one, a plain, plastic, concave number. There were no posters on the walls to hide things behind. A pale blue cotton sheet had been tacked up over the front window in place of curtains. I checked the window ledge behind that, but I wasn't really expecting to find anything.

Now I was just moving around the room to keep myself from freezing in panic. The bed base was a double with a single foam mattress – stained, mouldy and damp – marooned in the middle. All class was Snow. At least it was light enough to lift with two fingers which was a real bonus. So too, I guess, was the big fat joint beneath it, but I wasn't in the least bit tempted. Obviously the cops who'd searched the room hadn't been either.

On the floor beside the bed a pair of blue jeans with a leather belt had been dropped as if their owner had just stepped out of them. They reminded me of 'the pale green pants with nobody inside them' that I used to read to Niki when she was little. The pockets were gaping open in what I swore, and knew I might have to in court, was an inviting way. 'The pockets said, "yes", your Honour.'

I squatted beside the jeans, my knees clicking in a way the cricket selector on the radio, presently defending his choice of wicket keeper, would have cringed at. Tentatively, I inserted my fingers into the first pocket. The lining felt clammy, and as I moved my fingers the stink of Snow hit my nostrils. My stomach clenched. The pocket was empty. Turning my face aside, I inserted my fingers into the other pocket, pulling the lining as far away from the crotch as possible. I think I'd just decided there was nothing in there either when my head exploded.

If you've ever been knocked unconscious you'll know that while you're out there in never-never land you have no sense of time passing, and so, 'coming to', as it's quaintly called, is nothing like waking up from a sleep. What it's like is, one second you're innocently going through someone's pockets, and a split second later you're – well, in this particular scenario I'm lying on the floor of a different room with two scowling women glaring at me. There's no waking, yawning, stretching, no 'Oh my gosh, I just had the most amazing dream' kind of feeling when you regain consciousness. Even if half an hour has passed by, you have no sense of it passing. I guess being knocked unconscious is the closest you could get to time travelling, but I wouldn't recommend it.

For one paranoid moment I thought that someone had used my eyeballs to nail my head to the floor, but then I realised I could see just fine. That was the good news. The bad news was what I was seeing: Snow's twin sisters, Peaches and Cream, the former casually swinging a Kookaburra cricket bat like a cheerleader's baton.

'She's awake,' Cream said, which was useful to know, given my befuddled state and pain level.

Feeling at a distinct disadvantage in my prone state, I dragged myself to a sitting position. The movement induced an eerie feeling that I'd left my body on the floor – so convincing was it that I looked back to see if this was true. It was such a genuinely cool out-of-body experience that I opened my mouth to share it with the twins, but had to clench my jaw shut to hold back the vomit that threatened to spill. My head felt three times its normal size and as if it was going to fall off completely if waggled or moved at all.

The white-out effect created by the searing pain in my head was accompanied by a high-pitched whistle, but when Peaches crossed to the stove and turned off the gas under a kettle the sound stopped, so chances are it wasn't in my head. I eased myself into a wooden kitchen chair.

'Jesus, Peaches, why did you hit me with a cricket bat?'

Peaches leaned the bat against the stove and poured boiling water into an old railways' teapot.

'There's something else you'd rather I whacked you with?'

She grinned at me, but I was having trouble seeing any humour in the situation. I tentatively fingered the back of my head. If it wasn't for the pain, feeling separated from my body was a sensation I might have found vaguely enjoyable. A very tender bump was already forming at the base of my hairline.

'Fuck . . .' I managed, but the rest of the sentence whistled off into the white space called oblivion . . .

I blinked back awake as Peaches swaggered across the room and planted a mug of tea in front of me. She was the only woman I've ever seen pull off a swagger in high heels. It was a relief she'd left the Kookaburra leaning against the stove. I'm no fashion Nazi but it wasn't an accessory that worked with the black cocktail dress and heels. The dress was the one she'd been wearing at her brother's funeral earlier in the day. Perhaps in an attempt to remove the funereal association of the outfit, she'd piled her hair up and clasped on big purple glass-drop earrings that rattled against her neck as she leaned towards me. She'd gone with a glossy lipstick the colour of raw liver, presumably to match her earrings. It wasn't the first mistake Peaches had made in her life.

'Oh, come on!' she sneered. 'I gave you a light tap and you went out like a light.' She sounded aggrieved, as if unconsciousness had been an unreasonable reaction on my part.

Cream clearly didn't do polite chatter. She came right to the point.

'What the fuck were you doing going through our brother's pockets?'

There was no point trying to bullshit these two even if my brain had been up to it.

'I was looking for anything of Niki's. I thought he might have kept a souvenir, and now seemed a good time to look. Him being dead and all.'

My voice sounded odd, a bit robotic and echoey, but I wasn't sure if it was my speech or my hearing that was affected. A look passed between the women, and unless my faculties were even more damaged than I realised, it told me they'd already found something. Something of Niki's.

Knowing I needed to concentrate, I forced myself to take a sip of the scalding tea. I asked for my bag and Peaches picked it up off the floor and passed it to me without comment. As soon as I clicked open the flap it was obvious they'd gone through it. Cream held up two twenty dollar notes which presumably she'd lifted from my wallet. Ignoring her, I took it slow, scrabbling around in my bag for aspirin, buying time for my brain to reboot. I swore at myself for having turned my phone off instead of flicking it to silent.

I was considering the odds of being able to switch it on surreptitiously and push the emergency dial number which would ring directly to the police station, when Cream banged her elbows on the table and leaned towards me.

'You're still trying to get Snow for killing your sister, aren't you? You always wanted him for it.'

I moved my shoulders in a noncommittal way. It seemed pointless to deny the obvious truth. Peaches leaned against the wall and studied me.

'Were you trying to plant something? We couldn't find anything in the bag, so maybe you've already done it.'

'What? No!' I said, genuinely affronted. 'I didn't come here to *plant* anything.' I was going to add something about always staying on the right side of the law but given how I gained access to the house I decided not to go there. The aspirin retrieved, I hung the bag over the back of the chair.

'I thought maybe he'd kept something of Niki's as a kind of trophy. If so, I wanted to get it back. And I wanted to see where he lived. See if I could figure out why he did it,' I added, going again for the honest approach.

It seemed to pay off. Both women visibly relaxed. I punched two aspirin from the foil and knocked them back, using the tea as lubricant.

Peaches joined us at the table. 'Yeah, Snow was a prime arsehole all right,' she admitted without rancour. 'I don't know if he killed your sister, but I wouldn't put it past him.' She stared into the sugar bowl. Maybe she was remembering the time her brother broke a bottle over her head. She would have been about twelve when Snow was charged. He was fifteen and it being his first offence, he'd walked away with the judicial equivalent of a slap on the wrist with a wet bus ticket. Sean told me that after Peaches was stitched up, she was dealt a beating from her mother for getting Snow into trouble.

Cream glanced at her sister, then stared directly at me. Though she kept going in and out of focus, I did my best to respond with an equally direct look.

'The thing is,' she said, 'arsehole or not – he's our brother. Just like your sister is your sister. And he's been murdered, just like your sister was murdered. In fact, exactly like your sister was murdered. We want to know who did it, just like you do. I used to think you were right, that Snow did your sister, but now I'm thinking the same bastard that killed her, killed him. Is that what that cop husband of yours thinks?'

'Ex,' I clarified. 'My cop *ex*-husband.'

'Same thing,' Peaches added morosely. 'You might hate it, but the truth is we're on the same side. Your sister was murdered and our brother was murdered. You and us – we're both victims.'

My mouth was open to refute this but luckily the words were forming too slowly and there was time for me to clamp it shut. I wanted to say that the Wilson twins and I had nothing in common – that we were worlds apart. I wanted to say that where Niki's death should have slowed the world on its axis, their brother's murder deserved a week-long raging celebration, and I would be the first to jump up on the table and rock on with my glass raised. But looking at these two, I knew I was wrong. They loved that arsehole brother of theirs, and who was I to say they hadn't loved him as much as I loved Niki?

One more glance between sisters, then Peaches scraped her chair back and indicated for me to follow. We walked in single file down the hallway, Peaches leading and Cream close at my back. I glanced into Snow's bedroom as we passed. The radio clock was still on and I glimpsed the time: 7.58. Subtracting the time spent having a pleasant chat with the twins, I figured I must have been out cold for at least ten minutes. The idea that these two had dragged me down the hall unconscious and left me lying on the kitchen floor while they rummaged through my bag was seriously unsettling. Realising that Peaches had left the Kookaburra in the kitchen, I thought of shoving her into the wall and making a run for the front door, but even if I could have outrun Peaches' high heels, I didn't have a hope against Cream, dressed and ready for action as she was in sweats and sneakers. The pain in my head had been replaced with a numb, icy sensation. When Peaches pushed open a door and flicked on the fluorescent light, the brightness pierced me with a pain so severe I bent over dry retching. The sisters waited patiently until I steadied myself.

This room, too, showed signs of sorting. Cardboard boxes were stacked against one wall, and two floral-patterned armchairs sat expectantly in front of a television screen the size of Australia. The floor was littered with hundreds of DVDs, some inside their plastic covers, the rest scattered over the floorboards. The light made them shimmer like some wild cosmic display, though the effect might have been enhanced by the blow to my head.

Peaches stepped her clicking heels through the discs, careful not to stand on them. I suspected it was so she wouldn't go sliding arse over kite, rather than care not to damage the merchandise. Cream, hands on ample hips, surveyed the floor.

'You know she was a whore, your sister, don't you?'

There was no derision in her voice; it was simply a question, naming Niki's occupation, not her personality type. Not trusting myself to speak, I nodded.

'Well,' Peaches said, 'she was in Snow's stable.' She scrabbled inside a plastic shopping bag next to the screen and pulled out a disc already labelled and dated. The word 'stable' evoked images of warm hay, the baby Jesus, and three kings bearing gifts, but I was pretty sure that wasn't what Peaches was referring to.

'You mean Snow was her pimp,' I said, needing to hear myself say it. I realised something else. 'So, he took a cut of her earnings then.'

'Yeah, whatever,' Cream responded, a little unhelpfully I thought.

Peaches pushed the eject button on the DVD player sitting on top of the screen, and when the drive slid out placed her disc into it.

'Snow told us he had a good thing going with your sister. She brought the guys here to fuck and he had some high-tech hidden camera set up to film them.'

Cream indicated one of the armchairs. It was definitely time to sit, and I carefully lowered myself into it. Peaches was acting as techno expert, turning the big screen on and hunting down the remotes, while Cream, warming to her role as narrator, dropped into the other armchair.

'The deal was, your sister would engage the trick in as kinky a scenario as she could get him to agree to. Most of the guys just wanted straight sex, and according to Snow, quite a few of them would have been happy just to sit and talk. Creepy,' she added with a shudder. 'Anyway, that kind of thing wasn't going to cut it, so she'd have to convince them they wanted other stuff. Wacko-type stuff. According to Snow, they nearly always agreed – eventually. And then while they were going at it Snow would be busy filming the whole thing. A couple of days later he'd send a copy to the trick and suggest he might like to pay up or have the little number of him in a nappy or whatever broadcast on YouTube, or sent to his wife or daughter. According to Snow, most of them paid up real quick, quiet and in full.'

Cream pulled a lever at the side of her chair which flew back to accommodate a half-lying, legs-in-the-air position with feet cushioned by a padded foot rest. She looked like she was settling in for an evening's entertainment. Peaches, too, having found the right disc and the right channel, was looking more animated than I'd seen her yet. I almost expected her to bring out the popcorn. She pointed the remote at the screen and an image sprang to life.

Niki.

'Hang on,' I yelled.

Peaches jabbed the remote and the image froze.

I held my hand up to block it. 'You're telling me Snow took a cut of whatever Niki earned for having sex and . . . and stuff . . . with these guys?'

Peaches and Cream both nodded enthusiastically, like I was a slow student finally getting a handle on what was being taught.

'And then he blackmailed them and took that money as well?'

The sisters actually smiled at each other before nodding. Next they'd be putting a star on the back of my hand for being such a quick little learner.

'Well, in that case,' I said, 'what the fuck was Niki getting out of this deal?'

The sisters shrugged, disappointed with me. They'd been sure I'd get there without their help.

'Drugs, of course,' Peaches finally answered.

'Snow was her supplier,' Cream added.

Okay, I admit I'd been slow, but not that slow. There must have been something in my look because Peaches suddenly became defensive.

'Hey, he got her off the crap P she was taking and found her a supply of good clean ice from offshore.' She pressed the point. 'He wasn't all bad, you know.'

The sisters were disappointed with me all over again when I refused to settle back and join them in watching Niki having kinky sex with her tricks.

Their opinion of me may have improved when I grabbed the remote off Peaches and told her that, unless she handed over every recording they had of my sister, I'd rip them both apart with my bare fucking hands.

They relinquished the plastic bag of discs with a minimum of fuss, assuring me this was 'all there was of Niki'. I'd like to think the phrase was just tactless and not intended to wound the way it did. Cream told me the cops were responsible for the discs being scattered over the floor, the result of their search, aka a ransack, of the place after Snow's death. She indicated the bag I was clutching to my chest and with a conspiratorial grin told me the pigs didn't know Snow's secret hiding place for the 'special' discs. It dawned on me that Snow and his sisters had grown up in this house, and so they'd known exactly where to look. I wondered what else they'd found in that secret hiding place. As if reading my thoughts, Peaches assured me there was nothing else in the house of interest to me.

They let me go, even holding the front door open for me. As I thumped down the path, Peaches repeated her assertion that we were on the same side. Their sudden politeness might have had something to do with the way my fists clutched that plastic bag, the way my jaw was clenched, the way I was breathing hard through my teeth. I was struggling to hold back a rage that beat like a trapped gull inside my chest. I strode down the driveway towards Aro Street, trying to hold back the memory flashes of my little sister on the bed. I'd only caught a glimpse of that freeze-frame, but it had been enough. More than enough.

There was a taxi in Willis Street and the driver assured me he knew the quickest way to The Tasting Room. On the way I turned on my phone and watched as it registered eight missed calls. Three were from Gemma's number, and the 'Robbie' appeared twice. I recalled punching his name into my phone's address book while in the hearse outside Wainuiomata station, and that memory brought up an image of Robbie's hitched grin. Checking the phone's clock confirmed I was about an hour late meeting up with Gemma, Robbie and his mate. Since Gemma didn't know anyone else was joining us, and since neither Robbie nor his mate knew Gemma, I doubted they'd connected up.

One missed call on my phone was from Sean. His number came up under 'X'. I made a mental note to change that next time I was in a more adult frame of mind. No telling when that might be, but probably not before my mortgage was paid off or hell froze over – whichever came last.

The other two calls were from numbers I didn't immediately recognise. I checked to see if my credit cards were still in my wallet, and was relieved to find that the forty bucks cash was all the sisters had taken. To be fair to them, forty bucks seemed a reasonable fee for my breaking and entering their family abode, though in my own defence nothing was actually broken except possibly my skull and my pride, and the sisters were responsible for both of those.

While the driver zip-zapped my credit card, I checked my face in his rear-vision mirror. I had a half-hearted, foolish idea of tidying myself up before heading into the bar, but one look told me a lick and a promise wasn't going to cut it. I looked a train wreck.

The only good thing was that I didn't look nearly as bad as I felt.

CHAPTER 13

It's handy that bars have security guards ready to step in if things get out of hand or ugly. I was counting on them to do just that if Gemma took it into her head to deal to me for being late. I didn't believe Robbie and his mate would still be there. They were expecting me at eight and who waits an hour for a no-show date? So it was a surprise when Robbie waved to me from a table at the window. And even more of a surprise that Gemma was at the table with him. Well, that solved the other little problem waiting to bite me in the butt – telling Gemma I'd set her up on a double date.

The Tasting Room is primarily a designer beer bar but they also have a good selection of wines and pricey but generous servings of breads and olives, or chips with golden aioli for those not too worried about, or failing to keep to, their diets. Patrons can choose to squat on stools at tit-height bar tables, or squeeze behind tiny wooden tables that make them look like they're holding an Ouija board on their laps. My group had secured one of those pinny-sized tables, tucked in an alcove against the window.

Robbie stood as I approached. He was wearing an open-necked white shirt over dark dress pants, the sort of shirt worn out rather than tucked in. Nice. He held out his hand for me to shake and then presented that amazing smile as an accessory. He looked even better in civvies than he did in uniform, and again I found that smile damn difficult to resist. I beamed stupidly back at him.

My goofy smile soon vanished when I saw Gemma's scowl, but having had a previous taste of Robbie's warm handshake I wasn't going to let her deprive me of another. A girl takes what she can get in the way of male contact when she's been celibate for as long as I have. We squeezed palm to palm, and when I released him Robbie introduced me to his mate, Wayne, and I leaned across Gemma to shake his hand too. With the same fair hair and wide shoulders as Robbie, Wayne had a sharp, alert, impatient look that suggested intelligence rather than nerves.

I squashed in to a tiny space beside Robbie and opposite Gemma and Wayne, who'd scored the uncomfortable skinny-legged wooden chairs. I rolled the top of the plastic bag of discs over and discreetly stashed it behind my ankles. From the way Wayne looked at me I figured he'd already noted that I was holding my head steady in an attempt to stop it falling off. I was betting Wayne was a detective, though all cops, uniformed or otherwise, get pretty quick at noticing things like that. Sean was a master at it. Nothing escaped him. Nothing except me, that is. Not that I'd been trying to escape, I'd just gone way out on my own somewhere and then couldn't find my way back to him.

I launched into my apologies for being late. I muttered about traffic, and having lost track of the time – entirely accurate – and being unavoidably delayed, along with variations on the theme.

There hadn't been time to make up a good fabrication, and I knew from ghastly experience that it was better not to try and lie on the spot. Instead I went for obfuscation and attempted to move the conversation to safer ground as quickly as possible. I was acutely aware of Gemma's droll gaze on me as I twittered on, though I did my best to avoid meeting it.

Wayne told me he and Gemma had met at a police negotiators' course about a year ago, and that this was the first time they'd met since. He glanced at Gemma and added that it was odd they hadn't banged into each other before now, given how small the police community was in the greater Wellington area. Gemma sipped her wine without response, which was churlish even for her.

I insisted on buying a round and asked the hovering waiter to bring another of whatever everyone was having. I was struggling with waves of nausea, and had the bizarre sensation that my pounding heart had relocated to the back of my head.

After ten minutes, hoping I'd papered things over enough to allow myself a breather in the bathroom, I excused myself, asking Robbie to keep an eye on my 'shopping bag' under the table. That incriminating bagful could more accurately be classed as 'possible evidence in a murder case' if one was to be pedantic. The pedantic one I had in mind was my ex-husband, C/O of the investigation into Snow's homicide, but I couldn't think too much about that or him right now. Reluctantly, I removed my leg from its warm contact with Robbie's and launched myself across the room to the Ladies. I made it without staggering. I think.

The washbasin wasn't a basin at all, but a long, flat slab of marble cambered for drainage at the back. Looked great, very trendy and all, but it didn't allow for a full facial immersion, which had been my plan. Going for next best, I rested my elbows on the marble, filled my hands with cold water, and lowered my face into it.

I'd done this several times before the door swung open and Gemma joined me in front of the mirror, which up until now I'd avoided.

'So, where the fuck were you, and what's the deal with setting me up on a double date without the courtesy of asking me if I want to go on a double fucking date?' Gemma was, as always, to the point. 'Jeez, you look like shit,' she added.

I braved a look in the mirror. She was right. I definitely did look like shit. If I'd been wearing mascara – about the only make-up I ever wear – I would have looked even worse, but that was small consolation.

I wiped my face with paper towels before launching into my explanation for lateness. I told her Snow's sisters had held me up – an entirely accurate description of what they'd done. I explained that we'd been talking, which was also accurate, and that I'd lost track of time – likewise.

Luckily, this being a week night, the toilets weren't in hot demand, and I was able to fill Gemma in on a fair bit of my conversation with the twins. I'd just told her about Niki's part in Snow's blackmailing scam – registering the fact that Gemma didn't look surprised by any of this – when we were rudely interrupted by women with the audacity to want to use the toilets.

Forced to relocate, we sidestepped through the drinkers and back to the table where Robbie and Wayne were having a conversation of their own. They stopped as we approached, and Robbie threw that smile at me again. It was a real Heath Ledger of a smile he had going there, and for a minute I completely forgot where Gemma and I were up to.

While she and Wayne checked out the snacks menu, bickering none too politely, Robbie rummaged in his jacket pocket and held out my car keys. I thought it was good of him not to mention the Day-Glo alien figure attached, and even better of him not to lecture me about leaving my car unlocked and with the keys in such an obvious location it would have been anathema to refer to it as a 'hiding' place. Knowing something doesn't necessarily mean you've learnt it, as far as keys and hiding places go.

'It's pretty much right outside.' He hitched his thumb towards Courtenay Place. 'About five or six cars thataway.'

I dropped the keys into my shoulder bag, and thanked him for bringing my car all the way into the city. When I added another apology for being late, he shrugged.

'That's okay,' he said. 'There's nowhere else I had to be.' He leaned ever so slightly towards me so that our arms connected. 'You had a pretty tough day, eh?'

The warmth of his body was heady, and I felt mine incline towards him in response. 'Yeah, a bit,' I admitted.

He let that statement lie between us, giving me time to pick it up if I wanted. I didn't, but the silence was comfortable between us. I filled him in on the little I'd learnt about our John Doe. I gave him a brief rundown of Smithy's preliminary autopsy findings. The only body injury Smithy could find was a broken ankle, which the JD certainly hadn't died from. Finding the missing skull might confirm if he'd been killed or if it was a suicide, but then again, it might not. Identifying a bullet hole in the skull wouldn't be a guarantee either way unless it was at a really odd angle such as at the base of the neck pointing up.

Robbie nodded and stretched across the table for the jug of water, holding it above my glass and lifting his eyebrows.

'Yeah, thanks. Great,' I responded.

He poured all four glasses while I rabbited on about the boot our John Doe had been wearing, and how I had narrowed down the earliest year our guy could have walked it into the forest. Robbie settled back with his arm running down the entire length of mine. I really had forgotten how pleasantly warm a man's body could be, but my body was sure as hell remembering it all over again. Robbie, either less affected by my body heat than I was by his, or really quick with numbers, did the maths easily.

'If 1969 is the earliest he could have been wearing those boots, and if Smithy's right about his being twenty something when he died, that makes him born around 1949. If he'd lived, he'd be sixty-odd now.' Robbie sipped his water as he thought through the implications. 'Which means his contemporaries – wife, brothers, sisters, friends – most of them should still be alive. Maybe even his parents. Nothing showed up on the missing persons at HQ?'

'Well, actually there was one,' I admitted, and told him about Steven Grigg and my meeting with Alphonse. He nodded, then without any change in tone asked how the back of my head was feeling. 'Ice packs really do work,' he added, throwing me one of his hitched half grins. I was still struggling with how to answer this when I caught Gemma staring at me.

'What?'

She leaned across the table. 'How did you get into Snow's house? Cause I'm betting the twins didn't invite you in.'

'Sure they did.' I gave her my most aggrieved tone. Hell, I would have believed me. 'More importantly,' I said, leaning to meet her halfway, 'how come you're not surprised to hear Niki was the bait in Snow's blackmailing scheme?'

Gemma held my gaze for some time before leaning back in her chair. 'Yeah, we knew about that. Snow even gave up the names of some of the guys he'd scammed when we hauled him in for questioning over Niki's death.'

I could see her words were harsher and more casual than she felt. This was just Gemma's way.

'We looked at some of those guys too, running the angle that maybe Niki got caught up in some payback – but we hit a blank wall with that line of enquiry.' She'd reverted to police-speak out of deference to the other cops at the table.

The guys seemed a bit embarrassed by this sudden change in the conversation. That we were talking a case, which is pretty much all cops do talk about, wasn't the problem. In fact I'm sure it was a relief to them both, but they'd picked up the tension between us, and no doubt they'd picked up the emotional heat coming off me. All my talk and behaviour screamed 'personal involvement' and it was freaking the hell out of them. I wasn't feeling too shit-hot about it either but I couldn't keep from pushing Gemma one step further.

'You knew Niki was using, didn't you?'

'Yep,' she shot back.

'Even when she was alive, you knew, didn't you?'

Gemma, hesitated, and then nodded. 'She was trying real hard to get off it.' She snapped up one of the starched linen napkins, frowned at it, then started smoothing it into pleats. 'She was making progress.'

'Why didn't you tell me? I could have done something.' My voice broke like a pubescent boy's and I swallowed hard.

'What?' Gemma leaned in again, elbows on the table. 'What could you have done, Diane?'

My anger was threatening to brim over. I knew I should stop now, but knew also that I wouldn't.

'Talked to her. And if that didn't work I'd have grabbed her arse out of there. I would have stopped her taking that shit, got her out of that . . . that place. Away from that prick who killed her!'

The only way I could stop myself from crying was to keep my anger up. I knew I was being unreasonable. Knew I shouldn't be talking to Gemma like it was her fault. Gemma turned her attention back to the napkin folding and pressing. I focused on her chipped nail polish, and tried to keep my voice steady.

'Look,' I said. 'I knew she was stripping. I think I even knew she was whoring. But drugs? Blackmail? I can't believe she was so stupid.'

There was silence at the table. I could almost hear my blood pressure dropping. Wayne was turning his wine glass round and round. Robbie had created a very effective-looking paper dart out of his napkin, which at any other time might have impressed me. Gemma was folding and refolding the linen into squares. No one was looking at me. They were all giving me time to get it together. I took a sip of water and a deep breath and managed half a back-pedal.

'Look, I'm not blaming you, Gem, really I'm not. None of us is to blame. Not you, not Sean, not me. Not any of her so-called friends. We all gave her plenty of chances.' I took another sip of water, pleased I hadn't said or done something I'd really regret. 'You know, I even offered her a job. All she had to do was straighten out her life and we could have gone into business together.'

I remembered Niki's excitement when I'd made the offer. She said, 'Really?' and hugged her knees like she was fourteen years old. 'All she had to do was get her shit together,' I concluded.

Gemma wasn't looking at me. She'd squeezed the napkin down to the size of a small mobile phone. Robbie and Wayne made no pretence of doing anything but staring at it, mesmerised by the tension and movement of her fingers. Gemma's eyelashes twitched on her cheeks as her eyes darted back and forth.

'Anyway,' I added. 'She made her own choices.'

I felt Robbie's attention shift, and glanced up. Gemma was looking right at me and the look was not pretty.

'You think she didn't try and get her shit together? Do you have any idea how hard she tried to stop using that shit?'

I wanted to lean back out of the range of Gemma's breath. It wasn't that it was bad. It was the intimacy of it, and I knew instinctively I was about to hear something I didn't want to. My legs twitched in a classic flight or fight response. But Gemma's gaze held me in check. She leaned even closer – so close I could see that latticework of age lines around her eyes.

'All Niki ever did was try and live up to your expectations. She never judged *you*, Diane. She was just a fucked-up kid trying to do her best. But her best was never going to be good enough for you, was it?'

Gemma shifted back into her chair, the napkin still captive in her fist, the knuckles as white as the linen. The hit from Peaches was nothing compared to this one. I took a few small breaths, waiting for the pain in my stomach to ease. Gemma's words were scrambled in my brain like a tipped-over Scrabble set.

I must have managed goodbyes, and I know I retrieved the plastic bag from under the table. Robbie stood when I did, and Wayne hitched his eyebrows in a gesture of goodbye, but Gemma stared out the window.

The southerly from Kent Terrace was a welcome smack in the face – its freezing blast numbed my headache on impact. It made my eyes stream. Well, that's what I would have told anyone who asked.

CHAPTER 14

It's bullshit that the innocent sleep soundly while those with guilty consciences toss and turn all night. I slept long, deeply, and dreamlessly, and woke befuddled, with no memory of how or when I went to bed. Possibly I was in denial. I pressed the tender spot on my hairline where Peaches had clobbered me with the cricket bat. I remembered that all right. Well, not the clobbering itself, but the after-effect. The scratches from my struggle with the sash window looked ugly, and a smudge of bruising was already forming across my shoulder. My neck was seriously sore when I pressed it, but I had more effective ways of hurting myself than pressing bruises. I couldn't turn my head fully without lightning-like pain, and there was a high-pitched ringing in my left ear which I spent an idle minute cupping my hand over then lifting off. That created an oddly appealing underwater *wha-wha-wha.* A single girl has to make her own fun in bed.

I was starting to get bored with this game when I suddenly realised there was another body behind me in the bed. I went very cold and very still as I tried desperately to remember what I'd been doing, and who I'd been doing it with, before I fell asleep. I drew a blank. Whoever he was, his breath was so foul I could smell it over my shoulder, and he had a very unattractive snore. Who the hell had I picked up? I was considering panic as an option, but, since whoever was pressing the duvet into the back of my legs was deeply asleep and clearly not expecting trouble, I reckoned I could probably handle him. I took a big breath, flipped over to confront my bedmate, and came nose to nose with my faithful hound. His good eye stared right back at me, the blind one at this close range as milky as an opal. I snorted my relief.

'Oh my, what big teeth you have, Wolf,' I said. I don't think he got the fairy tale allusion, but it's hard to tell. I suspect he makes a point of not laughing at my jokes until I'm out of sight. At this thought I gave myself a stern talking-to about anthropomorphism and the need to get out more, which reminded me of seeing Robbie last night, which in turn reminded me of Gemma and what she'd said about my relationship with Niki – and that got me out of bed and into the shower pretty damn fast. I wasn't ready to excavate that little number yet.

While Wolf scooped his jaw methodically through his breakfast biscuits, I crunched on a slice of toast with Marmite and thumbed through yesterday's missed calls on my phone. The prefix of one unknown number was the same as Robbie's landline, which led me to conclude the call had been made from Wainuiomata.

I rang the number and it was answered so quickly that I had to shift a mouthful of toast before I could speak. It was Scott Wilborough, the ranger who'd found my John Doe. He told me Robbie had asked him to ring to set up a time to take me to where he'd found the body. Now was a good time if I was free because he was heading back in there to check on his possum traps. I got the distinct impression Scott wasn't keen on taking me anywhere, and that he wasn't expecting me to be able or willing to accompany him out to the Rimutaka State Forest Park on such short notice. While he talked I walked to the eastern side of the house and peered out towards the Palliser coast. Grey rain pounded down from a grey sky on to a grey harbour, blocking any evidence of the Rimutaka Range from where Scott was speaking. I guessed he was staring out at the rain and wearing a malicious grin.

'Beaut,' I said. 'I'll be there in forty-five minutes.'

He grunted, and warned me the hike into the hut was steep, and would be difficult in this rain, '. . . what with slippages and run-offs and all', but should only take a couple of hours each way if I didn't 'dawdle'. I suspected that Scott's version of a dawdle was what I'd call a brisk jog, but I knew if I wanted to see where the body had been found I had to agree to the ranger's terms. He spoke in short huffs, away from the mouthpiece, which made him hard to understand, until I asked if I could bring my dog along.

'I've got kiwi and other ground-dwellers up there, and I don't want some yappy, fluffy piece of city-dogshit tearing around undoing all my work.'

He must have heard me grinding my teeth, because he added that it was dangerous to take a dog in because there were a lot of dead possums and bait where we were headed. As a topper, he said that poisoning was a terrible way for a dog to die. Rather than argue, I wrote a note telling Damian that Wolf hadn't been walked today, and I was likely to be gone until early evening. I refused to acknowledge the doleful look Wolf threw at me as I left. You spend one night in bed with your dog and he acts like you're going steady.

By the time I drove into the Rimutaka State Forest Park the rain was even heavier, but despite the rain and the grisly reason for my visit, my heart lifted at the sight of all that green. I muttered a short prayer as I forded the creek; my car had once been caught in a flash flood, and I wasn't keen to repeat the experience. But it turned out to be a doddle, the water barely reaching halfway up the tyres. There was a moment of surge when I felt the car lean like a compliant dancer, but then the wheels made traction, I gunned the engine and shot out the other side.

I spotted the ranger as soon as I pulled into the car park where we'd arranged to meet. He was a real Sir Ed of a man, mountainous and clearly impervious to the inclement weather. His oilskin stopped abruptly just below his crotch. Bronze, hairy legs went all the way down to sockless hiking boots. He stood very straight, looking like a staked tomato being watered, as he waited for me to approach. The absence of socks I could deal with. Eccentricity isn't a problem. But I did send up a heartfelt prayer that the ranger was wearing shorts under that all-too-truncated raincoat.

After the briefest of introductions I slung my daypack over one shoulder, and we set off at a brisk pace into what's known amongst amateur trampers and family walkers as the Orongorongas – a state-owned forest abutting a hilly Department of Conservation-managed area of native bush shot through with small rivers. The first section of the track is used mainly by dog walkers and groups of picnickers. After that it's a good couple of hours' hike in to the first hut, and from there on, hidden away in the bush, are more basic shelter huts for trampers and hunters.

By international standards there's not much to trophy-kill, but the area's been used by generations of hunters looking for the odd pig or deer. It's regarded as a win-win situation for both the hunter, and DOC who view these animals as pests. I guess it's not such a win-win for the deer or pigs, but the scarred and staunch pig dogs I've passed on the tracks always seem intent on having a good time.

Scott wasn't a talker which was fine with me. Going at the pace he set, I wouldn't have had a hope in hell of keeping up my end of a conversation anyway. I was content to try and not fall too far behind or slide down slips that suddenly appeared, or lose my footing and disappear without trace into a hidden water hole. Peaches' Kookaburra had left my head feeling like a cricket ball after a three-day test match and I was doing my best not to jar it. We walked abreast for the first twenty minutes of the main track, and despite the rain I warmed up pretty quickly.

Where the trail was about to descend towards the river, Scott parted an enormous fern to reveal a track leading up the hill. I'd never been into that area of the forest and hadn't known the track existed. I presumed that we were heading to a DOC or tramper's hut, or that the ranger had a hut of his own. He hefted himself up the first step, grunting at me to follow, and so I did. We climbed steadily for about ten minutes, before the track once again flattened out. Apart from keeping a watch for ankle-twisters, there wasn't much to do except put one foot in front of the other. With Scott in front, we tramped on in silence for another hour or so.

There's something companionable about tramping together through wet bush, even if you're not too keen on the company, and I soon sensed Scott had walked himself into a better mood. When he stopped letting branches flick back in my face, I knew his feelings towards me had improved, and when he actually held his hand out for me as we clambered up a slick, muddy bank, I knew our relationship had entered a new phase. By the time we reached the hut, things were downright amicable even though we still hadn't spoken a word to each other.

We dropped our packs on the tiny veranda, Scott pocketed a bottle of water, and we continued for twenty minutes through dense bracken and manuka until the ground grew boggy and demanded careful footwork. The rain was relentless, and I'd completely lost my sense of direction when Scott finally pointed out the spot where he'd found my John Doe.

I paused to catch my breath and surreptitiously put a cooling hand on my bruised neck as Scott hunkered down and uncapped the water bottle. After a moment's hesitation he held the bottle out to me – an act of good manners in the bush. I dropped down beside him, leaned against a manuka and drank deeply. Before handing the bottle back I wiped the mouthpiece. Hey, I could do bush etiquette too.

Scott pointed at the big rata tree facing us, and told me how he'd come through there from a hut five kilometres to the north-east. He was laying traps as he went, and when he spotted the rata from up on the ridge he decided it would be a good place. It was a beautiful tree, at least a hundred years old, and he was keen to help its chances of survival. The tree would also act as a marker when he came back through to see what he'd caught.

He stood and pointed up the ridge to show me the direction he'd come from, then stood with hands on hips, breathing easily, watching me and waiting for any questions. We listened to the sounds of the bush: the raucous call of the tui, the *peep peep* of piwakawaka, the drone of wasps, and below us, the trickle of a stream, all dampened down by the hiss and shush of the rain.

Straightening, I felt a cramp in my thigh muscles, but I wasn't going to give Scott the pleasure of seeing me wince. I don't know a lot about trees but I remember being told that the roots of a tree spread out to roughly the circumference of its canopy. I titled my head to see the treetop etched against the marble sky, an action that reminded me painfully of the effect cricket bats have on the back of skulls. Fine rain drifted through the canopy onto my face, along with the occasional big splosh down my neck from the rata's branches. I estimated the roots would stretch nine metres from the base of the trunk to the furthest reach of its branches, and I turned a full circle, to get a sense of the space this tree had colonised. I could hear the trickle of the stream directly below, but even though the much bigger river wasn't far away, I couldn't hear it. The bush muffles sound, which explains why people get lost so easily. You can be ten steps from a river, but if the bush is dense enough, you won't hear it. You could scream your head off and not be heard by someone fifty paces away. It was an unnerving thought.

Scott was using his hand as a rain visor as he stared up the ridge again. Then he turned and pointed at my feet. 'It was right where you're standing. He was lying facing the tree, curled round it a bit, like a baby, but with his arm lying across his . . . where his head would've been.'

I took a step back, partly because it felt wrong to be standing on the exact spot the body was found, but also to put some distance between me and the ranger. He was a big guy, and now, lulled by the rhythm of the walk, I realised how very solid and male he was. As if sensing my shift in mood he approached the tree and struck a classic male pose, with one hand against its trunk and the other on his hip, as he continued his story.

The details fitted what he'd written in his report, but with enough embellishments to reassure me that he wasn't spinning a story by rote. He finished by saying he'd looked around for the head but couldn't see any sign of it and suspected it was long gone. To dampen any sense of unease, I squatted at the base of the tree and carefully moved aside the pine needles and rotted humus. I didn't know what I was looking for, but as they say, you never know until you find it.

I glanced up to see Scott give the trunk a gentle pat as if it was a highly strung horse in need of reassurance. Maybe this guy did the odd bit of tree-hugging when he was alone. I kind of hoped he did. I mean, who has ever been molested by a tree-hugger? Apart from trees, that is.

I looked around at the topography. From this side of the tree, something was obvious that hadn't been in the photos.

'His body was washed down from up there on the ridge somewhere, wasn't it?' I indicated the mist-shrouded hill face. 'The rata stopped the body from going all the way down to the river.'

Scott took off his cap and used his forearm to wipe the rain from his forehead, taking his time to answer. 'Yeah, that's my guess. You get massive rains in here. I reckon there was a big dump, his body got sluiced down, and the trunk snagged it. If it hadn't, he'd have gone all the way and chances are we'd never have found anything.'

I peered up the ridge, trying to calculate how difficult a climb it was going to be. The dense, misty rain clung in clouds to the canopy overhead.

'You didn't mention that in your report,' I pointed out.

'I was asked to write a *report*. I wasn't asked my *opinion*,' he responded with a shrug.

The guy had a point, and since I needed him to find my way out of this place I decided not to argue about it.

'If you *were* asked your opinion, how far up the ridge do you think the body was? Before the big rain, I mean.'

Scott pushed himself off from the tree and started to clamber up the incline. Within seconds he'd disappeared and all sound of him was gone. I hesitated, wondering if he'd gone off for a pee, or if he was mad at me and needed a few minutes on his own. Not having much in the way of choice, I headed after him. I'd only gone about fifteen paces when I banged right into him as he waited patiently, holding up a thorny branch for me to climb under. I muttered a thanks but he didn't respond. This truly was a man of very few words.

We'd climbed about a hundred metres up what felt like a vertical rock face, and I was about to admit defeat, when Scott spoke his first words since we left the big rata.

'We're here,' he said, and though I had no idea where 'here' was, I swear I'd never heard a sweeter phrase. Scott handed me his bottle again, and for the next minute or two I swallowed and thought what a wonderful, life-affirming substance water is. I'd been licking rain from my lips but it hadn't quenched anything. By the time I'd recovered, Scott had moved to the end of the little clearing, and was squatting in the entrance of a cave-like bite in the stone bank.

'I reckon he holed up in here.' He indicated the dark recess. 'It goes a fair way back.'

I hesitated. I really didn't know this odd, surly, sockless man, and here I was miles from possible help, no dog, no weapon apart from a very blunt pocket knife on my key ring which, now that I thought about it, was in the pack I'd left at the hut. And I hadn't told anyone where I was going, besides Wolf, who wasn't a big talker. How did I even know this *was* the ranger? I'd followed this mountain man into the bush without making any attempt to confirm who he was. I looked again at his lanky legs and sockless tramping boots. Everything about him screamed DOC worker, and no matter how I tried to excite myself into a vision of a mad killer, it didn't ring true. He was the ranger all right.

In a crouch, I duckwalked into the entrance of the cave ahead of Scott, while he crawled on all fours behind me. He indicated for me to go ahead down the naturally formed tunnel. I'd gone seven or eight metres when the roof pitched down suddenly, and I baulked. The cold was bone-chilling and the smell of decaying humus had a disturbing effect on my soft palate. The reassuring, outside sounds of birds and wind in the trees had already been smothered out of existence, and I could no longer hear the cosy patter of rain on leaves. This place was already seriously grave-like, and I wasn't crazy about crawling into a space the size of a coffin. I've always been a bit claustrophobic, and this was becoming nightmarish.

'Duck under the ledge, and when you come out the other side she opens up.'

Scott's voice was intimately close, and the plain humanness of it helped suppress my rising panic. His hand on my back urged me to kneel, then he shuffled back to give me room on the muddy ground. On all fours, I curled shoulders, then head, and scraped forward until my front half was under the ledge. I could feel the cave open out in front of me, but it was so black I thought for a moment I'd gone blind. I hesitated again, resistant to entering a blackness so total it was a force in itself. The dark space that opened out ahead didn't feel like an absence of light, but like a living, breathing void – a nothingness that had little to do with absence.

Except for the awareness that my arse was directly in front of Scott's face, I doubt I'd have been able to move forward but, as every girl knows, pride can override all fears. I dropped my butt, marine-elbowed my body through the gap, and once inside, with hand on already damaged head to cushion any contact with the ceiling, straightened myself gingerly until I was at full height. I heard Scott shuffle into the cave behind me, then sensed him move some paces further in. I reached out to touch him, but there was only air.

'It takes about ten minutes for your eyes to fully adapt, so just keep one hand on the wall until you start making out shapes. It'll start at the edges first.'

Despite the intense cold, sweat broke out on my scalp, and every one of my hair follicles stood up. I held my hand in front of my face and moved it closer and closer until it touched my nose. Nothing. I could see absolutely nothing. I placed my hands on my cheeks, partly for warmth, mostly for comfort. I really did not like this place. Just when I was about to can out, I caught a very faint gleam from the corner of my eye and recognised it as light filtering from the hole we'd just climbed through. Looked at directly, it was nothing but blackness, but with my head angled I could catch the faintest of glimmers.

I jumped as Scott touched my shoulder.

'Sorry,' he said. At least I hadn't screamed, but it had been close. 'Last time I was here, I had a torch.'

I thought of reasons he might have been in this cave. There were some I didn't like.

'I was collecting giant cave wetas for the sanctuary in Karori.'

Outsized creepy crawlies had been second on my horror list.

'Look here on the wall, just above the entrance,' he murmured.

I murmured back for the comfort of hearing my own voice. 'What is it?'

Scott's cold hand came to rest on mine. Taking my fingers between his, he ran the tips gently over the stone. At first all I could feel was stone so cold it was as if my fingertips had been dipped in ice. Then I began to make out a rough indentation the shape of the letter L. Despite my fear, I felt a buzz of excitement.

'It's a name?'

'Well, yes and no.'

He was so close I could feel the warmth of his breath on my neck. His hand still held my fingers. He drew my index finger over the cave wall. I said the letter aloud as we traced each indentation.

'L . . . A . . . R . . . A.' He lifted my finger off the wall but kept my hand in his.

'Lara?' I said. 'But that can't be my John Doe!'

Scott didn't bother to respond. He placed my finger on the wall again, finding the 'L', then he lifted it to the left.

'I think your John Doe holed up here all right, but he must have gone outside to die. Or maybe he went out for water or something, and got caught in a storm. Who knows?'

My eyes had finally adapted enough to see the odd gleam of light on the whites of his eyes.

'But I'm betting this is a note from him.'

We traced along the cold, smooth surface until we met the rough edge of another indentation. This time I didn't say the letters aloud. I let Scott guide my finger over the whole word, and when we'd traced the final letter he let my hand go.

Apart from the odd grunt and *whoa!* from me as we slid down from the ledge and made our way back to the hut, we were pretty much silent. I think we were both pondering the number of situations that could have led to our John Doe's death. And wondering what he'd been referring to when he wrote that message to Lara. Then again, for all I know, Scott was thinking about which freeze-dried meal he would have for dinner. I was running through scenarios, but every one brought me back to the same two questions. Who was Lara? And why had my John Doe etched the single word 'sorry' to her before he died?

Back at the hut, I was hoping for a nice cup of gumboot before we headed down, but the ranger was keen to check a few traps before nightfall, and first he had to walk me back to where the ridge track joined the main path. I knew I'd be okay from there. Eager to be rid of me, Scott immediately strode on, but I called him back, saying I wanted to use the long drop before we set off. It was as much as anything an excuse for five minutes' breather before we continued on our iron-man return trek.

The long drop was a classic of its kind – a wooden throne arrangement with a hole in the middle. I'm never too keen on baring my butt over a deep hole in the ground. I've heard too many horror stories about snakes and wetas. Flies droned, and I didn't know how long I could mouth-breathe, so I peed as fast as I could and reached for the toilet roll.

The roll was sitting inside a boot. A very old boot. I held it up to the light and examined it closely. I knew this boot. It was the partner to the one I'd left for Damian to take home for me. The one I'd traced back to its manufacturer in Germany. This was my John Doe's left boot.

CHAPTER 15

By the time I reached home it was late afternoon. Damian had left the evidence box on the desk in my office with a note saying he'd be back later to take Wolf for an evening stroll. Wolf was having a pre-prandial doze and appeared to be quite sanguine about that arrangement. Old dogs – they're pretty chilled about everything, really.

I spent a few minutes comparing the new boot with the other. There was no doubt they were a pair. It was damp from years in the long drop so I set it to dry in front of the blow heater under my desk, took the phone into the bathroom, and listened to my messages while I ran a bath and plopped in some big, fizzing, smelly balls of bath salts.

There was a message from Smithy saying he'd called in a few favours and had managed to collate some early forensic results about our John Doe that might be useful. Then he talked for so long about carbon and pollen dating, and esoteric stuff about the effects of rain and soil on human tissue, that I'd already stripped off one-handed and was slowly lowering myself into the near-boiling bath water by the time he got to the information I needed.

The results confirmed Smithy's initial belief that the skeleton belonged to a male in his mid twenties, and that the body had been in the elements for thirty-five to forty years.

By the time I'd submerged my entire body, a slow process given the extreme temperature, I'd thought this through to its logical conclusion: there was only one match in the police database for a guy in his twenties reported missing between 1968 and 1974. That was Alphonse Grigg's missing brother Steven, and I'd already discounted him as our John Doe.

One other man was reported missing within that time frame. I hunted around in the backblocks of my memory for his name – Robert something. Or was it Malcolm? Malcolm Robertson. That was it. But he was described as thick-set, and more importantly had a height of five foot seven. Assuming that height was correct, he couldn't be our John Doe, whom Smithy had estimated at a willowy six foot two. Even without his head the JD would have been almost as tall as Robertson.

The hot water stung the scrapes on my shoulder but was bliss for the bruising on the back of my neck. Whoever John Doe was, for some reason he'd never been registered with the police as missing. I swirled the water around to create steam twisters as I went over the most likely reasons for this. Maybe he was involved with a criminal underworld, and had been taken into the bush and killed, and those who knew about it also knew better than to tell. Possible, but usually some word or rumour of a murder leaks out eventually, and so far I hadn't found any evidence of, or reference to, that.

It could have been a suicide, of course, but it was unusual for a guy in his twenties to have no one close enough to eventually report him missing. I'd worked on cases where older people had cut all ties with relatives, and had no regular friends to notice or care if they were around any more, but that would be strange for someone in their twenties. Surely he had a parent, sibling, workmate or girlfriend who cared enough to notice he'd disappeared. The only clue I had to his identity was a pair of boots and possibly a message to 'Lara', telling her he was sorry.

Scott had agreed to send an email out to all members of the NZ Trampers' Association asking for the person who'd left the boot in the long drop to get in touch with me directly. I was hoping that person would be able to fill me in on exactly where they'd found it. I figured that was probably where the boot had been taken off, and I was interested to know how far away it was from where the body was found. When the boot was dry, I'd have a closer look at it.

But first I had to thaw out. By the time I'd tramped back to the car park I'd been drenched and my car's ineffectual heater didn't even begin to stop me shivering. I glanced at the Wainuiomata Police Station as I drove past, thinking I might see Robbie, but was relieved when I didn't. It wasn't just that I looked like shit, though that was definitely a factor. I was getting the yips at the idea of starting something with him. With anybody. I understood the whole 'moving on' thing in theory, but in reality I didn't know if I could move on from Sean. I didn't know how.

I stirred the water around my limbs. Baths are good places to think, so that's what I did. I thought about Niki and how it turned out that I didn't really know her. I thought about Sean and how much I missed him. I thought about him becoming a dad and was surprised at the effect that had on my stomach.

It hurt. I thought about that, too. I swirled the water around some more, then I thought again about Robbie and how badly I'd behaved on our first date. I'd have to apologise for that. I was remembering that great grin of his, and smiling back at the image, when my phone rang. Without thinking, I picked it up off the bathroom floor. As if I'd conjured him like a genie out of the mist, Robbie said, 'Gidday.'

I lay very still, hoping like hell he wouldn't realise where I was. There are very few people in the world I can talk to on the phone when I'm in the bath or on the toilet. Robbie, at this delicate stage of our relationship, wasn't one of them. The bath, that is. The toilet – probably never.

Robbie asked me how the reccy into the Rimutakas had gone, and keeping very still I told him about the second boot, and about Smithy's message, and how it was looking as if our John Doe had never been reported missing. While Robbie responded with some reasons why this might be, I watched Wolf push the door open with his nose and lumber in to check on me. I eased myself with extreme caution into a sitting position so as not to make any bath-type noises.

'If I can pinpoint exactly where the boot was found it might throw up something,' I said, reaching in slow-mo for a towel. Misinterpreting the gesture, Wolf moved towards my hand.

'No sign of the skull then?' Robbie asked.

'No, but Scott did show me a cave where he thinks our guy died. There was a message scratched into the wall.'

'What kind of message?'

'Two words: Sorry Lara.'

Realising I was in a huge water bowl, Wolf lowered his head for a deep slurp. I cupped my hand around the mouthpiece.

'If we can find Lara, then we can find out why he was sorry and who *he* was,' I said loudly. Wolf was going for it now, and the more I tried to push him away the more he took it for encouragement. I gave up on my plan to apologise for my rudeness the other night, and finished the phone call as quickly as I could, promising to let Robbie know if any emails about the boot turned up and cutting short his offer of help. I thought as I dressed that I'd probably made matters worse between Robbie and me, which really did piss me off. But right now, defrosted, dressed and determined, I had one more thing to do before I tried to set things right with him.

It took me a couple of hours to grab the images I wanted off the blackmail discs Snow's sisters had given me. The first few were the hardest, but then I got the procedure down to a fine art. I'd drop the disc in, shut my eyes until the whirring of the disc drive quietened, count to twenty, then open my eyes, keeping my focus on the door on the right of the screen.

In each scenario, as soon as the trick entered the frame, he glanced towards the camera. I figured the camera was hidden behind a mirror, and it was the image of themselves – the movement as they entered the room – that caught their attention and spooked them. Whatever it was, it was useful for what I had to do. I'd hit pause and then save the screen image, and while the hard drive did as it was instructed, I'd rummage for the next disc, ready to drop it into the drive as soon as the saved icon appeared.

That way I managed to avoid looking at my sister tied to the bed, spreadeagled on a mattress or dressed in whatever fetish outfit the particular john had agreed to – or not agreed to, for all I knew. I managed not to look at Niki at all. Mostly the guys were in normal clothes, sometimes with coats or jackets still on, so presumably they undressed or dressed up once they were inside the room. All of that was probably recorded in full-colour action but I didn't need or want to see any of it.

When I'd done maybe a dozen discs, I saved all the grabbed images in a folder and printed off the gallery of photos on one page, rolled it up image-side in, pinged a rubber band around it, and dropped it into my shoulder bag. Then I deleted the digital file. The plastic bag of discs I put in an archival box labelled 'Tax Year 2001–2002', and stacked it on my shelf between other boxes similarly labelled. Most of these had photos of body parts from previous police jobs, so the discs were in like company.

The heater had done its work on the left boot and the room now smelt of wet leather and a cloying compost smell that I hoped was just humus and not something more connected to one of the big Ds: disease, defecation or death. I placed the left boot in the box with its mate and locked it in my office. The boots would have to wait.

In the grey, flat light of early evening Pussy Galore looked depressed and scruffy. The flashing lights were working hard to glamour things up, but the passersby seemed more interested in getting home to TV dinners and an early night in flannel pyjamas. The Bookends were yawning and stretching their neck muscles as they went about preparing the place for business. They greeted me with identical hitches of an eyebrow, and the broader of the two politely held the door open for me. They didn't ask for money, so either they were giving me free entry out of deference to Niki, or every night in this place was ladies' night. The phrase 'ladies a plate' jingled in my head as I once again entered the world of prepaid sex.

There were only a few girls perched on the bar stools at this early hour, and already they looked bored and listless. Maybe they'd worked all day and were waiting for the night shift to relieve them. The spinning lights did their best to sparkle, but the daylight made the girls' feathers and harem silks appear lacklustre and shabby. In this half-daylight the whole place looked grungy, and not in a good way. It reeked of alcohol, sweat, old socks, cigarette smoke, talcum powder, and something that reminded me of disappointment.

I ordered a tomato juice from a tall, dead-eyed girl behind the bar. I thought our being the only two females with clothes on might make for a bonding experience, but she didn't seem in any mood to talk so I took my drink over to where the girls leaned against the wall each with one buttock hitched on their stools. A blank-faced girl was plucking at a length of shocking-pink faux fur wrapped like a feather boa around her neck. I asked her if Chloe was in yet. She glanced at me briefly, then towards the back of the room, before returning to her plucking.

Chloe didn't looked thrilled to see me again, and even less happy when I said I wanted to ask a few more questions about Niki, but she slid onto the nearest vinyl sofa, looped one leg over the other, aligned one breast with the other, and studied her claws – all of which I took to indicate that I should fire away. The claws were tusk-white, curved, and about half the length of her thin, pale fingers – they had me wondering how she performed certain intimate acts. I forced myself to focus on why I had come.

'I've found out quite a bit about Niki since the last time we talked,' I said, and waited. Finally her thin shoulders went up and down in a shrug, but she kept her mouth shut and her eyes on her talons.

'Look, Chloe, I know she was working as a prostitute,' I said, trying not to sound prim or accusatory. 'I know about the blackmail scam Snow had going.'

She flashed her heavily made-up eyes at me, and I saw her lip twitch before she went back to studying her fingers. At least it was a reaction, but I wasn't quite sure what it meant. I took a stab in the dark.

'Did Snow try to get you involved?'

Chloe adjusted her g-string, placing the talon of her index finger under the shoestring strap across her hip bone and sliding it along to the loop of the bow. I watched the goosebumps form along her bikini line, the raised flesh whiter than the sunbed bronze of the rest of her skin.

'No way.' She sighed theatrically to make the point that I

was boring her. She uncrossed her legs and for the first time looked directly at me, her voice the sullen whine of the teenager she was. 'Look, I gotta start work soon, so, like, what do you actually want?'

I took out the rolled-up sheet of photos and slid off the rubber band.

'I want you to look at these and tell me if you know any of these men,' I handed the sheet to Chloe. I kept my eyes on her as she studied the gallery, partly to watch for any reaction, and partly so as not to look at the images.

Chloe spent a lot longer looking at Niki than I'd been able to. She seemed to show no interest in, or recognition of, any of the guys, but I couldn't have sworn to it. She handed the sheet back to me. With the other hand, she tapped her illuminated nipple ring into life. It flickered like a Christmas tree light with a bad connection.

'Never seen any of them before.' She gave me a flat look. 'Can I go now?'

We eyeballed each other for a bit, and just when my anger was about to bubble over, I felt it slip away.

'Look, Chloe, I'm sorry, okay? I can't expect you to tell me who you know.' I waited ten seconds, hoping she might anyway. 'Well, can you tell me what other girls Snow was using for the scam?'

She swapped legs and swung her ankle, the bright red toenails peeking though the transparent plastic upper of her stiletto.

'Why should I tell you anything? So you can rescue us all, like you didn't save your innocent little sister?' She had all the world-weary sass of a seventeen-year-old who's seen too many bad movies. This girl made me feel a hundred years old. Niki did that sometimes – tried to sound ironic and knowing. She'd never fooled me, and neither did this kid.

'No,' I said, with as much honesty as I could muster. 'I just want to find out who paid Snow to murder her.'

I saw Chloe flinch and for the first time she looked unsure.

'Well, I don't know who did that,' she said defensively. She blinked those Barbie false eyelashes at me again. 'But, there's something you don't know. Something you've got totally wrong.'

A premonition fingered my spine. Chloe glanced over her shoulder then leaned towards me, lowering her voice to a whisper.

'It was the other way round. Niki didn't work for Snow: Snow worked for Niki.' She sounded spiteful, but I couldn't tell if that was directed at me, at Snow, my dead sister, or just anybody in her line of fire.

I kept my voice steady. 'How I heard it, Snow ran the scam. He arranged for Niki to have weird-shit sex with guys and then he blackmailed them. He paid Niki in drugs.'

'Wro-ong,' Chloe said, and added a game-show loser's buzzer sound to emphasise her point. She was animated suddenly, confident and chirpy, her little foot jiggling and her talons flashing. 'It was Niki's show all along. Her idea, her scam. *And* she made a shitload of money out of it.'

'Snow worked for Niki?' I said, trying it out loud. It didn't sound nearly as stupid as I wanted it to.

'Yup,' Chloe agreed. 'He called himself her enforcer.'

It was the clincher. I'd got it all wrong. Again.

'She never asked me to work for her,' Chloe added. I detected an edge of disappointment in her voice. She glanced over her shoulder again. The sassiness gone, she seemed genuinely nervous of being overheard. 'But I know she got Vex to. Work for her, I mean. Vex didn't want to, but she must have owed Niki or something, I think, and Niki must've got her to work off the debt.'

Chloe cupped both breasts and did a lift and drop action. I wasn't sure what this was supposed to accomplish, but it seemed to appease her sharp-eyed assessment of them. She flashed me a brilliant smile.

'Promise you won't tell Vex I told you, or she'll totally kill me.'

CHAPTER 16

I opened the front door to Wolf excitedly tap-dancing on the floorboards. Although I didn't show it in quite the same way, I was just as happy to see him. It had been one hell of a long day. I felt like I'd never completely thawed out from the cold of the Rimutaka forest, but maybe it was something about the atmosphere in Pussy Galore that had given me the shivers. Whatever. It felt good to be home.

Wolf's food bowl was empty, and even though his expression swore black and blue that he hadn't eaten a single thing all day, a note from Damian confirmed that he'd been walked, fed and smooched. I suspect the smooching is part of a communion with nature Damian enjoys with herb and hound. I wouldn't be surprised if he spent a good part of the walk sitting somewhere on Mt Victoria stroking Wolf's ears and blowing dope smoke rings for him. Not that Wolf would object, though as an ex-police dog he might suffer some guilt. Maybe he just doesn't inhale.

It was late. There was no real food in the fridge, so I defaulted to my favourite fast-food supper – a bowl of cornflakes washed down with a glass of Pinot. Actually, a glass of anything alcoholic would have been fine, but I happened to have a bottle of the good stuff, and the fine cuisine à la cornflakes deserved top shelf.

I retrieved the John Doe boots from my office and placed them on a sheet of newspaper on the table. They looked forlorn, curled up at the toes and gaping. I poured a second glass of wine, then pulled the anglepoise lamp around for more light. The manufacturer's name had already enabled me to age the boot to somewhere between thirty-five and forty years old. The right boot, found on the body, was in worse shape than the one from the long drop. The decomposing flesh had rotted away the cushioning leather at the Achilles area. In fact, almost the entire inside of the right boot was rotted and stained a disturbing maroon colour.

I took another spoonful of cornflakes and sip of Pinot before examining the left boot. Its much better condition made me suspect it had been in the dunny for a number of years. Hopefully, the finder of the boot would get in touch and I'd be able to confirm that.

As I reached again for the wine glass, my wrist hissed on the halogen bulb – shit! I wrenched my hand back, knocking the lamp head. Lit from this new angle, faint lettering appeared on the inside where the heel nestles. Sucking my wrist, I shifted the lamp further. It *was* writing. Faint. Very faint. But I was sure now. My heart was racing, and I couldn't resist a little victory dance. Wolf wasn't impressed but I didn't care.

For the next hour I angled the hell out of that poise without much success. I could decipher some of the letters, but not enough to make out a name that made sense. Then, despite or because of the third glass of Pinot, I had a brainwave.

Anyone who's doctored a digital photo of themselves to remove evidence of cellulite or scars (or an annoying ever-present frown) knows what a brilliant programme Photoshop is. It worked a treat. I took a few photos, downloaded and enlarged them. The handwritten lettering in the boot was the capital letter B followed by the name Crossen. There was no Crossen in the White Pages, but there was a Sarah Crossen-Smith.

I blew on my burnt wrist and counted ten rings before a woman answered. She sounded grumpy, like she'd just woken up.

'Hi, my name's Diane Rowe and I work for the police,' I said, and heard her sharp intake of breath. 'It's okay. Nothing's happened. This is just a routine enquiry.'

'If it's nothing then why the hell are you ringing me at two in the morning?' she shot back. Shit, I'd completely lost track of the time.

'Your surname is Crossen-Smith?' I asked. She didn't answer but I could hear her breathing. 'I'm trying to contact relatives of a Mr B. Crossen.' Still just the breathing, but I forged on. 'I'm sorry to ring so late, but if you could assist us, we'd be very grateful.' I tried to make it sound like the entire police force would be whooping it up.

'What about him?' She was awake now.

'I'd rather not talk about it over the phone. Can I come and talk to you tomorrow?'

'Sure. Why not.' She didn't sound too enthusiastic.

I crossed my fingers and asked my question again. 'So you *are* related to a Mr B. Crossen?'

There was a long pause before she finally answered.

'Yeah, you could say that.'

Trying to keep the excitement out of my voice, I made arrangements to meet the next day. Well, actually, it wouldn't be the *next* day – it would be later *today*, as she coolly pointed out. I could take her sarcasm because I was already fantasising about how I'd deliver the solved missing persons' file onto McFay's desk, i.e. with a flourish. Definitely a flourish.

I'd need to find out why Sarah hadn't notified the cops when our Mr B. Crossen went missing, but that was small print. Tonight, I told myself, I could sleep the deep, satisfied sleep of someone about to close a case. Partly that was an instruction to myself. I was warding off nightmares. That suffocating black cave had given me the willies, and I was hoping it wouldn't invade my dreams with claustrophobia.

But it wasn't like that at all. I dreamt I was standing on a wide open plain with a big, empty, blue sky above me. And then I realised it wasn't the countryside at all. I was in the middle of a huge, manicured golf course that went on and on forever. It was an exaggerated version of the place where Niki's body had been found, but in my dream it was endless and very, very empty. I was searching, hunting for some sign of her, but there was nothing. She was so gone, so utterly not there, it was as if she'd never existed.

It was the worst nightmare I'd ever had.

CHAPTER 17

Wide-eyed, tit-balanced Chloe had reluctantly agreed to give Vex a note from me, but she'd clapped her hands over her ears when I began to explain what the message said. Giving Vex the note was 'the totally last thing' Chloe was going to do for me, '*ev-er*'. I hoped the hundred dollars I gave her as payment meant one less blow job Chloe had to give. In reality, I'd probably just scored her a line.

I didn't really expect Vex to turn up, but just in case, I was at The Sandwich Bar early. I'd ordered my second coffee by the time the lowing lunch crowd stampeded in. I'd written in the note to Vex that I'd be wearing an orange jacket and my habitual scowl. I thought I'd leave it to her to approach me.

I didn't want to scare her by letting on that I knew what she looked like. I wasn't sure I'd recognise any of the other girls I'd seen at the club, but the fact that Vex had clothes on when she was dancing made it easier somehow.

Vex's dance routine had disturbed me in ways I'd still not got a handle on. She'd seemed so young and innocent with that swinging ponytail and the mesmerised dance routine aimed at her own reflection, yet she must have been aware of the effect she had on the men watching her. So? What was my problem with that? I still couldn't figure out what was niggling at me. Most likely it was because she reminded me of Niki. If it was true that Vex worked for Niki, then she was the closest link to my sister I'd found so far, and I needed to play this meeting very carefully.

Suddenly Vex was at my table, clutching a bottle of Diet Coke and holding out a small, cool hand for me to squeeze.

'Diane? Hi. I'm Veronica.'

'Veronica,' I echoed as the thin, cool fingers slid from mine.

She perched on the edge of the chair and unwrapped herself from a lengthy sky-blue silk scarf. 'It's a terrible name, isn't it? Sounds like something out of a 1950s comic. I don't know what my mum was thinking. Sometimes I think I should change my name to Vex, full stop.'

I was about to speak but didn't get the chance.

'I don't mean Vex Fullstop,' she giggled and took a sip of her Coke. 'But anyway, I don't mind if you call me Vex.'

'Okay,' I said. We hadn't made eye contact yet.

'Oh gosh, listen to me,' she said, as if I had any choice. 'I'm talking non-stop because I'm nervous.'

She took a deep breath, and then for the first time since she'd arrived she looked directly at me. Grey eyes, the whites startling in their healthiness. No mascara. No make-up at all that I could see. With a sand-sprinkling of freckles across her nose, she had the complete girl-next-door look. Although, actually, none of the girls I'd lived next door to were very nice. One stole my trike when I was four, and another stole my boyfriend when I was fourteen. That might explain why I'd never understood girls next door getting such a good rep.

From close up, in midday light, no make-up, and hair pulled back sharply from her face, Vex should have looked a lot less pretty than she did under the flattering club lights. If anything, she looked younger and, well, sweeter than before. She swallowed hard, and when she did speak her voice was strained.

'You look so totally like Niki.' She dropped her eyes to the Coke but not before I saw them flood.

I felt my throat thicken in empathetic response. 'Yeah,' I said. 'We used to get that a lot when we were young.' There was silence while we both fought to hold back tears. 'I think we both secretly liked it but pretended to each other that we didn't.' I realised suddenly how much I missed having someone look like me. With no mother, no children, no sister, there wasn't a single person in the world who resembled me. A feeling of loneliness engulfed me, surprising me with its intensity. Sensing this, or maybe still thinking of Niki, Vex touched her cool fingers to my wrist, and then quickly withdrew them and picked up the bottle of Coke.

We were distracted for a minute by a woman asking if she could take the spare chair from our table, looking from one to the other for approval. Thankful for the break in the spell, we nodded enthusiastically and 'yesed' and 'of coursed'. When she finally left, I took a deep breath and started.

'Well, thanks for coming.' I watched Vex attack the Coke bubbles with her straw. 'I really do appreciate it.'

She prodded the bubbles some more. 'When I first saw you through the window I thought, no way can I go in there and talk to her. I mean, I thought it would just be too weird, if you know what I mean.'

I nodded and knocked back the dregs of my coffee. Cold. Bitter.

'So I walked up and down the street for a while trying to work up the courage, and then I thought . . . ' She leaned her elbows on the table and dropped her voice almost to a whisper. 'I thought that talking to you would be like the closest I'd ever get to talking to Niki again.' She leaned back in her chair and fixed those grey eyes on me. 'And I thought that would be *so* cool.' The whites of her eyes were slightly bloodshot from the tears. 'So, ta-dah!' she said, like a magician's assistant whipping back a curtain. 'Here I am.'

Indeed she was.

I started with basic questions about the blackmailing scam – straightforward stuff that I already knew the answers to. Vex was nervous and watchful at first, glancing around furtively at the lunchers, but eventually she relaxed. With that same innocence and candour I'd seen in her dance routine, she told me about her role in the scam. She had agreed to do some jobs for Niki, and although she was a bit scared at first, my little sister had apparently been 'such a good boss' and 'really fair about the money side of things', offering Vex not just a fee for 'the job itself', by which I assumed she meant the sex, but a share of 'the big money' when the guy being blackmailed paid up.

The trick for me was to keep my tone as conversational as hers as I probed for the details I wanted, while avoiding those I didn't. When the first wave of lunchers were scraping back their chairs and stretching arms into coat sleeves, I thought it was time I started on some of the hard questions.

I asked Vex what happened if the guy being blackmailed refused to pay up. She glanced defensively at a group of women at the table close by as if they had asked the question, but turned back to answer me.

'They nearly always did. Occasionally one of them would

come over all macho and say he didn't care if we went public and all, but that hardly ever happened. The truth is, they all care about people knowing that kind of stuff about them.'

She glanced again at the women behind her then tilted her head, captured her bronze ponytail, and glided the hair between thumb and finger before grabbing the top again. She repeated the movement several times. The petting routine seemed to calm her. I kept my voice quiet and conversational, like I was asking about a recipe. *'But what if I didn't put the baking powder in . . . ?'*

'But what if they *did* refuse to pay up?'

'Well, then Niki would send Snow round to the guy's house. He would kind of remind the guy what he had to lose if the neighbours found out he liked to have sex with someone dressed as, you know, whatever.' She draped the ponytail over her shoulder and stroked it like a sleeping kitten. 'But Snow was a jerk.' With a flick of her fingers she threw the kitten over her shoulder. 'Niki was really fair and gave him, like, a cut of the pay-up as well as his fee and everything, but I think he was getting paid both ways.'

'You mean Snow kept some of the blackmail money for himself? Money that Niki didn't know about?'

Vex captured the kitten by the neck and ran it rhythmically through her palm again.

'Niki knew about it. I told her. Snow thought he was so shit-hot, ripping Niki off, but he wasn't.'

'You'll have to explain to me how the scam actually worked,' I said, manoeuvring my hands under my butt. It was the only way I could stop myself slapping the hair out of hers. 'Financially, I mean. Who got what money?'

Thankfully, Vex used her fingers to count off the details, laying them out for me like I was really slow.

'Well, *for example*,' she said, pushing back her index finger, 'Niki would do her thing with the guy who would pay her, like, say, two hundred, two-fifty, whatever.' The middle finger was pressed back. 'Then she'd pay Snow, like a thousand to make the guy pay up. They call that "shaking down",' she added helpfully.

'Got it. Thanks. And how much were the guys "shaken down" for?' I tried not to sound prim.

'Well, let's see . . . um, this one guy, *allegedly* . . . ' She waited for my acknowledgement that this was confidential. I thought better of patting the side of my nose in the time-honoured gesture. She was the wrong generation, and would probably think I was asking her to score me a line. A nod seemed to do the trick, and she picked up where she'd left off.

'Well, this guy, he had heaps of money, so he was supposed to pay up, like, ten thousand dollars. So that was all cool. Snow showed him the photos from the vid he'd taken, said he was going to send them to the guy's wife and his daughter and his boss *etcetera* and the guy paid up the ten thousand *in cash*.'

I searched for an ambiguous response. 'Wow,' I managed.

'Totally. But then scumbag Snow told Niki he'd only been able to shake this guy down for like, maybe, eight thousand, and Snow kept the rest for himself.'

This was new. 'Snow told you this?'

'Yeah! Can you believe that? Like he thought I'd keep his stupid little rip-off secret to myself. The jerk.'

I watched her anger spark, then dissipate just as quickly. She went back to sipping her Coke and twirling her hair round her finger. She had the faraway, blank look a cat gets when it pads a cushion. There was a lot about Vex that made me think of cats – the sudden spats of anger, the expressive but unreadable, wide, grey eyes. I was sure she was capable of a convincing purr as she curled around on her hapless clients' laps, too. My thoughts about cats had taken my attention off Vex who'd finished her Coke and was looping the long scarf around her neck, preparing to leave.

'So let me get this straight.' I leaned forward into her eyeline. 'You told Niki that Snow was ripping her off.'

She stared at me with those big, healthy, grey eyes. 'Sure. I mean Niki was a really cool boss, so, like, when it was me who did the job, the sex and all, Niki paid me the two hundred or whatever, *plus* twenty per cent of whatever the guy eventually paid up.' She blinked rapidly. 'Which is another reason Snow was totally dumb to tell me he wasn't giving Niki all the money, because that meant he was ripping me off too!'

From her startled expression and the way she yanked her scarf in a final loop around her neck, I suspect that this had only just occurred to her.

'And,' she added, pausing as if to get it sorted in her mind, 'she paid Snow his thousand dollars, just for him doing, like *nothing*.' She mulled this over. 'All Snow had to do was show the guy the photos, and say he was going to send them to other people. Like how difficult is *that*?'

I might have argued the point with her, but hell, I wasn't Snow's agent. Someone else could fill her in on the finer and not-so-fine challenges of his job.

'What did Niki say when you told her what Snow was up to?'

'I remember exactly what Niki said: "I know he's ripping me off. I've factored that in".' Vex smiled proudly as if the words were her own. '"Factored it in",' she repeated, shaking her head. 'She was a really cool businesswoman, you know. Smart as. She could have done anything.' Vex reached for her coat and laid it across her lap before giving me her feline stare. 'She was going to go into business with you, wasn't she? Once she'd got herself totally clean.'

My mouth went dry. 'She told you that?'

'Actually, that's why she started the whole blackmail business. She said she wanted to have some money of her own, so that when she went into business with you she could hold her head up.'

As if to emphasise the phrase, Vex freed the end of her ponytail from the scarf and tilted her chin up. It was an oddly childlike gesture of defiance, one that I'd seen Niki perform. Maybe Vex had learnt it from her.

'Niki was real cool,' she repeated, as if I'd suggested otherwise.

Niki was cool, all right. I watched Vex do up each of the oversized buttons on her duffle coat, and pet her ponytail some more, while I waited for my heart to stop thumping. Then I asked the question I'd been holding on to for some time.

'Vex?' I waited until she looked at me. 'Do you know who killed Snow?'

She clasped both hands in her lap, staring at them, taking her time before answering.

'I think it was probably one of the guys that Niki had . . . you know . . . '

'Blackmailed,' I added helpfully.

'Yeah, blackmailed,' she agreed, with a tiny shrug of her shoulders. 'I think Snow probably pushed some guy for money, and the guy's thought, I'll just kill him, and then I don't have to pay anything. Something like that.'

'Snow went on shaking them down even after Niki was dead?'

She gave that tiny shrug again. I waited to see if there was more, but she seemed spent. The nervous energy gone, she looked even younger. How old was this girl – seventeen? Eighteen?

'Do you have any idea who that guy might be?'

'I hope it wasn't one of the guys I . . . did. That would be too creepy.' She shivered, and sought comfort in her ponytail. 'But I only did it, like, a few times. More as a favour to Niki, really, and I . . . ' She glanced at me nervously. 'I owed her money for some *stuff* she'd got me ages ago, and she agreed I could pay her back in, you know . . . '

‘Sex.’

‘Yeah, sex. I mean, it was *her* business. Her “baby”, she called it. She did, like, a hundred times more guys than me. She worked really hard.’

I sincerely hoped Vex was the exaggerating type. I didn’t want to imagine that number of men having sex with my little sister. It was no easier when I flipped it and had my little sister on top having sex with that number of men. I couldn’t figure out how the Niki I knew and the Niki that Vex knew were the same person. Maybe neither of us really knew her. I was having trouble getting it straight in my head. My little sister, whose favourite book was *The Little Prince*, had been running a blackmail sex scam. That Niki, *my* Niki, had made this naive cat-girl pay off a drug debt to her by having her perform all kinds of weird and dangerous sex with men – so that Niki could then blackmail them.

It made me feel sick to hear that this kid sitting opposite me twiddling her ponytail had been grateful to Niki for this. I could feel a cold anger towards Niki growing in me. It was bad enough that she had been doing this crap herself, but the idea that she lured other young girls into the business with her made it so much worse.

Yet by far the hardest thing to accept was that Niki had done all this so she could ‘hold her head up’ when going into business with me. I’d suggested the whole business thing one night when Niki had called round, and I told her about a missing persons’ case I’d been working on. I’d managed to track down a woman who’d been ‘missing’ for twenty years, and had put her and her family back in touch. It had been one of the rare win-win results – everyone was happy, including me, particularly when I realised that the client had added a healthy bonus into my overdrawn bank account – and after a wine or two I think I was probably bragging a bit.

Okay, I’m sure I was bragging. I’d suddenly caught myself at it. I'd turned the conversation back round to Niki, and asked what she was doing. It was then that she'd said how much she'd love to be doing work like mine, and I'd said well, why not join me? I remembered how thrilled she'd been at the idea, and we played with it for the next few hours as we polished off two more bottles of wine. It was fun, we had a good night, but the truth is that I'd not really given it much thought after that.

I was so caught up in my thoughts I hadn't noticed Vex watching me.

'You think Snow killed Niki, don't you?' she said. 'That's what I heard.'

I dragged my attention back to the present. The very least I owed this girl was honesty.

'Yeah, I did think that. Now I'm not so sure.' I watched for a sign from Vex. Any sign that would tell me I was on the right or the wrong track. 'Now I think that maybe whoever killed Snow also killed Niki.'

She'd gone completely still. When she finally spoke it was so quiet I had to ask her to repeat what she'd said.

'Snow did kill her,' she said. 'He told me he did it.' A sweat broke out on my forehead. 'He said Niki told him she wasn't going to do the blackmailing any more. That she was going into a legit business with her sister.' Vex threw me an apologetic smile. 'He tried to get me to do it instead of her, but no way was I going to work for Snow! I mean, it was okay to do it for Niki, but not for that creepstake!'

'And you think Niki wanting to end the blackmail racket was enough to make Snow decide to kill her?'

She thought about it for a bit, and then nodded. 'Uh-huh.'

I took out the sheet of photos, checked that there was no one directly behind Vex, and handed it to her.

'Well, I think Snow probably did kill Niki,' I said quietly. 'But I think someone put him up to it.'

She showed no emotion as she examined each image. I'd

gone this far, so I decided I might as well try out the rest of my theory on her.

'I think someone offered Snow more money to kill Niki than he got working for her.'

Vex looked up at me. I could see her thinking this through. Saw it make some kind of sense to her. She turned her attention back to the photos.

'And you think that person might be one of these guys?'

'Maybe.'

I watched as she studied the last photo on the sheet. She'd already spent more time looking at this one than any of the others. I felt a little shiver of excitement. Vex ran a finger gently over the image of my sister. In this particular photo Niki was dressed in a school pinafore, her hair in high pigtails. She was licking a big swirl of fake lollipop. At least she had some clothes on. Vex stabbed her finger at the face glancing wild-eyed in the direction of the camera.

'Chris Ross.' She stabbed at it again. 'Niki hated him. Said he *deserved* to be blackmailed for the stuff he was into. She said she didn't have to make anything up with him – he was already way ahead of anything she could think up. Chris Ross was the genuine thing.' She rolled up the sheet of photos and snapped the elastic band on one end. 'One totally sick jerk.'

'Do you know if he paid up?' I asked.

'Last I heard, Niki sent Snow around twice to threaten him, but Ross was digging his heels in, refusing to pay up. And it wasn't like he didn't have the money. He was loaded.'

'When was this? When was Ross being blackmailed?'

Vex's hand suddenly flew to her mouth, and her eyes widened as she put two and two together.

'It was just before Niki was killed. Oh my god! It was him, wasn't it? Chris Ross paid Snow to kill Niki!'

Yep, I thought. It sure sounded like it. What I still couldn't figure out was why Ross had waited another whole year before killing Snow. Maybe he'd heard that Snow had blabbed to an undercover cop about the killing. Word of Gemma's attempt to snare Snow would have leaked out through the legal fraternity, and who knows what connections Chris Ross had. He might even be a lawyer or a judge for all I knew. Maybe Ross realised that as long as Snow was alive, he would remain vulnerable.

I pulled up the collar on my too-thin orange jacket and watched Vex hustle her way through the business crowd towards the taxi rank. Seeing her approach, the cab driver leaned across and threw open the front passenger door. I watched his face tilt up hopefully as she leaned in and gave him directions, then slump in disappointment as she opened the back door and climbed in. The driver pulled the front door shut and adjusted his rear-vision mirror so he could glance at Vex as he drove. I didn't blame him. There was definitely something about Vex that made you want to look at her.

As the taxi passed me Vex raised her hand in a small wave. The driver's head bobbed as his eyes flicked rapidly from the road to the rear-vision mirror. I watched until the car had passed the Police HQ on the corner and exited on to the motorway. I'd parked in the HQ building, so figured I could spend a couple of hours on my John Doe report before going to see Sarah Crossen-Smith and wrapping up the case.

As I stepped out from between two parked cars, another taxi whooshed past. I arched back quickly, feeling like a batsman bowled by a mean bouncer. The taxi changed lanes suddenly, causing a blast of horns, and sped through an orange light on to the motorway. I stepped back to safety, and stared in the direction the taxis had gone.

I'd glimpsed a man leaning forward from the back seat, pointing out the front window as he urged the driver on. It was Stoke, the guy I'd watched at the club. The guy who was at Snow's funeral. The guy I'd been told was in love with Niki.

Maybe it was a coincidence that he'd caught the taxi directly behind the one Vex had climbed into. I gave myself a talking to – Molesworth is a one-way street so it was no surprise both cars drove off in the same direction. And taxis cutting lanes? Well, that was hardly an indication of anything suspicious. I told myself Stoke probably wasn't following Vex at all. I told myself I had an overly fertile imagination. That's what my father accused me of each time I told him that his live-in girlfriend – numbers three, four and five – didn't like Niki or me.

And just like back then, when the little voice inside told me I was right about Dad's girlfriends, that same little voice told me I was right about this. Stoke had been watching while I talked to Vex, and was now following her. I didn't have Vex's phone number, and had no idea where she lived. What would I say to her anyway? I had no proof Stoke was following her. All I knew was that he was in a taxi going in the same direction as hers. Hardly enough to warrant an armed offender turn out. There wasn't anything I could do except feel uneasy. I'd learnt a long time ago not to discount feelings of unease, so I nursed them in my gut as I made my way across the road towards Police HQ.

Joey was on front desk security again, placating a man with a face the shape and colour of a beefsteak tomato, who was arguing his right to a just and fair hearing. Why he thought that was on offer at Police HQ was a bit of an enigma. Joey had his hands up, palms out in a calming gesture, but it didn't seem to be working on tomato-face. Catching sight of me, Joey called my name, but I scooted past, waving my new security pass in a 'I can let myself in' gesture. It was only when I reached the lifts that I realised why Joey had called out to me. It had nothing to do with my security clearance or beefsteak man. It had been a warning.

Sean had one hand on the elevator up button, the other resting protectively in the curve of a woman's back. He saw me in the same instant I saw him. The woman had her back to me, and only turned when she saw Sean's sudden change of expression. I'd never met Sean's new partner Sylvie but I was in no doubt this was her. At about five foot five to my five-eight, with styled, short blonde hair framing a bright little made-up pixie face, she exuded a kind of optimistic confidence, as if the world had always been good to her and she expected nothing less from it.

First impressions told me she was everything I wasn't. If I was crass enough to think 'types' – and crass is something I've never baulked at – then Sylvie and I were definitely at opposite ends of the type spectrum. Where I was tall, she was short. Where I scowled at the world, assuming the worst, she smiled in expectation of good things to come. Where she appeared composed, tidy and guileless, I was jittery, scruffy and suspicious. Sean made the awkward introductions, and Sylvie stepped forward to shake hands. It was yet another indicator of how trusting she was. It obviously didn't occur to her that I just might deck her. Sean stepped up protectively beside her – I'm fairly sure the possibility had occurred to him.

'It's nice to meet you at last,' she said, as if she meant it.

'Nice to meet you, too,' I lied.

'Nice' was probably the very last thing in the world this meeting was. Sean and I shuffled and avoided looking directly at each other. Sylvie beamed her open gaze from one to the other of us as if amused by our awkwardness, but still neither of us could manage any social chit-chat to help smooth things over. The silence became deafening. In the brief moment before the bell signalled the arrival of the lift, I thought I saw a flicker of doubt on Sylvie's face.

The lift doors slowly parted, and Sean ushered Sylvie into the lift ahead of him. He was in such a hurry to escape that he almost man-handled her right into the slowly opening doors. Even though Sylvie had her back to us, neither Sean nor I took the opportunity to make eye contact. As the lift doors began to close, Sean threw his arm out to hold it for me.

'Sorry. Are you going up, Di?' he managed.

The lift door stuttered, then clanged wide open again. I couldn't have moved my legs even if someone had yelled 'Fire!'

'No, I'm good, thanks. I'm going down,' I replied truthfully.

Instead of closing, the lift doors perversely now stayed wide open, framing Sean and Sylvie directly in front of me. I had to do something, frozen as I was with a scowling, sickly grin on my face. I thought I might as well take advantage of the moment.

'Hey, Sean,' I said, managing to keep my voice steady. He looked up from studying his shoes. 'Have you looked at a guy called Chris Ross for Snow's murder?'

Sean's lips tightened in a way that I knew so very well.

'Jesus, Diane,' he said, and punched the lift button with his index finger. 'Would you leave it alone!' The bell pinged in anticipation of the doors closing.

'You know Niki was blackmailing Chris Ross, don't you? Well, I think Ross might have paid Snow to kill her.' The doors began to glide together. 'Then a year later, when things heated up again, Ross killed Snow.'

I'm not sure if Sean heard the entire last bit before the doors closed. He sure as hell wasn't looking at me, and I reckoned, knowing Sean, if Sylvie hadn't been in the lift, he would've put both hands over his ears and sung 'lalalala' loudly, just to be sure I got the message. Knowing Sean.

Instead he'd rolled his eyes heavenwards, and pretended to ignore me. I guess that must be the new grown-up Sean. The one I didn't know. The one who was having a baby with that bright little blonde pixie in the lift. Sylvie and I had looked each other in the eye before the lift door slid shut between us. I wouldn't go so far as to say we bonded, but there was a definite acknowledgement this had been no fun for either of us.

I watched the numbers light up as their lift rose through the floors. It stopped at the seventh. Legals. Maybe Sean was seeing someone there about the Snow homicide. Or maybe Sylvie had some work there, and Sean had accompanied her for some reason. Maybe they'd just had lunch together.

Maybe they'd gone home to bed for lunch, like *we* used to.

The lift began its descent to the ground floor. As I watched the numbers light up and then extinguish, I was thinking about Sylvie and me. Why was I comparing us, when after all, I was pretty sure the only thing we had in common was Sean. That was the weird thing – if Sylvie and I were totally different types, as far as Sean was concerned, which of us was the aberration? Sylvie or me?

The doors whooshed open. The lift was empty. What did I expect? Sean coming back down to check if I was okay?

I thought about going up to the third floor to start on the John Doe report. I even stepped into the lift, and had my finger poised over the third floor button – but I stepped straight back out again. I'd caught a whiff of perfume. Chanel N° 5. I've never liked it. Too cloying. Too feminine. Just too bloody . . . nice.

CHAPTER 18

The national library, two blocks down the road from Police HQ, has a publicly accessible internet system with fast broadband. There's an okay café, a brilliant newspaper room, comfortable seats, and clean toilets. They even supply, free of charge, scrap paper and HB pencils sharpened to exquisite points. The atmosphere in the huge high-ceilinged research rooms is cool and hushed. No one looks at you. No one speaks. No one points and laughs at your mottled, cried-out face. No one asks about your red-rimmed eyes or the snail tracks down your cheeks. Don't believe those articles in magazines that tell you to splash cold water on your face to hide the crying blotches – instead of a smoothed, serene, professional look, you end up with the same swollen red face accessorised with big, wet, mock-turtle teardrop blobs on the front of your T-shirt.

To add to the god-awful picture I presented to the mirror, the bruise from Peaches' cover drive had spread a jaundiced mottle from my neck to my throat. Sean used to run his fingers along the line of my clavicle. He said it was one of the sexiest things about me. I wondered if ten minutes ago he'd even noticed that my sexy clavicle had a dirty purple bruise across it. The best thing to do with mirrors is not look at them. It's the only way to shut them up. Amazingly, Chris Ross's address was listed in the online White Pages: Ambrosia Court, a dodgy apartment block rumoured to hire rooms on a twelve or twenty-four hourly basis. Mostly the place was used by fences shifting hot electronics, and drug dealers needing a discreet place to do business. Its popularity owed a lot to the apartment block's elaborate security measures. Around the perimeter of the building was a high, mock stucco wall effectively creating a gated community, with security cameras perched at each of the four corners. Cameras also peered down from either side of a set of electronically controlled gates which were the only entry point for vehicles.

The place was a rathole because of both its design and the behaviour of its inhabitants. Every apartment had tortuous narrow stairwells for entry and egress. This made the apartments difficult for cops to raid without alerting the occupants in plenty of time for them to make an easy, if admittedly undignified, getaway. Which was why, of course, it was so popular with those people in the melodramatically named 'criminal underworld'. Ironically, what the occupants of Ambrosia didn't know was that their every action could be viewed in detail from a run-down penthouse perched at an oblique angle at the top of the office building opposite.

When I was last there, a bit over a year ago, the 'penthouse' – little more than a converted shipping container, really – was being used as a photographic studio by a bunch of polytech students. I'd gone there to ask if a young student named Marie Wilson could come down to the station to identify a ring that had turned up in the gut of a small shark caught off Mana Island the previous day. Marie's brother had disappeared six months earlier and was presumed drowned. The last sighting of him had been at Plimmerton beach. Marie's brother suffered from bouts of depression and he had a history of suicide attempts.

Marie asked for a few minutes to prepare herself before looking at the ring and in that time, while I made small talk and she drew deep breaths, I watched two separate deals go down in one of the Ambrosia apartments opposite. When I couldn't hide my distraction any longer, I asked Marie if she was aware of what was going down in the apartments across the road. It was no news to her. She explained to me the odd positioning of the penthouse – how it was tucked under a low-hanging eave at an oblique angle. Also, her window – the one with the bird's eye view – had an unusual type of reflective coating to minimise the amount of light getting into the studio. So, unless you knew exactly what you were looking for, from Ambrosia's point of view, Marie's place didn't exist.

The two other students who shared the studio with Marie referred to the one-way viewing window as their 'entertainment unit'. Marie told me that on Friday nights the three of them would crack open a cask of wine, line up the beanbags, and spend an entertaining couple of hours watching whatever was going down in Ambrosia. They'd witnessed various drug deals – even the occasional orgy.

Trying my best not to sound like a school prefect, I'd asked why they hadn't told the cops about it. According to Marie they held a vote every month to decide if they should, but so far, the majority had always been in favour of maintaining the status quo. As she explained it, they had to weigh up the entertainment value of one big blockbuster of a police raid versus a nightly crime drama series, and the consensus, up until the time of my visit anyway, had always been to stay with the nightly event. And, she pointed out, there was always the risk the cops would make the raid when the students were at class, which would mean they'd miss out on the blockbuster *and* have no evening entertainment either.

They'd obviously discussed the pros and cons in some detail. Up to their necks in student loans, they couldn't afford anything like concerts or big screen televisions, and were keen to hang on to their free entertainment for as long as it lasted. I remembered Marie referring to it quite accurately as 'good value'. I'm sure on some level her parents, who I knew were both accountants, would have been proud of her budgeting skills. She asked me not to tell anyone at work about it. Since 'work' was Police HQ, and since I was, at that stage, married to a cop, and since I was at the studio on police business, I'd struggled with the ethics of my silence for a full ten seconds. At nine seconds I went with 'a girl has to get her entertainment where she can' and agreed to keep quiet about it. What was the harm?

That had been over a year ago and I hadn't thought about Ambrosia or the studio's little 'window of opportunity' since then. There was always the chance that the students had voted for the blockbuster option over the nightly crime drama, and the place had been raided and dealings shut down.

It seemed unlikely that Marie and her two student buddies would still even be there. A lot had happened to me in that year since we'd met. My sister had been murdered, my husband had left me and gotten a pixie pregnant, I'd lost and subsequently semi-regained my job, and my sister's killer had been murdered.

Maybe I lead a particularly full and busy life. Maybe the three girls were still there and had changed little more in their lives than their brand of shampoo. There was only one way to find out. I still had an hour and a half to fill before meeting Sarah Crossen-Smith and putting my John Doe case to bed. I decided I might as well go and check out if Marie was in residence at the studio, and if her entertainment unit was still functioning. I just might be able to catch a glimpse of Chris Ross in his apartment, or better still, Marie might be able to fill me in on any extracurricular activities Ross had going on.

Access to Marie's studio was via the next-door building which housed seven floors of car parking. Car park buildings are creepy places. I hate them and do my best to avoid using them. It's nothing to do with a fear of being attacked. I never believe those movies. In my experience car park buildings are too well monitored, too busy and too bloody cold for anything much at all to happen in them, even crimes. Criminals feel the cold too, you know. The occasional skateboarder sneaking in to have a smoke and ride down seven floors of ramps is about the most heinous crime committed in them.

Car park buildings creep me out because, as a Wellingtonian, I've always got my antennae out for the next big shake – there's nowhere worse to be in an earthquake. Seven floors of concrete slabs neatly arranged one on top of the other – well, as soon as I drive up the first ramp I break into a sweat imagining how the floors would squash down one on top of the other at the first shudder. Give me an attacker any day.

Despite the stink of piss and petrol and the smattering of condoms, I walked up the entire seven flights of stairs. Being in a car park building when an earthquake hit would be the pits, but being inside a coffin-sized elevator would be even worse.

At the top of the final flight of steps were two doors. One led to the rooftop, the other, lurid with Day-Glo graffiti, sported a keypad but no handle. Unless you knew it led to the studio, you'd think it was the door to a storeroom or utilities cupboard.

The doorbell screamed like a fire alarm. In fact, I'm pretty sure it *was* a fire alarm rigged to the little plastic button by the keypad. A tall, bearded guy in his early twenties wearing leprechaun-green skinny jeans and a T-shirt emblazoned with 'art sucks' opened the door. I figured the studio was still occupied by students. When I asked if Marie was there he blinked myopically at me through his '50s-style tortoiseshell frames, then turned and walked back into the gloom. I took that as an invitation and followed his hunched shoulders and flapping canvas camo boots through the plywood anteroom. I tried and failed to forget that this was the bridge between two seven-storeyed buildings.

I explained to the guy's back that I'd met Marie a year ago and wanted to ask her about the Ambrosia Court apartments across the road. Without turning, he nodded enthusiastically as he led me into her room. Well, what used to be her room. Now, there was nothing in it except a row of three factory-clean Lazyboys facing the windows. Leprechaun-pants continued nodding as he lowered his frame into one of them, and levered himself back. It was only then that I saw the earphones and realised he hadn't heard a word I'd said. The reason for the fire-alarm doorbell became clear. I leaned over and yanked the plug out of his ear. He let out a yelp as if I'd unplugged his life support, which maybe I had.

'What's your problem?' he said, blinking rapidly at me.

'My problem,' I said, pushing his chair further into its reclining position, 'is that I'd like to talk to Marie.'

Leaning over him made me feel like a dentist. The sensation wasn't as bad as being a dentist's patient, but it still wasn't pleasant. What I'd thought at first sight were whisker bristles, I could now see, from this uncomfortably close surveillance, was a small but well-stocked forest of blackheads.

'I don't know where she is,' he said, returning his chair to a sitting position. 'I paid her twenty bucks for an hour's viewing, and she gave me the door code.' His attention shifted from the window to me long enough for him to appraise and dismiss me as unworthy of attention. 'She didn't tell me there was going to be anyone else here.'

'You paid Marie twenty bucks to view the apartments?' Clearly Marie's entrepreneurial skills had developed since I last saw her.

'Yeah. I always do Thursdays,' he grinned and added in explanation, 'Benefit day. It's when most of the deals go down.'

'Right. Of course,' I said, failing to sound cool and in-the-know.

'P's the drug *du jour*,' he explained, 'but sales for weed are still strong for the ACC guys with *actual* pain.' He checked the time on his phone. 'That's not for another hour yet, though.' His attention went back to the window. 'Meantime, I'm watching the cartoons.' He darted a suspicious look at me. 'Is Marie giving you a freebie?'

It was easier just to play it out. 'Nah,' I said, lowering myself into the adjacent chair, 'I'm paying. I just didn't know I'd have company.'

'Same,' he said, and stuck his earphones back in.

I watched him settle his chair back into a viewing position, all attention now on his 'cartoons' across the road. The Lazyboy was extremely comfortable and, apart from the farting sound it made every time I moved, made for perfect drama-viewing. I had direct sight into three separate Ambrosia apartments. They were identical in layout: an open-plan living area next to a bedroom, and ceiling-to-floor glass doors across both rooms opening out on to a small deck area. The three decks were separated by concrete partitions so that no apartment could see what was going on in any of the others – the irony being that from my personal 'gold lounge experience', I had prime viewing of the interiors and the decks of all three.

There was nothing going on at the southernmost apartment – the one furthest from my sight line. My fellow voyeur's attention was focused on the middle apartment. At first shocked glimpse, I thought he was watching a middle-aged man attacking a young woman. She was clutching the back of a sofa to stop herself being dragged backwards by the man pressed up to her. He had her long hair wound around his fist, and had wrenched her head so far back I thought her neck would snap. His other hand was on her throat. I was about to leap out of my Lazyboy – never an easy task – but the little pleasure grin on Leprechaun's face made me look again. The man released his hold on the woman's hair and fell forward. He stayed like that, resting his forehead between her shoulder blades as he slid out of her. The woman wriggled her skirt back down over her hips and straightened her back.

Leprechaun, not surprisingly, hadn't registered my mistake, but I still felt myself blush. I had a sudden flash memory of the first time I ever saw the sexual act. I hadn't recognised it for what it was then, either, but I was probably only about seven at the time, so had total lack of experience as an excuse. I'd stumbled upon a couple of dogs going for it on the back veranda of the house. I thought the male was attacking the bitch – she seemed so helpless and resigned to the male's grinning, slobbering violence. Well, that's how it seemed to me at the time. Needless to say, my attitude changed once puberty hit.

The woman stretched the kink out of her neck, and secured her hair back into a clasp. The man turned away and lit a cigarette. The dogs I'd watched as a kid had shown more affection afterwards. At least they'd licked each other's face.

Despite the cold, the glass doors of the third apartment, the northernmost one directly in front of me, gaped wide open. The living area was such a total mess I decided it had either been ransacked or been the setting for one hell of a fight. The sofa cushions had been ripped open, and the stuffing spread around the room. A glass-topped coffee table had been tipped on its side, and bottles and glasses were scattered everywhere. Stains formed continents on the beige carpet. A hole, suspiciously the size and shape of a head, had been punched in the wall. In the bedroom, the mattress had been half dragged off the bed, and a fully clothed man lay face up, spreadeagled across it. Another was slumped in a corner of the room. Both were asleep, dead, or unconscious. Since I'd nearly made an embarrassing mistake about what was going down in the middle apartment, I decided to play it cool with this one and not jump to any hasty assumptions.

Chris Ross's apartment had been listed in the White Pages as number four. I fart-noised my way out of the chair and, pressing my forehead against the window, tried to figure out which one of the three was his. There were three identical apartments under the ones I was surveying. Presuming they were numbers one to three, that would make number four either the apartment directly in front of me – the one with the two sleeping beauties – or the empty one at the southern end of the block.

Leprechaun whistled for my attention, and pointed to a pair of binoculars on a hook beneath the windowsill. They were padlocked to the wall, but the chain was long enough to allow viewing from the full width of the windows. Marie was obviously keen to provide a totally positive shopping experience. That girl will go far, I thought.

I scrabbled around in my shoulder bag for the sheet of photos, and then focused the binocularss on the spreadeagled guy. He was breathing. And he was Māori. I checked the photo of Ross just to be sure my memory was correct. Ross was dark-haired and olive skinned but definitely not Māori. I picked out the other guy slumped in the corner of the room. His knees were drawn up with his arms encircling them, head resting on his forearms. He looked about the same body type as Ross, but I couldn't see his face well enough to tell if it was him or not. I decided I could either come back some other time when Marie was there, and quiz her, or wait until this guy regained consciousness. I had about forty minutes before I was due at Sarah's, and I'd just decided to pack it in and come back some other time when I saw movement on the deck of the southernmost apartment – the one I'd thought was empty.

Chris Ross had been standing on his deck the whole time I'd been checking the Ambrosia out, but he'd been masked by the concrete partition between his place and the middle apartment. As I watched, he stepped out of the shadow of the dividing wall, used the toe of his boot to stub out a cigarette, and leaned on the deck railing. His body was still and attentive, like a cat watching for a rat in a compost heap. He seemed to be looking down at an alleyway that ran between Ambrosia and the two-storeyed building next to it. I couldn't see what he was looking at, and couldn't quite figure the layout of the buildings.

I left a twenty dollar note under a beer-themed fridge magnet in the kitchen, and let myself out. I'd asked Leprechaun if he knew what Marie was up to these days. He said she was spending all her time taking photos of sharks. When he asked me, 'How weird is that?' I really had no answer for him. On my previous visit Marie had identified the ring found in the shark's gut as the one her missing brother had always worn.

The car park building had the same piss and petrol smell, the same condoms, but it was easier going down seven flights of stairs than up them. I'd never noticed the narrow alleyway between the Ambrosia block and the art deco building next to it before. It was barely wide enough for two people to walk side by side, and definitely too narrow for vehicles.

The view from the pavement across the road wasn't nearly as good as from Marie's studio, but even from here I could make out Chris Ross's rapt attention as he leaned on the balcony's safety rail and peered down at the alleyway. There was something about his stillness that bothered me. Dodging traffic, I jaywalked across the busy street to the alley's entrance. From here, I was directly below Ross, but if I kept tight to the building the overhang of his deck meant I was invisible to him.

It was a dank, pissy, dead-end lane with mossy drainage run-off from buildings on either side. A freezing southerly sent plastic bags and newspaper pages swirling up to slap at the building truncating the lane. Tragic pigeons cooed on ledges, the white and green streaks announcing they'd taken up undisturbed residence some years ago. There was an exit door out of the building at the closed end of the lane. A single bare bulb in an old-fashioned copper housing hung above it.

I couldn't figure out which building this door exited from. A sudden flurry of wings too close to my head made me look up. Chris Ross was leaning over the railing of his deck and staring directly down at me. Heart pounding, I adopted an air of nonchalance. Wandering up the alley, I tried my best to look like a city council inspector or land agent. I even jotted a few things in my notepad. Actually I was writing 'Shit! Shit! Shit!' – which would have been equally appropriate if I had, in fact, held either of those jobs.

It was only after I'd given the driver Sarah's address and settled myself into the back of the taxi that I figured out which building backed on to the alleyway – which building Chris Ross had been so interested in. It was Pussy Galore. I remembered Niki telling me about the euphemistically named 'discreet entrance', promoted as a private entry and exit for 'gentlemen' who preferred their visits to the club to be confidential.

In reality, it was used to heave out punters who'd thrown up all over themselves. The pissy lane was also where any strippers' jealous boyfriends were dragged and nunchuked into behaving reasonably. Niki told me she'd taken to using the discreet entrance to go to and from the club. She said it was less hassle than trying to leave by the front entrance. I realised now, with shame, that I hadn't asked her what she'd meant by 'less hassle'. I reckoned a good evening's entertainment could be had watching the lane – perhaps not as good as Marie's 'window of opportunity', but arguably better than being inside the club itself. Thinking back over my own Lazyboy experience, I realised that there was probably a bit of the voyeur in all of us, and Chris Ross's viewing platform, looking down as it did on the back entrance to a strip club, was the ultimate location to watch from.

What was Chris Ross up to? Was it just a coincidence that a guy Niki had blackmailed had a prime location for viewing the 'discreet' entrance to the club she worked at? The entrance she used to leave by in the early hours of the morning? I thought about what he must have felt when he realised Niki had set him up. If my theory was right and Ross had paid Snow to kill her, he must have had to pay a hefty sum. Niki dead would have meant a big drop in Snow's earnings, and Ross must have offered a generous cash incentive for him to do it.

I hoped my little real estate act in the alleyway was convincing. It was dumb to have made myself visible to Ross, and I knew it. I'm not normally that reckless. Well, not by accident, anyway.

CHAPTER 19

Sarah Crossen-Smith was a compact, fox terrier of a woman. I judged her to be in her early sixties, which fitted with the age John Doe would have been had he lived. Her steel-grey hair was cut in a mannish style, longer at the top but bristling short at the neck. There was a lot about Sarah that bristled. Her suspicious little eyes darted over me as she dropped into a chair and planted her elbows on the table. She had the look of someone gleefully anticipating a bloody good argument. I suspected this was how Sarah approached most things that entered her world unexpectedly.

I started by asking her what Christian name the initial 'B' stood for.

'B for bastard,' she shot back, flicking the few strands of hair that had dared to move out of place. I decided it was time to ask what her relationship was to Mr 'B for bastard' Crossen.

'My relationship?' she sneered, using the heel of her hand to wipe the corner of her mouth. 'He was my fiancé.'

I half expected her to spit. I was getting the distinct impression that learning 'B for bastard's' body had been found wasn't going to be all that traumatic for Sarah. She may have read something in my expression.

'I can't be expected to go on grieving forever,' she added defensively. 'Brian died over forty years ago.'

I made a noncommittal noise. She glared at me for a while, then shrugged in response to some internal dialogue she'd been having.

'You want a drink?' she asked, hauling out a wine cask from the fridge. I noticed there wasn't much else in there.

'Sure,' I said.

There was enough of the Irish blood sloshing around in my veins to make a drink obligatory when talking about the dead. Or about nuns. Or mothers. Actually, there was quite a long list of conversational topics that made a drink obligatory. Sarah clasped two large-sized Marmite glasses in one hand, and banged them on the table between us.

'I'm guessing you found him, then. Brian.'

She acknowledged my nod by filling the glasses to the top and knocking hers back in one gulp. I'd never seen anyone do that with wine. She just opened her throat and threw the full glass of wine down it.

'Where'd you find him?' she asked, refilling her glass to the brim.

'In the Rimutaka State Forest Park. A ranger found him.'

I took a sip to give her time to take it in. She grimaced, but I couldn't tell if it was the wine or a reaction to finding out where her fiancé's body had been found.

'Did you bring him with you?' she asked, peering at my shoulder bag as if I might suddenly whip him out of it. I couldn't figure out if she was winding me up. Sarah didn't seem the joking type.

'Do you mind if I ask you a few questions?' I said, biting the cap off my pen.

Sarah shrugged. 'Fire away,' she said, then opened her throat again for more wine. The way she drank reminded me of a sword swallower.

'Brian Crossen was your fiancé,' I said, printing it in clear large letters so she could read it. I've always found that people open up more easily when they can see what you're writing.

'We were engaged in November 1968,' she said, hefting the wine carton to her ear and shaking it. There was a faint slosh of wine against plastic – the sound seemed to depress rather than please her.

'When did you last see him, Sarah? Do you remember?' I asked.

She ripped the cardboard box open, reached in, and pulled out the plastic bag before answering. Wine in plastic bags always makes me think of catheters.

'I remember exactly when I last saw him. Four thirty p.m. on the 10th of September 1969.'

It was obviously not the first time she'd reeled this off. I wrote, 'Last seen 10 September 1969'. When I looked up, she was staring at what I'd written. In the fifteen minutes I'd been there, Sarah had efficiently thrown five glasses of wine into her stomach and was now, suddenly, drunk. The alcohol had softened her edges. All her little bristles were flattened, and her face had fallen into soft folds as if she was melting. I'd managed to get away with only taking a sip, but even if I'd drunk my whole glassful I doubt she would've refilled it.

'10th of September 1969,' she repeated, and then stuck the little white nozzle of the cask in her Marmite glass and used both hands to squeeze the remaining wine out of the plastic bag. She gave the nozzle a little practised shake like a man does when he's finished peeing.

'It was his stag night. We were getting married the next day.' She let the last of the wine sit on her tongue before swallowing. There was a little crusty sugar line on her bottom lip.

'Stag night,' she slurred, with the sort of contempt only a drunk can muster. 'His mates took him off to the pub, started drinking, and never stopped. That's what you do on a *stag night,* apparently.' She stared malevolently at my glass of wine until I pushed it towards her. 'Bastards,' she added. She drank half of it in one mouthful, and kept hold of the glass. 'They'd got him a stripper. Some slut.' She dragged her head up to look at me, but her eyes slid away from mine before they could make any real purchase. 'The bitch even had the . . . shit . . . to turn up at his funeral.' She took another mouthful, being careful to leave a dribble in the bottom for later.

What funeral? John Doe couldn't have had a funeral. No one knew he was dead. I was starting to get a really bad feeling about this, but before I could clarify things with Sarah, she was off again.

'Totally pissed, he fucks some slut. Then he gets in his car and writes himself off on the motorway. Kaput. Fucked. Night before we were getting married.' She was so close I could smell the sickly sweet, diabetic smell of wine on her breath. 'S'pose you're wondering where I was, while he was having his stag night.'

No, I wasn't wondering that at all. I was wondering why my John Doe had been wearing boots with Brian Crossen's name in them, but I didn't have the heart to interrupt her story. I had the feeling nothing would have stopped Sarah anyway, so I nodded. I don't think she noticed that either. Sarah was her own audience – I was nothing more than an accidental hostage.

'I was playing pin the tail on the fucking donkey with a

bunch of other stupid bloody women just as bloody stupid as me.' She belched into one cheek and released the fumes slowly before resuming. 'There he was with his mates, getting pissed, fucking some whore, and writing himself off, and there was me, four months' pregnant, playing kids' party games with a bunch of other stupid chicks. What did we call those nights? They weren't called showers then. Hen's Teeth or something . . .' She drained the last of the wine and belched violently. 'Can't remember. Pin the fucking tail on the fucking donkey. If it wasn't so fucking dumb it would be tragic.'

Sarah staggered to her feet and yanked open the fridge door. 'I was going to be Mrs Brian Crossen the next day. I'd even practised writing my new married name.' She swayed in the cool air of the open door and glared at its meagre contents. 'So anyway, after he was dead, I changed my name by deed poll, added his on to mine. He owed me something, so I thought I might as well take his name – he didn't give me anything else worth keeping.'

'Was Brian a tramper?' I asked. 'I think I might have his, ah, boots.' It sounded pretty lame even to me, and the look Sarah attempted to level at me suggested she thought the same.

'I thought you said you'd found Brian, not his boots!'

I took a breath and laid it out for her as clearly as I could. 'A body was found in the Rimutaka Forest Park wearing boots with the initial B and the name Crossen written inside. We think the body had been there for about forty years. I'd presumed he was your fiancé, Brian Crossen.'

Sarah showed no emotion at all, but she did release another belch as she let the fridge door sigh shut.

'Nah, that's not Brian,' she said, hefting a new carton of wine from under the table. She suddenly seemed quite affable. Helpful, even. She used her thumb to push back the little flap in the carton, and wrestled out the plastic tap. 'Three weeks in intensive care before he died. I was there every day for him.

I even held his hand when they turned off the life support.' She paused with the tap positioned over her glass. 'And you know what I was thinking?' She didn't wait for my reply. 'I was thinking that the last thing he did, the last thing he'd remember, was getting drunk with his mates and fucking a whore.'

She repeated this several times, shaking her head in disbelief each time she said it, but she perked up again as her glass filled.

'I wore my wedding dress to his funeral. People gave me a hard time about it, but I didn't care.' She looked genuinely happy at the memory. 'What the fuck else was I going to do with it?'

I still couldn't figure out why she thought I might have had Brian with me. Sarah was addled but not that addled. As if reading my thoughts she started up again.

'I kept him on a shelf in the garage. Well, his ashes. Same thing. I wanted my son to remember how his father died. I thought maybe seeing his Dad there every time he got in and out of his car might stop him speeding. Couple of months ago he went missing.'

'Your son?' I said.

Sarah looked away from me. 'Jayden was killed in a hit-and-run last November.'

I murmured an inadequate 'I'm sorry,' but Sarah didn't seem to know I was there any more.

'I'd forgotten all about Brian being on the shelf until I went in there a couple of months ago to do something or other,' she said. 'And I saw he was gone. Someone must have nicked him.' Her eyes finally acknowledged me. 'I thought you might have found the box of him somewhere.'

Making a getaway wasn't difficult. Sarah had settled in for the evening. I'd said my goodbyes and made it as far as the letter box when she hailed me from the doorway.

'I remember the boots, though,' she called out. 'They were quite flash. He hadn't had them long. I gave all his gear to the local Sallies. I guess your dead guy must have got them from there.'

Walking away from Sarah's, I thought about dead ends. I'd been so sure I'd found someone to claim my John Doe. Someone who'd take the sad little pile of bones off Smithy and have them buried. Someone who'd say, 'I loved him,' and maybe even lay a gentle hand on the remains. Someone who wouldn't see a pile of bones, but the armature of a life lived. Wouldn't see the creepy articulation of a skeleton, but would remember legs running, fingertips on warm flesh, the gentle rise and fall of chest, arms embracing, sunshine on warmed skin. Would maybe remember golden hairs on delicate wrist bones. Maybe. And I thought about other dead ends. About how some people live out their entire lives as if they're barrelling towards a dead end, and just don't care any more.

I decided to walk back to collect my car from HQ rather than getting a taxi. I felt exhausted after being with Sarah; not the healthy kind of exhaustion you get from physical tiredness, but the sapped, depleted feeling you might get from spending an hour watching an animal tied to a stake – tugging at the rope occasionally but resigned to being held captive. It seemed to me that one event can totally screw up your life. One terrible incident can define you, set you off on forty years of rope-tugging or maze-running. I thought about Sarah, and how her fiancé's death had become the defining event in her life, and then I started to think about Niki and the effect her death had had on me. I only thought about that for a little while, and then I heard that '*Danger, Will Robinson. Danger*' warning inside my head, and decided to stop thinking about it. For now, anyway.

It had been a long day. It began with a lesson from Chloe about the details of my little sister's business acumen in the sex industry, and was finishing with dead-end Sarah. Add in the trauma of meeting Sean's pregnant girlfriend for the first time, and lay on top of all that, less than four hours' sleep, and all I really wanted to do now was hang out with some good company. Since I hadn't spoken to Gemma after she'd hit me with a few home truths about myself in the bar that night, and since I wasn't ready to rip open that suppurating little wound just yet, it seemed to me I really had only one other option.

An hour later, I chucked the dog bone and a boil-in-bag rice dinner for one into the back of the car and started the engine, but instead of reversing out of the supermarket car, park I sat staring out the windscreen at the plastic bags and bits of rubbish being blown around. Shoppers scurried across the forecourt with shoulders hunched and collars pulled up against the slanting rain, their faces tight and closed to the weather and anything else that might be coming at them. The gusting southerly juddered the lamp post lights, and sent reflected colours scattering across the puddles. It could have looked pretty but it didn't. Suddenly, the whole scene depressed me – the supermarket, the slouching figures, the rain. I nearly didn't bother answering my phone, but when I picked it up I saw Robbie's name pulse at me from the screen.

He wanted to know if I'd checked my Outlook today. Given my despondency, it took me a minute to figure out which outlook he was talking about. The one I'd been staring at through the car window wasn't exactly rosy.

'There's a bunch of emails gone back and forth between the ranger and the tramper who found our John Doe's left boot,' he explained.

He must have mistaken my silence for disapproval because he added, a tad defensively I thought, 'They cc'd me in.'

I switched off the engine, and listened while Robbie filled me in. The tramper had emailed that he'd found the second boot about eight years ago in a place roughly a mile south-west of the hut where I'd found it being used to house a roll of toilet paper. Robbie said he'd rung and talked to the tramper, was pretty confident he could find the spot, and thought he'd head in there tomorrow morning with the hope of finding something else belonging to the John Doe – like the dead guy's head, for example.

There was a pause while I listened to Robbie's breathing, and then he said he wondered if I might like to go with him. It was definitely a weird idea for a date, but sadly, I've had worse offers. I felt a smile spread across my face, and that seemed to kick-start a chain reaction of good feeling right from my scalp's hair follicles to the soles of my feet and everywhere in between. Tragic, really.

Grinning, I asked if I could bring my dog, and Robbie sounded like he was grinning too when he said, 'Sure.'

I offered to pick Robbie up from the Wainuiomata Police Station so we could drive the rest of the way in one car, but he rather bashfully admitted that tomorrow was his day off, and suggested it might be better to meet at the car park entrance to the forest. He asked if 6 a.m. would work for me, and then it was my turn to say 'Sure' – and I was *definitely* grinning. We giggled like a couple of naughty schoolkids when he reminded me that the ranger had a bit of an attitude about dogs so we might have to keep out of his way. I let myself enjoy the sound of his breathing in my ear for a full ten seconds before I rang off.

Truly, truly tragic.

The evening's cross-species tête à tête didn't turn out to be quite as intimate as I'd planned. With exquisite delicacy and good manners, Wolf had taken the bone from my hand and loped off to his special gnawing place to spend quality time with it, and I'd just squeezed the steaming rice out of the bag onto a plate, only burning myself twice in the process, when Gemma turned up clutching a couple of bottles of Pinot. We both knew they were peace offerings, and that she'd come to apologise for what she'd said about my relationship with Niki.

Her heartfelt and genuine apology took the form of not mentioning it or referring to it in any way at all – which was just fine with me. I doled out two plates of rice since neither Gemma nor Wolf was too keen on sharing his bone for dinner. Two bottles of wine later our relationship was back on track, almost like nothing had happened. Almost. It certainly wasn't Gemma I was holding a grudge against. It was me. Gemma was right. I'd judged Niki, holding myself up as the success story to the mirror of her failure. I'd need to look at all that more closely one day. One day soon, in fact.

But first, I had to find out who killed her. Not just who put the knife in her back. I was still convinced Snow was the jerk who'd actually done it, but I was pretty sure someone had taken out a hit on my little sister, and that person was probably the guy who'd killed Snow to cover his tracks. Chris Ross was number one on my suspect list. Whoever he was, I couldn't and wouldn't stop until I'd found out. I'd lost too much already to turn back now.

Gemma finally did say something before she lowered herself into the taxi. She told me Niki loved me, and that I'd been a great sister to her. For one blissful minute I took it as the gift it was and even believed it. I must have been drunker than I thought.

CHAPTER 20

Robbie and I tramped at a much easier pace than the one the ranger had set, and once we were in the shelter of the bush the soft rain was hardly more than a fine spritz, making the walk relaxed and easy. Wolf put all that police training bullshit behind him, and drunkenly zigzagged ahead of us, sniffing and peeing self-importantly while we ambled along behind.

I told Robbie about my meeting with Sarah, filling him in on how the boots ended up at the Sallies where our John Doe must have bought them. We agreed it was unlikely the boots would have stayed in the shop for long, so we were still looking at an earliest possible date of late 1969 for when he went missing.

Robbie found the side track we were to take and that got us

talking about dead ends, and the next thing I knew I was telling him about me and Sean. Maybe it was because we were walking while we talked and didn't have to make eye contact, or maybe it was because Robbie is one of those really easy people to talk to – whatever it was, I'd tracked my marriage to Sean, told about our break-up, and even described the ghastly meeting with the new pregnant girlfriend in the lobby of Police HQ the previous day, before I realised that this was the first time I'd been able to talk about any of it without wanting to run.

Admittedly, since I was already walking, I guess I was part way there – but still, this was an achievement. And the weird thing was, in telling Robbie about it, I didn't feel sad. I stole a glance at him. He looked relaxed. Maybe a little thoughtful, but not too deeply affected by my having laid out my whole marriage break-up, and pathetic, sad life on what, in effect, was only our second date. He must have felt me looking at him because he threw me one of his easy smiles.

'Sorry,' I said. 'You ask one question and I fill you in on my entire life story.'

Robbie whistled a soft two-note call and, to my surprise, Wolf came crashing back towards him through the bracken.

'Not your whole life story. Just the first instalment,' he said, and gave Wolf a good strong slap on the haunch before signalling, with a minute head-tilt, for him to go on ahead. Robbie caught my leery expression as I watched my dog do exactly as instructed by a complete stranger. Apart from Sean, and occasionally me, Wolf had never responded to anyone else's instructions. In fact, he'd been trained not to react to anyone except us, and yet here he was at this stranger's beck and call.

Robbie ducked his head in apology.

'I was a handler,' he explained. 'When I first started out, that's all I wanted to do, work with dogs. My granddad had a farm just out of Gore, and I spent a lot of my time there as a kid, so I grew up with dogs.'

Figures, I thought. He probably loves kids too.

'I'm useless with kids,' he added, and threw that grin at me as if he'd read my thoughts. 'And women,' he added. 'But dogs and me get on okay.'

I was about to ask him why he was no longer a dog handler, when he pushed ahead through some scrubby manuka into a clearing, and I saw we'd arrived at the same hut but from a different track than when I'd gone there with Scott.

I rested against the veranda, and watched Wolf follow at Robbie's heels as he strode off to find the entrance to the south-west track that we hoped would lead us to where the John Doe's left boot had been found. He located it almost immediately, and we decided to set off again without a break. The days were lengthening but we both knew darkness fell early in the bush, and that we'd need to be back on the main track well before sunset.

For the next mile or so the bush was dense, and pockets of tangled supplejack made the going slow, tough, and at times painful. The track itself was pretty much non-existent so conversation was on hold while we tore, scratched and crawled our way forward, all the time keeping an eye out for the little orange plastic ties that indicated the original track.

Wolf was thrilled by this intrepid behaviour, and showed it by crashing ahead then circling back to herd us into his orbit, all the time grinning, slobbering, and periodically letting out little yelps of pleasure. I suspect Robbie would have behaved in the same way if I hadn't been there. In fact, I was thinking that if they could have ditched me without any fuss, they'd probably have run off together grinning and licking each other enthusiastically.

Okay, I admit it. I was jealous of my dog. Because the fact was, Robbie's body heat was having a similar effect on me. Well, maybe not the slobbering, but as for the grinning, licking and little yelps of pleasure – most definitely.

For the last five hundred or so metres we crunched our way up a stony creek bed, criss-crossing the ankle-deep, icy water to avoid the muddy eddies that might be concealing waist-deep water holes. By the time Robbie dropped his pack at the base of an ancient rimu, I was out of breath, red in the face, covered in mud, and my feet were numb with cold. I knew I looked like shit but I felt fantastic.

Like a magician, Robbie produced a thermos from his pack, and while I leaned against the rimu and sipped the steaming coffee, he clambered over a couple of rotting tree trunks. Wolf lowered his butt onto my boot, and we both watched Robbie disappear from sight. For another thirty seconds I could hear the crack of his boots snapping on branches, and then even that was gone.

Wolf lay down, neck flattened, snout stretched between his paws in the direction Robbie had taken. I refused to be quite so obvious, and instead stamped around in circles in an attempt to get some feeling back into my feet. I'd just drained the last gritty dregs of the coffee when Wolf suddenly leapt up whining, and seconds later I heard Robbie's whistle.

It took me a few minutes to make my way to where he was standing, a camera to his eye and that smile hitching his face like a cinema curtain. Wolf saw it before I did, and let out one sharp bark, then immediately sat at heel, his attention riveted on the tangle of undergrowth at Robbie's feet.

The frame of the pack was rusted and pitted, the canvas bleached to a pale mint colour. At first glance it looked like an old 1960s postie's bag. It was undoubtedly our John Doe's pack. I didn't mind telling Robbie I was impressed.

He shrugged. 'Once I'd located where the tramper said he'd found the boot,' he said, pointing back over my shoulder, 'it was just a matter of following the natural curve of the land, and figuring out the direction big dumps of rain would have dragged anything that didn't have good roots.' He shook his head, annoyed at himself. 'First time I came in, looking for the skull, I approached from a different track. Guess that's why I missed it.'

We left the pack undisturbed, and spent the next fifteen minutes scouting out the area, Robbie taking photos and making notes of the surrounds. We walked about halfway back to the big rimu, he showed me the place the tramper had found the boot, and from there we tracked back towards the pack, calling excitedly to each other as we pieced together what we thought was the most likely sequence of events. Wolf joined in with the odd explanatory bark, and by the time we hunkered back down in front of the pack we'd all agreed that our John Doe had probably slipped and fractured his ankle somewhere near the old rimu, and had managed to limp, or more likely hop, for a hundred metres or so before he'd taken his boot off, maybe to strap the ankle, or maybe just to ease the pain. Realising he couldn't walk out, he'd probably slid and crawled, dragging his pack with him until he reached the naturally formed dugout just above where Robbie had found the pack.

We'd need to get a map to confirm it, but as far as Robbie could make out, and as far as I could pretend to follow the geography he described, the cave John Doe had eventually holed up in, where he'd scratched his message to Lara, was about two miles as the crow flies from where we now stood. We were both silent as we contemplated this. It must have taken him days to crawl that distance, and he would have been in excruciating pain the whole time.

'And hungry,' Robbie added. 'He probably stayed here until he ran out of food.'

My stomach rumbled in sympathy. 'The fact that he tried to crawl out rather than wait to be found suggests he knew no one was going to come looking for him.'

'And he was right,' Robbie agreed.

I felt a surge of anger so powerful and unexpected that I

had to put my hand on a tree trunk to steady myself. How was it possible that with all the billions of people in the world, someone could die alone? How was it possible for a young man to be missing long enough to starve to death without anyone realising he was gone? Surely someone had loved this man at some time in his life? How could any human live twenty-odd years on this planet and have so little impact on it that they die alone, and then, for the next forty years, no one so much as registers they're missing?

I didn't trust myself to speak. Robbie was silent too as he stared at the backpack, perhaps also thinking what a lonely way it was to die. A couple of tuis weren't. They crooned and clacked and argued with each other in the canopy.

I had a flash of Niki on the peppermint-green of the golf course, felt the pain of the boning knife going in, Snow leaning over watching her as she died. His leering face would have been the last thing she'd seen.

Robbie's voice brought me back to the present. 'Let's have a quick look,' he said, and started dragging the pack out of the tangle of weeds that had colonised it. 'We're going to have to hoof it back if we're to get out before nightfall,' he added, looking towards the gloomy hills.

It took a bit of dragging and chopping, but finally we had the pack upright, resting on its metal legs. I tried to pull the canvas tags through the buckles but they were weathered closed and my fingers were numb with cold. Eventually, we resorted to cutting. Inside, the pack was surprisingly dry, though when we opened the main flap there was a distinct waft of rotted vegetation. Could have been worse.

I lifted out a woollen jersey, and then felt something hard at the centre of it. My mouth went dry with excitement. It was a notebook wrapped carefully in a piece of soft leather, a thin strip of handwoven tapestry looped around it. Holding the book in one hand, I managed to untie the strip and carefully open the cover. It was dry now but, despite the leather wrapping, at some time enough water had trickled in and stuck all the pages together.

I gently peeled back a page. It was like lifting off a sheet of sunburnt skin. The page – all the pages – were blank. No writing at all. Nothing.

Robbie and I shared a disappointed look. I held the book up to catch the light. The pages had a very faint blue tinge, like veins under the skin of a newborn baby's skull. It was all that remained of whatever John Doe had written. Whatever message he'd left was now nothing more than a gentle blue wash on bleached paper. He'd been dead, his body unclaimed, unmissed for forty years, and now even his last words had been erased. His voice silenced forever.

CHAPTER 21

It took us more than three hours to reach the car park, by which time it was completely dark. Robbie had brought a torch with him but the night was clear and the moonlight strong enough for us to manage the last half hour of the track without it. Normally I'd have loved this night bush walk. Wolf certainly did. He seemed to have nothing on his mind except the moonlight and the intriguing night smells around him, but I'd been nursing uneasy thoughts and fell silent.

I couldn't help wondering about John Doe's spirit or his soul or whatever it is that continues on, waiting all those years, a lifetime, for someone to claim his body. Waiting for someone to say a prayer or a mantra or pour a shot of scotch on the soil as a final gesture of farewell. Waiting for someone to give him a so-called 'decent' burial. Waiting for tears. For words. The tree planted to mark the spot, the cross, or the cairn of stones. Even elephants return to their loved ones' bones to stroke the whitened remains in remembrance. Everybody deserves some ritual of burial.

But this man had received none of it, and that made me deeply sad and uneasy somehow, as if it was now up to me to put him to rest. When Robbie paused to retie his bootlace I told him what I'd been thinking.

'I don't think a soul can rest until their body's been claimed,' I said. I felt a bit silly using the word 'soul' but I was saved by the semi-darkness, and anyway, right here and now I couldn't think of a better word for it. 'Everyone deserves that.'

Robbie swapped feet and retied his other boot, his face thoughtful in the moonlight. 'Yeah,' he agreed. 'It doesn't seem a lot to ask, does it?'

We set off again at a quickened pace, as if the thought of being dead and unclaimed had given us both the yips. I think it had. We were quiet, thinking our own thoughts for a while, and then Robbie said he'd send photos of the notebook, the leather wrapping, and the strip of tapestry to a couple of newspapers, and see if someone out there recognised them – but we both knew this was a long shot. Worst of all was not finding the skull. We'd stayed and hunted for it as long as we could, but finally had to admit defeat. The excitement of finding the backpack and the notebook, only to have my expectations dashed with the discovery of the erased words, had left me feeling gloomy.

When Robbie said he felt the same, I realised there was some comfort in feeling gloomy *with* someone. In fact, learning that we felt gloomy together immediately cheered us up, and by the time I'd helped him to load John Doe's pack into the boot of his car, and Wolf had spread himself across the back seat of mine with what might as well have been a 'do not disturb' sign plastered across his forehead, Robbie and I were happily making arrangements to meet up for a late meal in town.

He suggested we could shower at his place first, and we grinned stupidly at each other, knowing that if we went to his place now we wouldn't be eating or showering any time soon. He opened my driver's door for me, and held his other arm out in a mock gesture of gallantry. His body presented to me like that was too much, too good to resist, and I stepped in against it. We stood pressed together, feeling each other's body warmth, and smiling inanely at each other for what felt like forever. And then very slowly he leaned in and took my bottom lip between his.

It's such a simple little phrase, 'a kiss'. A tiny phrase to describe such a sweet, moist prelude to lovemaking. He tasted and smelt delicious. The Joni Mitchell line, 'I could drink a case of you', sang in my head. I was thinking, bugger the shower and the prelude, but just as I slid my hands inside his shirt the lights of an approaching vehicle angled across the clearing, and we automatically stepped apart.

Once home, Wolf put up a good argument for spending the night exactly where he was, and it took quite a bit of coaxing to get him out of the car and into the house. The airbed mattress and Wolf both made the same collapsing sound as his body dropped on to it, and with one profound groan he went back to sleep. I looked at him lying there like an aged dragon, body curled with his muzzle resting on his haunch, his lips luffing like an unsecured sail each time he breathed out. For the first time I noticed all the grey on his muzzle and around his eyes. He was an old dog. It must have happened in the last year, but somehow I hadn't noticed. The walk, all those flamboyant canine antics and efforts to impress Robbie, had taken it out of him. His exhaustion confirmed my suspicions that his usual walks with Damian were more meditative than aerobic, which, given the state of him now, was probably a good thing.

I showered, soaped and perfumed my body, and wondered if Robbie was doing a male version of the same. The thought of Robbie in the shower made me break out in goosebumps. I spent some time agonising over what underwear to put on. I hadn't bought new undies for a long time and, scrabbling through my euphemistically named lingerie drawer, I realised my options were either sexy and shabby or sensible and smart. Easy decision. I've never been sensible and now was no time to start.

Before leaving the house, I did a quick check of the bedroom to make sure there was nothing too personal in it. If Robbie came back home with me, which I sure hoped he would, I didn't want him stumbling on anything that would embarrass either of us. I knew there were no photos of Sean around – I'd removed them all some months ago. There were photos of Niki and me as kids and as adults, but that was okay. It didn't mean I'd have to talk about what happened to her.

Knees clicking, I hunkered down for a quiet talk with Wolf. I warned him I might be bringing a friend home, and that he wasn't to get jealous if the friend climbed into bed with me. He didn't even open an eye, which could have meant he was traumatised at the thought of me sleeping with a man other than Sean or, more optimistically, judging from the way he'd acted with Robbie during the day, it meant he was giving his full canine approval. I decided to go with that reading of his non-response, told him he was a good dog, and then, feeling like a teenager sneaking out on a date, tiptoed out of the bedroom.

We'd arranged to meet at Kazu, a cosy upstairs Japanese bar that served skewered tuna and other tasty titbits grilled over a tiny charcoal barbeque. The atmosphere was smoky from the grill, and intimate in a noisy, friendly, boozy kind of way. It was my favourite bar – one of the few it was possible to go to without being hit on. It just wasn't a hit-on kind of place.

Kazu became my watering hole in the months after Niki died – the place where I'd drink methodically until either Sean picked me up at the end of his shift, or I staggered down to a cab in Courtenay Place. Robbie said he'd spent a fair bit of time in Kazu as well, and we expressed surprise at not having seen each other there. Maybe he *had* seen me during that time and was just been being polite, or maybe the time for seeing each other just wasn't right.

I could still remember the first time I set eyes on Sean. Straight away I knew . . . well, I knew something. I knew we were going to slam into each other in every way it's possible for two people to slam. I knew he would turn my world inside out and upside down. I knew I was going to fall in love, and I knew that eventually it was going to hurt like hell, and I knew too that it would be worth it. There hadn't been anything like that when I'd met Robbie, no big premonitions, but the man was undoubtedly having an effect on me, and I was liking it.

Too wired to stay inside, I walked out to the curb to wait for my taxi. All that agonising over which undies to wear had made me late. The night was clear and still, the moon shone brightly, and all the street lamps were lit, so there was no excuse for me not to pay more attention to the man walking towards me, his collar turned up against the non-existent rain, his head bent on non-existent thoughts.

Lost in the future, I didn't even notice him until he was up in my face saying something about a light. Before I could register a response, his punch landed in my gut with such force that I fell into him, winded, retching and in agony. Pain roared in my senses and blocked out any thoughts trying desperately to register. As I was half dragged, half carried across the pavement, in some stuttering part of my brain I could hear Wolf barking and bashing his paws against the window, but it was distant, removed somehow, as if the world had become an old super-eight movie running at the wrong speed – frames dropping out entirely, or flickering, blurred. My yell became nothing more than drool and a retching groan. It had all happened so damn fast.

I registered the car I was being dragged into as a big, black four-door Holden Commodore sedan, probably about six or seven years old. I even noted the tyres were Turanza ER 300s – the ones with the asymmetrical tread – before I was slammed head first into the gap between the front and back seats. With no time to raise my hands to soften the crash, I went straight down, cracking my forehead on something on the way. My legs were shoved in after me, the force of it ramming my head further under the front passenger seat. A nasty carpet burn stung my cheek, and I tasted the saltiness of blood. I heard the car door slam shut, and before I'd even thought of trying to pull my head out from under the seat, the driver had started the car and slid it quietly out from the curb.

I spent the first thirty seconds trying not to pass out. When the next big black wave rolled towards me I rubbed my grazed cheek into the flooring, hoping the pain would keep me conscious. The carpet smelt of bubblegum. Okay, I figured, if I could smell, it probably meant my nose wasn't broken. That was something. My knee, I wasn't so optimistic about.

A high-pitched screaming noise was going on and on – for one truly weird minute I thought it might be me making the sound. The taste of my own blood was strangely comforting. A voice suddenly cut through the screaming, and as I tried desperately to make sense of his words, the high-pitched wailing sound receded to background noise. So it wasn't me screaming, then. Good.

That stutter-frame film thing was still happening, and at first I could only register every second or third word he said. I heard 'bitch' and 'cops', and then the word 'blackmail' crashed through. I gritted my teeth, blocked out the pain my body was screaming at me to do something about, and tried to focus on each word, but still I couldn't make sense of what he was saying. It wasn't until I heard 'Bonnie' that I truly focused. Bonnie – Niki's working name.

'. . . bitch sister of yours destroyed my life and I'm not going to let you start that all over again.'

Even though I'd never heard him speak, even though my 'bitch sister' had probably destroyed a lot of men's lives, I knew immediately which one this was. Chris Ross. The man who'd hired Snow to kill Niki, and then killed Snow to shut him up. Spying on Ross from the alleyway had been a stupid mistake and I'd known it at the time. Being busted by Ross in the act of doing it was even stupider. Fuck! If I hadn't already figured it, I knew now, without any doubt, that I was in very deep shit.

Fully conscious now, my brain was working in 'oh shit!' hyper-survival mode while my body had effectively switched into sleep function. I had no feeling at all from my neck down. My brain told me it had been forced to turn off its pain awareness sector while it got me to wake the fuck up and start thinking! If my body position had allowed it, I'd have kicked myself. From the moment we'd pulled away from the curb I should have concentrated on the route, counted the turns and directions the sedan made, and registered the sounds we drove past that might give me a clue to where my kidnapper was taking me. I concentrated really hard, but all I heard was the noise of a grinding universal and Ross's ranting.

'Janine wouldn't even let me see the kids. Said I was a sad, sick fuck and she didn't want her children exposed to that. I'd already paid Bonnie everything I had, and then Janine went and took the rest.' He paused in his rant and I felt his weight shift in the seat.

'Well, I'm not going to have you fuck me up all over again.'

His voice was louder as he turned to look over his shoulder. He's changing lanes, I thought, and couldn't resist a smile at my cleverness as I felt the car surge to the left, then straighten up again. Carefully, quietly, I inched my head back out from under the front passenger seat. I needed to get my face turned around so I could see out the car window. Even prone on the floor, I was hopeful I'd be able to glimpse high-rises or advertising hoardings, and maybe get a bead on where I was.

It was a slow and excruciating process, and I had to block out the worst of the pain signals that flared through my brain's temporary barrier. Ross raved on but I wasn't listening any more. It took maybe two or three minutes but eventually I got my head out from under the seat. Still lying on my stomach, my legs thrust up beneath me, I managed to twist my shoulders and neck around to face the passenger window directly behind Ross. I could see the back of his head, the black woollen jacket collar pulled up, thinning greasy hair combed close against his scalp. Blue-black sky. Nothing else. No buildings. No advertisement banners. No neon lights.

I let my head fall back to the floor and rested my cheek against the carpet while I took in a couple of deep breaths. Okay, I thought, we're not in the CBD then. I shut my eyes and tried to gauge the speed we were travelling at. Too fast for Courtenay Place. I'd have caught a glimpse of high-rises. He wasn't stopping for traffic light changes, so that counted out both Lambton and Aotea Quay. The car hadn't slowed for some time. No one gets that many green lights, I thought, and then congratulated myself: okay, good, you're doing good. And we hadn't gone through enough intersections or turns for this to be the suburbs. Very slowly, I turned my head again. Suddenly a big, oblong orange light flew past the window. Moments later, a car horn directly behind my head blasted, and I saw Ross glance out the passenger window. We were on the motorway. That explained why the car interior was so well lit.

I felt a wave of euphoria at this little success, which just goes to show that sometimes you can take happiness from even the most ghastly situations in life. Now I just had to figure out which motorway we were on. Either we were heading north on state highway 1, or we were on highway 2 heading out towards the Hutt Valley. If we were on SH1, I reckoned by now we would be some way past the Johnsonville off-ramp. If we were on SH2, I'd know it when we hit the winding hill road over to the Wairarapa. Niki used to rather gleefully call it 'Diane's Vomit Hill' for obvious reason, and lying as I was on the floor of the car, I knew I would react in technicolor to the first major bend we hit. I tuned Ross in again. He hadn't paused in his rant since he'd thrown me in the back.

'. . . the cops after me saying I killed her . . . whole fuckin' nightmare started up . . . and then you're snooping around my place setting me up again . . . no way, man, no way am I going to have my life destroyed all over again . . . ' He had a glottal click, probably caused by too much spit. He needed to swallow more, or talk less.

Concentrating on sounds and analysing them was working – my panic was beginning to subside. Unfortunately, as the adrenalin settled, the pain started to filter through. It was nudging at my senses already, impatient to be registered. I knew when the pain did successfully breach my brain's flimsy resistance, it would be brutal. I needed to know where I was, and I needed to know before the pain hit.

Tuning Ross's voice out again, I focused all my attention on the other sounds. The Holden's motor had the whine of a sleep-deprived three-year-old. It sounded to me like the transmission was shot. That was going to be a costly fix for Ross, I thought, and was not surprised at the lack of sympathy I felt about that.

The low hum of traffic shifted in register as the car drove up what felt like a ramp or turn-off, veered right, then down again. An overbridge? We slowed, then accelerated through what might have been a roundabout, and then the car slowed and stopped, engine idling. Traffic lights. I heard the whirr of the driver's window sliding down, the rustle of a wrapper being crushed in Ross's fist. I focused on the new sounds through the open window – something soft, repetitive and familiar. The sound tickled at the edges of my memory, but before I could place it, the window whirred back up and the car lurched forward. Pain was pushing solidly at me now, demanding to be acknowledged. I had two, maybe three heartbeats before I'd have to let it take over. I wrenched my head around so that both ears were off the carpet. Stereo. Two things happened at once. I realised what the sound I'd heard was. Waves. Little shushing waves. The other thing that happened was an electric jolt of pain so fierce, so encompassing, so overwhelming, that I felt myself lurch into blackness.

CHAPTER 22

I surfaced to a kind of wakefulness, and then sank again. It was as if I was floating on a sea of consciousness. A wave of awareness would swell beneath me, and I'd open my eyes to a race of clouds whipping across a pastel-blue sky. Occasionally a break in the clouds would reveal a glimpse of the moon, or maybe it was the sun. I didn't care. The howling wind and the lonely cry of seagulls surrounded me always. My thirst was a terrible thing. I could hear the sound of teeth grinding. Was it me? Was I doing that? My hand wouldn't move, caught somehow. I let myself sink again into the deep, long, oily blackness.

I surfaced again. I knew time had passed. Deathly cold. Maybe I'm dead, I thought. Maybe this is what death is. A surging, swelling kind of nothingness. With that thought came a little bubble of fear. I noticed my legs were shaking so hard my ankles thumped on a concrete floor. Your body can't shake if it's dead, I told myself. I'm alive – and with that, I gratefully sank again into a kind of semi-death.

That time, long, long ago, when Peaches had walloped me over the head with a cricket bat, there had been no sense of time passing. One second I was in Snow's bedroom, and then, wham! In what seemed like the very next second I was in a different room with one hell of a sore head, and the incongruous sight of Peaches in an evening dress swinging a Kookaburra.

But this time I surfaced again and again from unconsciousness, and at each surfacing, though I didn't know where I was – didn't care where I was – I knew more time had passed, and that at every surfacing I was colder and thirstier. And then eventually I became aware of myself in a place – a freezing, windy, lonely place. And then I sank again into the sweet, soft, breathing darkness.

Time surged by. An achingly slow, painful torture of minutes passed like a nightmare where you try and run but can't move. After what must have been hours, maybe days of this, I drifted back up, and this time, like the flipside of going under an anaesthetic, I made myself stay there, counting one, two, three – willing myself to wakefulness. It was like slowly rising out of a deep hypnotism.

At twenty I opened my eyes. A whip lashed across my eyeballs, and I felt warm liquid dribble down my cheeks. I immediately fell back into the comforting blackness. Minutes, maybe hours passed, and then I was aware of myself again, and again I forced myself to stay conscious by counting. This time when I reached twenty I kept my eyes shut and focused on myself. It was like opening a floodgate as the awareness of pain and thirst smashed into me.

The torture of thirst was far greater than the pain. My

tongue had swollen to an enormous hard dry muscle. It feels like a parrot's tongue, I thought, and rested on the image of a parrot – took refuge in remembering the sweet beauty of garish feathers, paint-box blue and Lego yellow – and from there my mind wandered to favourite children's stories I'd read aloud to Niki. Lines from *The Lighthouse Keeper's Lunch* echoed in the distant, timeless void – out there? In my mind? I couldn't tell the difference any more. I tried to remember the name of the lighthouse keeper – Grinland? Grinning?

A part of me knew what was happening: my brain was comforting me with pleasant memories, free-wheeling from one anodyne thought to another, trying to help me out by imagining pleasant, comforting, everyday things, so I wouldn't have to face the horror of my reality. I felt a welling of gratitude for that and observed myself weeping. But there were no tears; everything about me was parched and dry as bleached, windswept driftwood.

I think it was hours later that I surfaced again. This time I lifted my eyelids fractionally, exposing only slits of eyeballs. Something lashed my cheek – a thick swatch of matted hair, crusted with blood and salt. So that's what the whip was – my hair.

I focused on my body. There was something wrong with my left hand. I couldn't move it. Okay, leave that for now. I forced myself to stay conscious as I took in the immediate surroundings. I was coiled up in an enforced foetal position, my body wrapped around an iron ring cemented into a concrete floor, my left wrist secured to it by a hard plastic pull-through handcuff. I was inside what appeared to be a three-sided bunker, my body curled towards a concrete wall built into the clay bank.

Okay, I congratulated myself. Well done. Now for the big one. I needed to know where the bunker was, and that meant turning my body to face the freezing wind at my back. I took a long, deep breath and rolled my body over. The wind slammed into me like a car crash. The open side of the bunker faced a heaving black mass of water stippled with moonlight. I counted ten deep, slow breaths, willing myself not to black out again. I knew where I was: Fitzroy Bay on the hill above the Pencarrow lighthouse. I was in an old WWII lookout bunker, dug into a hill above the deep, unsettled waters of Cook Strait.

Grinling. That was the name of the lighthouse keeper whose wife had fought so valiantly to stop the seagulls eating her husband's lunch. It was Grinling.

A couple of years ago, Sean and I had hired mountain bikes and cycled around the winding clay and shingle coastal track as far as Fitzroy Bay where the Pencarrow lighthouse winked at the ferries, and container ships hacked their course between the North and South Islands. I remembered it as a pleasant, easy jaunt of maybe six or seven kilometres from Eastbourne to the bay. The memory of that was reassuring. Beyond Fitzroy, the track became rougher, stonier, and much more difficult to ride on, and then increasingly tricky for some twenty kilometres before it finally reached Palliser Bay.

We'd decided the lighthouse was far enough for us that day. We weren't doing the ride for fitness, and were happy to lie around on a little grassy knoll above the lighthouse and lick salt spray off each other's skin. I suddenly remembered with a lurch of excitement that there was a lake, somewhere inland and not far from this bunker. Rather than return by the same coastal track, we'd ridden our bikes inland from the bay looking for a shortcut back to town, and we'd come across a small reedy lake where we stopped to watch the resident ducks skidding in to land on the water, their webbed feet stuck out in front like toppling waterskiers.

The memory of the lake was excruciating. I knew I didn't have a hope of finding it again. Reluctantly, I forced myself to abandon the possibility, and turned my thoughts back to the coastal road. Presumably Ross had driven his Commodore in from the Eastbourne end, but I had no idea how he'd gotten me from the dirt track up the hill to the bunker. Maybe I'd climbed with him; maybe he'd dragged or carried me. I couldn't remember anything after realising his car was heading along the foreshore of Petone.

I imagined myself dying up here on this wild, windswept outcrop of land, and merged that image with one of Niki dead on the manicured lawn of the Island Bay golf course. There was a strange sort of rightness to it. Niki had always been the tidy one, had never lost her compulsion to put things in order, tidy them away. She'd stopped counting lamp posts once I'd convinced her that the *Good Luk!* knickers would work their charm, but she'd continued to snip, trim and pluck at herself obsessively. She tried to keep it hidden from me and I let her think she'd succeeded, but there was little she could keep secret from me. That's what I'd thought anyway, until recently.

I slitted my eyes open again, and this time made out a sprinkling of the city's lights in the distance. So it was coming on to evening. I let this thought ping-pong around in my brain for a while until I worked up the courage to accept what it meant. This wasn't the same night I'd been kidnapped. One whole day at least had passed while I'd risen and fallen in and out of consciousness. I had to work very hard to hold down the panic that threatened.

Broken glass, graffiti, and the remnants of a fire meant people had been here in the bunker at some time. The thought brought some comfort. I wouldn't let myself dwell on the possibility that the debris was years old. I wouldn't let myself think about what a godforsaken place this was. Bikers and even walkers did the coastal track, but that was way below where I was. No matter how loud I screamed, only the seagulls would hear me, and they didn't care. I couldn't make any noise anyway. My swollen tongue made even breathing difficult.

Some hardy, intrepid off-road bikers might take it into their heads to come up here, but it was unlikely.

I took a ragged breath, and opened the floodgates of sensation again. Thirst. My whole being craved water. I pushed that down, down. What else? Cold. Freezing. Ice cold. Wind. I realised I was still lying down, wrapped around the concrete plinth in the middle of the floor. I dragged myself inch by inch into a half-sitting, half-crouched position. The plastic tie had sliced into my wrist and the wound was raw and oozing, crusted with dried blood. There was a lot of blood too on my free hand, my face and hair. I figured it must have come from my smashed nose. The light summer dress I had put on for my dinner date with Robbie was filthy with blood and whatever else I had been lying in – it smelled like shit and urine from some animal, possibly human. Possibly me.

Both my legs were scratched, knees grazed. No one ever died of grazed knees, I told myself. No shoes. No feeling at all in my feet. Numb with cold. With my free hand I systematically prodded and pressed every part of my body, forcing myself to register pain so I'd know how bad a shape I was in. I was sore from bruises and abrasions over roughly eighty per cent of my body, but no bones were broken as far as I could tell. There may have been some smashed cartilage in my nose – it seemed to be encrusted with a mix of blood and salt from the freezing southerly whipping spray up off Cook Strait – but my face was entirely numb so no matter how hard I pressed I couldn't feel anything.

There was something I still had to check. My brain told me not to do it but I ignored that advice. My undies were gone, vulva swollen and sore to touch, pubic hair caked with dried semen. I registered what this meant. My brain said, 'I told you not to do that', and then everything went black again.

This time I knew I was dead. I was in a freezing cold hell. Spirits screamed all around me, and Satan's eyes with their burnt-amber vertical irises studied me impassively. I tried to cry out but there was no sound from my swollen, parched throat. I was beyond thirst. Even the sibilance of the word 'thirst' tinkling in my head drove me mad. The constant shushing of the waves below was a torture.

Dawn. Cold, harsh, white dawn. The devil was no longer there but the thirst was worse than any pain I'd ever endured. I'd have done anything for water. I'd have killed for water. What a beautiful word it was. Water. I went over all the words – water, moisture, stream, liquid . . .

Seagulls circled overhead, screeching insults at each other. So, that was the sound I thought was the screaming of spirits. It was only seagulls. If I was to survive, I knew I had to use my desperate craving for the one and only thing I still cared about – water. I thought again about the lake Sean and I had found, but I knew I could roam for days in these barren hills and never find it. I wouldn't last days.

Reluctantly, I let that thought go, although the fantasy of it – a big blue mass of shining water – still shimmered in my imagination. Then, with a yip of pleasure, I remembered a trickle of water, maybe a mile or two back along the coast road: a beautiful little run-off trickle of water that drooled down the hill and across the shingle into the surf. Sean and I had stopped to watch a line of ducklings follow that trickle across the track. The memory of it was a sweet torture. It was little more than a two-finger-width dribble of water, but it was a thing of shimmering beauty in my memory. If I could just get my hand free I could go to it, I could drink. The plastic tie looping my hand to the iron ring looked flimsy enough but proved to be unbelievably resistant to everything I tried. Yanking and tugging opened the wrist wound until it oozed and then poured, but even using the blood as lubricant I still couldn't pull my hand free. My thirst was dreadful. I whimpered in a kind of shame as I licked at the blood.

What must have been an hour of rhythmical sawing on the rusted iron ring resulted in nothing more than a few scratches on the plastic handcuff and a lot more on me. I tried using my mouth but my cracked lips bled profusely before my teeth could get any purchase. I persevered, starting with my front teeth. I tried to snip at the tie and when that failed I snarled my lips back for the bicuspids to have a go. I worked away at it for a long time before I rewarded myself with a look at the result – just the faintest of fraying to one edge of the handcuff, plus bleeding gums, a cracked cuspid and painfully split top lip. This wasn't going to work.

From the position of the sun, I figured it to be late morning. I forced myself to do the maths while I scrabbled around looking for anything sharp I could use as a tool. Start with Tuesday. I was kidnapped on Tuesday night. My fingers closed on a small round stone and I tried rubbing that against the plastic handcuff. I was pretty sure a whole day had passed since then. A whole day of bright light and seagull cries. A whole day that my brain had slammed a 'Do Not Disturb' sign up on.

The stone was useless. I put it in my mouth for comfort while I systematically searched every centimetre of the floor within my reach. Okay, after that full day, I'd seen the lights across the harbour as night was falling. That would have been Wednesday night. And now it was day again. So, it must be Thursday. Late Thursday morning.

For the first time I allowed myself the luxury of a thought that until now I hadn't let myself indulge: they'll be looking for me. Someone will be looking for me. I'd been missing for two nights and a full day. As if in response to this realisation, my stomach clenched.

Manoeuvring my bum as far from the shackle as possible, I held my dress away from the hot, stinging shit that burst out of me. When I was sure the spasms were over, I used my bare foot to kick loose leaves and rubbish over the stinking, acrid mess.

Squatting back at the concrete ring, forehead resting on my handcuffed wrist, I fought back waves of nausea. I'd never believed in tying dogs up, and vowed if I was freed from here I would never, ever tie any animal up, ever.

Dog-god must have been listening. I'd just finished making the vow when I saw it: the rusting lid of an ancient tin can. Whimpering in anticipation, I lurched towards it, almost severing my wrist in the process. It had been hidden under the leaves I'd scuffed up to cover my foul-smelling discharge. With some clever toe work I managed to slide the lid close enough to grab it with my free hand.

Half an hour of sawing and slicing at the plastic tie and I was free.

I stood and fell over half a dozen times before accepting that my legs wouldn't hold me upright. There was no option but to slide down the hill on my arse. It ended up being more a scrabble than a slide. What looked like a smooth slope of tussock turned out to be deep clay furrows with ridges covered in hair-plug tufts of sharp reeds. Forced to grab at them to stop myself pitching forward was like being stabbed by a handful of bamboo skewers.

As I scrambled, crawled and skidded my way down, I thought this is why girls should never wear dresses – in case they're abducted and raped, have their underwear stolen, and are held captive on top of a hill in freezing cold weather and forced to slide down a slope covered in tufts of pick-up-sticks. But sliding was still easier than trying to walk down the practically vertical slope with legs that didn't work any more. When I'd manoeuvred myself about halfway down, the sounds that had been background noise for what seemed like my entire life became louder and more distinctive. What I'd thought was the grinding of teeth was the rattle of beach pebbles being clawed back under by possessive waves.

When I couldn't slide any more, I crawled on hands and knees. Half-moon shapes pitted the cracked, dry mud tracks. My spirits lifted. Hoof marks. Sheep! Not that sheep necessarily meant farmers but I let myself nurse this tiny spark of optimism.

The clay was softer now, and my heart pounded in anticipation of there being a puddle at the bottom of the hill. It helped me do what I had to do next. My knees refused to carry me any further. Stretching my body along one of the ridges, stomach flat against the tussock, chin tucked into my chest, I pitched myself off the edge. Niki and I used to roll down sand dunes. It was one of our favourite games. Actually, it was my favourite game because I usually won. We'd roll ourselves in beach towels until we looked like brightly coloured cigars, and then we'd throw ourselves off the top of the dune. The one who rolled the furthest won. Only now did it occur to me that I'd rolled further because I was bigger and heavier than Niki. At the time, both of us had credited it to my incredible older-sister skill.

At the bottom of the hill was a small depression like a gutter where the track met the incline, and in the middle of it was the most beautiful sight I'd ever seen in my life: a little pool of water the size of a saucer. I crawled towards it, whimpering pathetically, and then, dropping to the ground, I rested my cracked lips in the puddle and licked.

It tasted of salt and the acrid bitterness of animal piss. It was divine. The salt on my split lip stung like a bastard. I knew I probably shouldn't drink it all but did it anyway. There's no way I could have stopped myself. It was a tiny cupful of urine-flavoured nectar of the gods.

I lay in the ditch holding the pain at bay and figuring out what to do next. The taste of water had given me new strength, but I knew I couldn't make it all the way back to Eastbourne. I knew too that I had no choice but to try.

Putting one foot down in front of the other, I could manage ten steps before my legs would fold under and I'd sink slowly to the ground like a camel. I'd count to a hundred, then make myself stand and put left foot, right foot again, one after the other, until I'd made another ten steps. I saw the blisters on my feet form, peel and then bleed. I didn't feel a thing. I was too numb with cold, or maybe just too numb.

I used the tyre tracks in the middle of the road for the first few blocks of ten steps, and then realised the chances of finding water on the hill side of the trail were better, so moved closer to the bank for the next block. I staggered along like this, ten steps at a time, searching for any little dribbles of water leaking from the clay bank. My left wrist leaked blood into the crook of my right elbow where it was cradled against my breasts.

That little trickle of water the ducklings had made use of had to be close by. I convinced myself it was just around each bend in the winding track, and each time it wasn't there the disappointment was overwhelming. I staggered on, ten steps at a time, and died a little death every time I came to a bend and it revealed another identical bay and no little trickle of water. There was no end to this track.

On the left side of the path, waves clawed and raked at the foreshore. Oyster catchers prodded their bright orange beaks at stones, trying to convince themselves a slimy morsel was underneath, and shags perched on jutting rocks, their iridescent wings outstretched as if offering an embrace. I remembered this was where the *Wahine* survivors had huddled together waiting to be rescued. I'd seen photos of survivors on the backs of pickup trucks, grey emergency blankets wrapped around their shoulders, their faces revealing nothing but a kind of shamefaced acceptance. They knew even then that they'd be known as 'the lucky ones' forever after. They'd seen their fellow passengers drown out there in the crazy madness of the storm, or pummelled and shredded on the rocks as they tried to swim to shore. Not many of the survivors wanted to talk about it afterwards, except perhaps to honour someone else's act of heroism. Mostly they wore that guilty look all survivors have. Why me? Could I have done more to save others? Am I pleased it was someone else who died instead of me? Was it a mistake? Were they supposed to live and was I supposed to die?

I must have been walking for half an hour, but it wasn't really walking, it was more of a shuffle, and progress was tortuously slow. I reckoned at this rate it would take about three days to get to the Eastbourne gate. I knew I couldn't make it, but was determined to keep going until I couldn't get up any more. Each time I slumped to the ground, it took longer to struggle to my feet again. And then, finally, I knew the next time I folded would be the last.

I stumbled around yet another bend, and there in front of me, right in the middle of the track, was a goat. We looked at each other, that goat and I. He was definitely the prettier sight. Those amber marble eyes gazed at me with no sympathy. It was as if he'd been waiting for me. Maybe it's a hallucination, I thought, and hobbled one step closer. It stood its ground and just looked at me. These were the devil eyes I'd seen as I slipped in and out of consciousness up in the bunker. The creature had massive devil horns too.

Despite my exhaustion, I was curious now. Was it real? Was this thing simply a goat, or had the devil come to claim me, as the nuns had always told me he one day would? I staggered another step towards it. It stamped a petulant hoof in response, and then turned its head to look behind. For one moment I thought that head was going to turn right around and back again like the possessed girl in *The Exorcist*, but no such luck – it turned its baleful look back at me before walking stiff-legged towards the bank and leaping up it. Swaying on my feet I watched those unlikely legs continue to climb the hill to where an audience of smaller goats huddled together, waiting.

I told my foot to lift but it wouldn't. I waited for my legs to fold – and that was when I heard it. The crack and pop of tyres on gravel. There was a vehicle coming towards me on the track. That's what had spooked the goat, not me. Unable to move, I waited in the middle of the track, focusing the last of my strength on staying conscious. The truth of it was that I no longer knew if I *was* conscious. The driver would have water. I was sure of that. But now, at the end, I almost didn't care about water. Didn't know if the mythical nectar I thought of as water even existed. Maybe I'd dream its existence like I'd dreamt of the devil.

I was aware of a car coming into view and skidding to a stop in the middle of the track in front of me. I was aware of the cloud of orange dust, the sound of a car door slamming, someone coming towards me. It was all I could do to lift my head to look at my rescuer.

It wasn't a rescuer. It was Chris Ross. He was carrying a rifle. He didn't need it. I was dead anyway. My legs gave way, and I sank to the ground. It was over.

CHAPTER 23

A hand, Ross's hand, clasps around mine, trying to close my fingers around something. Plastic. Cool. My palm is bleeding, raw from all that crawling. The thing he wants me to grasp drops to the ground, bounces once then just lies there. It's a bottle of water. The water refracts light through the transparent plastic. I don't care any more.

Ross picks it up, squeezes a little pool of the liquid into the palm of his hand, places his other hand on my neck and tilts my face into the water. I don't want to drink, don't want to help my captor bring me back to life, but at the taste of what it's been craving my unfaithful body responds. I lick and suckle his palm obscenely, and then, when he lifts the plastic nozzle to my lips and squeezes a cool stream of water down my throat, I gulp the pure life-giving ecstasy of it until my gullet aches.

I hear his murmur in my ear telling me just to sip it, and a desperate fear comes over me that he'll take the water away. I grab the bottle off him and squeeze it and gulp the liquid until there's none left. My stomach heaves, and there's stinging bile in my throat, but I swallow it back down, gagging.

Maybe time had passed, maybe not. Sitting on the road directly in front of me was Ross, the rifle rested casually on his raised knees, his back against the Holden's number plate. He was talking, but I'd tasted water and now all I could think about was how to get more of it. Instead of sating my thirst, that little tease of water had increased my craving tenfold. I had to have more.

I dragged my attention back to focus on what Ross was saying. I watched his mouth flap up and down, open and shut, noise coming out . . . I forced myself to concentrate. It was an unpleasant mouth, too sensuous for a man. Big lips the colour of loganberries with a darker defining line around the edges, as if he spent a lot of time licking at them.

Concentrate! The lips were saying . . .

'. . . embarrassed? Damn right I was. I sure as hell never told my wife about it. No need, anyway. I was never going to ask her to be involved in something like that. I always wanted to be a good husband. Good father. I did my best to lead a normal life. Then it all just started to wear me down. I couldn't control it. Eventually I rang one of those helplines. They told me to get help. I said, 'That's what I thought I was ringing you for,' and the little faggot says, "We don't give *that* kind of help," like I was some . . . I don't know. He said, "You need to get *professional* help." And so I did. I'd never been to one before. Never really wanted to. I thought they were dirty. Diseased, you know. All that.'

His words were coming at me and I heard them, but they had

little meaning. To me, anyway. It didn't look like they meant much to him any more either. I don't know why he chose me to confess to.

'I met the other one first and she set it up, and that's how I met your sister. Tell you the truth, I really liked Bonnie. She was . . . sweet. I thought she was a nice girl. Shows what kind of judge of character I am, but at the time I'm thinking, this isn't so bad. I mean, no one's getting hurt here. It was kind of expensive, but you know, it wasn't like I had to do it that often or anything. Some people would spend more than that on booze or cars or whatever.'

He hefted the gun and I waited for him to point it at me but he just laid it on the ground, his hand resting on it.

'A week later my twelve-year-old daughter brings me in a package she says was on the doorstep. It was a movie of the whole thing. Your sister had set me up. I knew as soon as I saw it the nightmare was only just starting. Sure enough, then came the big freak demanding money. I paid up. Yeah, I know, stupid sucker that I am. And it just went on and on. Even after she was dead, it went on. In the end I had nothing left to give. I was going to lose my house. I had no choice. I decided to come clean, I mean, my wife loved me, our relationship was okay I thought. I didn't expect her to understand or anything but I thought she'd . . . I don't know. So anyway, I told her. I told my wife about my – my problem. And I told her how your sister set me up, and that I'd paid, but she was still after me. Some part of me thought maybe she'd . . . I don't know.'

He looked directly at me and I tried to look back, but I could feel my eyes sliding away from him.

'Have you seen it? The movie? Have you seen what Bonnie and me did?'

I managed to shake my head. No, I hadn't seen what he'd done to my sister. I'd seen the still photo of Niki dressed up in kid's clothes sucking a lollipop in a twisted, distorted version of what a child is. That had been more than enough for me. I didn't ever want to see the film of him fucking my little sister dressed like that. I remembered her too vividly as a child. She'd been such a lovely kid. I remembered the soft down on her shoulders when she was really little. Those fragile little shoulder blades like the promise of wings.

As if reading my thoughts, Ross leaned forward. 'I didn't have sex with her, you know. We didn't have sex. It wasn't like that. It wasn't sexual. It was just dress-ups. We both dressed up as . . . ' His voice broke with the difficulty of confession, but he picked it up again. 'We dressed up as kids and played at having a . . . a tea party. That's it. That's all we did. That's all I . . . had a need for. That's what she threatened to put on the internet. That's what I had to tell my wife.'

I heard part of what he was saying, all broken up and fragmented, but that gorgeous bottle of water he'd given me had been miraculous. I was alive. I was pain-searingly, ecstatically, *I am going to survive this even if it kills me*, alive.

Ross was sitting about four metres away from me. He'd picked up the gun again, and it was now cradled in his lap, his hand held loosely around the stock. Maybe at any other time I'd have felt sympathy for Ross. Okay, dressing up as a little girl and having a tea party isn't my idea of normal, but if he was telling the truth and there was no sex, then really it was more sad than bad.

But if I was ever going to feel sorry for him, it wasn't now. I didn't feel sorry for anyone or anything, not even me. I didn't feel anything really. Feeling could come if I ever survived this.

I wondered if I was strong and quick enough to run at him and wrestle the gun from his grasp. I knew I wasn't, but was about to make my move anyway, when suddenly he stood, gun hanging at his side, index finger resting on the trigger. I'd left it too late.

'I didn't kill Bonnie,' he said. 'I didn't kill anyone. Not even that big freak who was threatening me. Though they both deserved it for what they did to my life.'

Given my history with Ross, I admit I probably wasn't the best judge of his character, but I had a strong hunch he was telling the truth. I didn't know how I felt about that, but now seemed as good a time as any to ask for another truth from him.

'Did you rape me?' I asked, lifting my head to watch him answer. 'I need you to tell me that.'

He was silent for a long time – long enough for me to know the answer.

'I used to come out here fishing with my brother when we were kids,' he said, squinting into the dull, flat light of the horizon as if the memory was out there somewhere.

Casually he hefted the gun, barrel pointed towards me. I wanted to look away, but was transfixed by that little round black hole. I wondered if I'd see the bullet coming towards me like in a cartoon, and then was amazed at how well I was taking this – my final moments. Maybe it's only possible to look death in the face for so long before it becomes just like any other face. Maybe you just give up. 'Learned helplessness' I think it's called.

Remembering the term made me angry. I hadn't been helpless since I was a baby, and I wasn't prepared to accept dying in such a pathetic way, sitting in the middle of a dirt track on a lonely windswept coast. I wasn't going to be slaughtered without a fight. Even that stupid goat would have charged him, and surely I had more fight in me than a bovid!

I'd just made up my mind to rush at Ross and tackle him, when he suddenly strode towards me. I hunkered down, waiting for the blow. He paused in front of my crouched body for a full ten seconds – I know because I was counting them – and then he walked on past me.

I just sat there, pulling air into my lungs and then releasing it. Breathing. Feeling my big, fat, red, alive heartbeat. I didn't turn my head to watch him go, but I listened to the sound of his feet on the gravel, heard the sound become fainter until eventually it was completely gone. The baaing of the goats on the hill started up again, and the seagulls picked up their argument exactly where they'd left off. I sat on the gravel track, listening to them squabble, and I waited. I was waiting to die or to be found. The choice wasn't mine. I was a disinterested bystander. It seemed to me that some time later I heard a shot in the distance, but maybe I dreamt it.

That's where the two hunters found me, slumped in the middle of the road. They saved my life, so it's a pity the subsequent Armed Offenders' Squad search for Ross put an end to their day's hunting, but at least it meant the stupid goats got to live another day too.

One of the hunters must have called it in while the other was helping me into their four-wheel drive, because Sean was already waiting for me as we drove up to the Eastbourne gate entrance to the track. There were half a dozen plain-clothed detectives milling around self-consciously. I recognised a couple of the big guys from Central wearing duffle coats and with beanies pulled down over their ears, and appreciated that they discreetly kept their distance as Sean wrapped a silver survival blanket around my shoulders and shepherded me towards an ambulance parked with its back door open to receive me.

I baulked and refused to get in. There was something about the smell of it, the white sheets and chrome coldness. I just couldn't do it. The paramedic wasn't too happy, insisting I needed immediate attention, but I was having none of it. I just wanted to go home and crawl into bed. When it looked like the medic was about to forcibly sedate me, I agreed to the compromise of having Sean drive me directly to the hospital.

He turned the car heater up to full and handed me a bottle of Lucozade to sip on the way. I burrowed down into the scratchy woollen blanket Sean had nicked from the ambulance, and fought the urge to sob my heart out. Sean knew better than to say anything. Well, he knew me, full stop. He drove the car fast and smooth and kept silent, giving me time. At Days Bay he leaned over and switched the car's radio on. The Phoenix Foundation were singing 'This Charming Van' – sweet, easy, and oddly comforting.

It was good of Sean to give me the time I needed, but I knew the guys back at Eastbourne would be twitching, pacing, waiting for any word about who had kidnapped me and where the perp was now. I realised with a guilty jolt that they needed to know Ross was armed.

'It was Chris Ross,' I said, and was amazed that my voice sounded so normal. A bit scratchy, but a lot stronger than I felt. Sean slowly leaned over to pick up the R/T, turning the radio down in the same movement.

'That was his Holden on the track where they found me. He's carrying a Browning A5 semi-auto.'

I stared out the passenger window while Sean relayed the information to the guys back at Eastbourne, keeping his voice relaxed-sounding, conversational, talking in police-speak code, partly for my sake, but more to keep the prying, police short-wave radio listeners off the scent. My feet were starting to thaw out, and the pain was already excruciating. I hoped I could get some painkillers into my system before I was forced to start screaming – never a good look in a police car.

Sean casually flicked the emergency flashing lights on, reached his arm out the window, and stuck a blue cherry on the roof. I didn't tell him not to. Without turning my head to look, I could sense him glancing in my direction, keeping an eye on me. For one unworthy moment I liked that, but it was fleeting and it wasn't fair.

'Quit worrying. I'm fine,' I said, and then realised it was true. I was hurt, damaged but not broken.

I saw Sean's shoulders relax. 'We've got men all over the hills and the coastline. We'll find him, buddy.'

The pet name. It was so tempting to bask in it, the salve of old love. I should have gone in the ambulance. I sipped the Lucozade. Sweet and salty. When I finally relinquished it there was blood on the rim of the bottle.

'You went after him, didn't you,' Sean said, making it a statement only this side of an accusation.

'Not exactly. I was checking out where he lived. I fucked up. Ross saw me, knew who I was, and got it into his head I was going to blackmail him like Niki did. So he came after me.'

I had a sudden flashback of Ross coming towards me, felt the punch. My body flushed hot then cold, and pinpricks of sweat broke out on my forehead. Shit. How long was this going to go on for?

'I told you I'd checked him out,' Sean said as he slowed, then sped through a red light. 'What set you off on him, anyway?'

I pictured Vex telling me how much Niki loathed Ross – what a sicko she thought he was.

'Vex picked him out,' I said. At that moment we hit the Petone foreshore stretch, and I saw a woman in an emerald-green coat throwing a stick for her dog, a Golden Labrador. Every time the dog leapt in the air it twisted its body, and the drops of water flew off its coat in an arc. It was beautiful. It was all beautiful – the green of the woman's coat, the joy of the dog as it threw its body in the air, the far-flung arc of the droplets.

I felt the lump in my throat swell again, and I knew that if I started to cry now I'd never stop. I forced down a painful swallow of Lucozade and waited for the lump to go away. Sean knew I was struggling, and pulled back from his questions. He wove the car expertly across the lanes, going well over the 100 kilometres per hour limit, but I felt safe. I'd always felt safe with Sean.

'Is Wolf okay?'

'He's fine.' I saw Sean glance sideways at me and make a decision to add, 'Trust you to take up with an ex-dog handler.'

I let that sink it. Let it wrap itself gently around me. Robbie must have been the one to realise something was wrong and set the alarm bells ringing. He must have contacted Sean . . . a wave of exhaustion washed over me. Not yet. I wasn't ready to piece together what had happened in the real world. I felt as if I'd been away in a foreign land, where I didn't understand the people, the place or the language. The last few days were already taking on the feeling of a dream, a nightmare I was still in the process of waking up from.

'I thought I had it figured,' I explained. 'I thought Ross paid Snow to kill Niki.'

Sean grunted, but kept his eyes on the road. I didn't know how much he knew of all this, but didn't see any harm in telling him what I'd learnt. 'And then when Ross heard that Snow was mouthing off about killing her, maybe even heard about the recording Gemma made, he realised that eventually Snow would lead you guys to him, so he had to kill him.' Sean was still giving nothing away. 'But now I'm not so sure,' I admitted.

Finally he said, 'I *am* working this case, Di. I wish you'd trust that.'

'You're 'pursuing active lines of enquiry', eh?' I said, but kept it light.

'Yeah, I am actually,' he replied, keeping it just as light right back at me.

'I know.' I offered this as a kind of 'I'm sorry', and he took it and smiled grimly to himself.

'What happened back there, Diane?' Sean's voice was still relaxed and normal, but I saw his Adam's apple go up and down and knew he was struggling to hold himself together. It dawned on me that he felt guilty for not finding me sooner. Sean knew me, but I sure as hell knew him too. I shrugged and looked out the window. The ferry was coming in, packed full of laughing, happy, carefree holiday-makers no doubt. My shrug fooled neither of us.

'Did he rape you?' Sean asked, keeping his eyes on the road.

I counted to ten before answering. 'No,' I lied. 'He didn't rape me.' I didn't bother to cross my fingers behind my back, and I didn't expect Sean to believe me, but I knew it would be unfair to tell him the truth. He was my ex-husband and he was a cop. The ex-husband would feel he had to play the role of comforter. The cop would have to report it as a crime. I didn't want either.

'Diane. You know . . . ' He took a breath – but I cut him off.

'Leave it, Sean. I know what I'm doing. If you catch him, the kidnapping's enough to put him away for a long, long time.' I looked at Sean – saw the sweat on his palms, a dribble of it running down his hairline. The temperature in the car was probably really high, but I was still shivering. 'I'll testify to him kidnapping me and everything else he did . . . but not to that.'

He was probably going to argue with me, but we were pulling into the emergency drive-in area of A & E and medics were already waiting. I saw a couple of uniformed cops talking to reporters, pushing them back away from the entrance. My car door was opened, and an orderly leaned in to help me out. There was a flurry as the stretcher was clattered towards the car and I was lifted onto it. At the last minute I turned my head to thank Sean. He was still in the driver's seat, his body slumped against the door, his head thrown back, cheek against the cool glass, eyes shut. He looked like a man who'd just come last in a marathon.

I insisted on a shower before I'd let them do anything to me. They put up a bit of a fight and I heard murmurs of 'DNA evidence' and 'rape kit', but after I'd told them emphatically that I had *not* been raped they finally agreed to the shower, on condition a nurse accompanied me. I agreed to it only because I knew I couldn't do it on my own.

Marcia was professional and matter-of-fact, and I was grateful for that. I sat on a pink plastic chair in the cubicle holding the shower nozzle while she used a flannel to gently wash away the filth. I was still in love with water and luxuriated at the abundance of it, holding the nozzle above my upturned face and letting the water run over my eyelids into my mouth.

Marcia handed me the soapy flannel, and suggested I might like to wash myself. She meant my vulva. From the way she avoided my eyes I was sure she knew.

She found what must have been the only thick, soft towel in the hospital to pat me dry. I'd avoided looking directly at my body, but what I'd glimpsed was diminished and mottled with colours predominantly in the purple to yellow range.

I tried not to be stroppy with the doctors and nurses who prodded, poked and pricked me. I knew they were just doing their job, but hospitals are no place to be when you're sick. I even took pity on the young constable who'd been given the job of photographing my injuries for evidential purposes. She was quick about it, probably keen to make her getaway as soon as she could. Marcia stayed with me as I was wheeled to various parts of the hospital where I was X-rayed, had my wrist patched up, and my nose 'readjusted'.

They smothered my feet in what looked and smelled like engine grease, and then coddled them in thick bandages. I was suspicious they'd done that just to stop me from walking out the door, which I'd threatened to do every fifteen minutes – but the fight was going out of me. Marcia had most likely added a sedative to the saline drip in my arm. By the time the orderly wheeled me up to the ward all I wanted to do was sleep. Marcia murmured there was a policeman wanting to see me, but I'd had enough. I closed my eyes.

I heard the click of claws on linoleum and a stifled whine of yearning, and by the time I'd opened my eyes his huge paws were landing on the bed threatened to capsize it, and his massive bony head thumped down on my chest. It hurt but it was a good hurt. I cupped my palm over his intelligence bump and told him I was okay. Told him I was fine. I felt his warm, dry fingers brush the hair from my face, felt his lips on my forehead. He smelled divine. He was warm. Warm and alive. My hand stroked the silky warmth of him. I felt the tears come. There was no crying sound, no hiccup or groan, just the steady run of tears. They pooled in the hollow of my throat. It was as if, now that I had some water in me, it was all going to leak out again. He licked the tears up, whimpering. He told me to sleep now. Said they'd both be here when I woke. That I was safe and they wouldn't leave. And with that I breathed in the warm, sweet, biscuit aroma of him, and slept.

When I woke they were both still there, Robbie slumped in the chair pulled up close against the bed, his hand holding mine; Wolf lying across his feet, alert, watching me. Wolf saw me wake and leapt to his feet, dancing from paw to paw and whining in excitement. He lifted his huge front feet onto the bed again, and gave into the temptation to give me a good licking. The smell of the graze on my face worried him, and I had to do a fair bit of reassuring before he agreed to drop back on his four paws. Robbie's greeting was a little more restrained but just as heartfelt.

He leaned in and kissed my forehead. 'Welcome home.'

I hummed something, not able to speak yet. The curtain had been pulled around the bed, and I had no idea of the time of day or night. It was good being in this little enclosed world with just the three of us. Robbie poured me a drink of water, helped me into a half-sitting position, and held it to my lips, all the time chatting quietly to me and giving the occasional instruction to Wolf.

Although he never changed his tone, I was amazed at how Wolf knew when the words were for him, and even more amazed that he immediately did as he was told. Then I realised

I had too. Done what I was told, that is. I'd done exactly as Robbie had asked – sipped my drink, leaned forward so he could put a pillow at my back, even responded to his questions about pain level without biting his head off. What was it about this guy that made both Wolf and me acquiesce so readily? I warned myself to look out for that.

There was a pause, a silence, and I realised Robbie was giving me time to speak if I wanted to.

'I don't want to talk about it yet.'

'Okay,' he said, and waited some more.

'Any update on our John Doe?' I asked, thinking that was as good a subject as any.

'As a matter of fact,' he said, and flashed his grin at me. It made my heart lurch, and with the lurch came the realisation that my heart still worked. 'I called in a favour from a dog handler mate of mine from Police College. I sent him back into the bush with our surly ranger to look for John Doe's skull.'

I reached for my drink but was snagged – I was still tethered to the saline drip. Robbie held the paper cup to my mouth, and I sipped tentatively – while he continued updating me. It was good thinking about something other than me.

'That first night you . . . ' He paused, then picked it up again. 'The night you went missing, I stayed up all night drawing up a topographical grid, going over the changes in watercourses and how they most likely would have shifted over the years. It, you know, it took my mind off . . . ' He trailed off and then made a big deal of throwing the cup in the rubbish and replacing it with another one, all the time with his back to me. Wolf was watching him intently, so he knew too.

'When did you know something had happened to me?' I waited until he turned back to face me. 'It's not like I have a great record of punctuality with you.'

'This time was different,' he said, and took my good hand in his again. 'When you didn't turn up at Kazu I tried ringing your mobile and got your voicemail. I was worried pretty much straight away. I mean, we'd had such a great day together, and I thought, I can't be *that* wrong.'

I squeezed his hand, not trusting myself to speak.

'So I drove to your house. There was no answer and the place was all locked up. Wolf had barked so much he'd pretty much lost his voice, but he was still bashing at the window.' Wolf's head swivelled round at the sound of his name. 'Platz,' Robbie said to him, and Wolf obediently subsided with his head between his paws. When I looked the question, Robbie bobbed his head apologetically. 'Sorry. I train all my dogs in German.'

I let the '*my* dog' go. For now.

'I talked to your next-door neighbour who said Wolf had been barking non-stop for an hour, and I knew then that something was badly wrong.'

He poured himself a glass of water and held it clutched between his two hands. I could see he was reliving it – could see, too, that the poor guy hadn't had a decent sleep in a long time. Probably not since I'd gone missing.

'So I rang it in. By the time the car arrived I'd found your bag in the bushes. Then it was all on. Sean was great. He had Ross pegged as the guy even on that first night.

Oh, super, I thought. He's bonded with my ex-husband. That's all I need.

I watched Robbie take a sip of water.

'The guys, everyone, went all-out to find you, Diane.' He hung his head, and I could see him struggle to get his voice steady before he spoke again. For the first time he looked directly at me and held my look. 'I'm sorry,' he said, and his voice broke.

I felt my lip split painfully as I tried to smile at him. 'What are you sorry for?'

'That we didn't find you. We should have found you.'

I patted him. It works for Wolf, and they seem to be pretty

simpatico, so I hoped it would work for him. After a couple of minutes he cleared his throat and we half grinned at each other.

'So you sent this guy in with a sniffer dog to look for the skull and told him where you thought it might be?' I said, picking up the John Doe story where he'd left off. 'How did he go?'

'It's in my car,' he said, sliding me the proud grin of a new father.

'You're kidding me! He found John Doe's skull?'

He lifted one shoulder. 'I'd been thinking about what you said about the guy's soul not resting until his body had been claimed,' he said, and was about to go on but then just shrugged again.

'Why haven't you taken it to Smithy?' I asked, unreasonably.

'That little job was next on my list,' he said, giving it right back at me.

'Go. Go now and give him the skull. The sooner he gets it . . .' I said, leaving the sentence unfinished. I saw him hesitate. 'Hey, I'm fine. Really. And anyway,' I added, when he still didn't look like moving, 'I want to pee. And I need help to do that.' I hoped that was the final impetus he needed.

It took a bit more pushing, but eventually they were gone with only one backward glance and a tail wag as they went.

CHAPTER 24

The worst part was having the thick bandages peeled off my feet, but after what I'd been through with Ross, normal, smarting, everyday pain somehow seemed easier to take. It wasn't easy to convince them to take the drip out of my hand. The doctor insisted I needed at least another twenty-four hours of rehydration, and that it was the easiest way to get the antibiotics into my system, but when she saw that I was determined to pull the needle out myself she agreed, on condition I sipped a full glass of water every half hour and took my drugs in pill form like a good girl.

I knew the hospital staff thought I was difficult. What they didn't know was that the tethering of my undamaged hand to the metal drip stand was sickeningly reminiscent of being shackled to the iron ring in the bunker. The wrist wound was already beginning to heal, but I was going to be left with a scar that would resemble a botched suicide attempt.

Detective Alex Bower came to take a full statement from me, and he introduced himself as the detective in charge of my case. It was a good move to give it to someone who didn't know me; it was easier for me to go over everything that had happened with a stranger than it would have been to tell someone I knew.

I started from the time Ross had punched me in the gut, and kept going until I got to when the hunters found me on the track. There were quite a few blanks I couldn't fill in, but I managed to give him more details than I'd thought I'd be able to. There's a real art to taking a statement from a victim or witness, and Alex was good at it – opening doors, asking questions without leading me to assumed answers, methodical without getting bogged down in useless details.

He used a Pitman's style shorthand which allowed me to talk at my usual pace, and that helped too. I didn't want to linger on any of it. When I'd described being tied up in the bunker, he asked straightforwardly if Ross had raped me. There were no piercing looks, no lowering of voice, just the question. I'd prepared myself for it, and answered just as straightforwardly that no, Ross hadn't raped me.

Detective Bower drew the little saucer-shaped hieroglyphic for 'no', and continued with his next question. He did spend some time encouraging me to remember the details of what Ross was wearing the last time I saw him. Of course, I realised with a jolt, they were still hunting for him. No doubt the media had been given the 'armed and dangerous and not to be approached' warning to print alongside his photo.

I did my best to picture Ross for young Alex Bower. There

was an image burnt into my retina of him sitting opposite me on the road, the gun resting in his lap. I remembered green trackies, camouflage green maybe, and fawn-coloured, thick, rubber-tread boots, but I couldn't be certain of any of it. All I could picture with any real clarity was the Browning A5 semi-auto and the bottle of water.

The statement took about an hour, and when we finished I felt oddly elated, as if by telling it all from beginning to end like a story I'd made it something that had happened to someone else. Purged myself of it somehow. It was a bit like confession. Maybe if I said three *Hail Marys* and an *Our Father* it would all disappear forever.

If Alex hadn't still been there I might even have tried it. Instead, I sipped my water and asked him if there'd been any sightings of Ross. He answered matter-of-factly that I was the last one to see him. AOS were still searching the peninsula, and both Eastbourne and Palliser Bay had extra cops on duty around the clock looking out for him, but by far the most likely scenario was that Ross had shot himself. According to Alex, 'the boys' were pretty hopeful of finding Ross's body out there in the hills somewhere.

He locked eyes with me before adding that there was always the possibility the body would never be found, and warned me I should prepare myself for this. He left me with that thought after assuring me that everyone was doing the best they could to find Ross, and my job was to rest and get better. Right. Got it.

The exhilaration I felt after giving my statement was short-lived. In fact I was feeling pretty low and sorry for myself half an hour later when Gemma turned up. I knew how much she hated hospitals, so it was really big of her to come and check up on me, but no sooner had she appeared at the foot of the bed than she was eyeing the exit.

'Pure cotton. None of your winceyette shit,' she said, reaching into a Country Road bag and slapping a pair of eggshell-blue pyjamas on the bed. 'I didn't imagine you as a nightie girl,' she added, glaring so effectively at an approaching nurse that the poor girl did a U-turn and left without a word. 'Bad enough being in this place without having to walk around with your arse sticking out the back of a hospital gown for everyone to perv at.'

It was good to see her and I said so, and then noticed something odd about her.

'Are you wearing make-up?' I asked, and even I heard it sound like an accusation.

'No,' she shot back, glancing at the corridor as if she was about to make a run for it. 'Well, you know, just a bit of mascara.'

In all the years I'd known her, Gemma had never worn make-up. Gemma wearing mascara was as incongruous as an All Black wearing lipstick, and then I remembered Ma'a Nonu's penchant for eyeliner and softened my tone.

'It looks good on you,' I said, not knowing what else to say.

Gemma shot me a look to make sure I wasn't winding her up.

'Yeah, well, you know,' she mumbled. She stepped around to the side of the bed, making sure the exit was still in her sight. 'You sure as hell gave us a fright.' She looked me over like I was a rusty second-hand car someone was trying to palm off on her. 'You're going to come through this okay.'

I couldn't tell if it was a question or a statement. 'Yeah,' I responded, just as ambiguously. 'I'm fine. It's all superficial.'

I watched as she glared at the chair before cautiously lowering herself on to it. Any germs would have been frightened off by that look. She was breathing through her mouth to avoid smelling any stray hospital smells.

'I hate hospitals,' she muttered.

'No kidding?'

She laughed, and with that laugh all the tension went out of her.

Though she claimed to have asked nicely, I suspect Gemma had bullied the nurses into letting her make me a real cup of coffee, but however she achieved it, I was grateful. For a while there, sipping scalding black coffee and chatting to Gemma, it was almost like nothing had happened. It felt like a long time since she and I had just hung out and talked bullshit to each other. Actually, it had only been a few days, but everything that had happened to me before Ross felt like a lifetime ago. The ghost of Niki was still there between Gemma and me but it wasn't blocking our communication with each other. After a while, when I knew her guard was down, I brought up the mascara again.

Gemma coloured slightly. 'I'm meeting Wayne later for a drink.'

It took me a minute to remember who Wayne was. 'Robbie's friend? The guy you were such a bitch to that night at The Tasting Room?'

'I can't have been that much of a bitch,' she said. 'He's asked me out three times already. This is the first time I've agreed.'

I tried to remember how long it had been since Gemma had spent a night with someone, and as if reading my thoughts she admitted, 'I've almost forgotten what they look like without clothes on.' She grinned. 'Almost, but not quite.' And this time she really coloured up, as if she'd been caught in the act of imagining it. Maybe she had.

'Good for you, Gem,' I said, and meant it.

I asked her if there'd been any sightings of Ross, and I must've sounded okay because she answered plainly that there'd been no sightings yet, but no body found either, so until he was confirmed dead they were still working on the assumption he was alive.

We rabbited on for a bit and I basked in the lovely, warm, safe feeling of friendship. At some point I must have fallen asleep.

I was back there in the bunker on the hill, my wrist still tethered, the cold leeching into my bones. Ross squatted on his haunches close by, hunched over with his back to me, head bowed. There was something odd about the way he was crouched, and then I realised he was cosseting something in his lap. I strained to reach him but the handcuff snagged me back.

And then I heard it: a faint mewling sound, a tiny cry. Suddenly my heart swelled, then faltered in fear. What was he holding in his lap? What was it he was huddled over so possessively, so guiltily? What was making that sound?

Ross turned his face towards me but kept his body bent over his catch. He wore a shamefaced smirk. He lifted one hand and sniffed it. He seemed confused by the amount of blood sticking his fingers together. Now there was only the faintest mewling from his lap. I didn't want to see, didn't want to know what he had there. But he showed me anyway. A small cat, a kitten really, barely alive. He held it up by the scruff of its neck, and it hung there, limp, blood still dripping from its torn mouth, drooling on to its pale, exposed underbelly, the little pink teats stained a lurid red.

Now it was me doing the mewling. I tried to grab it off him. Snatched and snatched at it, but each time I lurched for it he swung his prize out of my reach. Although Ross's mouth wasn't moving I could hear him repeating over and over, 'I had to do it. It wasn't my fault. You made me do it.'

I jolted awake, knowing exactly what the dream meant. If Ross was still alive, Vex was in serious danger. I couldn't believe how stupid I'd been. Couldn't believe I hadn't thought of it sooner. Vex would be next on his list.

I was already halfway out of bed, but my next thought froze me to the spot. Maybe he already had her when he had me. Maybe he'd kept us both captive at the same time.

I remembered Ross's absence when I was up on the hill. He could already have had her tied up somewhere too – could have gone from one of us to the other. He was a lot of things, Ross, but he wasn't stupid, and he'd have known it was Vex who'd told me about him. He knew she was involved in Niki's scam. If he was hell-bent on punishing me, he'd want her to pay too.

I counted the days since I was abducted, and my heart sank. She couldn't have survived this long. I'd been close to death when I was found, and that was thirty-six hours ago.

My first thought was to ring Sean and tell him to go to Vex's place and make sure she was safe. If she wasn't there, he should check if anyone had seen her in the last few days. If the gods were on our side and she was okay, then someone needed to keep an eye on her until Ross, or Ross's body, was found.

I found my shoulder bag slung over the back of the armchair, and to my relief my phone was in it, fully charged. I tapped on Contacts and then double-clicked Favourites. There he was, still saved as 'X'. It really was time I did something about that.

I was about to press the Call icon, but paused. Sean was always my first thought and it was a habit I needed to break, for both our sakes. Seeing him slumped in the car, eyes closed, head against the window when I was being wheeled into the hospital – I'd known then that it was time to let him go. Let him get on with his life. Whether it was with the pixie or with someone else, it wasn't any of my business. I'd blown it with him. I'd thought what Sean and I had was unbreakable, and then when Niki died I'd recklessly thrown our love around the room, expecting it to hold together no matter what.

And it didn't. It shattered into pieces. I *could* drag Sean back into my world – I'd realised that when I saw him slumped against the car window – but I had no right to drag him anywhere. I let the image of Sean fade away, and with the fade it was almost as if I did let him go – as if I felt him slip out of me and away.

When Robbie's voice message kicked in, I almost expected to hear, 'Leave a message for Robbie or Wolf', since those two were hitting it off so well. I didn't want to leave a message. I thought about ringing Gemma, but then remembered the mascara. There was no way I could bring myself to interrupt her date with Wayne. Bugger it, I thought. I'll just have to go check on Vex myself.

It's almost as hard to get out of a hospital as it is to get in these days. My pleading and cajoling of the formidable ward sister did me no good at all. But then I remembered I wasn't in prison, they couldn't *make* me stay. In the end it was a simple matter of signing a form saying I was responsible for my own wellbeing and confirming that they'd advised me against leaving but that I was out of there anyway – or words to that effect.

Marcia called out to me as I waited for the lift and for a minute I thought I'd have to make a run for it, but all she did was hand me a paper bag of dressings and bottles of antibiotics and painkillers, and kiss me on the cheek. If she'd taken my arm and led me back to the nice, safe, white bed I think I'd have gone without a struggle, but she just wished me well, turned on her squeaky-soled shoes, and walked away.

I had no idea where Vex lived, but I knew someone who did.

CHAPTER 25

The Bookends blessed themselves as I approached so I guess I looked pretty bad. The taxi driver had been silent all the way from the hospital. If he had any questions about why I looked the way I did or why I was going from the hospital to a downtown strip joint, he didn't ask them. He didn't show any interest at all. I guess some people are just naturally inquisitive. Others – not so much.

The Bookends slid together like lift doors, effectively barring my entrance to the club, and I knew I didn't have a hope in hell of wrestling my way though them. I explained that I needed to know where Vex lived so I could check she was okay, but they stared at me like I'd risen from the dead – an overrated trick that, in my opinion, Christians are ridiculously impressed by.

Before I could take advantage of their superstition, one of them pushed a button and the little, highly strung manager swung out of a side door like a cuckoo out of a clock. I hadn't realised there was a door in the panelling until he popped out of it. Gavin waved his hands in a histrionic fashion and yelled at me.

'Go away. You look terrible. Even worse than before. You go now before I call police.'

I stood my ground, mostly because I had no choice. My reaction time was down, and I was still pretty unsteady on my feet. I had to choose carefully before making any fancy moves, like taking a step forward or back.

'Look, all I want is to check that Vex is okay,' I said.

'Vex good. Vex no problem. *You* problem. You go away,' he said, doing that sweeping gesture that I found really irritating. As Gavin advanced towards me I sensed a shuffle from the Bookends. I knew instinctively that if it really came down to it, they'd back me, not him, but I was hoping it wouldn't come to that. I held my hands up in peace-offering submission to discourage Gavin from stepping any closer.

'I'll leave if you let me see Vex. That's all I want. I just need to talk to her for five minutes, that's all, and then I promise I'll be out of here.'

Before Gavin could respond, the bigger of the two Bookends put a baseball glove-sized hand on his arm.

'Vex isn't here, sis,' he said to me. 'She hasn't been in all week.'

My heart thumped. There was no reason for him to lie.

'You go now. You got answer,' Gavin said, plucking the huge hand off his arm and glaring at the big guy for having dared to touch him.

At that moment, the main doors slid open and a couple of punters came out of the club. The Bookends moved aside to let them past, and in the brief moment before the doors closed behind them, I glimpsed Richard Brownlee through the haze of swirling lights, one buttock hitched up on a stool at the bar, his head tilted towards the girl serving him. Then the doors slid closed again. It was early evening, around eight, but the club was already pulsing with music, lights and sex.

'Have you tried to ring her? Have you checked she's okay?' I asked, but Gavin was already writing something on the back of a business card.

'This her address. You go see her at home. Tell her come to work,' he said, shoving the card at me. 'She not have phone so you tell her for me, "Come to work."'

I looked at the three guys. The massive Bookends and tiny Gavin in front formed a weird little tableau. A very odd kind of family. I decided now was not the time to lecture Gavin about giving out the girls' addresses.

'Let me get this straight,' I said. 'No one's seen Vex for a week?'

All three shook their heads in reply. There was a really bad feeling in the pit of my stomach. If Vex hadn't been seen all week, then she'd been missing since around the time Ross had kidnapped me.

The address Gavin had written on the card was in Hataitai, a ten-minute cab drive from the club. I thought again about ringing Gemma and telling her about my fears for Vex, but couldn't face the lecture I'd have to endure for having signed myself out of hospital.

I decided I'd check out Vex's house, that was all. Maybe she just had a cold or had decided she needed a break from doing blow jobs on guys at the club for a week or so, in which case I'd tell her about Ross, suggest she go away for a while, at least until he was caught or his body was found. If she wasn't at her house or there were signs of something wrong, then I'd call Gemma and get her to sound the alarm.

I'd failed Niki. I wasn't going to fail Vex.

I paid off the cab at the Hataitai shops, deciding to foot it the rest of the way. I don't know why I did that – some gut feeling that I should approach Vex's place unseen. It wasn't an easy decision. Despite the drugs I'd taken, the pain in my feet was excruciating.

I don't know what kind of house I'd assumed strippers lived in, but this wasn't it. It was a large, two-storeyed 1940s wooden number painted a lustrous white with mint-coloured window surrounds. The grey tile roof and white picket fence announced doctor or lawyer rather than sex worker, but, hey, who was I to say? The begonias edging the path had me checking the house number again, but sure enough, this was the address Gavin had written on the card.

I stopped outside a house diagonally across and along from Vex's. It had a driveway with enough head-high shrubbery for me to step into the shadows while I surveyed her house for signs of life. The outside lights were on, casting a pool of golden light on the begonias and the interior of the carport – empty except for a sack of kindling stacked neatly in one corner. A cool security light illuminated the far side of the house.

There were no interior lights on that I could see from this side of the road, but I did detect a faint glow on the lawn at the back, possibly created by a bathroom, porch or security light at the rear of the house. I'd need to get closer if I was to check that out.

There was nothing lying on the closely cropped lawn that would give a clue about the inhabitant, and the house itself gave nothing away. I still couldn't reconcile this as being the home of a teenage sex worker – couldn't picture Vex living here. There was no sign of life at all, no sounds of music, no banging of cooking utensils, no voices, no twitching curtain.

I was just about to cross the road towards the house when something caught my eye – a movement inside a dark blue

Honda Civic parked close to where I was standing, and in direct eyeline to Vex's house. It's true, you know, the hairs on the back of your neck do actually rise – well, that's what it feels like, anyway. Luckily, I was still hidden from view, my body tucked in behind the shrubbery.

I took a calming breath and angled my head for a better look. There was a man behind the wheel of the Civic, his collar pulled up to above his hairline and a beanie pulled down over his ears. He was slumped in the seat as if he'd been there a long time. His head was turned towards the house opposite. Vex's house.

It was Ross. It had to be Ross. My bowels loosened, and for one horrible moment I thought I was going to shit myself.

I patted my pockets, cursing that I had little on me in the way of a weapon, defensive or otherwise. The packet of breathmints and my wallet just weren't going to cut it. My phone wasn't much use either – I couldn't risk using it this close to Ross. I thought of knocking on the door of the house whose driveway I was huddled in, but didn't want to risk Ross driving off while I was trying to explain things to a nervy neighbour. The way I looked now, most likely the occupants wouldn't even open the door to me.

I was determined not to give up what might be the only chance to capture Ross. If he was never caught, I'd spend the rest of my life looking over my shoulder for him. No way. I looked around the driveway for anything I might be able to use as a weapon. Nothing. Then I spotted a garden rake leaning up against the fence. Not exactly my weapon of choice, but probably more effective than breathmints. The wooden handle felt good, solid in my hand, if a bit unwieldy. My only advantage was the element of surprise. I knew I'd have to make the most of that. I gripped the handle and readied myself.

All I had to do was get to the driver's door, throw it open, and smash Ross in the face with the metal end of the rake. Apart from scratching at his neck with his index finger, he hadn't moved since I'd spotted him. I was confident he hadn't seen me. The important thing was not to hesitate.

First, I'd have to cover the distance from the driveway to his car door without him hearing me. I figured it at ten paces. I'd squeezed my bandaged feet into the rubber-soled sneakers Robbie had left under the hospital bed for me. Those ten paces would hurt but, as long as I didn't yelp, at least the run would be quiet. It was now or never. I steeled myself, gripping the handle of the rake, waiting for my breathing to steady. I could do this. Ten steps, that's all it would take.

The night was unusually still for Wellington, and even the sound of my breathing seemed loud. No cars had driven past in the ten minutes or so I'd been sheltered in the driveway. There'd been no sound or movement from Vex's place, either. My knees were going a bit wobbly and my feet hurt like bastards. I knew I had to make the run now. Clutching the rake in my right hand, I braced myself. Five, four, three — At 'two' the rake was wrenched out of my hand and a palm smacked across my mouth.

'What the hell do you think you're doing?' Gemma hissed at me, and smartly removed her hand to avoid being bitten.

Relief and confusion hit me in equal measure. I blurted out about Ross being in the car and Vex being in danger, but I could sense straight away that I'd got something terribly wrong. And when 'Ross' climbed out of his car and walked towards us, even I could see it wasn't Ross. In fact, sandy-haired and freckled, he was pretty much the antithesis of Ross, in appearance anyway. And when he eyed up the rake and followed that with an amused look at me, I figured his personality type was pretty far removed from Ross's as well.

I hardly needed her to spell it out for me, but being Gemma she did it anyway.

'The night you were abducted, Sean had Vex picked up and taken somewhere safe. She's going to stay hidden until we're sure she's no longer in danger. Young Detective Williams has been keeping an eye on her house in case Ross turns up here.'

I smiled sheepishly at him, and from behind Gemma's back he returned the smile.

'Ryan's not the sort of guy to hold a grudge, but he might have resented a rake in the kisser, and he might have even been forced to lay a complaint against you if he knew for sure that assaulting an officer was your intention.'

I opened my mouth to speak, but Gemma's look made me shut it again just as quickly.

'Which is why,' she continued, 'Ryan is relieved to hear that smacking him one was most definitely *not* what you had in mind, Diane.'

Gemma stepped back so that Ryan and I were face to face. We must've looked like two kids caught scrapping in the playground with the teacher insisting we shake hands and make up. Ryan waited politely for my apology, which I offered wholeheartedly. He didn't seem too perturbed by his close shave with the rake, but as I turned away I caught a gesture from Gemma to Ryan that she owed him one, so maybe he was playing it cooler than he felt.

I assumed Ryan had spotted me and phoned Gemma, but she admitted she had a 'source' in the hospital under strict instructions to ring her if I freaked out, did a runner, or otherwise caused a ruckus. She added that there was an office sweepstake at Central on odds that I'd do one of the latter two. I didn't know whether to be flattered or insulted.

'I found the cabbie who'd taken you to the club, and the boys on the door were very helpful,' she explained, eyeing me a little suspiciously. 'You've got a fan club of two there, I think.'

'Sorry, Gem. I freaked out at the thought Ross might go after Vex. And, you know, I didn't do so good looking out for Niki . . . ' I left the rest unsaid.

'You could have rung me, you know,' she said.

'I didn't want to interrupt your date.'

She made a scoffing sound that I wasn't sure how to interpret. 'Go home, Di,' she said. 'You look like shit. I'll put someone else on here and Ryan will take you home.'

I started to argue that I could find my own way home, but she gave me a flat look that I knew not to argue with. Ryan opened the door for me, and I carefully moved his jacket and MP3 player into the back before folding my tired, bruised body into the front seat. The interior of the car smelt of mandarins. Either Ryan had been having a healthy snack, or he used a particularly fruity kind of aftershave. I listened to Gemma and Ryan's murmuring outside the car for another five minutes. I felt comfortable and comforted in the car.

I woke with a start as the car door slammed shut on a waft of cold night air and coffee. Ryan handed me a steaming polystyrene cup. He used one free hand and his teeth to rip open a packet of biscuits.

'I got you a latte with one sugar – I figured that had all the main food types covered,' he said, offering me the packet. Chocolate chippies. I nearly kissed him.

'Thanks,' I said, already in the process of dunking. 'Sorry about falling asleep like that.'

'Hey, it's preferable to smashing me with a rake,' he said, firing the engine up and easing out of the forecourt, coffee in one hand, chocolate chippie clenched between his front teeth. He slid his eyes at me in a way I knew meant he was just winding me up.

We didn't say much the rest of the way to my place. He told me he'd been instructed to stay parked outside my house until morning, by which time Gemma would have organised someone to keep an eye on me until Ross was found. I didn't object. In truth I was relieved to know Ryan would be nearby. Ross walked away from killing me once. It's never smart to push your luck. Ryan pointed out, without sounding in the least bit judgemental, that there had been a plan in place for keeping a watch on me once I was released from hospital, but that I'd jumped the gun a bit by releasing myself before they'd put that plan into action.

He made no comment when I tilted the pot plant up for the key underneath, nor when I put the key back under it, but once inside he suggested I find a new 'hiding place' for it tomorrow. He managed not to sneer at the phrase. Ryan walked ahead of me through the house, opening all the doors and checking each room thoroughly, even the wardrobe and broom cupboards, and then he swished back the shower curtain and checked there too. The sound of his size 12 boots walking through the house was reassuring. By the time he called, 'all clear' I was feeling safe and confident there was no one in my little house except us.

The house search was undoubtedly just for my benefit, but I was grateful for his committed performance. I told him he was welcome to stay in the house rather than in his car but he declined, saying he was better out there. It was one of those ambiguous remarks I would normally question, but not this time. I was keen to climb into bed and sleep. I offered him anything he might like to take from the fridge, but he didn't seem tempted by week-old milk and a couple of suspect jars of pickles. Clearly a fussy eater.

As he headed down the path to his car, I locked the front door behind him just like he'd told me to, and even double-checked the back door to make sure it too was bolted. The bedroom seemed very empty without Wolf. It's a sad state of affairs when it's your dog you miss from your bedroom and not a man. And in thinking that, I realised I missed Robbie. How was it possible to miss him when I'd never had him?

In the bathroom I changed into my favourite old pyjamas and carefully brushed my teeth, avoiding the cracked cuspid and split lip, and all the time making sure I didn't catch sight of myself in the mirror.

The bedroom window was covered in Wolf's slobber and scratches from his frenzy at the sight of Ross attacking me. I'd need to replace the curtains at some time too – the bottoms had been shredded by his claws and teeth. Outside I could see Ryan was settled back in his car, chomping through on his packet of biscuits. He gave me a friendly little wave and I waved back, before pulling the curtains closed.

I gulped a glass of delicious water, filled a litre bottle from the tap for beside the bed, collected up the cordless phone, and listened to my messages while I climbed in between the cool, fresh sheets. There was only the one message from Smithy telling me that the John Doe skull Robbie had dropped off was completely intact and showed no signs of bullet holes or blows from either blunt or sharp objects. On the strength of that and his fuller examination of the rest of the remains, he was calling it an accidental death. He waffled on uncomfortably for a while, admitting how worried he'd been about me, and ended by saying he looked forward to seeing my lovely, frowning face again as soon as I was feeling better. He even offered to take me out to dinner which, given my impressions about his latest diet craze, I wouldn't be in a rush to take him up on.

Actually, hearing his stumbling but clearly genuine words of concern, I had to fight the urge to weep. I was afraid that if I started I might never stop. The messages Robbie had left the night I was abducted were gone, in fact there were no messages before this one of Smithy's. Robbie must have erased them. That was okay. I didn't want to hear his worried voice asking where I was. I didn't want to be taken back to that night in any way, shape or form. I was just about to put the phone down on the bedside table when it rang, loud enough to make me jump and my entire body flush with fright. It was Robbie.

His voice was calm, and he managed not to sound accusing as he explained that he'd phoned the hospital to check on how I was and had been surprised to hear I'd signed myself out. He didn't give me a hard time about it, and I was immensely, pathetically grateful for that. Again I felt that damn crying thing coming on, and had to bite my bottom lip to stop it happening.

In the silence, Robbie apologised for having Wolf at his place and offered to bring him over. I managed to say it was okay, and explained that I had a policeman parked outside the house keeping an eye on me, and since there were only a couple of hours until sunrise I reckoned I was fine. I badly needed to sleep. I'd been knocking back painkillers every thirty minutes or so, and they'd left me more than a little light-headed. I wouldn't have been surprised if an entire herd of wildebeest wearing techno-coloured nighties had wandered into the bedroom. I might have overdone the painkillers a bit.

I could feel myself drifting, and it was most pleasurable. Robbie told me he'd received an email about the John Doe notebook and tie we'd found. He'd put a photo of them up on the police website, and a woman had emailed to say she knew who the items belonged to. Robbie had arranged to meet her and thought I might like to come with him. At least I think Robbie said all this, but given my painkiller count I may have dreamt it. Either way, Robbie's voice was like warm candle wax in my ear. I must have fallen asleep with the phone still attached to it.

I lurched awake with that awful, heart-thumping knowledge I'd been woken by a sound. What was it? What had I heard? I lay completely still, listening intently. The loudest sound was my breathing. I could hear the scratching of a kowhai branch on the bathroom window. That wasn't what had woken me. I knew that sound. It was so familiar I usually just zoned it out.

The fridge made a low humming noise, and the house creaked as old houses do, particularly in Wellington where there's always wind. Nothing. Just the thudding of my heart. A lone dog barked in the distance. Still nothing. I'd almost convinced myself I'd imagined the noise when I heard it again. This time I knew immediately what it was – the squeak of a rubber-soled shoe on wooden floorboards. And I knew exactly where the sound came from – the hall outside my bedroom.

Someone was in the house, walking very slowly towards me. Ross. This had to be Ross. But how the hell had he got past Ryan? Given the amount of drug overdosage I'd engaged in it was hard to tell how long I'd been asleep. It felt like five minutes, but from the faint blur of light through the curtains I suspected at least a couple of hours had passed and it was now very early dawn.

I knew I had to move fast or I'd freeze and be unable to move at all. If I could make it to the window I'd only have to pull the curtains back and wave at Ryan, and I knew he'd be in like a shot. Unless, of course, he'd fallen asleep. Another creak from the hallway, closer this time to the bedroom door, almost had me losing my nerve. I thanked the gods I'd closed the bedroom door. It's not something I usually do. I slid out of bed and, keeping my body low to the floor, ran in a crouch across the room to the window. In one movement I stood to my full height and yanked the curtain open.

Ryan's car was gone. I couldn't believe it. Ryan had driven off, abandoned me, and now Ross was in the house. There was no way I could wrestle the window open and escape – I'd accidentally painted it shut the previous summer and had never got around to fixing it.

There was no time to whimper. No time to let fear take over. I crouched again, listening hard, and keeping a close watch on the little gap under the closed door. The security light over the back porch threw a faint light down the length of the hall, and I knew I'd see the shadow of feet when Ross was directly outside the bedroom door. If my hearing was accurate I figured that last creak put him half a dozen steps away from the door.

Another creak, and my stomach turned to ice. Between me and the door there was nothing that even vaguely resembled a weapon – there wasn't even a photo on the wall that I could smash him over the head with. Cautiously, I edged my way along the wall towards the door, figuring I could at least hide behind it. It wasn't the greatest plan I'd ever had, but it was *a* plan and it kept my brain ticking as I figured out if I could reach the door before he did. My fingertips brushed the gib board as I crept along the wall, the soft *tsk* of my bare feet sounding as loud as gunshots to me.

Hanging on the back of the door was a terry-cloth dressing gown. I used it to wipe the sweat from my face as I flattened my back against the wall. Optimistically, I searched the dressing gown's oversized pockets, but there was nothing except an old scrunched-up tissue. It didn't quite cut it as my weapon of choice. The door handle slowly turned. My only hope was that he'd push the door wide open and wouldn't see me tucked in behind it. If Ross turned around and saw me, I was done for. I looked at the dressing gown still clutched in my hands. If I moved fast enough, then maybe, just maybe, with the element of surprise on my side, I could bring him to ground. Though the dressing gown was one of those luxurious deep-pile numbers, it was probably not quite fluffy enough to stop a bullet, and I assumed Ross was still carrying his Browning semi-auto. If I could land him so his body was between me and the gun, I might have a chance. Not a very big one, but right now I'd take any chance I could get.

The door started to open. I pressed my back against the wall, planted my bandaged feet apart for balance, clutched my dressing gown at the ready, and held my breath. The door opened.

CHAPTER 26

By my reckoning Ross was a good six foot and weighed in at about seventy-seven kilos. He didn't look all that fit but he was solid, and I knew from experience that he delivered a dirty punch with plenty of force behind it – which is why I was proud of myself for bringing him to ground so easily. Admittedly I had surprise on my side. I jumped him from behind, threw the dressing gown over his head, and leapt on his back in one single, painful, ungraceful movement. Now here he was pegged to the ground with me on his back pummelling his head into the floorboards, and his only resistance was a bit of half-hearted leg and arm flailing.

Niki used to put up a stronger fight than this when we

play-fought, and she'd been a lot younger and lighter than Ross. Something was wrong here. I stopped thumping his head against the floor and pulled the dressing gown back. There was enough cold, blue, early morning light for me to see quite clearly that this was someone younger and skinnier than Ross. Someone who didn't know how to fight.

I flipped him over. It was Stoke. His nose was flattened and bloodied and he was having trouble breathing, but I had little sympathy for him.

'Get off! Get off me! I can't breathe!' he gasped.

I shifted my weight from his chest to his stomach. Even that concession wasn't enough to stop him grizzling about me trying to kill him.

He was starting to look a bit waxy, so I eased my weight off a little more.

'What the hell are you doing here?' I dug my knees into his ribs. 'Why'd you break into my house, arsehole?'

'I wasn't going to rob you,' he sulked. He clearly felt the house-breaking suggestion was an uncalled-for slur on his character. 'Well, not much. I just wanted, like, something of Bonnie's. Something of hers I could keep to remember her, type of thing,' he mumbled. 'I'd of looked after it.'

I studied him, trying to figure this guy out. Vex had said he was in love with Niki, and a crazy thought was developing in my slowed-down brain.

'I thought it was a good time to get something, that's all,' he said. 'With you in hospital and that scary bloody dog of yours off with your new cop boyfriend.' He spent the next couple of minutes coughing, while I waited impatiently, gathering my thoughts.

'Please,' he managed between coughs, 'please, get off of me.'

I wasn't prepared to sit my butt anywhere lower on his anatomy, so I lifted my weight, but kept my knees angled into his ribs just in case. He was at an obvious disadvantage, prone like this, but even carrying injuries I knew I was in no danger from this guy.

'The key was just sitting there under the pot plant,' he whined, which sounded like the old 'you were asking for it' argument to me. Normally I'd have pointed this out, but right now I had more important things on my mind.

'Why did you want something of Niki's?' I asked.

'She wouldn't of minded. I'm not saying she owed me or anything like that, but you know, I did get a sort of justice for her . . . ' He started in on the coughing again, and while he did that, I let the realisation dawn on me. I had to wait until he'd finished that racket before I could ask for confirmation. What a drama queen. A bit of pummelling and head-bashing, and the guy turns into a hypochondriac!

'You killed Snow, didn't you,' I said. It wasn't a question.

'Yeah.' He threw me a bashful smile as if I'd just patted him on the back for a job well done. I wasn't prepared to go that far, but I did climb off him and offer a hand to help him up. He mistook the gesture and gave me an affable handshake.

'Get up,' I said, gruffly. 'Go fix up your nose while I make us coffee.'

I heard him running the water in the bathroom. I'd never realised before how beautiful the sound of running water is, and I lost thirty seconds of my life listening to the exquisiteness of it. I heard Stoke yelp as he tried to put his nose back into shape, which wasn't nearly as pleasant a sound as the water. I still couldn't breathe through my own nose, so I knew what it felt like. Sean's coffee perc was hooting by the time Stoke entered, looking very sorry for himself. I ignored the look. He settled in at the table, and I put a mug of coffee in front of him. I had a lot of questions and was still trying to figure out which one to open the batting with, but Stoke made it easy by starting right on in.

'Snow deserved to die for what he did to Bonnie,' he said, and ducked me a complicit look. 'I know her name was Niki, eh, but I knew her as Bonnie.'

I nodded my understanding, not wanting to break the spell.

'That's why I killed Snow the same way he killed her. I wanted him to feel what she felt.'

He took a sip of his coffee, and I lowered myself into the chair opposite him, keeping my actions slow and quiet like you do with an animal that spooks easily.

'Vex told me Snow was mouthing off about killing Bon, like he was *the man*, you know?' he said, blinking rapidly. I couldn't tell if he was fighting tears or his smashed nose was bothering him. 'As soon as I found out he'd done it, you know, killed her, I was going to do him straight up, but Vex was like, "No, no, you'll just get into trouble yourself, it's not worth it", and all that blah blah and for a while I didn't do it, and then one day I just like snapped and thought, whoa!'

I had to concentrate to follow his scattergun dialogue with its odd tics, voice impersonations, and half-finished sentences, but the message was clear enough. Stoke had killed Snow as revenge for Niki's murder.

'Vex is a cool chick you know, and she really loved Bon–, I mean Niki.' He glanced nervously at me, unsure how much about my little sister I knew. I knew a lot more than I did a week ago. 'Bonnie had a bit of a drug problem, eh.'

It wasn't a question but I nodded anyway, and he relaxed and took a sip of his coffee.

'Vex was trying to help her with that,' he added.

There was no reason I could think of why Stoke would lie, but I wanted to be sure.

'Tell me how you killed Snow,' I said, keeping my voice easy, my body relaxed.

Stoke took another sip of coffee, then started right in like he was telling me a bedtime story. 'Well, first off, I wanted to hear it from the horse's mouth, so I drove him up to the golf course where she was found, and I asked him straight up, I said, "Did you kill Bonnie?"' He threw me an apologetic look. 'I called her Bonnie to him because that's what he called her.'

I nodded again and just kept nodding to encourage him to continue. I didn't trust myself to speak, anyway.

'He 'fessed right up. Like Vex said, he was proud of doing it. Then he got out and just stood there, looking around and grinning to hisself, like probably remembering it. And I just got like *the frenzy* and I stuck him in the back. I didn't know until right when I did it that I would, you know, do *it*.'

I remembered Smithy's 'frenzied and unexpected' description of the attack on Snow and made a mental note to tell him he was right.

'He so wasn't expecting it.' He took an enthusiastic sip of his coffee and smiled at me, as if I'd congratulated him. He must have been telepathic.

We sat in silence for a minute.

'And then you dropped his body out of the car in Cuba Street?' I offered.

'Yeah. I meant it like it was a message, leaving him there with the rubbish and all that. That's what he was, you know? Rubbish.' He grinned, but then his face fell. 'But I don't think anyone got it. And there were recycle bins out, so maybe people thought I meant something like he might come back again or some reincarnation shit or something.'

'I got the "rubbish" message,' I said. Well, I had!

His face brightened. 'You did?' He nodded, pleased with his work. 'Cool,' he added, rubbing his hand up and down his thigh and nodding enthusiastically.

We sat in silence for a while. Then, with a surreptitious glance at me, he started up again.

'I thought it would be, like, cooler than it was. I thought I'd feel something like retro-whatsit.' He looked to me for help.

'Retribution,' I offered.

'Yeah, retro-bution. I thought I'd feel the retro-bution, but it didn't work out like that. I didn't feel, like . . . righteous.'

He was reliving the moment of Snow's death. It felt almost pornographic to watch him.

'But, like, in the end, I don't have a regret for it. He shouldn't of done that to Bonnie,' he said. He drained his coffee, at peace with himself. His personal moral compass had swung in his own favour, and he was content.

'You loved her, didn't you? You loved Niki,' I said.

He used the back of his hand to wipe the coffee grinds from his lips. 'She didn't feel that way about me, but that's okay,' he explained, simply. 'I wasn't in her league.'

I let that sit quietly between us. There was nothing I could say, and he didn't seem to expect me to contradict him. When a decent interval had passed, I tried another question.

'Do you have any idea who ordered the hit on Niki?'

He went very still like a dog does when it thinks it's heard a sound. 'Snow did it. I thought you knew that,' he said, confused by my ignorance.

'I know he was the one who stabbed her,' I said. 'But I think someone else paid him to do it. Snow . . . ' I hesitated, trying to find a way to refer to the recording Gemma made without actually mentioning it. 'Snow told someone that he was just "the enforcer", which means someone else was behind it. For a while I thought that someone was Chris Ross. But now, well, now I'm not so sure.'

He studied me for a long time before pushing the empty mug across the table towards me.

'I don't know anything about that,' he said.

'Snow didn't say anything? Before you killed him?'

He thought about that before answering. 'We didn't talk much,' he admitted. 'I just asked him if he did it and he said "Yeah", and that was about it.'

I poured him a second cup and pushed the sugar bowl closer.

He ladled four heaped teaspoons into his cup while I sipped my coffee and thought some more.

'I'm sure someone was behind her killing,' I said, but it sounded like I was trying to convince myself. Actually, I was wondering if I'd got stuck in that tunnel vision thing cops always warn about. 'I just can't believe Snow would have killed her without good reason. I mean, he was making a lot of money out of Niki's blackmailing scam. Plus she was paying him for her drugs. It wasn't in his interest to kill her.'

Stoke didn't respond. He seemed less concerned by the contradiction in Snow's motivation than I was. Then again, Stoke had killed the man in revenge for murdering Niki, so he had more invested in believing in Snow's singular guilt.

'He said he hated working for a chick,' Stoke added, colouring up in anger. 'He called Bonnie the c word.' Stoke paused to rein in his anger. 'But she wasn't that – she was an angel,' he summed up with conviction. He said it without a flicker of sarcasm or irony. He said it and he meant it, and I saw that he truly did love her. In every way I could think of Stoke and I were worlds apart, but we both loved Niki and that bonded us. Love of her was the only thing about Niki that lived on. She was gone, gone, gone – but as long as we loved her, some part of her still existed. I loved her. Stoke loved her. *We* kept her alive. I hunched my body towards him until I'd captured his full attention.

'You see, Stoke,' I said, 'I was thinking that one of the guys Niki was blackmailing – Ross or maybe Richard Brownlee or some other guy that I don't even know about yet – maybe they decided they'd had enough of being blackmailed by Niki, and offered Snow more money to kill her than she paid him to work for her.'

I could see Stoke was struggling to keep up with this. He wasn't the sharpest knife in the drawer, but in his defence I'd smashed his head around a fair bit, and it was early in the morning. He smiled sheepishly at me, as if he'd failed a spelling test.

'Nah, I can't see it,' he admitted. 'Sorry.'

Not that I rated Stoke's opinion all that highly, but I had to admit, I might have gotten it wrong. Maybe there was no one else involved, it had simply been Snow's idea to kill Niki. I thought back to Gemma pretending to hire him to run down her fictitious husband. Snow had described in ghastly detail how he'd killed Niki. He'd made no mention of anyone else's involvement. In fact he'd been keen to take all the credit himself.

Belatedly, I realised I should have been writing Stoke's statement down as he talked. I scrabbled around in my bag until I located my notepad and a pen. Stoke was studying me. I could see he was working up the courage to ask something.

'What?'

'What happened to you?' he asked. 'Your face and shit.'

'It's a long story,' I said. I flicked through the GST workings and shopping lists looking for the first empty page on which to write Stoke's statement. The last page I'd written on was from the night I'd made notes while talking to the Bookends at the strip club. That was on the very first night – the same day I'd heard from Sean that Snow had been murdered. I read what I'd written and let out a little yelp of surprise. Stoke looked at me expectantly.

'You're coming with me,' I told him.

It said a lot about Stoke that he didn't ask where we were going. It said even more about him that he looked quite happy to be going there.

CHAPTER 27

Gemma's eyes shifted from me to Stoke to me again, and then with a theatrical sigh she stepped back to allow us entry. Stoke bobbed his head nervously, and she returned his anxious glance with a steely glare. When I introduced her as Detective Patterson I saw his shoulders slump. It had probably only now occurred to him that I was handing him over to the cops. Gemma indicated the couch, and Stoke sat with knees pressed together and his head bowed. Gemma rolled her eyes but I think that was just for my benefit.

'Stoke's got something he wants to tell you, Detective,' I said meaningfully. 'Something that if he voluntarily confesses to, then things might go a lot easier for him further down the track.'

Gemma's arms were crossed over her chest in the classic 'I'm giving away nothing' pose. She stared at me for a long time, and then very slowly turned her attention to Stoke. There was a pause in which I assumed Stoke was considering whether he should confess to killing Snow or make a run for it. I was really hoping he'd do the former.

But Stoke wasn't considering either of these options; he was thinking about something else entirely.

'Could I have something to eat?' he asked, and when we both stared at him, gobsmacked, he added, 'It's just that I'm starving and I haven't had any breakfast yet.'

Gemma's eyes did that eyes-popping-out-of-the-head thing that I thought only cartoons could do. I shot Stoke a warning look.

'Tell Gemma what you did, Stoke. Tell her what you did for Niki. And while you're doing that I'll go see if there's anything in Gemma's fridge to eat.'

Gemma shot me a look of outrage but I ignored it.

The murmur of their voices filtered through to the kitchen while I made some toast and a cup of tea. The bread looked a bit mouldy but not once I'd cut into it strategically. Despite Gemma's hard-arse demeanour, I could hear her voice was quite gentle as she talked to Stoke. Needless to say, there wasn't a tea tray, Gemma not being the Sunday-brunch-in-bed kind of girl, but I found a semi-clean breadboard to carry the breakfast on. Stoke looked pretty depressed, but when I placed the board on the coffee table he cheered up immensely.

Gemma was on the phone asking for a car to come and collect an arrest from her house. She had that barely suppressed excitement that always accompanies a collar. Having a crim confess a major crime is definitely a high point in a cop's life, and though I was pleased for Gemma, I felt a bit like a well-trained hunting dog who'd just delivered her a dead duck. The image was tragically apt for poor old Stoke. It felt mean handing him over for doing something I'd only dreamt of but never had the guts to carry through. Instead, I poured him a cup of tea and offered the plate of strategically cut-up bits of toast.

A little flush of pleasure bloomed on his cheeks. 'Oh, cute,' he said. 'You made shapes out of them. No one's ever done that for me before.'

Gemma's mouth opened, but I shot her a look and thankfully she shut it again. What the hell. Let him think I'd cut toast shapes for him. He'd taken out my sister's killer because he loved her, and now he was going to prison for it. Shaping toast was the least I could do in return.

Gemma poured herself a cup of tea but wisely declined the toast. She appeared relaxed but her body was on alert, keeping an eye on Stoke in case he suddenly had a change of heart and either made a run for it, or jumped us. Neither seemed very likely to me. He was much more interested in breakfast, and rather tragically seemed to genuinely enjoy our company.

'So how come you two hooked up at this ungodly hour of the morning, anyway?' Gemma asked, eyeing me over the rim of her cup. 'Last I heard you were tucked up in bed.'

Stoke shot me a look. He'd admitted to Gemma that he'd murdered Snow, but had clearly failed to mention the bit about breaking into my house. I spoke up before the urge took him to confess. Stoke was definitely a spontaneous-combustion kind of guy who needed to be carefully watched. I reckoned he was in enough trouble without landing himself a breaking and entering charge.

'Stoke came to see me at home early this morning,' I said, avoiding his eyes. 'He wanted to give himself up for Snow's . . . death,' I explained, carefully avoiding incriminating words like 'killing' or 'murder'. 'And he asked me to help with that.'

Stoke looked momentarily confused but then grinned at me around his toast slice.

'Yeah,' he agreed, nodding good-naturedly.

Gemma wasn't buying it, but she let it go.

'What happened to Ryan?' I said, hearing the peevish tone in my voice. 'I thought he was staying outside my place until morning.'

Gemma hesitated, glancing in Stoke's direction, as if weighing up what she could say in front of him. I felt a little frisson of premonition.

'What?'

'Ross is dead. His body was found about an hour after Ryan dropped you off home.'

I felt the relief flood over me. 'How?'

Stoke seemed to have zoned us out completely. I watched him claim another piece of toast. He was alternating between honey and Marmite – and here I'd thought that loving Niki was the only thing we had in common. It helped to watch his rhythmical, enthusiastic chomping while I waited for the details of Ross's death.

'He blew his brains out. With Ross dead there was no reason for Ryan to stay outside your place any more, so we sent him home.' She stared meaningfully at Stoke. 'Maybe we should have left him there since you never can tell who might try and break into your house.'

I half expected Stoke to immediately confess, but he seemed to be enjoying his breakfast too much to have picked up his cue. Gemma turned back to me.

'Ryan decided you needed your sleep more than you needed to hear about Ross being dead, so he didn't wake you.'

'That was nice of him,' interjected Stoke, smiling benignly.

Gemma shook her head, staring at Stoke with an expression of amused bewilderment.

I wanted to laugh, but I had something on my mind that I needed to work through. I hadn't come here just so Stoke could confess – that was a bonus gift for Gemma, really. I came here because I had a suspicion about Niki's death. Something I'd noted down way back when I met the Bookends on my first visit to the strip club.

I asked Gemma if she'd edited anything out of the recording she made of her 'conversation' with Snow. She glanced uneasily in Stoke's direction, not keen to talk about it in front of him, but when she saw he was happily pouring himself another cup of tea and seemed completely uninterested in our conversation, she relented.

'Yeah, sure, I did,' she admitted. 'You have to remember, when I gave you the tape you didn't even know Niki was turning tricks. You sure as hell didn't know she was running a dirty sex scam and blackmailing her clients – so, yeah, I edited those references out and just gave you the last bit of the recording. Even then, you learnt more than you wanted to,' she reminded me.

'Have you got it? The full tape? The unedited one?'

She jutted her lower lip out. 'I think so. Yeah. Sure.'

Stoke stopped sipping and chewing. His eyes shifted from me to Gemma. He could feel the tension. Not surprising since I was standing with my fists clenched.

Gemma was looking at me too. 'What? You mean, now? Can't it wait?'

'No.' It sure as hell couldn't.

For what felt like a full minute Gemma just stared at me. Then, with a shrug, she left the room, returning with an old-fashioned cassette tape and a pair of cracked vinyl-padded headphones which she jacked into the stereo.

Stoke must have heard something that neither Gemma nor I did, or maybe he sensed something. His head spun round to face the door, and a split second later there was a knock. A knock like only a policeman can make. Stoke looked at Gemma, a frightened look, but as I slotted the tape into the deck I saw Gemma give him a reassuring pat on the shoulder. He relaxed and helped himself to the last piece of toast while she let the uniformed cops in. I put the cans over my ears. The silence was sudden and complete.

I listened to the full tape of the conversation between Gemma and Snow as a soundscape to the cops taking Stoke into custody. The younger of the two cops wanted to handcuff him but Gemma motioned that it wasn't necessary, and both Stoke and I were grateful for that. Even though the cop's handcuffs were metal and not the plastic type favoured by Ross, I'd broken out in a sweat as soon as they appeared.

I'd listened all the way through the unedited tape and had reached the section where Snow described Niki's *Good Luk!* undies when Stoke was led to the door. I didn't need to hear any of that again and flicked the stop button and removed the cans. Stoke offered me a rueful smile and a wee wave, and I gave the same right back to him. Gemma closed the door behind them and turned to look at me.

'Jesus,' she said. 'You look like you've seen a ghost.'

'Not exactly,' I said. 'But I *do* know who killed Niki.'

CHAPTER 28

I wasn't allowed to confront the person charged with procuring my sister's death until after the guilty plea was sorted out with various lawyers, and once the legal bigwigs had argued over the finer points of the Crimes Act 1961, number 43, section 66, 1 (d). Sean tried to insist on coming to the prison with me, but that was something I had to do on my own. I needed to hear the confession face to face. That was all I needed from Niki's killer. Nothing more.

Prisons always remind me of health camps. Maybe it's that 1950s colour scheme, or maybe it's because I've loathed health camps ever since Dad sent me to one when Niki was born. When Mum died, that is. I waited in the barren dining room for the prisoner to be brought through, mouth-breathing to avoid the stench of sweat and overcooked corned beef.

At first I didn't recognise Vex without her bronze ponytail. Her hair was now cut short and framed her face in a little bob the colour of dishwater. Dressed in avocado-green prison overalls, she looked like a ten-year-old. Ten going on eighty. Those grey eyes had a blankness to them I hadn't noticed before, but maybe they'd always been like that.

The prison guard remained by the closed door as Vex approached the table and sat opposite me. This meeting was part of her 'deal' with police, and she looked relaxed and ready to see it through. She didn't smile or act like we were friends, and I was pleased about that. I sipped my bottled water and worked at keeping my heart rate and voice low and steady. An orange plastic mug of water had been placed in the centre of the table. She took a sip, and then rolled the mug between her palms before finally looking up at me.

'So, where do you want me to start?' she asked.

It was my cue and I jumped right in. 'It was your scam wasn't it? The whole sex and blackmailing thing – it was yours, not Niki's.'

I didn't tell her that I'd figured out *she* was the 'chick boss' Snow had referred to moments before he was killed – not Niki, as Stoke had presumed. Didn't tell her that the beautiful Samoan Bookends at the club had given me the clue that very first night when I'd written 'Snow – Vex' into my notepad. They'd told me the two were connected but I hadn't put it together. Didn't tell her I should have guessed she was the puppetmeister when I saw Stoke follow in her wake up Molesworth Street.

'Sure. Niki worked for me,' she said, tilting her chin up proudly. 'The deal with Niki was that she'd front it – she'd get to act like she was the big "boss lady".' She waggled her head sarcastically. 'I didn't want anyone to know I was running things, so it was a win-win.' Vex offered me a long, amused look, edging on a sneer, but I refused to be baited. I wanted to hear everything from her, which meant I needed to keep my cool.

'She wanted to develop her "business skills" as she called them.'

I could tell she was quoting Niki. I could just imagine my little sister saying that. We both knew Niki had been practising her "business skills" because she wanted to impress me.

'Whatever,' she laughed. 'It wasn't her *business* skills that made me money.' She shook her head and laughed again. 'That girl made me rich doing things with men I sure as hell wasn't ever prepared to do.'

I kept my voice steady. 'And when she tried to get out of it, you had Snow kill her.'

Vex opened her mouth to answer, but the thrumming of a bee against the window pane distracted her. She turned to watch the bee batter its little body against the glass in a futile attempt to escape. Finally, she turned back to answer me, but some of the heat, the sarcasm, had gone out of her voice.

'It wasn't quite like that,' she said. 'It wasn't like I planned it from the start. Niki just got so uppity. She kept talking about this legit business you and her were going into.' She shrugged before adding. 'It really annoyed me.'

Vex drained her glass, and turned again to watch the bee buffet against the pane. I took the opportunity to take in a deep breath, not trusting myself to speak until I'd gathered myself together. Niki had been brutally murdered because she'd 'annoyed' Vex? The seconds ticked by while I tried to focus on my next question, but Vex, eyes still on the bee, started up again of her own accord.

'Actually, she hated doing it, but she was good at the sex stuff, I'll give her that. Even the really ghastly stuff. She made me a shitload of money.' Again, the little shrug. 'She was using every day, but that suited me as long as the clients didn't know. They don't like junkies. They like them young and fresh-looking, you know? Girl-next-door types.'

She turned her gaze back to me for confirmation. Yeah, I did know what she meant, but before I could answer, Vex turned back towards the bee. It had become tangled up in a spider's web in the corner of the pane, and its hum was now at a higher, more desperate pitch.

'I had a good offshore supply of ice I fed her through Snow, so the money was going in a nice little circle back to me.' She flicked those flat grey eyes back at me, expecting a reaction I think, but when I just returned the look, she made that little shrugging gesture again and continued. 'But then she got it in her head she could go clean. They all say that, you know, but they never do it. But Niki surprised me. She cut right back and the next thing she's talking about how she's going to ask you to help her come off it completely – going on at me about how she's going to admit to her "big sister" that she had a "drug problem" and ask you for help. I knew once she started talking to you she'd never stop – it would all come out, and I'd go down for the drug supply *and* the whole blackmail scam. She'd told me about your cop connection.'

I felt the air go out of me, as if I'd been punched. Vex dragged her eyes away from the desperate bee, and leaned back in the chair before delivering her body blow.

'So yeah, I got Snow to kill her,' she said.

'Just like that?'

'Yeah. Just like that,' she answered with that little shrug of her shoulder.

'And the cops never suspected you?'

'Not me. They had Snow lined up for it. That ex of yours was on him night and day and, to tell you the truth, for a while there, I thought Snow would buckle and tell them everything, but then suddenly all the heat was off and no one was asking questions any more. Until that woman cop set Snow up and got him on tape confessing to knifing Niki. Jesus, what a pain in the arse that was. It was real dodgy for a while there. But eventually even that blew over and everyone forgot about Niki again.'

I hadn't forgotten about her, but I wasn't going to mention that now. Vex had become quite chatty, rolling the whole sordid scenario out in front of me like a red carpet. She seemed to have forgotten that this was my sister she was talking about. Or maybe she didn't care enough about Niki or me to try to soften the blows.

'Snow was a jerk-off,' she added. 'A waste of space. I have no regrets about having him killed.'

Whether she had any regrets about having Niki murdered lay between us, but I couldn't bring myself to ask. She levelled those cool grey eyes at me but didn't offer an answer to my unasked question.

'If the heat was off, why did you have Snow killed?'

She sighed as if tiring of the subject, and folded her arms across her chest. The bee was humming in little staccato bursts of panic. It was giving up the fight.

'The cops had shelved Niki's case because they had no evidence, but Snow started yabbering to anyone who'd listen about how he'd knifed her. What was he *thinking*?'

It was a joke – Snow didn't *think* – and she grinned in my direction, complicit, inviting me to join in the comedy routine. I sipped my water, not wanting to buddy up to her, but not wanting her to stop talking either. I could feel her eyes on me, and eventually she continued.

'He was *so* totally a liability. He was going to lead the cops to me eventually. I had to get rid of him.'

Her eyes swivelled again to the window. Now there was only the occasional burst of sound from the captured bee.

'And then Stoke presented himself to you on a plate,' I said.

She smiled. 'Poor old Stoke. He was totally gaga over

Niki. Sure enough, Stoke totally leapt at the chance to play little Niki's avenging angel, so I guess I was right about him, wasn't I?'

'Yeah, you were right.'

She dragged her eyes from the bee's final struggle and levelled that gaze at me again, and then she pushed back her chair. The screech of it made the hairs on my arms stand on end. The guard stepped forward, her hand hovering over the taser on her belt. Vex turned to face the guard, holding the plastic mug up and indicating the sink bench beside the window. When the guard nodded, Vex crossed to the sink.

It was time to leave. I retrieved my jacket from the back of the chair and shrugged my arms into it. When I turned back to the table, Vex approached but in deference to the watchful guard positioned herself on the other side of it again.

She held the plastic cup towards me. 'Let it go?' she asked.

We looked at each for what felt like a very long time, and then I took the cup from her hands. I could feel the vibration as the exhausted bee hummed and rolled in the bottom of the cup. Yeah, sure. I'd set it free. I'd release the bee into the warm, pollen-filled summer air somewhere way beyond the confines of the prison where I hoped Vex would be held captive for a very long time.

CHAPTER 29

The woman who'd emailed Robbie claiming to know the owner of the John Doe diary and its distinctive, handwoven tapestry tie, had signed herself 'Mrs J. O'Neill', so it seemed unlikely this was the Lara our JD had written 'sorry' to on the wall of the cave. On the drive to her house, Robbie suggested he do the talking, at least at first, and that seemed reasonable given his police-uniform status and the email relationship they'd already formed.

When Mrs O'Neill gasped and attempted to close the door in my face, I realised Robbie's suggestion wasn't because of any special bond they'd formed, but because I wasn't the greatest-looking person to go door-knocking with. I didn't take her response personally; I pretty much did the same thing every time I caught sight of myself in the mirror. The bruises on my face had shifted into the hepatitis B colour range, and the many grazes and abrasions had reached the scabby stage of healing that sets people's teeth on edge. I'd taken to wearing a terry-cloth '80s-style sweatband to cover the wrist gash, but the wound still occasionally drooled blood like a stigmata – not a good look outside of Catholic churches. I probably looked like someone who'd failed a suicide attempt, with Robbie as my police escort to ensure I didn't give it another go.

Robbie flashed his ID at her – a bit of overkill I thought, given his full police uniform – and used his most assuring tone. When she continued to stare at me with suspicion, I lied spectacularly about my 'recent car accident'. Finally, Mrs O'Neill told us to call her Jane, and stepped back to indicate that we should enter.

I put Jane O'Neill down at sixty, plus a year or two, but she was one of those women who I suspect had embraced older-woman status some time in her fifties, so may, in fact, have been quite a bit younger. Her long grey hair was split down the middle and secured tightly by a rubber band in a rat-tail at her neck, the tips of her ears peeking out through her hair like little pale scallop shells. The style was aggressively unflattering. She wore a long black skirt, flat shoes, and a metallic grey blouse buttoned nunlike to the throat. It was as if she was working at repressing any spark of sexuality that might make a brazen attempt to reveal itself.

When Robbie hefted John Doe's backpack on to the sink bench, Jane's hands flew to her cheeks and her eyes filled with tears. They just stayed there, those tears, enlarging her eyes like miniature spectacles, refusing to drop. To my horror I realised mine were filling in sympathy. This was new. I'd developed quite a thick skin in my years on the job. I'm not sure if it was working with the dead or working with the cops, but whichever it was, the result had been a definite drop in empathetic response.

I put the lapse down to recent trauma. Luckily, neither Jane nor Robbie seemed to have noticed. He placed the diary on the spotless, stainless steel sink bench beside the pack. I took a chair beside her so as not to be in her direct eyeline. I didn't want my face to interfere with her grieving process.

I wondered how Robbie was going to play this. I'd done this sort of thing so many times I was interested to see how someone else went about it. Jane was still staring at the items on the bench, but showed no sign of wanting to inspect them, and no inclination to speak. Robbie waited, apparently in no hurry.

'He's dead, isn't he?' she said.

It was as if she'd been waiting for this moment her whole life. The tension in the room was as powerful as at a séance, and I almost expected John Doe's voice to answer her from inside the backpack, but it was Robbie who responded.

'His body was found in the Rimutaka State Forest out past Wainuiomata. We suspect it's been there for a long time. Possibly since as early as 1970.'

She nodded once, keeping her eyes fixed on the pack, and then with some effort wrenched her gaze away and spoke directly to Robbie.

'His name is Boris Pasternak.'

I placed my notepad on the table quietly so as not to disturb her flow.

'When his mother was still just a young woman she was standing in the front line of a Moscow parade of some kind, and the famous author Boris Pasternak saw her and leaned over the protective railing and kissed her on the lips.' Jane paused to smile to herself. 'At that very moment she made a vow that her firstborn son would be named after him.' Jane let go of the image, and shrugged. 'Or some such story.' She glanced at the shorthand hieroglyphics I'd made on the notepad. 'That's what he told me, anyway,' she said, throwing me a complicit smirk. 'But he was a born liar,' she added for Robbie's benefit, though I was pretty sure he'd got that. 'And sexy as all hell.'

I saw Robbie's lips twitch in a grin, but he didn't look at me. In my best Pitman's I dutifully wrote down 'sexy as all hell', thinking maybe I'd been wrong about Jane.

Robbie asked if she was ever called Lara, and she laughed softly.

'No. My name is Jane. Plain Jane,' she added, and gave a secret smile.

So, she'd been a beauty in her day. Studying her closely, I could see the ghost of it in the large luminous eyes, the high cheekbones, the full bottom lip, but now everything about her had softened and draped. 'But I was his Lara,' she said. 'That's what Boris called me. His Lara.'

She stared at Robbie again as if searching for her long-lost lover in his looks, and then she turned away, disappointed.

'I thought your email said there was nothing written in the diary,' she said. 'You said all the writing was gone. So how did you know Boris called me Lara?'

She was looking at me so I answered her. 'We think he broke his ankle and spent some time sheltering in a cave in the bush. It was there that we found a message scratched on the wall.'

She was watching me with an intense expression of excitement, as if she thought I had a key of some kind, one that would unlock everything she'd closed away all these years. I spoke quickly to put her out of her misery, picking my words carefully, so there'd be no confusion. The message had been for her and I owed it to Boris to deliver it as he'd intended.

'He wrote the words "Sorry Lara". He may have written more, but that's all that survived.'

'"Sorry",' she repeated, flatly.

It wasn't a question, and from her look I'd say it sure as hell wasn't an answer either. She sat there, slumped into herself, her lip trembling with the weight of the 'sorry' still on it.

Robbie picked up the diary, and with one hand on top and one underneath he presented it to her like an altar boy. She stared at his hands, and then tilted her head to look up into his face.

'I think Boris wrote everything in here, Jane, everything he felt for you, everything he wanted to say. He'd wrapped the diary tightly and tucked it carefully in his pack. I'm sure it was all written in here, before the rain washed it clean.'

She smiled gratefully at him, and then she took the diary and rested her cheek against it. She stayed like that for a long time, her eyes closed, and a faint, secretive smile on her lips. I kept my head bent as if in prayer, but I wasn't praying.

Finally, she opened her eyes and smiled. 'He was always so eloquent,' she said, as if she'd heard him speak.

Jane made us tea, and told us her husband had died a month ago after thirty years of marriage.

'A reasonably happy one,' she added, and paused in her tea-making as if surprised by the realisation. I wrote it down, realising as I did that Jane had lost her husband about the same time as her lover's body had been found. I didn't think I'd draw her attention to it.

Robbie sipped his tea and crunched his way through a plateful of biscuits, helping Jane out with the occasional narrative nudge, while I jotted down the relevant dates and details for the report I'd need to write up for McFay. She was relaxed, happy to display her memories for us, like a draper throwing a roll of cloth across a table – all the flaws, the wefts and weaves on display for our inspection.

She was vague on some of Boris's background details, but she did remember he'd told her he had decided 'on a whim' to go to sea. At eighteen or nineteen, fit, strong, and keen to see the world, he'd had no trouble signing up on a Russian fishing vessel about to set sail. Whether this was true or a romanticised version of the truth, Jane didn't know, but she'd believed Boris when he told her that he'd left his family and his life in Russia without a backward glance, and that he would never return.

When he subsequently abandoned her, or so she'd believed until now, she assumed that was his pattern when things got tough. Boris had hated the sea, had been intimidated by the constantly drunk captain and violent crew, and when the vessel docked in New Zealand, Boris had simply jumped ship. By the time Jane met him he'd already been living here as an illegal alien for a couple of years. It didn't surprise me he could do that. It was easy to fly under the radar in those days before electronic ID and the internet. He would have been fine as long as he stayed out of trouble.

'I'm a sixty-two-year-old grandmother now and no doubt you can't imagine me as a young woman,' she said, aiming it at Robbie, 'but we were madly in love.' She shivered at the memory. 'He was, quite simply, the love of my life.'

I followed her gaze to a little three-legged occasional table on the far side of the room. On it was what looked like a memorial selection: a dramatic Greek-style urn of ashes surrounded by a horseshoe of family photos. This, no doubt, was all that remained of Mr O'Neill. I wondered if he'd known that Boris Pasternak was the love of his wife's life through their thirty years of 'reasonably happy' marriage.

A plastic-framed photo sat proudly beside the urn. It was a snapshot of the deceased pointing to someone and smiling, beaming in their direction, but the person he was pointing to had been excised from the photo. Maybe it was Jane he'd been so proudly drawing the photographer's attention to, but with her gone it appeared as if he was wasting that expansive smile on his own urn – as if he was pointing at his own ashes with a boyish 'Hey, check *this* out!' gesture.

Suddenly the ashes, the photo, and the talk about corpses were oppressive. I slid the notepad and pen across to Robbie, excused myself, and went through to the bathroom where I threw cold water on my face, luxuriating in the sparkling wetness of it.

I didn't need to pee, but since I was there I thought I might as well sit and fill in a bit of time. The bathroom was of the pink fluffy kind, full of female accoutrements. Chiding myself, I checked out the medicine cabinet. No shaving brush or razor. No nose hair clippers or snoring remedy. *Mr* Jane O'Neill, it seemed, had been quickly and thoroughly tidied away. Erased.

I sat on the lid of the toilet and wondered what it would be like to live in a marriage for thirty years knowing your partner always held that special place in their heart for someone else. All the time she was married to Mr O'Neill, Jane didn't know Boris was dead, although she must have considered the possibility. If Boris had lived – if they'd married, had kids, all that – would he have remained the love of her life? I think for some people it's easier to hold onto the dream or the memory of love than to put it to the test by living it.

Neither Jane nor Robbie looked up as I re-entered the room. Jane was deep in storytelling mode, and I suspect enjoying the attention of this honey-eyed man. I could understand that. Robbie slid the notepad back to me but kept eye contact with Jane so as not to disturb her flow. He'd drawn a little smiley face in the corner of the page. I flicked back through what Robbie had written, catching up on their conversation while I'd been out of the room.

'We had what you'd probably now call "a volatile relationship",' she said, and then gave that secret smile again before adding, 'Russians are like that.'

'Can you remember the last time you saw him?' I asked. 'Any idea of the date?'

She shifted around to face me as if only now realising I

was back in the room, and took a good thirty seconds before answering. I think she'd held these memories close and secret to herself for so long she was shocked to hear herself sharing them.

'We had a fight. An argument,' she said tightly, and turned back to face Robbie. 'And, you know, over all these years I've tried to recall what we were arguing about, and for the life of me I can't remember.' Jane stared at the heavily cushioned sofa across the other side of the room. 'He sat on the couch, put his boots on, picked up his pack, and left. That was the summer of 1972.' She took a deep breath before continuing. 'And that was that. I waited. He never returned. Eventually I had to accept the truth: he'd abandoned me just like he had his family.'

She glanced again in my direction. 'That's what I thought anyway, until I saw the piece in the paper and then the photo of his pack on the police website. I'd always imagined he was in Canada, for some reason. A grandparent, like me.' She turned her gaze back to Robbie. 'I want you to tell me where you found his body. I want to know everything that happened to him.'

I listened as Robbie laid it all out for her, explaining about the body being found by the ranger, and then later our finding the pack with the diary inside. He didn't mention the head being found at a different time and place from the rest of the body.

She listened without interrupting, her head bent, big splashes of tears dropping into her lap. She made no effort to wipe them away but just let them fall. I'd never seen anyone cry that way – it reminded me of an *Alice in Wonderland* illustration. When Robbie reached across the table and put his hand on hers I realised I could have done that and probably should have.

'All these years I thought he'd abandoned me, but he hadn't,' she said, that little secret smile appearing again. 'He didn't mean to leave me.'

Robbie suggested the scenario that perhaps, after their

argument, Boris wanted to be alone for awhile, wanted to walk it out of his system.

'Maybe he wanted to be alone to think,' Jane agreed. 'He did that sometimes,' she added, and smiled at Robbie as if he'd given her a gift.

'It looks like he broke his ankle and couldn't make it back to the hut to call for help,' Robbie concluded.

'How long did he survive?' she asked, determined to know.

I saw Robbie hesitate, weighing up how much to tell her.

'He survived for some time in the cave,' I said. 'That's where he wrote the message to you.'

She nodded without turning to face me.

Robbie picked it up from there. 'It looks like he may have crawled out of the cave to look for water, and then was unable to climb back up.'

I saw her take this in. So did I. For the first time since my kidnapping I realised how Boris had actually died.

Jane voiced my thoughts. 'Oh my God. He died of thirst.'

I allowed myself a single lip-lick. 'No, we don't think so,' I lied. 'Most likely he died of exposure. It's one of the most painless ways to go. He would have just drifted off.'

In the silence I could feel both Robbie's and Jane's eyes on me. By the time I looked up again Robbie was talking to Jane about the body, asking if she'd like to claim the ashes, but before she could answer, the door opened and a big blond-haired man filled the doorway. His smile faltered as he took in Robbie's police uniform and my battered appearance.

'This is my son,' Jane said by way of introduction.

Robbie held out his hand to the man. 'Robbie,' he said simply.

The big man smiled tentatively at his mother as he shook Robbie's hand.

'Mischa O'Neill,' he said. 'What's all this about?'

'Nothing,' Jane answered, before we had a chance to respond.

'Apparently there have been burglaries in the neighbourhood, and they're going door to door reminding people to lock up.'

Mischa glanced at the backpack on the sink bench.

'I found it in the attic,' she said simply. 'Now that I don't have your father to worry about, I thought I could go for a tramp. But it's a bit past it.'

On the drive home we talked about Jane's lie, and I admitted to Robbie that I wasn't a very polished fibber. I said he needed to know that if we were, you know, going to see more of each other. Without taking his eyes off the road Robbie grinned, and said that was fine with him, because he was a bit of a truth-fan himself. Except when it came to avoiding telling people the gorier details of how their loved-one died. That kind of lying was cool with him. We drove in silence for a while. It was a first-class silence, and right in the middle of it I noticed that Robbie had very sexy wrists.

He pulled the car up outside my place but kept the motor running. Wolf barked once – his greeting bark. He'd recognised the sound of Robbie's car. Robbie screwed up his face in apology.

'We kind of bonded,' he admitted.

'Yeah, I noticed,' I said. 'Okay – he lives with me, but you get visiting rights. Deal?'

He turned that grin in my direction. 'Deal,' he said, and took my fingers in his. We sat like that, fingers entwined. It felt good. It felt more than good.

'Give me a day or two, okay?' I said. 'I need to let some bruises heal.'

'Okay,' he said, giving my fingers a little squeeze. 'You let me know when you're ready. I'm not going anywhere.'

He kissed my fingers, an odd, courtly gesture. Sexy as all hell.

CHAPTER 30

Four or five years ago, two men, brothers, went fishing at dawn off the Island Bay coast. Experienced boaties, big strong blokes in their forties who, according to their families and friends, should have been able to swim to shore from pretty much anywhere. Nobody knows what happened: neither their bodies nor their little fishing boat came home that day.

The families set up a vigil on the shore. Every day and every night someone was there on the beach peering out at the Strait, willing the men to come home. Of course it was on TV and in the local papers – one of those stories you get caught up in despite yourself. The frightened huddle of the kids, siblings and cousins, squabbles and rivalries forgotten for now; the wives staunch and proud. The kind of people who never ask for help from anyone, but asking for it now: *Could yachties keep a look out for any sign of the men?*

As the days went by, the story was no longer front page or even second or third page news; and then, when weeks passed, I had to search the paper to find any reference to it . . . a second and then a third unsuccessful search . . . and then, finally, nothing. The men never did return. Their bodies were never found.

I thought about the brothers a lot in those first weeks, hoping against hope they'd managed to clamber ashore somewhere and were waiting for someone to collect them. I was eager for the big breaking story of their being discovered by the captain of a fishing vessel, or sighted on some unlikely rocky outcrop. A few kilos lighter, maybe, and shyly grinning through a couple of weeks' growth, saying, 'Nah nah, it wasn't all that bad – the worst was having to listen to him snoring.' Something like that.

But that story never happened, and eventually I forgot about the brothers. I forgot about the little huddle of cousins waiting for their dads to come home. And then a couple of months after they first went missing, I was walking Wolf around the rocky coast and stumbled upon a little cross made of driftwood with a dirty, old woollen beanie stuck on top of it. When I looked closer I saw a handcarved message in the upright stick. It said, simply, 'We love you Dad'. The cross was surrounded by a collection of little offerings: a handmade bracelet of tinfoil trinkets, a plastic miniature truck, a paua shell with kisses scratched into it. I guessed they were love-gifts and messages from the men's children, or maybe little charms, amulets to lure the men's spirits back to shore. I knew these men were good dads, and I knew too that no matter what you believe happens to you when you die, somehow, somewhere, those two brothers would be keeping an eye on their brood of kids left behind. If anything was going to hitch this world to any other one, those heartfelt, powerful little love totems would do it.

The handmade cross wasn't there any more, and the beanie and talismens were long gone, but the spot still held a magic for me, still felt sacred. Tapu. I sat nearby, balanced the simple little cardboard box of Niki's ashes on my knees, and looked out across Cook Strait towards the South Island. I could tell from the jagged horizon line that there was a big swell out there, and my heart swelled with it.

I told Niki I was sorry. Sorry for everything. And I told her it was time for me to let go. Not let go of her, but time to let go of trying to make it better for her, of trying to control her. I didn't want 'retro-bution' as Stoke called it. I didn't want revenge. I didn't even want to understand *why* Vex had ordered her death, or why Snow had killed her. Like Gemma said, that way lies madness. All I wanted was to remember Niki with love.

I rubbed a smooth shell between my thumb and finger, and watched Wolf enact a wildebeest fantasy as he dragged a pile of seaweed along the narrow piece of sand between the rocks. I told Niki to rest easy in my heart and memory. In the distant horizon I could just make out the snowy peaks of the Kaikouras. I remembered the words of the Baxter poem:

Alone we are born
    And die alone;
Yet see the red-gold cirrus
    Over snow-mountain shine.

He was only nineteen when he wrote that, and the thought made me smile. I continued the rest of the verse.

Upon the upland road
    Ride easy, stranger:
Surrender to the sky
    Your heart . . .

But I didn't need to recite the rest of the line. That was enough. I didn't care if anyone heard me. It was time for Niki to ride easy, and if anyone should surrender their anger it was me.

I did a lot of letting go on that wild, windy coast. I let Niki's ashes go with the gentle northerly, and watched them disappear into the surf and sand beneath. And then I asked those two missing fishermen if they'd mind very much keeping an eye on my little sister for me. I asked if they'd make sure she keeps warm and that she laughs a lot.

And I let the tears go too. I howled all the tears right out of me. I put my fists between my legs, aware of the bruise left by Ross, and hugged myself, and then I let him go too.

Gemma had told me that, when Ross abducted me, Sean had Vex removed to a safe house. I assumed it was to keep her safe from Ross, but his reasoning was more complex than that: if she was innocent she needed protecting; if she was guilty he'd know exactly where she was. I'd underestimated Sean. Maybe I always had. And with that thought I let Sean go too. Gone, gone, gone.

As I drove away from Island Bay, my heart felt light, and I realised I was ravenously hungry. It felt like my first real hunger in years. I'd call Gemma and see if she wanted to join me for fish and chips and a beer on Lyall Bay beach. I heard Wolf's little yelps of pleasure as his tongue flapped in the wind. And I'd buy him a battered sausage, and he could run around on the sand pretending he was a young dog again.

And maybe tomorrow I'd ring Robbie and ask if he was free.

THE NEW ZEALAND SOCIETY OF AUTHORS–PINDAR PUBLISHING PRIZE

The 2010 NZSA–Pindar Publishing Prize – the first of its kind in New Zealand – has been a resounding success. We received over 500 entries, from overseas and around the country, all vying for the prize of a complete publishing package. A shortlist of five was open to online voting, and the Readers' Choice Award went to Anne Stubbings for 'Chasing the Moon'.

The inaugural winner, Donna Malane, won the opportunity for her book to be professionally edited, produced, marketed and distributed throughout New Zealand.

Her novel, *Surrender*, was produced by Pindar in association with NZSA and Creative New Zealand, and printed by AstraPrint. *Surrender* is being promoted by *The New Zealand Herald* and offered for sale at all Whitcoulls and Borders stores nationwide. As a result, Donna's novel will receive unprecedented publicity and attention, as it well deserves.

The NZSA and Pindar wish to thank all of our sponsors for their generous input into this prize. We would also like to recognise the huge effort made by the judges – Linda Herrick, Graeme Lay and Mia Yardley.

THE NEW ZEALAND SOCIETY OF AUTHORS

PINDAR

Whitcoulls

BORDERS. where minds meet

The New Zealand Herald

astraprint

creative nz

ARTS COUNCIL OF NEW ZEALAND TOI AOTEAROA

Donna Malane is an award-winning television producer and scriptwriter. She has written for all genres of television, including drama and sketch comedy, and is the author of a successful humorous sports book, *The Girls' Guide to Rugby*, and a young adult story, *Alien Time*.

Surrender is her first adult novel and the winner of the inaugural 2010 New Zealand Society of Authors–Pindar Publishing Prize. *Surrender* is intended as the first in a series.

Donna lives in Wellington with her partner, novelist Ian Wedde, and whichever of their five kids needs a bed for the night.